汉英对照

中国古代散文选

CHINESE-ENGLISH SELECTIONS OF ANCIENT CHINESE PROSE WRITINGS

周向勤 郑苏苏 译

Translated by Zhou Xiangqin and Zheng Susu

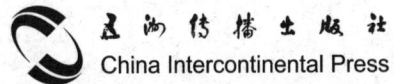

China Intercontinental Press

图书在版编目（CIP）数据

汉英对照中国古代散文选 / 周向勤, 郑苏苏编译.
-- 北京：五洲传播出版社, 2018.8
ISBN 978-7-5085-4026-9

Ⅰ.①汉… Ⅱ.①周… ②郑… Ⅲ.①古典散文—散文集—中国—汉、英 Ⅳ.①I262

中国版本图书馆CIP数据核字(2018)第198696号

汉英对照中国古代散文选

译　　者：	周向勤　郑苏苏
出 版 人：	荆孝敏
责任编辑：	宋博雅
封面设计：	北京丰饶视觉科技有限公司
内文制作：	北京优品地带文化发展有限公司
出版发行：	五洲传播出版社
社　　址：	北京市海淀区北三环中路31号生产力大楼B座6层
邮政编码：	100088
发行电话：	010-82005927，010-82007837
网　　址：	http://www.cicc.org.cn，http://www.thatsbooks.com
印　　刷：	北京浙京印刷有限公司
版　　次：	2019年1月第1版第1次印刷
开　　本：	710毫米×1000毫米　1/16
印　　张：	32.5
字　　数：	470千字
定　　价：	198.00元

一本可以做中英文教材的好书

凌鼎年

我妻子曾就读于上海市六女中,她最要好的一位同学兼闺蜜,嫁给了原本在九江外事办工作,后来调到无锡外事办从事翻译的郑苏苏先生。在他们调动前,正好我领了结婚证明,准备旅游结婚,时在1979年金秋。我妻子的同学劝我们在她调动前去庐山一游,好接待我俩。就这样,我们去了九江,去了庐山,与郑苏苏有了一面之交。

郑苏苏夫妇调无锡十来年后,于1990年移民去了澳大利亚。这一晃30多年再没见面。

前不久,我妻子说:郑苏苏与扬州大学外语学院周向勤教授合作翻译了一本书,想就出版问题咨询我。就这样,我与郑苏苏重续旧缘了。

等收到资料,才知郑苏苏与周向勤教授翻译的是金元明清时期的古典散文。我查看了目录,除少量篇章是金代与元朝的,大部分是明清的散文名篇,不少还是进入教科书的。我在中学时代与大学课本里就读到过宋濂的《送东阳马生序》、刘基的《卖柑者言》、马中锡的《中山狼传》、归有光的《项脊轩志》、魏学洢的《核舟记》、林嗣环的《口技》、姚鼐的《登泰山记》、龚自珍的《病梅馆记》等。特别使我高兴的是,两位译者选的散文里有王世贞与张溥、吴梅村的作品,这三位都是我家乡太仓的历史名人,在中国文学史上也是赫赫有名。王世贞是明代"后七子"领袖，独主文坛20年，相传《金瓶梅》就是出自他手。太仓有王世贞的弇山园与王世贞的墓。张溥是明代复社领袖，他倡导的"兴复古学，务为有用"红极一时，他领导的复社相传一度"遥控朝政"。太仓的张溥故居至今保存完好。张溥的《五人墓碑记》是《古文观止》的压轴篇，300多年来影响深远，打动过无数学子，激励过无数志士仁人。张溥故居有《五人墓碑记》完整而清晰的碑刻拓片。吴梅村被叶君远教授誉为"清代诗坛第一家"。吴梅村以诗闻名于世，其实他的散文也是不可多得的上品。2009年时，在笔者的策划下，太仓举办过"纪念吴梅村诞辰400周年学术研讨会"。我注意到，集子中还翻译了归有光的《项脊轩志》。归有光系昆山人，有人就想当然地认为项脊轩在昆山，但在20世纪70年代前的版本中，凡注释通常都写明"项脊轩在今江苏省太仓"。我查核了太仓的古地图与古地名，太仓在明清时，确实有项脊泾。太仓学者有专门的考证文章。至于近年出现的版本写项脊轩在昆山境内，那是以讹传讹。昆山归氏与太仓的关系非同一般。归有光的曾孙归庄抗清失败后，就隐居在太仓乡间，为了纪念他，这个小镇后来就被命名为归庄镇。

　　平心而论，两位译者在选择作品方面还是很有眼力的，我很佩服两位的审美与品味。所选其人其作，或是一代名人名流，如元好问、宋濂、刘基、高启、方孝孺、归有光、王世贞、李贽、袁宗道、张岱、张溥、夏完淳、黄宗羲、李渔、顾炎武、侯方域、蒲松龄、方苞、郑燮、袁枚、钱大昕、姚鼐、龚自珍等；或是被公认的脍炙人口的精品佳作，如刘因的《辋川图记》、李孝光的《大龙湫记》、马中锡的《中山狼传》、魏学洢的《核舟记》、魏禧的《大铁椎传》、林嗣环的《口技》等；也有两位的个人偏好，独家选择，从浩瀚的古书堆里钩沉索隐、披沙沥金翻找、挑选出来的。总之，这些作品都是值得一读的优秀之作、经典之作。

近年，中国的党和国家领导人在多种场合强调：中国文化、中国文学要走出国门，走向世界，也公布了奖励"经典中国"的翻译、出版项目。但中国文化、中国文学走向世界的步伐并不很快，业绩也不尽如人意。原因何在？一言以蔽之，翻译是瓶颈。据说中国的翻译队伍很是庞大，其中人才济济，如果让他们把海外的作品翻译为中文，绰绰有余。但把中国作品翻译为英文、法文、德文、日文、西班牙文等，实力就很有限了。因为这些翻译人员长期生活在中国，生活在华人圈子里，对欧美国家的语言习惯、语言变化多少有些隔膜。他们直译的多，而有些中国的俗语、俚语、歇后语、成语或方言很难找到相对应的精彩语言；还有些中国近年冒出的政治术语、精简语言、网络语言、民间语言，如果对海外语言了解不深不透，要想翻译得恰如其分，让西方读者心领神会，确乎有相当的难度。由于有些翻译者用中国式语言习惯、中国式语法翻译，翻译出来的作品有一种"隔"的感觉，欧美国家的读者读起来很吃力，很拗口，或者读不懂，甚至有莫名其妙、不知所云的感觉。这就是中国翻译界的一个软肋，中国翻译者翻译的书籍也就很难在海外、在欧美读者市场被普遍认可。据讲，莫言的小说作品能获奖，一个重要的原因是翻译者都是生活在海外的著名汉学家，他们的二度创作，使莫言的作品更能为海外读者接受、欣赏。

郑苏苏与周向勤教授的合作翻译，是一种取长补短，是一种珠联璧合。周向勤教授是扬州大学外语学院的专职英语教授，已翻译、出版过多本文学作品，有翻译的实战经验。郑苏苏曾多年从事外事翻译工作，又在澳大利亚生活了近30年，对海外读者的阅读方式、阅读习惯，对中英文的各自表述，对中英文的语法、修辞、逻辑、词汇等之间的微妙差异，显然要比长期生活在汉语圈的中国翻译家内行得多。翻译，其实就是为不同民族、不同国家的读者在阅读时架设桥梁，是一种功德。我不敢轻易下结论说：郑苏苏与周向勤教授的翻译，已达到了"信、达、雅"的层次与境界。但他们的合作是成功的，他们的努力是应该被看到，应该被肯定的。

周向勤与郑苏苏的自序，已对翻译的作品有了较为全面的分析与评点，提纲挈领，言简意赅，很是到位，我就不再啰嗦。

我最后想说的是，这本中英文对照的中国古代散文选，可以成为中国在海外500多家孔子学院与数千家汉语学校很好的教材，也是海外对中文，对中国文学、中国文化有兴趣的朋友极好的自学教材，同时，也是中国读者学习英语的辅助教材。

2016年4月4日（清明节）于江苏太仓先飞斋

凌鼎年系中国作家协会会员、作家网副总编、"一带一路"中国文化促进会会长、中国微电影与微小说创作联盟常务副主席、世界华文微型小说研究会秘书长、中华凌氏宗亲会会长，美国纽约商务出版社特聘副总编、香港《华人月刊》《澳门文艺》特聘副总编。

序　言

周向勤　郑苏苏

　　随着中国的崛起，世界上学习汉语言、研究汉文化的人越来越多，星罗棋布于世界各地的孔子学院便是明证；更何况每年来华留学的世界各国的学生犹如潮水一般，还不算通过其他途径进行学习的人。总之，学中文已成为一股世界性的潮流。尤其是习近平主席提出"实现中华民族伟大复兴的中国梦"以来，影响所及，这股潮流显得更为壮观。他们不仅努力学习中国的现代文化，而且热衷于中国的传统文化，因为众所周知，中国有5000多年的文明史，而且中华文明是世界四大古老文明中唯一一个连绵不断、历久不衰的文明，其辉煌灿烂、博大精深令人神往。正如习近平主席所说："中华优秀传统文化是中华民族的精神命脉，是涵养社会主义核心价值观的重要源泉，也是我们在世界文化激荡中站稳脚跟的坚实根基。"作为中国人，我们深为中华民族5000多年的文明史感到自豪；同时，我们又觉得应当为传播这5000多年的中华文明做点儿什么。那就要像习近平主席所说的那样："结合新的时代条件传承和弘扬中华优秀传统文化，传承和弘扬中华美学精神。"

　　文化以语言为载体，而文学的语言最为丰富多彩。散文是中国文学的正宗（朱自清语），而明清时代的散文又离现代文明最近，因而较易学习。于是，我们首先想到了编译一本汉英对照的明清散文选，辅之以汉英双语注释和英语译文，以帮助英语国家的人，或是通过英语这一媒介，帮助世界各地的人读懂这一时期的中国散文，达到传承和弘扬中国传统文化的目的。后来又考虑到金元时期是中国文学史上的特殊时期，散文作家和作品篇数都很少，不宜单列，一般都与明清划为同一时段，于是又将明清散文选扩大为金元明清散文选。虽然，在人们的心目中，金元明清时期的散文在中国文学史上的地位不算很高，提到中国古代散文，人们所津津乐道的往往是先秦两汉、魏晋南北朝时期的散文，特别是"唐宋八大家"的散文，而对金元明清的散文谈论较少，但其实，金元明清散文中也不乏美文佳作。

金代王若虚的《焚驴记》就是一篇出色的寓言小品，托物兴讽，寄寓了对现实的不满，对世情的激愤。元好问的《送秦中诸人引》虽是常见的赠序之作，但不落窠臼，写来意趣高迈，涵盖甚深。

元代散文寥寥无几，可数者仅戴表元的《送张叔夏西游序》、刘因的《〈辋川图〉记》、李孝光的《大龙湫记》和钟嗣成的《〈录鬼簿〉序》。《送张叔夏西游序》以作者与友人张叔夏的三次相见，写其颠沛身世，勾勒了由宋入元一代知识分子的形象，手法简约有度，曲折有序，渗透着情感。《〈辋川图〉记》通过对《辋川图》及其作者王维的人品、节操的评述性议论来宣扬忠臣烈士的封建纲常和文人学者的修身治己的准则，同时也隐晦曲折地鞭笞了由宋降元的一般文人的软弱气质。《大龙湫记》细致传神地描写了浙江乐清境内雁荡山的瀑布大龙湫的奇丽景象，时时有游人感受的穿插，遂使诗情画意形于一体。《〈录鬼簿〉序》是戏曲作家钟嗣成编的杂剧作家小传和作品目录集子的序，总共不到380字，短小精悍、幽默泼辣。

经过元代的沉默，至明代，散文开始中兴。明初宋濂的《送东阳马生序》是勉励当时太学生刻苦读书的赠序。他教诲后辈不板着面孔,而是叙述自己刻苦求学的经历,借以勉励他人,文词恳挚畅达。刘基的《卖柑者言》言近而旨远,深刻地揭露了元代那些官僚们"金玉其外,败絮其中"的腐朽本质。而他的《楚人养狙》简直就是个动物界的"造反"故事。被称为"吴中四杰"之一的高启,以其"近《史记》"(林纾语)之笔所写的《书博鸡者事》,紧扣博鸡者性格的主导面——见义勇为,选取几个行为侧面,如惩治豪民、为袁守申冤等,加以表现和充实,从而写得栩栩如生。

明朝初年,诗文曾流行以点缀升平为统治者歌功颂德的"台阁体",追求形式的典雅工丽。这在山水游记中也有反映。而同时期的薛瑄所作的《游龙门记》却匠心独运,不事雕琢,显得自然逼真,使人如亲临其境;该文以时间为序,描述井然,文中妙喻如珠,倍增形象感。马中锡的《中山狼传》以寓言的形式抨击了生活中的忘恩负义之徒,讽刺了那些滥施善行而自食恶果的"东郭先生"们。这篇寓言在情节安排上很有特色,它处处为表现寓言形象服务,而用墨饰色,无不栩栩传神。崔铣的《记王忠肃公翱事》,善于选材,选取了人事调动及物品馈赠这两方面各一典型事例,集中表现了主人公王翱廉正刚烈的性格,塑造了一位清官的典型形象,即在反腐倡廉的今天亦仍有教育意义。何景明的《说琴》,旨在说理,却并非直陈其理,而是借物喻理,说物明理,是古代说理散文中的一篇颇具特色的佳作。

明代散文中值得注意的是归有光的散文,描写日常生活的琐事、情景,与明代市民小说审美思潮一致,表明文学走向生活的趋向。其《项脊轩志》情调隽永,围绕项脊轩的前后变化展开描述。先写其狭小、破漏与昏暗,继写经过修葺之后的优美、宁静与恬适。

轩内积书，轩外花木，白日小鸟，月夜桂影，构成了一种谐和清雅的小天地。而居于这个小天地的作者清贫的生活，高洁的志趣，怡悦的心境，于不知不觉中显露了出来。老妪和祖母的心理都刻画得十分细致。清桐城派姚鼐选大型总集《古文辞类纂》，即以"唐宋八大家"及明归有光等文为基础（朱东润语）。

公安派袁氏三兄弟，宗道、宏道与中道，文学上主张独抒心灵，散文风格清新明快。袁宗道的《极乐寺纪游》，袁宏道的《满井游记》及《晚游六桥待月记》则是本书试译的起始篇目。《满井游记》中对冻河的描写："于时冰皮始开，波色乍明，鳞浪层层，清澈见底，晶晶然如镜之新开，而冷光之乍出于匣也"，使人很容易联想起柳宗元的《小石潭记》等山水游记。难怪张岱说："古人记山水手，太上郦道元，其次柳子厚，近时则袁中郎。"他充分肯定了袁宏道（中郎）的山水游记在中国散文史上的地位。

几乎与公安派同时，又产生了以钟惺与谭元春为代表的竟陵派。钟惺的《夏梅说》是一篇托物寓意的论说文。作者因友人咏夏梅的诗而发生感触，写了这篇文章，集中地反映了竟陵派"幽深孤峭"的风格。他的《浣花溪记》生动地描写了浣花溪畔杜甫草堂一带清幽曲折的景色，对于诗人杜甫在穷愁奔走之际还能择胜而居的安详胸襟寄以敬意。谭元春的《再游乌龙潭记》描写了大夏天游乌龙潭时忽逢雷阵雨的情景，气势飞动，神态逼真，把大自然惊心动魄的壮美景象生动地呈现在眼前，在竟陵派的游记文学中算得一篇上乘之作。

说到游记，不能不说到徐宏祖，他就是我国明代著名的旅游家徐霞客，钱谦益曾为之作《徐霞客传》，列述其生平和旅游之地。徐霞客本人写成的《徐霞客游记》文学价值很高，以日记体的形式出现，如本书所选的《游黄山日记（后）》就写他第二次遍游黄山绝景天都、莲花二主峰,尽览天下奇观。本文写景、抒情、发议融为一体,以写景为主,寓情于景,藏议于景。

魏学洢的《核舟记》用的是缩龙成寸的表现手法,把人物情态描绘得传神尽致。张溥的《五人墓碑记》是一篇众口交赞的散文。一般"墓志"为达官贵人所写,而张溥的这篇却是为下层人民所写。全文情绪激越,紧扣五壮士和东厂斗争的中心,夹叙夹议,甚至以议为主,在善与恶的搏斗、正与反的对比中对下层人民的正义行为和崇高品质给予大力肯定和热情赞扬,实是一篇战斗的小品文。

张岱继"公安""竟陵"两派之后,是晚明散文家中一位卓有成就的名家。他的《西湖七月半》和《湖心亭看雪》向为人们所传颂。《西湖七月半》一反历代文人把自然景象作为直接描写对象的作法,不涉墨于景,只着色于人,描述游西湖的几种人的情态,毕露无遗,又各个形成鲜明对比。《湖心亭看雪》则以经济绝妙之笔来写湖中雪景:"雾凇沉砀,天与云与山与水,上下一白;湖上影子,惟长堤一痕、湖心亭一点与余舟一芥、舟中人两三粒而已",描写了雪天的壮美景象,意境以大小对衬,形成了朦胧美。

明末清初,异族入侵,王朝更迭,民族矛盾特别尖锐,反映在散文中,爱国主义主题突显。《〈奇零草〉自序》的作者张煌言本人就是一位著名的抗清将领、民族英雄,曾率军奋战17载。虽然最终在清政府的镇压下失败了,但他大志难酬,壮怀激烈,"思借声诗以代年谱","欲以有韵之词,求知于后世",于是搜集他业已零落散佚的诗稿汇编成集,即《奇零草》。他为该诗集写的这篇自序,将写诗、编集的经历和生活、斗争的道路联结起来,作双线交织的叙述,字里行间洋溢着爱国热情。年仅十七岁的少年抗清英雄夏完淳的《狱中上母书》充满了爱国主义的热情,表现了崇高的民族气节，虽言家事，但实议国事，表现出视死如归的情怀，感人至深。稍后的全祖望的《梅花岭记》以悲壮天地的笔墨刻画了明末史可法死守扬州，为民族尽节，抵抗异族侵略，视死如归的崇高形象，也是足以惊天地、泣鬼神的。

明清之际思想家、史学家黄宗羲的《原君》，曾被梁启超称为"真极大胆之创论"。文章托古论今，古今对比，扬古贬今，抨击暴戾君制，措词激烈，意义深远。周容的《芋老人传》所写，虽是野老鄙夫，却有过人之识，由食芋细事，论及人伦法、德行操守，出言发语，惊世骇俗。

清王朝入主中原，对中华各民族一方面实施武装镇压，另一方面进行思想钳制，大兴文字狱，在广大知识分子中造成极度恐惧的心理，使得明末清初刚刚兴起的爱国主义热情又迅速沉寂下去。人们在这样的社会背景和社会氛围中，思想受到严重禁锢，不敢稍有创见，只好埋头"做学问"。所谓"康乾盛世"所产生的以方苞、刘大櫆、姚鼐为代表的桐城派，鼓吹古文"义法"，即以儒家思想为"义"（思想内容），以结构语言的简洁劲爽为"法"（艺术形式），形成一种"清真雅正"的文风。方苞的《左忠毅公逸事》是一篇写人的散文，它以细节点染的方法，着力表现左光斗爱护贤才、不计个人荣辱的可贵品质，使其刚烈形象跃然纸上。《狱中杂记》是方苞在狱中写成的，因对狱中生活有亲身体验，故能将清代狱政的黑暗腐败写得很有艺术感染力。刘大櫆的《骡说》是一篇短小精悍的小品文，富有新意，堪与唐代韩愈的《马说》媲美。姚鼐的《登泰山记》全文不足500字，却写得情景如画，既有概括描述，又有具体绘写，虽记登山经过和山上各种景物，却重在描述观日出的胜景，形象而又生动，文笔洗练优美，因此为人们所传诵。

彭端淑的《为学一首示子侄》讲的虽是"为学",即求学,阐发的却是做事难与易的辩证关系,从而告诉人们,只要坚忍不拔,难事也能变成易事,道理至深。蒋士铨的《〈鸣机夜课图〉记》塑造了一位相夫教子的古代妇女的形象。作者的母亲钟令嘉不仅在教子方面是慈母,而且在相夫方面是贤妻,在事亲方面是孝女。文章从这三方面组织材料,扣住一个"贤"字,突出她的美德,加以颂扬,其特点是以情感人。"檐风几烛,若愀然助人以哀者"及"铨诵声琅琅然,与药鼎沸声相乱",都是情景交融、声情并茂的好文字。

以绘画闻名于世、被称为"扬州八怪"之一的郑燮(板桥)的《范县署中寄舍弟墨第四书》,娓娓叙家常,发自肺腑,无处不动人。该文手法清新,自然流畅的文笔,高风亮节的品德,都使其不失为一篇情真意切、直抒胸臆的好文章。《聊斋志异》作者蒲松龄在300多年前经历了一场大地震,并把它描述出来,以时间为经,以空间为纬,既写物,又写人,纵向发展,横向扩延,物人俱陈,因果相对,构成了一个多层次、多侧面的艺术立体:《地震》。

诗歌理论家袁枚的散文《黄生借书说》,与明初宋濂的《送东阳马生序》相似,也是一篇鼓励后生刻苦读书的好文章。他提出"书非借不能读也"的新颖独特的见解,并以自己少年贫穷只好借书而读,因而特别珍惜,故能细想牢记的亲身经历,阐述了一番意味深长的治学道理,发人深省。袁枚的《祭妹文》是他痛悼三妹素文的不幸遭遇、怀念兄妹间往日深厚情意的一篇抒情性祭文。他主张诗文要写"性灵",认为"情从心出,非有一种芬芳悱恻之怀,便不能哀感顽艳",而他与三妹既如此情深意笃,三妹又遇人不淑,命运乖蹇,过早去世,且葬身异乡,故而这篇祭文写得如血泪凝成:"呜呼!身前既不可想,身后又不可知;哭汝既不闻汝言,奠汝又不见汝食。纸灰飞扬,朔风野大,阿兄归矣,犹屡屡回头望汝也。呜呼哀哉!呜呼哀哉!"真是字字出肺腑,句句断肝肠!

刘开的《问说》是一篇典型的议论文,全文观点鲜明:"君子之学必好问",论据充分,结构严谨,条理清晰,是颇合桐城派古文家"有物有序"原则的好文章。

桐城派"义法"差不多风靡整个清代文坛。讲究文词的"雅洁"固然不错,但语言的生气不足也是一大缺点,须得有人起而冲破之,才能发展。这个重任就落在了龚自珍等人的身上。龚自珍的《病梅馆记》是他的代表作,写江南梅树因受人工的束缚而变得病态而又畸形,借以控诉封建统治者禁锢思想、扼杀人才的罪恶;又写他辟病梅馆疗救病梅,借以抒发解放人才和个性自由的思想。寓意深刻。他写于鸦片战争前夕,即清宣宗道光十九年(1839年)的《己亥六月重过扬州记》,是一篇抒情记事散文。该文因小见大,从扬州的由盛转衰,写出整个时代的由盛转衰,目光十分敏锐。

以上概述就像导游带领读者诸君畅游了一番金元明清时期的散文百花园,但不管我们说得如何天花乱坠,也都是走马观花式的游览,不能代替各位驻足观赏,即亲自研读。正如毛泽东所言:"你要知道梨子的滋味,就得亲口尝一尝。"希望读者诸君参考注释与译文研读原文,体味其精神、脉理、气势、韵味、格调、词采;一句话,领会中华优秀传统文化的美学精神。

中国古代散文的英译是一项艰辛的工作。在整个翻译过程中,澳大利亚友人 Lynette Hennigar 自始至终给予我们热心的帮助,她对我们的译文做了不少修改和润色工作,对本书的成功出版起了不小的作用。在此,我们向这位热心的国际友人表示衷心的感谢。同时,感谢扬州大学出版基金会对本书出版的支持。

目 录

2　焚驴志 / 王若虚

8　送秦中诸人引 / 元好问

14　送张叔夏西游序 / 戴表元

20　《辋川图》记 / 刘因

28　《录鬼簿》序 / 钟嗣成

34　大龙湫记 / 李孝光

40　送东阳马生序 / 宋濂

50　楚人养狙 / 刘基

54　卖柑者言 / 刘基

60　书博鸡者事（节选）/ 高启

70　指喻 / 方孝孺

76　游龙门记 / 薛瑄

84　中山狼传（节选）/ 马中锡

100　记王忠肃公翱事 / 崔铣

Contents

3   An Appeal from a Donkey at the Stake / Wang Ruoxu

9   On the Departure of My Friends from Qin / Yuan Haowen

15 A Farewell Note on Zhang Shuxia's Departure for the West / Dai Biaoyuan

21 The Picture of Wangchuan Mountain Villa / Liu Yin

29 Preface to the *Records of Ghosts* / Zhong Sicheng

35 The Great Dragon Pond / Li Xiaoguang

41 A Farewell to Young Scholar Ma from Dongyang / Song Lian

51 A Monkey-Raiser from the Chu Area / Liu Ji

55 A Fruit-Pedlar's Words / Liu Ji

61 The Brave Deeds of a Cockfight Gambler (excerpts) / Gao Qi

71 The Enlightenment from a Sick Thumb / Fang Xiaoru

77 A Trip to Longmen / Xue Xuan

85 The Zhongshan Wolf (excerpts) / Ma Zhongxi

101 The Noble Deeds of the Revered Mr. Wang Ao / Cui Xian

108　说琴 / 何景明

120　项脊轩志 / 归有光

128　任光禄竹溪记 / 唐顺之

136　题《海天落照图》后 / 王世贞

142　题孔子像于芝佛院 / 李贽

146　极乐寺纪游 / 袁宗道

150　满井游记 / 袁宏道

154　虎丘记 / 袁宏道

162　与丘长孺书 / 袁宏道

166　晚游六桥待月记 / 袁宏道

170　山居斗鸡记 / 袁宏道

176　江行日记二则 / 袁中道

180　夏梅说 / 钟惺

184　浣花溪记 / 钟惺

190　避风岩记 / 张明弼

200　再游乌龙潭记 / 谭元春

204　游黄山日记（后）（节选） / 徐宏祖

212　核舟记 / 魏学洢

109	The Secret of the Musical Instrument, *Qin* / He Jingming
121	The Hut Called Xiangjixuan / Gui Youguang
129	Guanglu Ren's Bamboo-Stream Garden / Tang Shunzhi
137	The Inscription on *The Sea and Sky in the Glow of the Setting Sun* / Wang Shizhen
143	Paying Tribute to Confucius in the Zhifo Temple / Li Zhi
147	Visiting the Happy Temple / Yuan Zongdao
151	Travelling to the Scenic Spot Manjing / Yuan Hongdao
155	The Tiger Hill / Yuan Hongdao
163	A Letter to Qiu Changru / Yuan Hongdao
167	Visiting the Six Bridges at Night to Await the Moon / Yuan Hongdao
171	Watching Cockfighting in the Mountain / Yuan Hongdao
177	Two Diary Entries about My Voyage on the Yangtze River / Yuan Zhongdao
181	The Summer Plum / Zhong Xing
185	The Flower-Washing Stream / Zhong Xing
191	The Wind-Shelter Cliff / Zhang Mingbi
201	Revisiting the Black-Dragon Lake / Tan Yuanchun
205	A Diary Entry about Touring Mount Huangshan (Second Visit) (excerpts) / Xu Hongzu
213	A Miniature Boat Carved from a Peach Stone / Wei Xueyi

220　西湖七月半 / 张岱

228　湖心亭看雪 / 张岱

232　五人墓碑记 / 张溥

242　海市记 / 吴伟业

248　《奇零草》自序 / 张煌言

260　狱中上母书 / 夏完淳

270　原君 / 黄宗羲

280　芙蕖（节选）/ 李渔

286　与人书 / 顾炎武

288　李姬传 / 侯方域

298　就亭记 / 施闰章

306　芋老人传 / 周容

316　大铁椎传 / 魏禧

324　口技 / 林嗣环

330　送王进士之任扬州序 / 汪琬

334　地震（节选）/ 蒲松龄

338　狱中杂记（节选）/ 方苞

356　左忠毅公逸事 / 方苞

221 The West Lake in the Middle of the Seventh Month / Zhang Dai

229 Viewing the Snow Scene from the Mid-Lake Pavilion / Zhang Dai

233 The Epitaph Inscribed on the Five-Men's Tomb / Zhang Pu

243 The Castles in the Air / Wu Weiye

249 Preface to *Sparse Withered Grass* / Zhang Huangyan

261 A Letter Written in Jail to My Mother / Xia Wanchun

271 On the Obligation of Monarchs / Huang Zongxi

281 Lotus (excerpts) / Li Yu

287 A Letter to an Anonymous Person / Gu Yanwu

289 The Story of Lady Li / Hou Fangyu

299 The Ready-Made Pavilion / Shi Runzhang

307 The Old Taro Man / Zhou Rong

317 The Story of Big Iron Club / Wei Xi

325 The Magic of Vocal Mimicry / Lin Sihuan

331 Seeing Off Palace Graduate Wang to His Post in Yangzhou / Wang Wan

335 The Earthquake (excerpts) / Pu Songling

339 The Events in a Prison (excerpts) / Fang Bao

357 Anecdotes of the Revered Mr. Zuo Zhongyi / Fang Bao

364　范县署中寄舍弟墨第四书 / 郑燮

372　游三游洞记 / 刘大櫆

378　骡说 / 刘大櫆

380　为学一首示子侄 / 彭端淑

384　梅花岭记（节选）/ 全祖望

392　黄生借书说 / 袁枚

396　祭妹文 / 袁枚

408　《鸣机夜课图》记 / 蒋士铨

426　弈喻 / 钱大昕

430　登泰山记 / 姚鼐

438　问说 / 刘开

448　病梅馆记 / 龚自珍

452　己亥六月重过扬州记 / 龚自珍

462　作家小传

365 The Fourth Letter to My Younger Brother Mo / Zheng Xie

373 Travel Notes on Touring the Sanyou Cave / Liu Dakui

379 About Mules / Liu Dakui

381 A Note about Study Written for My Sons and Nephews / Peng Duanshu

385 The Plum Blossom Ridge (excerpts) / Quan Zuwang

393 Advice to Young Scholar Huang on Borrowing Books / Yuan Mei

397 Lamenting for My Younger Sister / Yuan Mei

409 The Picture of Teaching while Weaving at Night / Jiang Shiquan

427 The Metaphor of a Chess Game / Qian Daxin

431 Ascending Mount Tai / Yao Nai

439 The Importance of Asking Questions / Liu Kai

449 The Home for Sick Plum Trees / Gong Zizhen

453 Revisiting Yangzhou in Early Midsummer of 1839 / Gong Zizhen

463 Brief Biographies of Writers

焚 驴 志

王若虚

岁己未①,河朔②大旱,远迩③焦然④无主赖⑤。镇阳帅自言忧农,督下祈雨甚急。厌禳⑥小数⑦,靡不为之⑧,竟无验。既久,怪⑨诬⑩之说兴。适民家有产白驴者,或指曰:"此旱之由也。云方兴,驴辄仰号之,云辄散不留。是物不死,旱胡得止?"一人臆倡⑪,众万以附。帅闻,以为然,命亟取,将焚之。

---

① 岁己未:金章宗承安四年(the 4th year of the Cheng'an Reign of Emperor Zhangzong in the Jin Dynasty, 1199)。
② 河朔:黄河以北一带(area to the north of the Yellow River)。
③ 迩:近(near)。
④ 焦然:禾苗枯焦的样子(the seedlings were scorched)。
⑤ 无主赖:没有依靠(have nothing on which to rely)。
⑥ 厌禳(ráng):祈祷解除灾难(pray to get rid of calamities)。
⑦ 小数:小法术(little magic arts)。
⑧ 靡不为之:没有不做的(there is nothing that has not been done)。
⑨ 怪:怪异(bizarre)。
⑩ 诬:无根据(groundless)。
⑪ 臆倡:胡乱提出(propose a wild guess)。

AN APPEAL FROM A DONKEY AT THE STAKE

Wang Ruoxu

In the 4th year of the Cheng'an Reign (1199), during the Jin Dynasty, a severe drought hit the area north of the Yellow River. All the crops, far and near, were scorched and people had no food on which to live. The commander in chief of Zhenyang District, claiming that he was worried about the farmers, urged his subordinates to pray for rain. All sorts of witchcrafts which were supposed to have superpowers for vanquishing calamities had been tried out but without any success. Before long, groundless assumptions and ridiculous theories followed. A white donkey happened to be born in the stable of an ordinary household. After this someone conjectured about the abnormal donkey by saying: "This animal is the cause of the drought. Look, whenever clouds gathered in the sky, this white donkey would raise its head and bray loudly. Every time it brayed, the clouds would immediately disperse. If this animal is not killed, how can we expect this drought to subside?" One man proclaimed this absurd proposition, thousands of people blindly supported it. The commander heard this story and believed it. He ordered his

驴见梦①于府之属②某曰："冤哉焚也！天祸流行，民自罹之，吾何预③焉？吾生不幸为异类④，又不幸堕于畜兽。乘负⑤驾驭，惟人所命；驱叱⑥鞭箠⑦，亦惟所加。劳辱以终，吾分⑧然也。若乃水旱之事，岂其所知，而欲置斯酷⑨欤？孰诬我者，而帅从之！祸有存乎天，有因乎人，人者可以自求⑩，而天者可以委⑪之也。殷之旱也，有桑林⑫之祷，言出而雨；卫之旱也，为伐邢⑬之役，师兴而雨；汉旱，卜式⑭请烹弘羊⑮；唐旱，李中敏⑯乞斩郑

---

① 见梦：托梦（appear in one's dream and make a request）。
② 府之属：帅府中的僚属（officials in the office of the commander in chief）。
③ 预：相干（relate to）。
④ 异类：非人类（species other than humans）。
⑤ 乘负：骑乘、负重（ridden by a person or bear a heavy burden）。
⑥ 驱叱：驱赶呵斥（drive and scold）。
⑦ 鞭箠：鞭笞，用皮鞭打（beat with a whip）。
⑧ 分：本分（one's duty）。
⑨ 酷：酷刑（cruel torture）。
⑩ 自求：问问自己（ask oneself）。
⑪ 委：听之任之（allow sth. to go unchecked）。
⑫ 桑林：地名，桑山之林（name of a place; the woods in Mount Sangshan）。
⑬ 邢：古国名，在今河北邢台市西南（name of an old state, in the southwest of today's Xingtai City, Hebei Province）。
⑭ 卜式：汉代河南人（Bu Shi: a historical personage of the Han Dynasty [206 BC – AD 220]; a native of Henan）。
⑮ 弘羊：桑弘羊，汉代洛阳人，汉武帝时任治粟都尉，领大司农（Sang Hongyang: an official in charge of agriculture in the time of Emperor Wudi of the Han Dynasty; a native of Luoyang）。
⑯ 李中敏：唐时陇西人，曾任监察御史（Li Zhongmin: a historical personage of the Tang Dynasty [618–907]; he was from the western part of Gansu and once held a post as a supervisory official）。

subordinates to find the donkey and burn it.

That night the donkey appeared in someone's dream and that person happened to be an official in the commander's office. It said to him: "I am a victim of injustice and I will soon be burnt to death. When a natural calamity hits this area, the local people suffer from the disaster. Does this have anything to do with me? Why should I be blamed for the disaster? I am unlucky to be born as something other than a human being. It is even worse that I found myself to be one of the domestic animals. At man's disposal, I always carry heavy burdens, ridden and driven by somebody. What's more, I am often abused and whipped. I consider it as my duty to endure hard work and humiliation all my life. Humble as I am, how can I know anything about this natural calamity? Why should I be put to the stake? I don't know who has framed me or why the commander believed the wrong accusation. Some calamities come from nature and some from man. If it is a man-made disaster, find out who is to blame. If it is a natural one, let things run their course. When a great drought was happening during the Shang Dynasty (1600 BC – 1046 BC), King Tang held a praying ceremony in the woods of Mount Sangshan. No sooner had the prayers been said than it began to rain. The drought which the State of Wei incurred prompted the launching of a punitive expedition against the State of Xing. It started raining as soon as the war began. When the Han Dynasty witnessed a severe drought, Bu Shi persuaded Emperor Wudi to kill Sang Hongyang. During the

注①。救旱之术多矣，盍亦求诸是类乎？求之不得，无所归咎，则存乎天也，委焉而已。不求诸人，不委诸天，以无稽之言，而谓我之愆②。嘻，其不然！暴巫③投魃④，既已迂矣，今兹无乃复甚？杀我而有利于人，吾何爱一死？如其未也，焉用为是以益⑤恶？滥杀不仁，轻信不智，不仁不智，帅胡取焉？吾子，其属也，敢私⑥以诉⑦。"

某谢⑧而觉⑨，请诸帅而释之。人情初不怿⑩也。未几而雨，则弥⑪月不解⑫，潦溢⑬伤禾，岁卒以空⑭。人无复议驴。

---

① 郑注：唐文宗时奸佞，惯于诬陷忠良（a crafty sycophant in the time of Emperor Wenzong in the Tang Dynasty, who always framed a case against officials loyal to their sovereign）。
② 愆（qiān）：过失（fault）。
③ 暴巫：让巫师在太阳底下曝晒求雨（order wizards to pray in the hot sun for rain）。暴，同"曝"（exposed to the sun）。
④ 投魃（bá）：驱赶旱神（drive away the god of drought）。
⑤ 益：增添（add）。
⑥ 私：私下（privately）。
⑦ 诉：申诉（appeal, complain）。
⑧ 谢：认错，道歉（apologize）。
⑨ 觉：醒（wake up）。
⑩ 怿：高兴（happy）。
⑪ 弥：满（full）。
⑫ 解：停止（stop）。
⑬ 潦（lào）溢：涝灾（crop failure caused by waterlogging）。
⑭ 空：没有收成（no harvest）。

Tang Dynasty, when a severe drought made people suffer greatly, Li Zhongmin appealed to the monarch to behead Zheng Zhu. There are many ways to subdue a drought. Why not learn from the ancient people and follow their example? If we desire something but fail to get it, we should not blame anybody for the failure. Our success and failure are all determined by Heaven and we should ask Heaven to give us the right answer. Now in this case, no wise people have been consulted and Heaven has not been asked for the answer. What has been used is the groundless accusation to frame me. Oh, how ridiculous it is! It is already silly to have wizards pray for rain in the scorching sun and try to drive away the god of drought. Now an even more stupid thing is being done. If to kill me would benefit human beings, I am willing to die. If this is not the case, did they do this to commit more crimes? It is not benevolent to wantonly slaughter innocent people and it is unwise to give ready credence to rumors. Why did the commander do such a heartless and unwise thing? You are his subordinate and I venture to make such a complaint privately in front of you."

  Having heard what the donkey had said, the official immediately apologized and then awoke. He asked the commander to release the donkey. At first nobody was happy with his story and suggestion. Very soon it began to rain and the rain did not stop for the whole month. The flood ruined all the crops and the year ended up with no harvest. After that, people did not talk about the donkey any more.

送秦中诸人引

元好问

关中①风土②完厚③,人质直而尚义;风声习气④,歌谣慷慨⑤,且有秦汉之旧⑥;至于山川之胜⑦,游观⑧之富,天下莫与为比;故有四方之志者,多乐居焉。

予年二十许⑨时,侍先人⑩官略阳⑪,以秋试⑫,留长安中八九月。时纨绮气⑬未除,沉涵酒间⑭,知有游观之美,而不暇⑮也。

---

① 关中:潼关以西,今陕西省境内(west of Tongguan, within today's Shaanxi Province)。
② 风土:自然条件(natural conditions)。
③ 完厚:美好肥沃(perfect and affluent)。
④ 风声习气:风气习俗(general mood and convention)。
⑤ 慷慨:意气激昂(in high spirits)。
⑥ 旧:遗风(a custom left by a preceding generation)。
⑦ 胜:景色优美(beautiful scenery)。
⑧ 游观:游览,这里指可供游览之地(sightseeing, here referring to scenic spots)。
⑨ 许:左右(or so)。
⑩ 先人:指其继父元格(referring to his stepfather Yuan Ge)。
⑪ 略阳:地名,在今甘肃省秦安县内(name of a place in today's Qin'an County, Gansu Province)。
⑫ 秋试:指三年一次的仲秋乡试(referring to the triennial examination held in each province in midautumn for the title of Juren 举人)。
⑬ 纨绮气:富家子弟的习气(bad habit of profligate sons of the rich)。
⑭ 沉涵酒间:沉湎酒色(overindulge oneself in wine and women)。
⑮ 不暇:没有空闲时间(have no free time for)。

ON THE DEPARTURE OF MY FRIENDS FROM QIN

Yuan Haowen

The natural conditions in the area west of Tongguan are perfect and affluent and the local people are straightforward by nature and loyal to friends. Its public morals and social customs, together with the exciting folk rhymes and songs seem to have inherited the spirit from ancient times as early as the Qin (221 BC – 206 BC) and Han dynasties. As to the beauty of its mountains and rivers as well as the number of its scenic spots, nowhere in the whole nation can compare with it. Therefore, those who are ready to offer their services wherever they are needed like to make their home here.

When I was about twenty, I looked after my stepfather who held an official position in Lueyang. Then I went to stay in Chang'an City for eight or nine months, to prepare for the imperial examination which was to be held in autumn. At that time, I still had the bad habit of a playboy, indulging in sensual pursuits. Though I knew there were quite a few scenic spots

长大来,与秦人游益多,知秦中事益熟,每闻谈周汉都邑①,及蓝田②鄠③杜④间风物,则喜色津津然⑤动于颜间⑥。二三君⑦多秦人,与予游,道相合而意相得⑧也。常约近南山⑨,寻一牛田⑩,营五亩之宅⑪,如举子⑫结夏课⑬时,聚书⑭深读,时时酿酒为具⑮,从宾客游,伸眉⑯高谈,脱屣世事⑰,览山川之胜概⑱,考前世之遗迹,庶几乎不负古人者。然予以家在嵩前⑲,暑途千里,不若二三君之便于归也。

---

① 周汉都邑:周都邑,指镐京,今陕西省西安市西南;汉都邑,指长安(Hao, the capital of the Zhou Dynasty [1046 BC – 256 BC], in today's southwest of Xi'an, Shaanxi Province; Chang'an, the capital of the Han Dynasty)。
② 蓝田:陕西省蓝田县(Lantian county, Shaanxi Province)。
③ 鄠(hù):鄠县,即今西安市鄠邑区,在今西安市西南(Huyi District, in the southwest of today's Xi'an City)。
④ 杜:杜陵,在陕西省咸宁县(Mound Du, in Xianning County, Shaanxi Province)。
⑤ 津津然:高兴的样子(happy air)。
⑥ 颜间:脸孔上(in the face)。
⑦ 二三君:指"秦中诸人"(referring to several friends from Shaanxi Province)。
⑧ 道相合而意相得:志同道合(cherish the same ideals and follow the same path)。
⑨ 南山:终南山(Mount Zhongnan)。
⑩ 一牛田:一头牛耕种的田地(a piece of land which can be tilled by one cattle)。
⑪ 营五亩之宅:经营五亩的田园(manage five *mu* fields and gardens)。
⑫ 举子:参加考试的文人(scholars who take part in the imperial examinations)。
⑬ 结夏课:在夏日集合起来温习作文(gather together during summer to review and write)。
⑭ 聚书:聚集一些书籍(collect some books)。
⑮ 为具:整理饮食器具(arrange utensils for eating and drinking)。
⑯ 伸眉:扬眉、得意(raise one's brow, looking very pleased)。
⑰ 脱屣世事:如同脱鞋一样摆脱世事(free oneself from affairs of human life just as shoes are dropped)。
⑱ 胜概:美丽的景象(beautiful scenery)。
⑲ 嵩前:嵩山之南(south of Mount Songshan)。

around, I did not have time to go there. As I grew older, I made more friends among the local people of the Qin area and became more familiar with the happenings over there. Every time I heard people talking about the ancient capital cities of the Zhou and Han dynasties or about the local scenery and customs of the vast area including Lantian County, Huxian County and Mound Du, I became so excited that my face would light up with pleasure. All of you are local people of the Qin area. When you were travelling with me, I had the feeling that we were friends sharing the same ideas and thoughts. I often talked with you about my plan to find a piece of land somewhere near Mount Zhongnan and there build a farm with a house and courtyard covering an area of five *mu* (one *mu* = 666.7 square meters). We collected a lot of good books to read attentively, just as a group of scholars usually did on summer days while reviewing their lessons before attending the imperial examination. We kept brewing wine and drinking to our hearts content. Sometimes we went sightseeing with visitors. Talking and laughing cheerfully, we shook off worldly affairs just as taking off our shoes. We would not let our ancestors down when we showed our affections toward the beautiful landscape of mountains and rivers and demonstrated our enthusiasm for exploring the ancient historical remains. However, my home is south of Mount Songshan and to get to the Qin area I will have to travel one thousand *li* (1 *li* = 0.5 km) on hot summer days. It is not as easy as your journey to go

清秋扬鞭，先我就道，矫首①西望，长吁青云。今夫世俗惬意②事，如美食、大官、高赀③、华屋④，皆众人所必争，而造物者⑤之所甚靳⑥，有不可得者。若夫闲居之乐，澹乎其无味，漠乎其无所得，盖自放⑦于方之外⑧者之所贪，人何所争，而造物者亦何靳耶？行矣诸君！明年春风，待我于辋川⑨之上矣。

---

① 矫首：举头（raising one's head）。
② 惬意：心满意足（be fully satisfied and content）。
③ 高赀：钱多（have a wealth of money）。
④ 华屋：华美的居室（magnificent house）。
⑤ 造物者：指上天（Heaven, Providence）。
⑥ 靳：吝惜（spare, stint）。
⑦ 自放：自我放纵（self-indulgent）。
⑧ 方之外：世外（outside the world）。
⑨ 辋川：今陕西蓝田县南，唐时王维筑别墅于此（Wangchuan: a place located in the south of Lantian County, Shaanxi Province, where Wang Wei, a poet of the Tang Dynasty built his villa）。

back home.

Now, breathing the clear autumn air and whipping your horses, you are ready to embark on the journey ahead without taking me with you. I, myself, with my head raised to look westward, saw an azure sky and uttered a deep sigh. Nowadays in society, delicious food, high positions, plenty of money, magnificent houses, and all such things are desperately sought after by everybody. Heaven is not generous in giving out his gifts, so not everyone can get what he wants. But the happiness of staying home leisurely, perhaps tasteless and insipid and so empty as not to have a thing in the world, is what those people who stand aloof from the world have been longing for. Would ordinary people be desperate for this kind of life? Would Heaven be unwilling to give this to those who like it? Please start out, my friends! Wait for me in Wangchuan next year when the spring wind starts to blow.

送张叔夏西游序

戴表元

玉田①张叔夏与余初相逢钱塘②西湖上，翩翩③然飘阿④锡⑤之衣，乘纤离⑥之马，于是风神⑦散朗⑧，自以为承平⑨故家⑩贵游少年不啻⑪也。垂及⑫强仕⑬，丧其行赀⑭。则既牢落⑮偃蹇⑯。尝以艺北游，不遇⑰，失意。亟亟⑱南归，愈不遇。犹家钱塘十年。久之，又去，东

---

① 玉田：张叔夏，号玉田（Zhang Shuxia, was alternatively named Yutian）。
② 钱塘：今杭州市（today's Hangzhou）。
③ 翩翩：举止洒脱（elegant manners）。
④ 阿：细缯（fine silk fabrics）。
⑤ 锡：细布（fine cloth）。
⑥ 纤离：古代北方国名，产良马（name of an ancient state in the north which produced good horses）。
⑦ 风神：风采神态（demeanour and manner）。
⑧ 散朗：潇洒明快（natural and lovely）。
⑨ 承平：太平盛世（time of peace and prosperity）。
⑩ 故家：旧贵族（old nobles）。
⑪ 不啻（chì）：不亚于，如同（not less than, as good as）。
⑫ 垂及：将要到（till）。
⑬ 强仕：指40岁（40 years old）。
⑭ 行赀：路费（travelling expenses）。
⑮ 牢落：无所寄托（no one to entrust）。
⑯ 偃蹇（yǎn jiǎn）：困顿失意（tired out and disappointed）。
⑰ 不遇：没有遇到被提拔的机会（have no chance to be promoted）。
⑱ 亟亟：赶快（at once, quickly）。

A FAREWELL NOTE ON ZHANG SHUXIA'S DEPARTURE FOR THE WEST

Dai Biaoyuan

My first meeting with Zhang Shuxia, alternatively named Yutian, took place on the West Lake in Hangzhou. On that day he looked elegant, wearing nice clothes made of pure silk and fine cloth and riding an expensive Xianli horse. His imposing appearance and graceful manner, so natural and unrestrained, could match that of a young man who was born to the family of a high official in time of peace and prosperity. However, by the time he reached his forties, he had lost all his wealth. So he had nothing to rely on and became worn-out and frustrated. Then he travelled north, trying to use his skill (in calligraphy) to achieve something but ended up in failure. Feeling disappointed, he immediately came back to the south but still made his trip in vain. He settled down in Hangzhou for ten years. Then he left his home again and travelled east to cities or county-seats which included Shanyin, Siming and Tiantai. Once again he did not gain anything from his trips, so he gave up and returned to the west.

游山阴①、四明②、天台③间，若少遇者。既又弃之西归。

于是余周流授徒，适与相值，问叔夏："何以去来道途若是不惮烦耶？"叔夏曰："不然。吾之来，本投所贤，贤者贫；依所知，知者死；虽少有遇而无以宁吾居。吾不得已违④之，吾岂乐为此哉？"语竟，意色不能无阻然⑤。少焉饮酣气张，取平生所自为乐府词，自歌之，噫呜⑥宛抑⑦，流丽清畅，不惟⑧高情旷度⑨，不可亵⑩企⑪，而一时听之，亦能令人忘去穷达⑫得丧⑬所在。

盖钱塘故多大人长者，叔夏之先世高曾祖父，皆钟鸣鼎食⑭，江湖高才词客姜夔尧章⑮、孙季蕃花翁⑯之徒，往往出入馆⑰谷⑱其

---

① 山阴：浙江会稽（kuài jī）山之北（to the north of the Kuaiji Mountain）。
② 四明：今浙江省宁波市（today's Ningbo City, Zhejiang Province）。
③ 天台：今浙江省天台县（today's Tiantai County, Zhejiang province）。
④ 违：离开（leave）。
⑤ 阻然：沮丧的样子（dispirited, depressed）。
⑥ 噫呜：悲切的音调（a plaintive tune）。
⑦ 宛抑：郁结（pent-up）。
⑧ 不惟：若不是（if not）。
⑨ 高情旷度：才情高妙，胸怀旷达（[a profound man] with open minds and deep affections）。
⑩ 亵：轻慢，亲近而不庄重（to be close to sb./sth. without proper respect）。
⑪ 企：企及，希望赶上（expect to catch up with）。
⑫ 穷达：困厄与显达（distressed or illustrious）。
⑬ 得丧：获得与丧失（gain or lose）。
⑭ 钟鸣鼎食：指贵族豪华生活（living an extravagant life of nobles）。
⑮ 姜夔尧章：姜夔，字尧章，南宋词人（Jiang Kui, who styled himself Yaozhang, was a *ci* poet of the Southern Song Dynasty [1127–1279]）。
⑯ 孙季蕃花翁：孙惟信，字季蕃，号花翁，词人（Sun Weixin, styled himself Jifan, alternatively named Huaweng, a *ci* poet）。
⑰ 馆：住宿（lodge）。
⑱ 谷：饮食（food and drink）。

When I was making a teaching tour which entailed going from one place to another, I encountered him and we had a chat. I asked him: "Why do you keep going and coming like this? Don't you feel tired of it?" He answered: "Listen to me. I have been moving from one place to another to seek refuge with somebody. However, when I tried to get help from an able and virtuous man, this man had become poor. When I tried to rely on a person, whom I knew very well, that person had passed away. Although occasionally I was lucky enough to have my ability appreciated, I still could not obtain a decent dwelling in which to settle down. So I had to leave for another place again. Do you think I prefer to move around like this?" Having finished his words, he looked depressed. Then, after drinking to his heart's content, his spirit was soon stimulated by the wine. He brought out the folk songs he had composed over all these years and began to sing the songs. His songs, laden with sorrow, sounded plaintively melodious and pleasantly cadenced. Only profound men with open minds and deep affections could fully appreciate the meaning and beauty of the songs. If ordinary men had a chance to listen to his songs, they would forget their poverty and sufferings.

In Hangzhou there used to be many able and virtuous men who were in high positions. Shuxia's great-great-grandfather and great-grandfather both enjoyed the extravagant life of noble lords. Celebrities such as Jiang Kui (he styled himself Yaozhang) and

门，千金之装，列驷①之聘，谈笑得之，不以为异。迨②其途穷境变，则亦以望于他人，而不知正复尧章、花翁尚存，今谁知之，而谁暇能念之者！

嗟乎！士固复有家世材华如叔夏而穷甚于此者乎！六月初吉③，轻行④过门⑤，云将改游吴公子季札⑥春申君⑦之乡，而求其人焉。余曰：唯唯。因次第其辞⑧以为别。

---

① 列驷：车马众多（many horses and carriages）。
② 迨：等到（by the time）。
③ 初吉：初一（the first day of the month）。
④ 轻行：轻装而行（to travel light; with a light pack）。
⑤ 过门：到家门来拜访（call on）。
⑥ 季札：春秋时吴国公子（the son of a prince of the State of Wu during the Spring and Autumn Period [770 BC – 476 BC]）。
⑦ 春申君：战国时楚国贵族（a noble of the State of Chu during the Warring States Period [475 BC – 221 BC]）。
⑧ 次第其辞：顺着他谈话的次序（according to the order of his talks）。

Sun Jifan (his alternative name was Huaweng) often came to stay and dine in their mansions. Here it was not unusual that during talking and laughing a very expensive robe or a luxurious gift of a beautiful carriage with a number of horses was given. So when the financial situation of Shuxia's family had greatly changed and he found himself in a difficult position, he immediately thought of those people who had had a close association with his family and he placed hope on them. Actually, he did not have any idea about whether Yaozhang, Huaweng and the others would still remember him or whether they would have time to even bother about him, if they were still alive.

Alas! There are some scholars whose talents and family background are as good as Shuxia's but they are even poorer than he. On the first day of the sixth month of the year, Shuxia, travelling with light packs, came to see me. He told me that this time he was going to visit the hometowns of Prince Ji Zha of the State Wu and Lord of Chunshen (of the State Chu) and there he wished to find someone who would appreciate his ability. I said "All right" and then, following the sequence of his story, wrote these farewell words on his departure.

《辋川图》①记

刘因

是图，唐宋金源②诸画谱皆有，评识者③谓惟李伯时④山庄可以比之，盖维平生得意画也。癸酉⑤之春，予得观之。唐史暨维集⑥之所谓竹馆、柳浪⑦等皆可考，其一人与之对谈或泛舟者疑裴

---

① 《辋川图》：即《辋川山庄图》，为唐诗人王维所画。辋川山庄乃王维所筑别墅（the Picture of Wangchuan Mountain Villa was painted by Wang Wei, a famous poet of the Tang Dynasty. The Wangchuan mountain villa was Wang Wei's property）。
② 金源：本指黑龙江省阿勒楚喀河发源地，是金国兴起的地方，后用为金国的别称（originally referring to the source from where the Alechuka River rose in Heilongjiang Province; as this was the birthplace of the State of Jin [1115–1234], hence it became another name of the State of Jin）。
③ 评识者：评论者（commentator）。
④ 李伯时：宋代著名画家李公麟，字伯时，号龙眠居士，安徽舒城人。龙眠山在安徽舒城县北五里，李公麟为泗洲参军，归老于此，自绘《龙眠山庄图》，苏轼为之跋（Li Gonglin, a famous painter of the Song Dynasty [960–1279], styled himself Boshi, alternatively named Lay Buddhist Longmian, was from Shucheng County, Anhui Province. The Longmian Mountain was situated five li north of the county. Li used to be a military staff officer of Sizhou and lived there when old. He painted the "Picture of the Longmian Villa," to which Su Shi wrote a postscript）。
⑤ 癸酉：元世祖至元十年（the tenth year of the Zhiyuan Reign of the Yuan Dynasty [1206–1368]）。
⑥ 维集：王维的集子（collection of Wang Wei）。
⑦ "竹馆""柳浪"：皆辋川山庄之景观（different views of landscape around the Wangchuan Mountain Villa）。

THE PICTURE OF WANGCHUAN MOUNTAIN VILLA

Liu Yin

The "Picture of Wangchuan Mountain Villa" was embraced by all the books of model paintings compiled in the Tang, Song and Jin Dynasties. Some commentators said that only the picture of Longmian Mountain Villa painted by Li Boshi could compare with it. Wang Wei himself might have considered this painting as his personal favorite work. In spring of the tenth year (1273) of the Zhiyuan Reign in the Yuan Dynasty, I had the pleasure to view it. What were described as "the Bamboo House," "Willow Waves" etc. in the *Tang History* and *The Collection of Wang Wei's Poems* could be found in this painting. That figure who was now chatting, now boating with the artist might be Pei Di (a friend of Wang Wei). The picture was so nice, with a beautifully painted landscape of magnificent mountains and graceful waters, glossy grass and elegant trees, that I kept approaching to touch it gently here and there and forgot to roll it up. While doing so, an idea suddenly came into my mind that I wished to have a cottage built

迪①也。江山雄胜②,草木润秀③,使人徘徊抚卷而忘掩④,浩然有结庐终焉⑤之想,而不知秦⑥之非吾土也。物之移人⑦,观者如是,而彼方以是自嬉者,固宜疲精极思⑧而不知其劳也。

呜呼!古人之于艺也,适意玩情⑨而已矣。若画,则非如书计⑩乐舞之可为修己治人之资,则又所不暇而不屑为者。魏晋以来,虽或为之,然而如阎立本⑪者已知所以自耻矣。维以清才⑫位通显⑬,而天下复以高人目之,彼方偃然⑭以前身画师自居,其人品已不足道。然使其移绘一水一石一草一木之精致⑮,而思所以文⑯其身,则亦不至于陷贼而不死,苟免⑰而不耻,其紊乱错逆如是之甚也。岂其自负者固止于此,而不知世有大节,将处己于名臣乎?斯亦不足议者。

---

① 裴迪:王维的友人(a friend of Wang Wei)。
② 雄胜:雄伟奇丽(grand and wonderful)。
③ 润秀:润泽秀美(glossy and graceful)。
④ 掩:指掩卷(close the book)。
⑤ 结庐终焉:在这里建筑房屋安享晚年(build a simple house to spend one's remaining years here)。
⑥ 秦:今陕西(today's Shaanxi)。
⑦ 移人:令人陶醉(make one intoxicated)。
⑧ 疲精极思:殚精竭虑(rack or cudgel one's brains)。
⑨ 玩情:玩赏情趣(take pleasure in one's interest)。
⑩ 书计:书写和计算(write and calculate)。
⑪ 阎立本:唐初著名画家(a famous painter at the beginning of the Tang Dynasty)。
⑫ 清才:清俊之才(remarkable talent)。
⑬ 通显:官位显贵(in high positions)。
⑭ 偃然:俨然(just like)。
⑮ 精致:精巧细致(exquisite and delicate)。
⑯ 文:熏陶(nurture and edify)。
⑰ 苟免:苟且免祸(muddle along to avoid disasters)。

here and to spend the rest of my life in this beautiful place. I did not realize at the moment that the Qin area (where the mountain villa was located) was no longer my homeland. Viewers can be similarly intoxicated by an object such as a good painting. Though the person who made it might have originally attempted to amuse himself, he must have devoted his entire mind and energy to his work without feeling tired.

Alas! Ancient people always took the attitude, toward any artistic skill, of doing it only for amusing themselves in accordance with their own tastes. In their mind, painting was not as good as writing and counting or playing music and dancing which could serve as a means of cultivating one's moral character or governing other people. They did not want to waste time on it as they thought it was not worth doing. Though there have been forerunners who pursued a painting career since the Three Kingdoms Period (220-280) and the Jin Dynasty (265-420), artists such as Yan Liben knew very well how his skill in painting had brought him disgrace. It was his remarkable talent that enabled Wang Wei to hold a high position and the whole nation saw him as a superman of amazing attainments. He himself posed as a born master painter but nothing good can be said about his moral character. Nevertheless, if he had thought how to nurture and edify himself with the same care and craftsmanship which he had put into his painting while drawing the waters, stones, grass and

予特以当时朝廷之所以享盛名，而豪贵之所以虚左①而迎，亲王之所以师友而待者，则能诗能画、背主事贼之维辈也。如颜太师②之守孤城，倡大义，忠诚盖一世，遗烈振万古，则不知其作何状③；其时事可知矣。后世论者，喜言文章以气为主，又喜言境因人胜，故朱子④谓维诗虽清雅，亦萎弱⑤少气骨，程子⑥谓绿野堂⑦宜为后人所存，若王维庄，虽取而有之，可也。呜呼！人之大节一亏，百事涂地⑧，凡可以为百世之甘棠⑨者，而人皆得

---

① 虚左：古人尚左，空出左边的位置以示尊敬（ancient people valued "left"; empty the left seat to show respect）。
② 颜太师：颜真卿。曾任太子太师（Yan Zhenqing used to be the crown prince's teacher）。
③ 不知其作何状：玄宗时，颜真卿为平原太守。安禄山反，河朔尽陷，独平原城仍为颜真卿所守，玄宗得知大喜，顾左右曰："朕不识颜真卿形状何如！"（during the reign of Emperor Xuanzong of the Tang Dynasty, Yan Zhenqing held a position as the chief of Pingyuan prefecture. When An Lushan rebelled, all the cities north of the Yellow River fell, only Pingyuan was still defended by Yan. Knowing this, Emperor Xuanzong was very pleased and looked at his attendants, saying, "It is a pity I have never seen Yan Zhenqing and I don't know what he looks like."
④ 朱子：朱熹（Zhu Xi, a famous philosopher of the Song Dynasty）。
⑤ 萎弱：衰弱（declined and weak）。
⑥ 程子：指宋朝理学家程颐（referring to Cheng Yi, an idealist philosopher of the Confucian school in the Song Dynasty）。
⑦ 绿野堂：唐代名臣裴度的别墅，故址在今河南洛阳市南（the Green-Field Hall, villa of Pei Du, a famous official of the Tang Dynasty; its former site is to the south of Luo Yang City, Henan Province）。
⑧ 涂地：即一败涂地（a complete loss）。
⑨ 甘棠：木名。据说召公循行南国，宣扬文王之政，曾憩于甘棠树下；人民爱戴召公，也因而爱护甘棠（name of a tree, i.e. birchleaf pear. It is said that the Revered Shao Gong went to the south to propagate the administration of King Wen. Once he took a rest under a birchleaf-pear tree. People loved the Revered Shao Gong and thus also loved this type of tree）。

trees, he would not, in order to remain alive, have surrendered to the enemy who had captured him. He would not have become so shameless as not to care about his dignity while begging for mercy. He would not have made himself so ridiculous that he mixed up right and wrong and confused friend with foe. He thought highly of himself. Was this the reason why he did not know the existence of loyalty in the face of adversity and thus he still considered himself as one of the outstanding ministers? However, this is not a topic worth talking about again and again.

Why did Wang Wei enjoy a high reputation in the royal court? Why did the noble men leave the seat on their left vacant to greet him? Why did the princes treat him as their teacher or friend? The only reason, I guess, was that those people and Wang Wei were birds of a feather and therefore they admired his talents in poetry and painting regardless of his wrong doing of betraying the monarch and serving the rebels. On the contrary, Yan Zhenqing (the crown prince's former teacher) was a righteous official who did not surrender to the rebels while leading his troop to guard an isolated city. His loyalty was hardly comparable in his time and his heroism has inspired generation after generation. The emperor had never seen him and did not know what Yan looked like. You can easily imagine the then political situation. Commentators from later generations are keen on the topic that the most important element of an article is the moral standard of the author. They also

以刍狗①之。彼将以文艺高逸自名者，亦当以此自反②也。

予以他日之经行③，或有可以按之以考。夫俯仰间④已有古今之异者，欲如韩文公⑤画记，以谱其次第之大概而未暇，姑书此于后。庶几士大夫不以此自负，而亦不复重此，而向之所谓豪贵王公或亦有所感而知所趋向焉。三月望日⑥记。

---

① 刍狗：古代结草为狗，供祭祀之用，祭祀完毕，随即抛弃，后比喻轻贱无用的东西。这里用作动词（in ancient times people wove a grass effigy of a dog to offer as a sacrifice to the gods. When the ceremony was over, this was thrown away. Later it is figuratively referred to a useless thing. Here used as a verb）。
② 自反：自我反省（reflect on oneself）。
③ 经行：经历与行为（experience and behaviour）。
④ 俯仰间：形容时间短暂（describing a short period of time）。
⑤ 韩文公：韩愈（Han Yu, a famous writer of the Tang Dynasty）。
⑥ 望日：农历十五日（the 15th day of a lunar month）。

like to say that a place becomes enchanting because of the fame of his owner. That's why Master Zhu (Zhu Xi) commented on Wang Wei's poems by saying that they were beautifully written but weak in spirit as they did not have much moral strength. While Master Cheng (Cheng Yi) said that the Green-Field Hall should be well preserved for later generations but Wang Wei's villa could be grabbed by somebody for possession. Alas! Once someone has lost his integrity, he will fail completely in everything. As a result, what are originally cherished as treasures have become things that everybody will reject. Those who would become well-known for their excellent literature and art works should draw a lesson from this event and reflect upon themselves.

I reckon that our future experience may help us, through analysing what are depicted in this painting, study the difference of the past and the present which took place within a short period of time. Originally, I was going to follow the example of Han Yu's *Notes on Paintings* to make a detailed description of this painting from head to toe but I did not have time to do so. Therefore I wrote this article instead. I hope that scholar-officials will not think highly of themselves because of their painting skill and no longer set store by the talent and skill in painting. I also hope that those so called nobilities can learn something from this story, thus knowing what kind of public morals should be held in esteem. Written on the 15th day of the third month.

《录鬼簿》① 序②

钟嗣成

贤愚寿夭③,死生祸福之理,固④兼乎气数⑤而言,圣贤未尝不论也。盖阴阳之屈伸⑥,即人鬼之生死。人而知夫生死之道,顺受其正⑦,又岂有岩墙⑧、桎梏⑨之厄⑩哉?虽然,人之生斯世也,但知以已死者为鬼,而未知未死者亦鬼也。酒罂饭囊⑪,或醉或梦,块然⑫泥土者,则其人虽生,与已死之鬼何异?此曹⑬固未暇⑭论也。

---

① 《录鬼簿》:作者所编元代杂剧作家小传及作品目录的集子(a collection of brief biographies of the drama writers in the Yuan Dynasty and the content of their writings compiled by the author)。
② 序:一种文体,有两种用途,一是叙事,二是议论。本篇不是叙事,而是议论(a type of writing which can be used for writing narrative or argumentative articles. This one is an argumentative essay)。
③ 夭:短命早死(die young)。
④ 固:本来(originally)。
⑤ 气数:命运(fate; destiny)。
⑥ 屈伸:收缩和伸长,指更替(contract and extend, here referring to replacement)。
⑦ 顺受其正:顺应自然法则(comply with natural law)。
⑧ 岩墙:高耸危险的墙(a towering and dangerous wall)。
⑨ 桎梏:镣铐(shackle, bond)。
⑩ 厄:困厄(dire straits)。
⑪ 酒罂(yīng)饭囊:酒囊饭袋(a person who can do nothing but eat and drink)。
⑫ 块然:无知觉的样子(unconsciousness)。
⑬ 此曹:这类人(this kind of people)。
⑭ 未暇:没有工夫(have no time)。

PREFACE TO THE *RECORDS OF GHOSTS*

Zhong Sicheng

It must be relevant to one's own fate that one was born to become either wise or foolish, to live long or die young, to die when one's life is at stake or to stay alive, to enjoy happiness or suffer from misfortune. This topic has also been talked by sages. The growth and decline of the opposite forces (negative and positive, or *Yin* and *Yang* in the Chinese version) in a human body are demonstrated in the form of life and death. If we know the reasons concerning life and death and are willing to comply with the natural law, why should we feel frustrated when we are surrounded by the walls of a prison or restrained by shackles? However, normally people living in this world only know that the deceased are ghosts. They do not know that some of the living are also ghosts. Those who can do nothing but eat and drink, always drunk or dreaming without doing anything useful are as senseless as clay lumps. Though they are alive, what difference can we see between these people and the deceased — ghosts? I do not have time to talk about these useless people. There are some others who

其或稍知义理，口发善言，而于学问之道甘为自弃，临终之后，漠然无闻，则又不若块然之鬼之愈①也。

余尝见未死之鬼吊②已死之鬼，未之思③也，特④一间耳。独不知天地阖辟⑤，亘古迄今⑥，自有不死之鬼在。何则⑦？圣贤之君臣，忠孝之士子，小善大功，著⑧在方册⑨者，日月炳焕⑩，山川流峙⑪，及乎千万劫⑫无穷已，是则虽鬼而不鬼者也。

今因暇日，缅怀古人，门第卑微，职位不振⑬，高才博识，俱有可录。岁月弥久，湮没无闻，遂传其本末，吊以乐章⑭。复以前乎此者，叙其姓名，述其所作。冀乎初学之士，刻意⑮词章⑯，使

---

① 愈：更加，尤甚（more, increasingly）。
② 吊：吊唁，哀悼（condole, pay last respects to）。
③ 未之思：即"未思之"，对此没有考虑过（have never thought of this）。
④ 特：不过，只（only, nothing but）。
⑤ 阖辟：从关闭到打开（from closing to opening）。
⑥ 亘古迄今：从古绵延至今（from time immemorial to the present day）。亘：绵延（be continuous; stretch long and unbroken）。
⑦ 何则：为什么（why）。
⑧ 著：留，记录（remain, recorded in）。
⑨ 方册：史册（history, annals）。
⑩ 炳焕：鲜明，辉煌（bright, glorious）。
⑪ 山川流峙：如水奔流，如山耸峙（flowing like rivers and standing like mountains）。
⑫ 劫（jié）：梵语，天地一毁一成为一劫（Sanskrit, meaning: from ruin to success of heaven and earth）。千万劫：经过极长一段时间（after a long, long time）。
⑬ 不振：不高（not high）。
⑭ 吊以乐章：指《录鬼簿》中给18位剧作家所写悼词（memorial speeches written for the eighteen drama writers in the *Records of Ghosts*）。
⑮ 刻意：用尽心意（painstakingly, sedulously）。
⑯ 词章：诗文（poems and essays）。

are more or less educated and talk well but are unable to persist in their study. These people, after their death, will become unknown to the public. In my mind, they are even more worthless than the above-mentioned ghost-like people.

I have seen the scene of living ghosts paying the last respects to the dead but at the time when I saw it I did not realise how little difference there was between the two. I should have known long ago that since the world came into being and from time immemorial there have existed numerous ghosts who have never died. What are they? They are the former sagacious monarchs and their able subjects, loyal and filial scholar-officials. Whether minor or great, their merits, once written in history, are as glorious as the sun and the moon and as everlasting as a big river or a high mountain. Therefore, although they are no longer living in the human world and have become ghosts, they still exist in our memory as if they were still alive.

Today I am free and have time to recall my departed friends. In spite of their humble family status or low positions, they were all learned and capable personages who deserve occupying a space in my book. For fear that long years will make them sink into oblivion, I have written their biographies as well as memorial poems for some of them. In my book, I also include those who lived earlier than these writers of drama, introducing their names and works. I hope that all the beginners, by constantly improving

冰寒于水①,青胜于蓝,则亦幸矣。名之曰《录鬼簿》。

嗟乎!余亦鬼也。使已死未死之鬼,作不死之鬼,得以传远,余又何幸焉!若夫高尚之士,性理之学②,以为得罪于圣门者,吾党③且啖蛤蜊④,别与知味者⑤道。

至顺元年⑥龙集庚午⑦月建甲申⑧二十二日辛未,古汴⑨钟嗣成序。

---

① 冰寒于水:语出《荀子·劝学》,"冰,水为之,而寒于水"(from "Master Xun's Advice on Study": "Ice coming from water but colder than water")。
② 性理之学:指宋以来的理学(referring to the Confucian school of idealist philosophy since the Song Dynasty)。
③ 吾党:我们(we)。
④ 且啖蛤蜊:意为不顾他人讥讽,自顾吃蛤蜊(meaning: in spite of others' ridicules, just eat one's clams)。啖:吃(eat)。
⑤ 知味者:指真正懂的人(the one who really knows)。
⑥ 至顺元年:1330年。至顺:元文宗年号(the reign title of Emperor Wenzong of the Yuan Dynasty)。
⑦ 龙集庚午:指1330年。
⑧ 月建甲申:这年的夏历七月(the seventh month of this year [of the lunar calendar])。
⑨ 汴:开封的古称(Bianzhou, old name of Kaifeng City, Henan Province)。

their writing skills, will one day surpass these masters. I would be very happy if later generations could excel the former ones. My book is entitled "the Records of Ghosts."

Alas! I am also a ghost. However, I would regard it as my good luck If I were able to make already-dead and still-alive ghosts live forever so that their merits could be passed on to further generations. Whereas those noble-minded scholars who believe in the rationalistic Confucian philosophical school might think I was offending the sages. I don't mind what they say. Just as when we are eating clams, we try to find people who may know the taste to talk with.

Written by Zhong Sicheng from the ancient city of Bianzhou (today's Kaifeng in Henan Province) on the 22nd of the 7th month in the first year of the Zhishun Reign (1330).

大龙湫①记

李孝光

大德七年②秋八月，予尝从老先生③来观大龙湫，苦雨积日夜。是日大风起西北，始见日出。湫水方大。入谷，未到五里余，闻大声转出谷中。从者心掉④，望见西北立石，作人俯势；又如大楹⑤。行过二百步，乃见更作两股相倚立。更进百数步，又如树大屏风。而其颠谽谺⑥，犹蟹两螯，时一动摇。行者兀兀⑦不可入。转缘南山趾⑧，稍北，回视如树圭⑨。又折而入东崦⑩，则仰见

---

① 大龙湫（qiū）：浙江省乐清县雁荡山一著名风景区，亦称大瀑布（a famous landscape on the Yandang Mountain in Yueqing County, Zhejiang. Also named the Big Waterfall）。湫：潭，池，湖（pond, pool, lake）。
② 大德七年：公元 1303 年。大德，元成宗年号（Dade was the reign title of Emperor Chengzong of the Yuan Dynasty）。
③ 老先生：蒙古族官僚，伯牙吾台氏，字兼善，好学嗜古，曾师事李孝光，因出身蒙古贵族家庭，后又做高官，所以作者称之为"老先生"(a Mongolian bureaucrat, named Boyawutai; he styled himself Jianshan and once had Li Xiaoguang as his teacher. He was from a Mongolian noble family and later became a high official; so called "the Old Man" by the author)。
④ 掉：惊恐（alarmed and panicky）。
⑤ 楹：堂屋前部的柱子（principal columns of a hall）。
⑥ 谽谺（hān xiā）：空而深的样子（empty and deep）。
⑦ 兀兀：心情紧张不安（nervous）。
⑧ 山趾：山脚（the foot of a hill）。
⑨ 圭：帝王所执玉质版符（tally made of jade held by kings）。
⑩ 东崦（yān）：东山（the eastern hill）。

THE GREAT DRAGON POND

Li Xiaoguang

In the eighth month (the first month of autumn) of the seventh year of the Dade Reign (1303), I followed the Old Man to visit the Great Dragon Pond. It had been annoyingly raining day and night but on the day when we were there, a strong wind came from the northwest and the sun began to appear. The pond suddenly looked magnificent. We entered the valley and no sooner had we walked five *li* or so than we heard an enormous sound coming from inside the valley. All the attendants were shocked by the noise. Soon I saw a mountain peak standing in the northwest. It resembled a bowing man and also looked like the front column of a big hall. When I saw it again after walking two hundred steps, the peak seemed to have two thighs which supported each other to stand. Having taken another one hundred or more steps, I found it as erect as a huge screen. Its top, split deeply in the middle, looked similar to the two claws of a crab, shaking from time to time. Feeling nervous, the travellers did not dare to go any further. So we turned to walk alongside the foot of the southern hill. I looked back when we were a little further north and saw that the peak was in the shape of a standing jade tally (a symbol of power held

大水从天上堕地，不挂著四壁，或盘桓久不下，忽迸落如震霆。东岩趾有诺讵那庵①，相去五六步，山风横射，水飞著人。走入庵避，余沫迸入屋犹如暴雨至。水下捣②大潭，轰然万人鼓也。人相持语，但见张口，不闻作声，则相顾大笑。先生曰："壮哉！吾行天下，未见如此瀑布也。"

是后，予一岁或一至。至，常以九月。十月，皆水缩，不能如向所见。今年冬又大旱。客入，到庵外石矼③上，渐闻有水声。乃缘石矼下，出乱石间，始见瀑布垂，勃勃④如苍烟。乍小乍大，鸣渐壮急⑤。水落潭上洼石，石被激射，反红如丹砂。石间无秋

---

① 诺讵那庵：罗汉庵（temple for arhats）。
② 捣：冲荡（rinse out, rush away）。
③ 石矼（gāng）：石桥（stone bridge）。
④ 勃勃：喷射出来的样子（spray out）。
⑤ 鸣渐壮急：水声渐渐宏壮急迫（the sound gradually becomes loud and urgent）。

by a monarch). While turning toward the eastern hill, I looked up and saw a flood of water falling from the sky onto the ground without touching any of the surrounding cliffs. It seemed to hover in the air for quite some time before falling down suddenly as powerful as a thunderbolt. At the foot of the eastern hill there was a temple called Nojuna, only a few steps away from us. The mountain wind blew sideways, spraying us with flying water. We had to take shelter in the temple but bubbles kept bouncing into the hall as if torrential rain was pouring outside our shelter. The waterfall, banging on the pond, made very loud noises as though thousands of people were beating drums. We were talking to each other but none of us could hear what was said, so everyone laughed merrily as he saw his counterpart's mouth movement without hearing the voice. The Old Man said: "How marvellous it is! I have traveled all over the country but never seen such a waterfall."

From then on I have come here once every year, often in the ninth month. In the tenth month water decreases and the view is different. This winter has witnessed another drought and this time I have come from outside this area. I was on the stone bridge near the temple and after a while I began to hear the sound of flowing water. I came down from the bridge and then walked through scattered stones. Suddenly I saw a waterfall hanging down from the sky. It was so slender that it looked like blue smoke and its size changed from time to time. As we were approaching, the waterfall sounded louder

毫①土气，产木宜瘠，反碧滑如翠羽凫②毛。潭中有斑鱼③廿余头，闻转石声，洋洋④远去，闲暇回缓⑤，如避世士然。家僮方置大瓶石旁，仰接瀑水。水忽舞向人，又益壮一倍，不可复得瓶。乃解衣脱帽著石上，相持扼腕⑥，欲争取之，因大呼笑。西南石壁上，黄猿数十，闻声皆自惊扰，挽崖端偃⑦木牵连下，窥人而啼。纵观久之，行出瑞鹿院⑧前。今为瑞鹿寺。日已入，苍林积叶，前行，人迷不得路，独见明月宛宛如故人。

老先生谓南山公也。

---

① 秋毫：极少量（so small as to be almost indiscernible）。
② 凫：野鸭子（wild ducks）。
③ 斑鱼：有斑点的鱼（spotted fish）。
④ 洋洋：众多，丰盛（numerous, copious）。
⑤ 闲暇回缓：悠闲自在（leisurely and carefree）。
⑥ 扼腕：牢牢地用手握住腕（hold one's wrist firmly）。
⑦ 偃：横卧（lie transversely）。
⑧ 瑞鹿院：雁荡山中的一座寺院（a temple on the Yandang Mountain）。

and more urgent. The fall, dropping onto the deep-set rock which appeared above the surface of the lake, splashed out and made the rock look as red as cinnabar in the reflection of the sunlight. There was not the slightest sign of soil on the rock, so if there were plants on it, they must not be luxuriant. However, the rock was covered with vegetation which was as green and glossy as the feather of kingfishers or wild ducks. A score or more fish with black spots swiftly swam away on hearing the noise of water hitting the rock. Leisurely and carefree, they looked like a group of hermits who had withdrawn from the human world. One of my servants put a big bottle by the rock, trying to catch water from the fall but the flying water, suddenly doubling its size, gushed at them and he lost hold of the bottle. The servants took off their clothes and hats and placed them on the rock. Holding each other's wrist firmly and yelling and laughing loudly, they tried to retrieve the bottle. On hearing the noise, dozens of yellow apes on the southwestern cliff became nervous and one by one they came down from the horizontally lying trees. Peeping at us from the edge of the cliff, they jabbered sadly. Having enjoyed the view around us for quite some time, we walked out of the valley and came to the front of the Ruilu Hall, today's Ruilu Temple. The sun had set and the ground of the dark green forest was covered with fallen leaves. We lost our way while heading for home and we saw the bright moon which was greeting us gracefully like an old friend.

 The Old Man was the respectable Mr. Nanshan.

送东阳①马生序

宋濂

余幼时即嗜学②,家贫,无从③致④书以观,每假借⑤于藏书之家,手自笔录⑥,计日以还。天大寒,砚冰坚,手指不可屈伸,弗之怠⑦。录毕,走送之,不敢稍逾约⑧。以是人多以书假余,余因得遍观群书。既加冠⑨,益慕圣贤之道,又患无硕师⑩、名人与游,尝趋⑪百里外,从⑫乡之先达⑬执经叩问⑭。先达德隆望尊⑮,门人弟子填其室⑯,未尝稍降辞

---

① 东阳:今浙江省东阳市(today's Dongyang, Zhejiang Province)。
② 嗜学:酷爱学习(be very fond of study)。
③ 无从:无法(unable)。
④ 致:得到(get)。
⑤ 假借:借(borrow)。
⑥ 手自笔录:亲手抄写(copy personally)。
⑦ 弗之怠:弗怠之的倒装(not slack about it)。弗:不(not);怠:懈怠(slack)。
⑧ 逾约:超过约定的限期(exceed a certain time limit)。
⑨ 加冠:古代男子20岁时将头发束在头顶上,戴上帽子,表明他已成年(when twenty, a man will tie his hair on the top of his head and put on a hat, showing he is an adult)。
⑩ 硕师:才学渊博的老师(a great learned teacher)。硕:大(great)。
⑪ 趋:赶往(hurry to)。
⑫ 从:向(from)。
⑬ 先达:有道德学问的前辈(predecessors of virtue and knowledge)。
⑭ 叩问:询问,请教(consult, ask for)。
⑮ 德隆望尊:德高望重(be of noble character and high prestige)。
⑯ 填其室:家里满是(his house is full of)。填:填塞(fill)。

A FAREWELL TO YOUNG SCHOLAR MA FROM DONGYANG

Song Lian

When I was still under age, I already had a great interest in acquiring knowledge from reading. My family was poor and I could not afford to buy books so I had to borrow from those who had books at home. Each time I borrowed a book, I would copy the whole book by hand and then return it to the owner on time. I did not slack off even when the weather was so cold that the inkstone froze and my fingers were stiff. I would rush to return the book as soon as I had finished copying it for fear that I would exceed the time limit. Therefore, those who had books were willing to lend them to me and I could read all kinds of books. When I had grown up, I admired even more the teachings of sages. Without any opportunity to be in the company of great teachers or famous scholars, I had once travelled one hundred *li*, carrying classics, to visit a learned man in my hometown. Having a high moral character

色①。余立侍左右，援疑质理②，俯身倾耳③以请④；或遇其叱咄⑤，色愈恭，礼愈至⑦，不敢出一言以复⑧，俟⑨其忻悦⑩，则又请焉。故余虽愚，卒获有所闻。

当余之从师也，负箧⑪曳屣⑫，行深山巨谷中。穷冬⑬烈风，大雪深数尺，足肤皲裂⑭而不知；至舍⑮，四支⑯僵劲⑰不能动，媵人⑱持汤⑲沃灌⑳，以衾㉑拥覆㉒，久而乃和。寓逆旅㉓，主人日再食，无鲜

---

① 稍降辞色：把言辞放委婉些，把脸色放温和些（with mild tone and gentle look）。
② 援：引（put forward）；疑：疑难问题（difficult questions）；质：询问（enquire, ask for）；理：道理（truth; hows and whys）。
③ 俯身倾耳：弯下身子，侧着耳朵倾听（bending one's body, inclining one's head and listen attentively）。
④ 请：请教（consult）。
⑤ 叱咄：训斥，呵责（rebuke; dress down）。
⑥ 色：神态（expression）。
⑦ 至：周到（attentive and satisfactory）。
⑧ 复：回答（answer）。
⑨ 俟（sì）：等到（wait until）。
⑩ 忻：同欣，喜悦（glad）。
⑪ 负箧（qiè）：背着书箱（carry a small suitcase on the back）。
⑫ 曳屣（yè xǐ）：拖着鞋子（drag one's shoes）。
⑬ 穷冬：严冬（severe winter）。
⑭ 皲（jūn）裂：皮肤因寒冷干燥而破裂（skins break with cold and dry weather）。
⑮ 舍：学舍（dormitory）。
⑯ 四支：四肢（arms and legs）。
⑰ 僵劲：僵硬（stiff）。
⑱ 媵（yìng）人：原指随嫁的女佣人，这里指服侍的人（originally referring to a maid accompanying a bride to her new home; here meaning a servant or a handyman）。
⑲ 汤：热水（hot water）。
⑳ 沃灌：浇洗（pour water on somebody to wash）。
㉑ 衾：被子（quilt）。
㉒ 拥覆：盖上（cover）。
㉓ 逆旅：旅店（hotel）。

and enjoying great esteem, this learned man always had his house full of his followers and disciples. His stern voice and countenance had never become mild. I stood aside, raising some questions and asking for explanations of some principles, bending down to listen attentively while he was making the explanation. When I was rebuked by him for raising a silly question, I would appear more reverent and respectful. I did not dare to say a word until I saw him in a merry mood and then I would again raise a question. Though I was not intelligent, I still gained benefit from his wisdom.

When I finally found a school where I could have teachers to assist with my study, I had to carry a small suitcase and drag my legs amid big mountains and giant valleys. It was midwinter and I was walking against a strong cold wind and stepping over heavy snow several *chi* (3 *chi* = 1 metre) deep. I did not know that the skin of my feet were chapped. On arrival in the school, my arms and legs were numb with cold. The servant, holding a container, poured hot water on me and then covered me with a quilt. It took quite some time to warm me up. I stayed in a hotel and its owner provided two meals a day but without fish and meat. All my school-mates were dressed in embroidered

肥①滋味之享。同舍生皆被绮绣，戴珠缨②宝饰之帽，腰③白玉之环，左佩刀，右佩容臭④，烨然⑤若神人；余则缊袍⑥敝衣⑦处其间，略无⑧慕艳⑨意。以中有足乐者⑩，不知口体之奉⑪不若人也。盖余之勤且艰若此。

今虽耄老⑫，未有所成，犹幸预⑬君子⑭之列，而承天子之宠光，缀⑮公卿之后，日侍坐备顾问⑯，四海亦谬称⑰其氏名⑱，况才之过于余者乎？

---

① 鲜肥：鱼肉（fish and meat）。
② 缨：系帽的带子（tassel tying one's hat）。
③ 腰：此处用作动词，系在腰间（here used as a verb, meaning tying around one's waist）。
④ 容臭（xiù）：香袋（perfume satchel）。
⑤ 烨（yù）然：光彩耀眼的样子（dazzling）。
⑥ 缊（yùn）袍：以乱麻或旧棉为絮的袍子（gown with old cotton as wadding）。
⑦ 敝衣：破衣（poor clothes）。
⑧ 略无：一点也没有（not at all）。
⑨ 慕艳：羡慕（admire and envy）。
⑩ 以中有足乐者：因为心中有足以自得其乐的事（because I have enough in my heart to enjoy myself）。
⑪ 口体之奉：指吃的穿的（referring to food and clothes）。
⑫ 耄（mào）老：八九十岁叫"耄"，这里泛指老（in one's eighties or nineties; here just meaning old）。
⑬ 预：参与（partake）。
⑭ 君子：这里指品学兼优，有社会地位的人（gentleman of virtue and knowledge）。
⑮ 缀（zhuì）：追随（follow）。
⑯ 日侍坐备顾问：天天侍奉在皇帝座旁，准备接受问询（daily attending upon the emperor, ready to be consulted）。
⑰ 谬称：错误地称颂（wrongly praised）。
⑱ 氏名：姓名（name）。

silk clothes, each wearing a cap decorated with jewellery and a girdle mounted with white jade and each carrying a sword on his left and a scent bag on the right. They looked radiant like celestial beings. Among them, I was the only one who was dressed in poor clothes, wearing an old cotton padded robe, but I did not have the slightest feeling of envy or admiration. I had enough in my heart to enjoy, so much and so nice that I did not feel my food and clothing were not as good as theirs. This was an example of my diligence and frugality.

Now I am an old man without achievement. Fortunately, I have the honor to be in the list of real gentlemen — men of noble character and profound knowledge, thus enjoying favor bestowed by the emperor and having the opportunity to follow high officials to go to the court, ready to be consulted by the emperor. I do not think that I deserved the compliments from inside or outside the imperial court, particularly from those whose ability exceeds mine.

今诸生学于太学①，县官②日有廪稍③之供，父母岁有裘④葛⑤之遗⑥，无冻馁之患矣；坐大厦之下而诵诗、书⑦，无奔走之劳矣；有司业⑧、博士⑨为之师，未有问而不告、求而不得者也；凡所宜有之书皆集于此，不必若余之手录，假诸人⑩而后见也。其业有不精、德有不成者，非天质⑪之卑⑫，则心不若余之专耳，岂他人之过哉！

东阳马生君则⑬，太学已二年，流辈⑭甚称其贤。余朝京师⑮，生

---

① 太学：古代设在京城的最高学府（the highest institution of learning established in the capital）。
② 县官：古指天子，这里指朝廷（referring to the emperor in ancient times, but here referring to the court）。
③ 廪（lǐn）稍：官府免费供给的粮食，犹言今之助学金（free grain provided by the government, similar to today's student grant）。
④ 裘：皮衣（fur clothing）。
⑤ 葛：夏布衣服（clothes made of grass cloth）。
⑥ 遗（wèi）：给予（give）。
⑦ 诗、书：这里泛指儒家经典（referring to Confucian classics in general）。
⑧ 司业：相当于今天大学教务长（the equal of today's Dean of Studies in an university）。
⑨ 博士：相当于大学中之教师（the equal of today's college professor）。
⑩ 假诸人：假之于人，向人借（borrow from others）。
⑪ 天质：天资（natural gift）。
⑫ 卑：低下（low）。
⑬ 马生君则：君则系马生的字（the student named Ma styled himself Junze）。
⑭ 流辈：同辈的人（of the same generation; fellow）。
⑮ 朝京师：到京都（南京）朝见皇帝。宋濂年老辞官以后于洪武十一年（1378）再到京都（having an audience with the emperor in the capital Nanjing. After resigning from office, in the eleventh year of the Hongwu Reign [1378], the author came to the capital again）。

The students who are studying in the Imperial College eat free meals every day provided by the government and wear seasonal clothes for the year round prepared by their parents, thus not having to worry about hunger or cold. Sitting in a big building, reading or reciting Confucian classics, they never experience the fatigue from doing a lot of legwork in pursuit of their studies. Having official lecturers and learned scholars as their teachers, they are sure to have their questions answered and their requests granted. All the necessary books are available here and they do not have to do what I used to do — to borrow books from other people and then copy them by hand. If any one of them fails to have a mastery of what he has learnt and also has failed to develop good moral character, a lack of talent is not the reason. No other person but he himself should be blamed for his failure as he is not studying as attentively as I.

A student named Ma Junze from Dongyang has been studying in this Imperial College for two years. People of the same generation regard him as a noble man. Ma came to see me one day as a young man paying a visit to the elder generation of his town. He brought a long letter as a present to me at first meeting. His letter was written smoothly and gracefully.

以乡人子①谒②余,撰③长书④以为贽⑤,辞甚畅达。与之论辩,言和而色夷⑥。自谓少时用心于学甚劳,是可谓善学者矣。其将归见其亲也,余故道为学之难以告之。谓余勉乡人以学者,余之志也;诋⑦我夸际遇⑧之盛而骄乡人⑨者,岂知⑩余者哉!

① 乡人子:同乡晚辈(the younger generation from the same town)。
② 谒(yè):进见长辈或地位高的人(call on a superior or an elder person)。
③ 撰:写(write)。
④ 长书:长信(a long letter)。
⑤ 贽(zhì):初见面时为表敬意送的礼物(gift presented to a senior at one's first visit as a token of respect)。
⑥ 夷:和悦(amiable)。
⑦ 诋(dǐ):毁谤(slander)。
⑧ 际遇:遭遇际会(referring to being appreciated and placed in an important position by the emperor)。
⑨ 骄乡人:在同乡面前骄傲(be arrogant before fellow villagers; here 骄 is used as a verb)。
⑩ 知:了解(understand)。

He spoke in a mild tone and with a pleasant countenance when we were arguing about some issues. He said that when he was a teenager he studied very hard. He can be regarded as a man who knows how to study. On the occasion that he is going to see his parents, I am eager to tell him more about the truth that study is a very hard job. If someone says that I am encouraging a townsman to study hard, I am well understood. However if I am accused of showing off my brilliant career before a townsman, I want to say, "How can you understand my aspiration!"

楚人养狙①

刘基

楚有养狙以为生者，楚人谓之狙公。旦日②必部分③众狙于庭，使老狙率④以之⑤山中，求草木之实⑥，赋⑦什一⑧以自奉⑨。或不给，则加鞭棰⑩焉。群狙皆畏苦之⑪，弗敢违⑫也。

一日，有小狙谓众狙曰："山之果，公所树⑬与⑭？"曰："否也，天生也。"曰："非公不得⑮而取与？"曰："否也，皆得而取也。"

---

① 狙（jū）：猴的一种（a kind of monkey）。
② 旦日：早晨（morning）。
③ 部分：部署、分派（arrange and assign）。
④ 率：带领（lead）。
⑤ 之：往（go to）。
⑥ 实：果实（fruit）。
⑦ 赋：征收（levy）。
⑧ 什一：十分之一（one-tenth）。
⑨ 自奉：供养自己（self support; provide for oneself）。
⑩ 棰（chuí）：鞭打（whip）。
⑪ 畏苦之：畏惧并认为很苦（think of it as suffering）。
⑫ 违：不依从（disobey）。
⑬ 树：此作动词，种植（[v.] plant, grow）。
⑭ 与：欤（a modal particle, used to express doubt, like 吗 or 呢）。
⑮ 得：能（can）。

A MONKEY-RAISER FROM THE CHU AREA

Liu Ji

A man in the Chu Area made his living by raising monkeys and was called Monkey Man by the local people. Every morning he would bring the monkeys together and assigned the eldest one to lead others to collect fruits from the mountain trees and bushes. He always levied one-tenth of the fruits for himself. If they refused, he would whip them. The monkeys regarded that as suffering but dare not disobey.

One day a young monkey asked the other monkeys, "Are the fruits on the mountains grown by Monkey Man?" They replied, "No, they are grown by Nature." The young one continued to ask, "Can only Monkey Man and not others collect them?" They answered, "No, anybody can have them." The youngster asked again, "In that case, why should he control and enslave us?" Before he finished his words, all the others had understood what he meant.

曰:"然则①吾何假②于彼而为之役③乎?"言未既④,众狙皆寤⑤。

其夕,相与俟⑥狙公之寝,破栅毁柙⑦,取其积⑧,相携而入于林中,不复归。狙公卒馁⑨而死。

郁离子⑩曰:世有以术⑪使⑫民而无道揆⑬者,其如狙公乎?惟其昏⑭而未觉也,一旦有开⑮之,其术穷矣。

---

① 然则:(既然这样)那么(in that case; then)。
② 假:凭借(depend on; rely on)。
③ 役:使唤(enslave)。
④ 既:已,尽(finish)。
⑤ 寤:悟(understand, realize)。
⑥ 俟:等待(wait till)。
⑦ 柙(xiá):兽笼(cage for beasts)。
⑧ 积:指积蓄的果实(saved fruits)。
⑨ 馁(něi):饥饿(hungry)。
⑩ 郁离子:作者别号(author's alternative name)。
⑪ 术:权术(political trickery)。
⑫ 使:役使(enslave)。
⑬ 道揆(kuí):道理、法度(reason, law)。
⑭ 昏:认识不清楚(confused)。
⑮ 开:启发(enlighten)。

That evening, they assembled and waited until Monkey Man was asleep and then destroyed the sheds and cages. They took away all the fruits which he had stored and hand in hand went into the forest. They never came back. Finally Monkey Man died of hunger.

Master Yuli says: "In the world, those who enslave people through political trickery and in a lawless way are like Monkey Man, aren't they? Only when the people are muddled and unaware can they do so. Once the people are enlightened, the trickery comes to an end."

卖柑者言

刘基

杭有卖果者,善藏柑,涉①寒暑不溃②。出之烨然③,玉质而金色④。置于市,贾⑤十倍,人争鬻⑥之。

予贸⑦得其一,剖之,如有烟扑口鼻,视其中,干若败絮。予怪而问之曰:"若所市⑧于人者,将以实笾豆⑨、奉祭祀⑩、供宾客乎?将炫⑪外以惑愚瞽⑫也?甚矣者,为欺也!"

---

① 涉:经历(experience)。
② 溃:腐烂(rot, putrid, decompose)。
③ 烨(yè)然:光彩灿烂的样子([of light] bright)。
④ 玉质而金色:质地像玉一样润泽,颜色像金子一样辉煌(be like jade in texture and like gold in colour)。
⑤ 贾:价(price)。
⑥ 鬻:卖,这里应是买的意思(sell but here should mean "buy")。
⑦ 贸:买(buy)。
⑧ 市:卖(sell)。
⑨ 实:充实(fill);笾(biān):祭祀时盛果品的竹器(bamboo ware for containing fruits when offering sacrifices to gods or ancestors);豆:盛肉食等物的木器(woodenware for containing meat)。
⑩ 奉祭祀:作为祭祀的供品(offerings to gods or ancestors)。
⑪ 炫:夸耀(show off)。
⑫ 愚瞽:指傻子与盲人(fools and blind persons)。

A FRUIT-PEDLAR'S WORDS

Liu Ji

A fruit pedlar in Hangzhou was clever at storing oranges. The oranges he stored lasted long and did not rot through summer and winter. When taken out from his storehouse, all the oranges were shiny and each looked like a piece of golden jade. In the market his oranges were sold at a price 10 times higher than the others but customers still went to his shop and fell over each other to buy his oranges.

I bought one from him. While cutting it, smoke burst out, entering my mouth and nostrils. I looked at the pulp and saw dry material similar to cotton waste. I felt strange and asked him: "Will this orange you are selling be used for filling sacrificial utensils to honor our ancestors, or used for entertaining our guests? You are deceiving foolish and blind people by giving the orange a dazzling exterior and you have done much to cheat customers."

卖者笑曰："吾业是有年①矣。吾赖是以食②吾躯。吾售之，人取之，未尝有言，而独不足子③所④乎？世之为欺者不寡矣，而独我也乎？吾子⑤未之思也。今夫佩虎符⑥、坐皋比⑦者，洸洸⑧乎干城之具⑨也，果能授孙吴⑩之略耶？峨大冠⑪、拖长绅⑫者，昂昂乎⑬庙堂⑭之器⑮也，果能建伊皋⑯之业耶？盗起而不知御，民困而不知救，吏奸而不知禁，法斁⑰而不知理，坐糜廪粟⑱而不知耻。

---

① 业是有年：从事这一职业已有好多年（be occupied in this trade for many years）。
② 食：饲（support, keep sb. alive）。
③ 子：对对方的尊称（a respectful form of address for "you"）。
④ 所：所需（what you need）。
⑤ 吾子：对对方的尊称（a respectful form of address for "you"）。
⑥ 虎符：虎形的兵符（a tiger-shaped tally held by a general as imperial authorization for troop movement）。
⑦ 皋比（gāo pí）：虎皮，这里指虎皮做的坐垫（tiger skin, here referring to mattress made of tiger skin）。比：同"皮"。
⑧ 洸（guāng）洸：威武的样子（looking mighty）。
⑨ 干城之具：保卫国家的将才（talent as a field commander defending one's country）。
⑩ 孙吴：古代著名军事家孙武和吴起（Sun Wu and Wu Qi, famous strategists in ancient China）。
⑪ 峨大冠：戴着高冠（wearing a high hat）。峨：高耸的，这里用作动词（high, here used as a verb）。
⑫ 拖长绅：拖着长带子（wearing a long girdle）。
⑬ 昂昂：高贵的样子（elitist manner）。
⑭ 庙堂：朝廷（royal government）。
⑮ 器：人才（a talented person）。
⑯ 伊皋：古代著名的政治家伊尹和皋陶。伊尹，商汤的贤相，曾辅佐商汤攻灭夏桀；皋陶，相传是舜的刑官（Yi Yin and Gao Yao, two famous statesmen in ancient China. Yi Yin was Shang Tang's good prime minister who assisted him to destroy Jie, the last ruler of the Xia Dynasty [approx. 2070 BC – 1600 BC]. Gao Yao was said to be Shun's official in charge of punishment）。
⑰ 斁（dù）：败坏（ruin, corrupt）。
⑱ 坐糜廪粟：坐着白吃国家仓库里的粮食（consume grain in the state granary without doing anything useful）。糜：耗费（consume）。廪：粮仓（granary）。

He laughed and said: "I have been in this business for years and I am doing it to earn a living. I sell oranges and customers buy them. No one has complained. You are the only unhappy customer. There are so many cheaters in the world. I am not the only one, but you are not considering this fact. Those who hold tiger-shaped tallies and sit on tiger-skin cushions have a commanding presence. Do they really possess the wisdom and capability which Sun Wu and Wu Qi had as military commanders? Those who wear high hats and long girdles sit imposingly in the royal court. Can they achieve political greatness like Yi Yin and Gao Yao? They do not know how to suppress the rampant robbers and bandits and do not do anything to help the poverty-stricken people. They are unable to control the treacherous officials and restore the now corrupted law and order. They do not feel ashamed of the extravagance and waste they have made. Look at those people who are living in grand mansions, riding giant horses, drinking expensive wine and eating luxurious food. Which one of them does not have a majestic appearance that holds you in awe? Which one of them does not have an eminent position that makes you envious? Wherever they go, all of them, no one excepted, are shining on the outside but rotten on the inside. Now you are blind to all these facts but critical about my orange."

观其坐高堂,骑大马,醉醇醴①而饫②肥鲜者,孰不巍巍③乎可畏,赫赫④乎可象⑤也?又何往而不金玉其外,败絮其中也哉!今子是之不察,而以察吾柑!"

予默默无以应。退而思其言,类东方生⑥滑稽⑦之流,岂其愤世嫉邪⑧者耶?而托⑨于柑以讽⑩耶?

---

① 醇醴(chún lǐ):味道醇厚的美酒(good wine with good taste)。
② 饫(yù):饱食(eat one's fill)。
③ 巍巍:高不可攀的样子(in a manner difficult to reach)。
④ 赫赫:气势很盛的样子(domineering manner)。
⑤ 象:效法(learn from)。
⑥ 东方生:指东方朔,汉武帝时大夫,善辞赋,性诙谐,常以滑稽之言进行讽谏(named Dongfang Shuo, a high official in the time of Emperor Wudi of the Han Dynasty. He was good at literary composition and humorous in character, often providing parable and expostulation for the emperor)。
⑦ 滑稽(gǔ jī):诙谐,机智(humorous and quick-witted)。
⑧ 愤世嫉邪:对世事表示愤慨,对邪恶表示憎恨(express one's indignation toward affairs of human life and hate toward social evils)。
⑨ 托:假借(make use of)。
⑩ 讽:讽劝。指用含义深刻的话进行劝告或指责(persuade humorously, i.e. persuade or criticise sb. with profound implications)。

I did not have anything to say. Later, when I was pondering what he had said, I realised that he was a witty man like Dongfang Shuo. He detested human injustices and used his orange to satirise the ugly side of human society.

书博鸡者事（节选）

高启

博鸡①者，袁人②，素无赖③，不事④产业⑤，日抱鸡呼少年博市中。任气⑥斗，为里侠者⑦皆下⑧之。

元至正⑨间，袁有守⑩多惠政⑪，民甚爱之。部使者臧⑫，新贵⑬，将按郡⑭至袁。守自负年德⑮，易之⑯，闻其至，笑曰："臧氏之子也。"

---

① 博鸡：以斗鸡作为赌博（to gamble on cockfighting）。
② 袁人：袁州人（a native of Yuanzhou, in Jiangxi Province）。
③ 素无赖：一向游手好闲，蛮不讲理（always idle about and behave savage and unreasonable）。
④ 事：从事（go in for, be engaged in）。
⑤ 产业：生计，生产（means of livelihood）。
⑥ 任气：任性（willful）。
⑦ 为里侠者：乡间当好汉的（brave men in the countryside）。
⑧ 下：服从（obey, be submitted to）。
⑨ 至正：元朝最后一个皇帝惠宗的年号（the reign title of the last emperor [Emperor Huizong] of the Yuan Dynasty）。
⑩ 守：太守，这里指总管。（prefectural chief in ancient China）。
⑪ 惠政：善政（benevolent rule in administration）。
⑫ 部使者臧：江西湖东道肃政廉访使臧某（a certain person called Zang, who was then an official in charge of supervision in Hudong Circuit in Jiangxi Province）。
⑬ 新贵：新登高官的人（a man newly appointed to a high official position）。
⑭ 按郡：视察所管辖的各路（inspect each prefecture in his jurisdiction）。
⑮ 自负年德：倚仗自己资格老，品德好（to flaunt one's seniority and good reputation）。负：凭借，依仗（rely on）。年：做官的年资（qualifications as an official）。
⑯ 易之：看不起他（look down upon him）。

THE BRAVE DEEDS OF A COCKFIGHT GAMBLER (EXCERPTS)

Gao Qi

A cockfight gambler from Yuanzhou was a rascal who disliked working and had the habit of holding a cock in his arms every day and call to the youngsters he met to gamble in the city streets. He was so willful and combative that even the most gallant men in town bowed to his superiority.

During the Zhizheng Reign (1341–1368) of the Yuan Dynasty, there was a chief of the Yuanzhou Prefecture who was held in high esteem by the local people because of his benevolent government. The circuit inspector named Zang, a newly appointed high official, during his tour to inspect each prefecture under his jurisdiction, would come to Yuanzhou. The prefecture chief, sure in his own seniority and reputation, looked down upon Zang. On hearing that Zang was arriving, he laughed and said, "A green hand from the Zang Family is coming." Zang was furious when somebody

或①以告臧。臧怒，欲中守法②。会③袁有豪民④尝受守杖，知使者意嗛⑤守，即诬守纳⑥己赇⑦。使者遂逮守，胁服⑧，夺其官。袁人大愤，然未有以报⑨也。

一日，博鸡者遨⑩于市。众知有为⑪，因让⑫之曰："若⑬素名⑭勇，徒能藉⑮贫孱⑯者耳！彼豪民恃⑰其资⑱，诬去贤使君⑲，袁人失父母；若诚⑳丈夫㉑，不能为使君一奋臂㉒耶？"博鸡者曰："诺。"即

---

① 或：有人（someone）。
② 欲中守法：想假借法律陷害太守（attempt to frame the chief in the guise of law）。中：击中（attack）。
③ 会：适逢（happen to）。
④ 豪民：强横而又富有之人（an unreasonable and rich man）。
⑤ 嗛（xián）：通"衔"，怀恨（nurse a hatred for）。
⑥ 纳：收受（receive）。
⑦ 赇（qiú）：贿赂（bribery）。
⑧ 胁服：强迫他认罪（force him to admit his guilt）。
⑨ 未有以报：没有办法对付（without any way with which to cope）。
⑩ 遨：游荡（loaf about）。
⑪ 众知有为：众知其有为，大家知道他有办法（all knew he could think of a way）。
⑫ 让：责备（blame）。
⑬ 若：汝，你（you）。
⑭ 名：号称（be known as）。
⑮ 藉：欺侮（bully）。
⑯ 孱（chán）：软弱（frail, weak）。
⑰ 恃：依仗（rely on）。
⑱ 资：资财（capital and goods; assets）。
⑲ 诬去贤使君：诬陷赶走了贤德的总管（frame and drive away the virtuous general director）。使君：汉朝时候对州郡长官刺史和太守的尊称，这里指总管（a respectful form of address toward the officials such as prefectural governors in the Han Dynasty, here referring to the general director, i.e., the chief）。
⑳ 诚：果真（if really）。
㉑ 丈夫：男子汉，大丈夫（true man; real man）。
㉒ 奋臂：振臂而起。这里是指动手帮助（raise one's arm and rise, here meaning: raise a hand to help）。

informed him about it and attempted to frame the prefect. It so happened that a local tyrant who had once been punished with the rod by the prefect heard that the inspector nursed a hatred for the prefecture chief. He fabricated a charge against the chief, accusing the latter of taking a bribe from him. The inspector immediately arrested the prefect, forced him to plead guilty and removed him from office. The local people of Yuanzhou were greatly angered by this happening but no action could be taken.

One day the cockfight gambler was wandering in the city street. Knowing that he could always find a way out in whatever circumstances, someone pretended to sneer at him by saying: "You are noted for bravery, but you cannot call yourself a brave man if you only know how to bully the weak. That despotic gentry took advantage of his wealth and influence to frame our able and virtuous chief, thus making us, the people of Yuanzhou, lose the parent-like prefect. If you are a real man, why don't you do something to help the good man?" The cockfight gambler answered, "Yes, I will do something!" He immediately went to the residential area where the poor people lived and called together dozens of strong young men to stand in the despotic gentry's way. The wicked rich man, brightly dressed, was on horseback followed

入闾左①，呼子弟②素健者，得数十人，遮③豪民于道。豪民方华衣乘马，从群奴④而驰。博鸡者直前捽⑤下，提殴之⑥。奴惊，各亡⑦去。乃褫⑧豪民衣自衣，复自策其马⑨，麾⑩众拥豪民马前，反接⑪，徇⑫诸市。使自呼曰："为民诬太守者视此！"一步一呼，不呼则杖⑬，其背尽创⑭。豪民子闻难⑮，鸠⑯宗族童奴百许人，欲要⑰篡⑱以归。博鸡者遂谓曰："若欲死⑲而⑳父，即前斗。否则阖㉑门善俟㉒。"

---

① 闾（lú）左：贫苦人家聚居处。古时富家居闾右，穷家居闾左（slum area which is crowded with poor people. In the old days, rich people lived on the right and poor people on the left of the gate of an alley）。闾：巷门，里门（the gate of an alley）。
② 子弟：年轻人（young men）。
③ 遮：拦住（hold back）。
④ 从群奴：后面跟着一群奴仆（followed by a group of servants）。
⑤ 捽（zuó）：揪住（seize）。
⑥ 殴：打（beat）。
⑦ 亡：逃（run away）。
⑧ 褫（chǐ）：剥去（strip away）。
⑨ 策其马：骑上豪民的马并鞭打之（ride his horse and whip it）。
⑩ 麾（huī）：古代指挥军队的旗帜，此处用作动词，即指挥（a flag for directing an army, here used as a verb, meaning: direct）。
⑪ 反接：两手反在背后（be bound with two hands behind the back）。
⑫ 徇（xún）：游行示众（parade sb. through the streets）。
⑬ 杖：用木棍打（beat with a wooden rod）。
⑭ 尽创：到处是伤痕（covered with scars）。
⑮ 难（nàn）：事变，乱子（trouble）。
⑯ 鸠：纠，集合（gather）。
⑰ 要：邀，拦截（intercept）。
⑱ 篡：夺取（take by force）。
⑲ 死：置之于死地（put him to death）。
⑳ 而：你的（your）。
㉑ 阖（hé）：关（close）。
㉒ 俟（sì）：等待（wait）。

by a group of servants. The brave gambler dashed to pull him down from the horseback and beat him. His frightened servants fled from the scene. The brave man stripped off the rich man's robe and put it on himself. Then he mounted the horse and told his followers to push the tyrant in front of the horse. With both hands tied together behind his back, the evil man was paraded through the streets. He was ordered to shout: "Look here! I am the one who has framed the prefect." He had to shout these words every time he took a step. He was flogged by a stick if he refused to do so and soon bruises were all over his back. On hearing this incident, the tyrant's son mustered over one hundred people including his clansmen and all the young servants. He attempted to obtain his father by force. The cockfight gambler said to him: "Come forward to fight if you want your father to die. Otherwise, stay at home and shut your door to wait. I will return your father to you as soon as I have finished the parade. He will be all right." For fear that his father would be killed by the flogging, the son did not dare to take any action. He soon withdrew his men and returned home. Many people had gathered to watch the event which later caused a great sensation in the whole city. The official in charge of the civil affairs in the prefecture was shocked by the happening and

吾行市①毕,即归若父,无恙②也。"豪民子惧遂杖杀其父,不敢动,稍敛③众以去。袁人相聚从观④,欢动一城。郡录事⑤骇之⑥,驰⑦白⑧府⑨。府佐⑩快其所为⑪,阴纵之⑫不问。日暮,至豪民第门,摔使跪,数⑬之曰:"若为民不自谨⑭,冒⑮使君,杖汝,法也⑯;敢用是⑰怨望⑱,又投间⑲蔑污使君,使罢⑳。汝罪宜死,今姑贷汝㉑。后不善自改,且复妄言,我当焚汝庐㉒、戕㉓汝家矣!"豪民气尽㉔,以额叩地,谢不敢。乃释之。

---

① 行市:徇示,游街示众（to parade sb. through the streets to humiliate him before the public）。
② 恙（yàng）:疾病,担忧（illness, worry）。
③ 敛:收敛,集合（restrain oneself; gather）。
④ 相聚从观:聚集在后面看热闹（gather to watch the scene from behind）。
⑤ 录事:掌管城中民事的官员（an official in charge of civil affairs in a prefecture）。
⑥ 骇之:对其事感到可怕（be frightened by sth.）。
⑦ 驰:飞奔（run quickly）。
⑧ 白:报告（report）。
⑨ 府:总管府（the prefecture government）。
⑩ 府佐:总管府中的辅佐官（assisting officials in the prefectural government）。
⑪ 快其所为:以其所为为快事（feel happy about what he did）。
⑫ 阴纵之:暗地里放纵博鸡者（secretly indulge the cockfight gambler）。
⑬ 数（shǔ）:数落,责备（scold）。
⑭ 谨:老老实实（behave oneself）。
⑮ 冒:冒犯（offend）。
⑯ 杖汝,法也:拷打你是依法治罪（to flog you with a stick is a punishment according to law）。
⑰ 用是:因此（because of this）。
⑱ 为怨望:生怨恨之心（have a grudge against sb.）。
⑲ 投间:钻空子（seek loopholes）。
⑳ 使罢:使……遭免官（have sb. dismissed from office）。
㉑ 姑贷汝:暂且饶了你（pardon you for the time being）。贷:饶恕（forgive）。
㉒ 庐:房屋（house）。
㉓ 戕（qiāng）:杀（kill）。
㉔ 气尽:气焰一点也没有了（to have no arrogance left）。

immediately went to report it to the prefectural government. However, the assistant in the prefect's office was happy with what the cockfight gambler had done and did not intend to do anything to restrain this man's behavior. When it was getting dark, the tyrant was taken to the door of his house where he was forced to kneel down on the ground. The brave man scolded him by enumerating his wrongdoings: "You are a citizen but you do not behave yourself, so I have ventured to flog you with a stick. I am acting according to the law. You seized an opportunity to vent personal grudges by slinging mud at the prefect to make him lose his position. You are guilty and deserve the death penalty. Today we will spare your life but if you do not amend your ways and shut your dirty mouth, I will burn your house and kill all your family members." Having lost all his arrogance, the local tyrant knelt and knocked his forehead on the ground, saying: "I don't dare to do it any more." He was soon released.

The hero asked the crowd, "Is it enough to repay the kindness

博鸡者因告众曰:"是足以报使君未①耶?"众曰:"若所为诚快②,然使君冤未白③,犹无益也。"博鸡者曰:"然。"即连楮④为巨幅,广⑤二丈,大书一"屈"字,以两竿夹揭⑥之,走诉行御史台⑦。台臣弗为理⑧。乃与其徒日张"屈"字游金陵市中。台臣惭,追受其牒⑨,为复守官而黜⑩臧使者。方是时,博鸡者以义闻东南。

---

① 未:同否(is it ... or not)。
② 诚快:确实(叫人)痛快(really make us happy)。
③ 未白:没有昭雪(has not been righted)。
④ 楮(chǔ):纸张。楮是一种落叶乔木,树皮可造纸(paper made of mulberry, a kind of arbor whose skin can be used to make paper)。
⑤ 广:宽(wide)。
⑥ 揭:高举(hold high)。
⑦ 行御史台:中央御史台在各重要地区的分支机构(branch organ of the central supervisory commission)。
⑧ 台臣弗为理:御史台的长官不受理他们的案子(the officials of the supervisory commission did not accept and hear their case)。
⑨ 追受其牒(dié):追认前状,受理了他们的诉状(subsequently confirm the previous complaint and accept and hear it)。
⑩ 黜(chù):罢免(dismiss sb. from his post)。

of the prefect?" They answered, "We are pleased with what you have done but it is of no help as the fabricated charge against our good man has not been redressed." The brave man responded by simply saying, "All right!" He soon used glue to join quite a few pieces of paper to make a two-*zhang*-wide (1 *zhang* = 3.3 m) banner on which a huge character of "injustice" was written. Then he fixed this banner between two bamboo poles and together with his followers, held it high. They marched to the branch office of the central supervisory commission and lodged a complaint of injustice but the officials there did not accept and hear his case. So every day he led his men, carrying the big banner, to parade in the city of Jinling. Feeling ashamed, the officials accepted and heard his case retroactively. To enable the prefect to resume his post, they dismissed the circuit inspector named Zang. Thus the cockfight gambler became famous for his brave deeds in the southeast of the nation.

指　喻

方孝孺

浦阳①郑君仲辨，其容阗然②，其色渥然③，其气充然④，未尝有疾色也。他日，左手之拇有疹⑤焉，隆起而粟⑥，君疑之，以示人。人大笑，以为不足患⑦。既三日，聚而如钱，忧之滋⑧甚，又以示人。笑者如初。又三日，拇之大盈握⑨，近拇之指，皆为之痛，若剟刺⑩状，肢体心膂⑪无不病者。惧而谋诸医。医视之，惊曰："此疾之奇者，虽病在指，其实一身病也，不速治，且能伤生。然始发之时，终日可愈；三日，越旬可愈；今疾且成，已非三月不能瘳⑫。终日而愈，艾可治也；越旬而愈，药可治也；至于既成，甚将延乎肝膈，否

---

① 浦阳：浙江浦江县的旧称（old name of Pujiang County, Zhejiang）。
② 阗（tián）然：丰满的样子（full）。
③ 渥（wò）然：红润的样子（ruddy, rosy）。
④ 充然：充足的样子（ample）。
⑤ 疹（zhěn）：皮肤上生的小疙瘩（rash）。
⑥ 粟：米粒那样大小（like a rice grain）。
⑦ 患：忧虑，担心（worry）。
⑧ 滋：增加（increase）。
⑨ 握：一把的容量（the full hold of a hand; here describing that a tiny object becomes so big that a hand can hardly hold it）。
⑩ 剟（duō）刺：割刺（cut or stab）。剟：刺，击（stab, prick）。
⑪ 膂（lǚ）：脊梁骨（backbone）。
⑫ 瘳（chōu）：病愈（recover from an illness）。

THE ENLIGHTENMENT FROM A SICK THUMB

Fang Xiaoru

Mr. Zheng Zhongbian from Puyang County looked very healthy having smooth and round cheeks, rosy complexion and a vigorous spirit. He had never looked ill. One day, a rash appeared on the thumb of his left hand. It swelled and looked like a rice grain. Feeling somewhat apprehensive, he showed it to others. They burst into laughter and told him not to worry. Three days later, the skin eruption on his thumb was as big as a coin and he became more concerned. Once again he showed his thumb to others and they laughed as the first time. Another three days later, his thumb swelled to the size of a fist. His other fingers near the thumb were also painful as if they were being cut or pricked. His limbs, heart and backbone all were aching. He was fearful now and went to see a doctor. The doctor was surprised to see the swollen thumb and said: "This is a peculiar disease. Though only the thumb looks awful, actually the whole body is sick. Unless treated at once, it will endanger your life. When it has just happened, it can be cured within a day. If the treatment has been delayed for three days, it will take ten days to cure the illness. Now that you have become very sick, your illness cannot be cured within three months. When it can be cured within one day, moxibustion is good enough for

亦将为一臂之忧。非有以御其内,其势不止;非有以治其外,疾未易为也。"君从其言,日服汤剂,而傅①以善药。果至二月而后瘳,三月而神色始复。

余因是思之:天下之事,常发于至微,而终为大患;始以为不足治,而终至不可为。当其易也,惜旦夕之力,忽②之而不顾;及其既成也,积岁月,疲思虑③,而仅克④之,如此指者多矣!盖众人之所可知者,众人之所能治也,其势虽危,而未足深畏;惟萌于不必忧之地,而寓于不可见之初,众人笑而忽之者,此则君子之所深畏也。

---

① 傅:同"敷"(apply)。
② 忽:不注意(inattention)。
③ 疲思虑:费了不少心血(cost / expend much painstaking effort)。
④ 克:克服(overcome, conquer)。

the treatment. When it needs more than ten days for the treatment, medication will be needed to cure the illness. When the patient has become very sick, his liver and diaphragm may have been affected. Even if this is not the case, the swollen thumb will become a curse to the relevant arm. Unless we give you an internal treatment, we will not be able to stop your illness from becoming worse. Nevertheless, if an external treatment is not carried out, you will never be free from the illness." Mr. Zheng accepted the doctor's advice, taking a dose of decoction of medical ingredients every day and applying an effective ointment externally. As expected, two months later, his illness was cured. Then another month later, his spirit and complexion started to return to normal.

Enlightened by this event, I have come to realize that similar things often happen in the world: a minor problem will eventually become a great disaster. When a problem has just occurred, people are inclined to think that there is no need to solve the problem. However, a minor problem may finally develop into a large crisis which is hard to tackle. When it is easy to handle, people are eager to conserve every bit of their energy. Owing to their negligence, no attention has been paid to the problem. Once it has become a great disaster, a long period of time has to be spent and a lot of energy and brains have to be used for overcoming the crisis. In the world, there are many happenings that are similar to what happened to the thumb. Therefore, when an event occurs, if it is already known by many people and can be easily handled, there should be no fear even though the situation appears desperate. We should only feel rather fearful about such an affair

昔之天下，有如君之盛壮无疾者乎？爱天下者，有如君之爱身者乎？而可以为天下患者，岂特①疮痏②之于指乎？君未尝敢忽之；特以不早谋于医，而几至甚病。况乎③视之以至疏之势，重④之以疲敝⑤之余，吏之戕摩⑥剥削⑦以速⑧其疾者亦甚矣！幸其未发，以为无虞⑨而不知畏，此真可谓智也与哉！

余贱，不敢谋国，而君虑周行果⑩，非久于布衣者也。传不云乎"三折肱而成良医⑪"？君诚⑫有位⑬于时，则宜以拇病为戒。洪武辛酉⑭九月二十六日述。

---

① 岂特：岂止（isn't that only ...）。
② 痏（wěi）：伤口（wound）。
③ 况乎：何况（let alone）。
④ 重：加重（aggravate）。
⑤ 疲敝：人力物力受到消耗（consumed in manpower or material resources）。
⑥ 戕（qiāng）摩：杀害，消灭（kill, wipe out）。
⑦ 剥削：搜刮（extort）。
⑧ 速：加快（quicken）。
⑨ 虞：忧虑（anxiety）。
⑩ 虑周行果：考虑周密，行动果断（careful in consideration and decisive in action）。
⑪ 三折肱（gōng）而成良医：多次折断胳膊后，渐通医术，遂成为一个好医生（if you have your arms fractured several times, you would become a good doctor）。
⑫ 诚：如果（if）。
⑬ 位：官位（official position）。
⑭ 洪武辛酉：洪武十四年，即公元1381年。洪武是明太祖年号（the 14th year [1381] of the Hongwu Reign; Hongwu is the reign title of the founder of the Ming Dynasty [1368–1644]）。

whose happening does not make people feel it is necessary to worry, whose hidden danger cannot be seen at the beginning and whose existence does not worry anybody as many people still ridicule it.

Was the world in the past free from any disaster just like Mr. Zheng who was originally free from any ailment? Among the people who love the nation, is there anybody who cares for the nation as much as Mr. Zheng cares for his health? Is the disaster which makes the whole nation suffer similar to the sore on someone's finger? Mr. Zheng did not overlook the sore on his thumb but in not to see the doctor early enough, he was almost beaten by the illness. However, while dealing with a social problem, people usually take an extremely careless attitude. Common people are already poverty-stricken but the officials still try to suppress and exploit them, quickening the process of making them even poorer. Fortunately, the world is still not in chaos. But if the rulers think there is nothing to worry about and they do not feel any fear, it cannot be regarded as a wise attitude.

Humble as I am, I dare not give any advice or suggestion to the imperial court. Whereas Mr. Zheng, careful in consideration and decisive in action, will not remain as a normal person for ever. There is a saying in *Zuo Zhuan* (the *Spring and Autumn Annals*), "If you have your arms fractured several times, you would become a good doctor." Had Mr. Zheng held an official position one day, he would learn a lesson from the illness of his thumb. Written on the 26th of the ninth month in the 14th year of the Hongwu Reign (1381).

游龙门①记

薛瑄

出河津县西郭门②,西北三十里,抵龙门下。东西皆层峦危③峰,横出天汉④。大河自西北山中来,至是山断河出,两壁俨立⑤相望。神禹⑥疏凿之劳,于此为大。

由东南麓穴⑦岩构⑧木,浮虚⑨架水为栈道⑩,盘曲而上。濒⑪河有宽平地,可⑫二三亩,多石少土。中有禹庙,宫曰"明德",制⑬

---

① 龙门:位于山西省河津与陕西省韩城之间(situated between Hejin, Shanxi Province and Hancheng, Shaanxi Province)。
② 郭门:城门(city gate)。
③ 危:高峻(high and steep)。
④ 天汉:银河(the Milky Way)。
⑤ 俨立:整齐地立着(stand in good order)。
⑥ 神禹:凿龙门导黄河的夏禹(Great Yu, the founder of the Xia Dynasty, who created a miracle to chisel the Dragon Gate to channel flood into the sea)。
⑦ 穴:这里作动词用,凿洞(make a hole of, here used as a verb)。
⑧ 构:这里亦作动词用,架木(put up, here also used as a verb)。
⑨ 浮虚:凌空(be high up in the air)。
⑩ 栈道:悬崖上架设木板铺成的通道(passageway erected over cliffs)。
⑪ 濒:临近(close to)。
⑫ 可:大约(about)。
⑬ 制:规模(scale)。

A TRIP TO LONGMEN

Xue Xuan

Going out of the western city gate of Hejin County and then traveling thirty *li* northwestward, we arrived at the foot of the Longmen Mountain. To both east and west we saw range upon range of mountains and high peaks, towering into the sky. The Yellow River was running from the gorge in the northwest and up here river waters replaced rolling mountains. Steep cliffs faced each other across the river. From here we could see the outstanding achievements of the great legendary Da Yu (Great Yu) who had tamed the flood by widening the gorge to dredge the waterways.

On the southeastern side of the mountain, holes were bored into the rocks at its foot for holding wooden brackets and a plank road winding up the mountain was built on them for crossing the river. A piece of flat land lay on the river bank. This land, 2 or 3 *mu* (1 hectare = 15 *mu*), had more stones than soil. At its centre stood a temple called "Mingde Palace." This magnificent hall was used to honour King Yu. I entered the temple and paid homage to this legend. Pondering over his monumental contributions, I stood there for quite some time

极宏丽。进谒①庭下,悚肃②思德③者久之。庭多青松奇木,根负④土石,突⑤走连结,枝叶疏密交荫,皮干苍劲偃蹇⑥,形状毅然,若壮夫离立⑦,相持不相下。宫门西南,一石峰危出半流⑧。步石磴⑨,登绝顶,顶有临思阁,以风高不可木⑩,甃⑪甓⑫为之。倚阁门俯视,大河奔湍⑬,三面触激,石峰疑若摇振。北顾巨峡,丹崖翠壁,生云走雾,开阖⑭晦⑮明,倏忽⑯万变。西则连山宛宛⑰而去。东视大山,巍然与天浮⑱。南望洪涛漫流,石洲⑲沙渚⑳,高原缺岸,烟村雾

① 谒:进见(pay one's respects to)。
② 悚(sǒng)肃:恭敬(with great respect)。
③ 思德:思念功德(fondly remember one's merits and virtues)。
④ 负:背着(carry)。
⑤ 突:穿(pass through)。
⑥ 偃蹇(jiǎn):高傲的样子(arrogant manner)。
⑦ 离立:并立(stand side by side)。
⑧ 半流:中流(midstream)。
⑨ 石磴:石级(stone step)。
⑩ 不可木:不可用木料建筑(can't be constructed with wood)。
⑪ 甃(zhòu):砌(build by laying bricks or stones)。
⑫ 甓(pì):砖(brick)。
⑬ 湍(tuān):急流(rapid stream)。
⑭ 阖(hé):合(shut)。
⑮ 晦:暗(dark)。
⑯ 倏(shū)忽:突然(suddenly)。
⑰ 宛宛:蜿蜒(winding; zigzagging)。
⑱ 与天浮:和天一起浮在空中(floating in the air together with the sky)。
⑲ 洲:水中陆地(land in water)。
⑳ 渚:小洲(small piece of land surrounded by water, islet)。

with my heart full of veneration for this great man. In the courtyard there were many pine trees and other unknown trees. Their roots broke through rocks and soil, stretching far and tangling with each other. Their branches, thick with leaves, made large areas of shade. Their rough trunks, tall and straight, stood firm and imposing, similar to warriors, each occupying a spot and none willing to yield. To the southwest of the temple gate, an isolated rocky hill rose abruptly from the river. We climbed to the summit by taking the stone steps and saw a pavilion called Linsige. It was built of bricks. Wooden construction might not be strong enough as it was too windy over there. Looking out from the pavilion window, I saw the rolling and roaring Yellow River. Its waves surged in three directions with such a mighty effect that the mountain top seemed to be vibrating. I looked at the gigantic gorge to the north and saw overhanging red rocks and sheer precipices covered by green plants. Clouds and fog seemed to be created from there and their gathering and dispersing made the sky at one moment clear, the next cloudy. A range of mountains extended continuously further to the west. A huge mountain stood imposingly in the east with its peak soaring to the sky. Looking south, I could see rolling and turbulent waves, lashing at rock islets and sandbars. I also saw the broken edges of the river bank and a high flatland on which villages and woods were enveloped in mist and fog. In the distance, sailing boats were visible now and then. Mount Huashan, Tongguan Pass and some big mountains in Shaanxi and Henan Provinces seemed

树,风帆浪舸①,渺茫出没,太华②、潼关、雍③豫④诸山,仿佛见之。盖天下之奇观也。

下磴,道⑤石峰东,穿石崖,横竖施木,凭空为楼。楼心穴⑥板,上置井床⑦辘轳,悬繘⑧汲河⑨。凭栏槛,凉风飘潇,若列御寇⑩驭⑪气在空中立也。复自水楼北道,出宫后百余步,至右谷,下视窈然⑫。东距山,西临河,谷南北涯相距寻⑬尺,上横老槎⑭为桥,踔步⑮以渡。谷北二百举武⑯,有小祠,扁曰"后土⑰"。北山陡起,下

① 舸:船(boat)。
② 太华(huà):华山,五岳之一,在今陕西华阴市(Mount Huashan, one of the Five Sacred Mountains, situated in Huayin City, Shaanxi Province)。
③ 雍:古九州之一,在今陕西、甘肃、青海一带(one of the nine administrative divisions of ancient China, in the area of today's Shaanxi, Gansu and Qinghai)。
④ 豫:古九州之一,在今河南省一带(one of the nine administrative divisions of ancient China, in the area of today's Henan Province)。
⑤ 道:取道(by way of)。
⑥ 穴:穿穴(make a hole of)。
⑦ 井床:井栏(well-sweep)。
⑧ 繘(jú):绳索(rope)。
⑨ 汲河:从河中汲水(draw water from a river)。
⑩ 列御寇:列子(Master Lie)。
⑪ 驭:驾驭(get control of)。语出《庄子·逍遥游》:"列子御风而行"(from Master Zhuang's "Wandering about at Leisure": "Master Lie travels by riding on the wind")。
⑫ 窈(yǎo)然:幽深的样子(deep and quiet)。
⑬ 寻:八尺(eight *chi*)。
⑭ 槎(chá):树干的分枝(branch of trunk)。
⑮ 踔(jí)步:两步相接走路(walk at a small pace)。
⑯ 举武:举步。古代六尺为步,半步为"武"(step forward. In the olden days, a step is six *chi*; half a step is *Wu*)。
⑰ 后土:土地神(land god)。

to be in view. What a spectacular sight all these have created!

On our way down from the peak via the eastern path, we saw an overhanging tower on a sheer cliff. This wooden structure was built by driving wooden brackets into the rock of the cliff and putting up timber building materials criss-crossed upon them. In the tower, a well-pulley was installed in the centre of the floor with a rope pendent passing through a hole, for drawing water from the river. Leaning against the rails of the tower, with a cool breeze blowing over me, I felt like the legendary Lie Yukou, who could command the wind, whilst standing high up in the air. We continued our downhill journey through the path north of the tower and passed by King Yu Temple. Having walked over one hundred steps from there, we came to the edge of a ravine on the right. I looked down into the ravine and could not see the bottom. Looking around, I saw a big mountain in the east and the Yellow River in the west. The ravine was more than one *zhang* wide from south to north. A trunk from an old tree had been placed across the ravine to serve as a bridge. We walked slowly and carefully across this bridge. North of the ravine about 200 steps away, there was a small temple with its name "Houtu" inscribed on a board above the door. The north mountain rose abruptly and its foot joined the river bank. This was the finish of the mountain path east of Houtu Temple. There was a cave nearby, large and empty like a big hall. Entering the cave, we saw stalactitic stones, in different sizes and shapes, hang from the roof. Some looked like human figures or birds' wings and

与河际①，遂穷祠东。有石龛②窿然③若大屋，悬石参差，若人形，若鸟翼，若兽吻，若肝肺，若疣赘，若悬鼎，若编磬④，若璞⑤未凿，若矿未炉⑥，其状莫穷。悬泉滴石上，锵然⑦有声。龛下石纵横罗列，偃⑧者、侧者、立者，若床、若几、若屏，可席⑨、可凭、可倚。气阴阴，虽甚暑，不知烦燠⑩；但凄神寒肌，不可久处，复自槎桥道由明德宫左，历石梯上。东南山腹有道院⑪，地势与临思阁相高下，亦可以眺望河山之胜。遂自石梯下栈道，临流⑫观渡，并⑬东山而归。

时宣德⑭元年丙午，夏五月二十五日。同游者，杨景端也。

---

① 际：交接（join; connect）。
② 石龛（kān）：石室（stone room）。
③ 窿（lóng）然：空空洞洞的样子（empty）。
④ 编磬（qìng）：古代乐器名，由16个发音不同的磬编挂而成（name of a musical instrument, made up of 16 chime stones of different sounds）。
⑤ 璞：未雕琢的玉（uncut jade）。
⑥ 炉：这里作动词"炼"解（used as a verb, meaning refine）。
⑦ 锵（qiāng）然：清脆（clear and melodious）。
⑧ 偃：卧（lie on one's back）。
⑨ 席：坐（sit）。
⑩ 烦燠（yù）：烦躁（irritable and restless）。
⑪ 道院：道士住的庙宇（temple where Taoist priests live）。
⑫ 临流：靠近水边（near water）。
⑬ 并（bàng）：通"傍"，靠（lean against）。
⑭ 宣德：明宣宗年号（reign title of Emperor Xuanzong of the Ming Dynasty）。

beasts' muzzles; some resembled livers, lungs and even warts on a human body. There were some others that reminded us of tripod cauldrons and bell chimes, as well as uncut jade and crude ores. To fully describe all these shapes is absolutely impossible. Spring water from above fell onto the stones, making a pleasant jingling sound. Numerous big stones lay vertically or horizontally on the ground of the cave. Some stones looked like beds, being low and flat, for people to sit; some resembled tables, inclining to one side, for people to rest on; while others copied erect screens for people to lean against. It was cool inside the cave. Though it was midsummer, we did not feel the heat at all. Gloomy and somewhat freezing, it was not a pleasant place to stay long. We walked over the trunk bridge again. Having passed the Mingde Palace on its left, we took the stone stairs to go up again and saw a Taoist temple halfway up the hill. It was situated at the same altitude as the wooden tower of Linsige. From here we could also sight the beauty of the River and mountains. Then we went downhill via the stone stairs and came back to the plank road. We stood on the river bank and saw the coming and going of ferry boats. After a while, we left and returned home by walking alongside the road east of the mountains.

  This took place on the 25th day of the 5th month of the 1st year of the Xuande Reign and my travel companion was a friend named Yang Jingduan.

中山狼传（节选）

马中锡

赵简子①大猎于中山②，虞人③道前④，鹰犬罗后⑤。捷禽鸷兽⑥，应弦而倒者不可胜数⑦。有狼当道，人立⑧而啼。简子唾手⑨登车，援⑩乌号⑪之弓，挟肃慎⑫之矢，一发饮羽⑬，狼失声而逋⑭。简子怒，驱车逐之。惊尘蔽天，足音鸣雷，十步之外，不辨人马。

---

① 赵简子：春秋后期晋国大夫，名鞅，实际是晋国执政者（a senior official of the State of Jin in the late stage of the Spring and Autumn Period; his name was Yang and he was actually at the helm of the state）。
② 中山：今河北省定州一带（area of today's Dingzhou, Hebei Province）。
③ 虞人：管理山泽的官吏（officials in charge of mountains and waters）。
④ 道前：在前面作向导（as a guide in the lead）。道：通"导"。
⑤ 罗后：成队地跟在后面（follow in teams）。
⑥ 捷禽鸷（zhì）兽：敏捷的飞禽，凶猛的野兽（swift-winged birds and ferocious beasts）。
⑦ 不可胜数：数不清（countless）。
⑧ 人立：像人一样直立（upright like a man）。
⑨ 唾手：向手心吐唾沫，表示将要做什么（eject saliva into one's palm, showing one is going to do sth.）。
⑩ 援：拉（pull）。
⑪ 乌号：古代有名的好弓（well-known good bows produced in ancient times）。
⑫ 肃慎：古代国名（现在吉林省内），出产名箭（name of an ancient state, famous for arrows）。
⑬ 饮羽：形容箭射进肉中很深，连箭末的羽毛都看不见了（describing an arrow shot so deep into muscles that the plume at its end cannot be seen）。饮：吞没的意思（meaning swallow）。
⑭ 逋（bū）：逃（flee）。

THE ZHONGSHAN WOLF (EXCERPTS)

Ma Zhongxi

Zhao Jianzi was launching a huge and grand hunt on Zhong Shan (Mount Zhong). The officials in charge of mountains and waters were leading the way with falcons and hounds bringing up the rear. Following the sounds of bowstrings, fast flying birds and ferocious beasts fell to the ground one by one without end. Suddenly a wolf appeared on the road, howling and standing like a man. Spitting into his palm, Jianzi immediately got on his carriage. He drew his top-class bow called "crow-wailing" and put onto it a good quality arrow made in the State of Sushen. The wolf was shot so deeply into the muscles with the arrow that the plume at its end could not be seen. Screaming with pain, it ran away. Jianzi flew into a fury and drove his carriage, chasing the wolf. The dust, kicked up by the carriage, blotted the sky and the horse hooves sounded like thunder. Ten feet away, it was impossible to distinguish men from horses.

Mr. Dongguo, a scholar who was a follower of the Mohist school of thought, was at the moment on his way to Zhong Shan

时墨者①东郭先生②将北适中山以干仕③,策④蹇⑤驴,囊⑥图书,夙行⑦失道⑧,望尘惊悸⑨。狼奄⑩至,引首⑪顾曰:"先生岂有志于济物⑫哉?昔毛宝放龟而得渡⑬,随侯救蛇而获珠⑭,蛇龟固⑮弗⑯灵⑰于狼也。今日之事,何不使我得早处囊中以苟延残喘⑱乎?异时倘得

---

① 墨者:信仰墨子学说的人(a scholar believing in the theory of Master Mo)。
② 东郭先生:古代寓言中常用的人名。东郭,复姓(a well-known character in ancient fables; Dongguo: a compound surname)。
③ 干仕:求官做(seek an official post)。
④ 策:马鞭,这里用作动词(horsewhip, used as a verb here, meaning: beat with a whip)。
⑤ 蹇:跛足,这里指行动迟缓(lame, here meaning slow action)。
⑥ 囊:(用口袋)装着(hold sth. in a bag)。
⑦ 夙行:早晨行路(walk in the morning)。
⑧ 失道:迷路(lose one's way)。
⑨ 惊悸:惊惧(palpitate with fear)。
⑩ 奄(yǎn):忽然(suddenly)。
⑪ 引首:伸头(poke one's head)。
⑫ 济物:周济万物(give arms to everything)。
⑬ 毛宝放龟而得渡:毛宝军中一兵士放生乌龟后,宝兵败而死,兵士投水,龟载之而生(a soldier of Mao Bao's army set a tortoise free; when Mao Bao was defeated and died, his soldiers drowned themselves in a river and were saved by the tortoise)。
⑭ 随侯救蛇而获珠:随侯看见一条大蛇受伤,给它敷药治好了,后来那条大蛇从江里衔出一颗大珠子来报答他(when Marquis Sui saw a snake was wounded, he applied ointment to cure it; later the snake, holding a large pearl in its mouth, came out from the river to repay him for his kindness)。
⑮ 固:本来(of course, naturally)。
⑯ 弗:不(not)。
⑰ 灵:聪明(clever)。
⑱ 苟延残喘:拖延虚弱的生命而不死(drag out a feeble existence)。

in the pursuit of an official post. He was walking with a lame donkey which carried a bag full of books. He had lost his way while taking an early morning trip. Seeing dust swirling in the air, his heart palpitated with fear. Suddenly the wolf came, craned its neck and looked at Mr. Dongguo, saying: "Are you ready to give a hand to people who need your help? A long time ago, a soldier in Mao Bao's army set a tortoise free. When Mao Bao was defeated and his soldiers drowned themselves in the river, they were saved through being carried on the tortoise's back. Seeing a wounded snake, Lord Sui applied medicinal ointment to cure it and sometime later the snake held in its mouth a big pearl from the river and gave it to him as repayment. Tortoises and snakes are not as intelligent as wolves. Why don't you let me hide in your bag so that I can survive this difficult situation? When one day my talent wins acknowledgement and I have power and money, I will follow the example of the tortoise and snake to find a way to repay your kindness of reviving me from this most critical condition."

Mr. Dongguo said: "Alas! If I secretly hide you at the risk of offending a high-ranking and influential official, what kind of trouble it may incur is hard to predict. Do you think that under such circumstances I still have any desire for repayment? However, according to Mohist theory of loving all equally, I will definitely try my best to save you. Even if I have to incur danger, I certainly

脱颖而出①，先生之恩，生死而肉骨②也。敢不努力以效龟蛇之诚！"

先生曰："嘻！私③汝狼以犯世卿④、忤⑤权贵，祸且不测，敢望报乎？然墨之道，'兼爱'⑥为本，吾终当有以活汝⑦，脱⑧有祸，固所不辞也。"乃出图书，空囊橐⑨，徐徐焉⑩实⑪狼其中，前虞⑫跋⑬胡⑭，后恐疐⑮尾，三纳之而未克⑯。徘徊容与⑰，追者益近。狼请曰："事急矣，先生果将揖逊⑱救焚溺，而鸣銮⑲避寇盗耶？惟先生速图⑳！"乃中踽跼㉑四足，引绳而束缚之，下首至尾，曲脊掩

---

① 脱颖而出：比喻才能一旦被人发现，就像口袋里的锥子穿透口袋露出来一样（figuratively meaning: talent shows itself just as the point of an awl sticking out through a bag）。颖：锥子的尖（point of an awl）。
② 生死肉骨：救活已死的人，长肉在枯骨上（bring the dead back to life and make flesh grow from one's skeleton, here 生 and 肉 are all used as verbs）。
③ 私：偷偷地庇护（protect secretly）。
④ 犯世卿：冒犯大官（offend high officials）。世卿：世代为卿的人，这里指赵简子（a man from a prominent family which has produced high court officials for generations, here referring to Zhao Jianzi）。
⑤ 忤（wǔ）：触怒（enrage）。
⑥ 兼爱：一视同仁的爱（love without exception）。
⑦ 吾终当有以活汝：我总要想法子救你的命（I'll manage to save you）。
⑧ 脱：即使（even if）。
⑨ 囊橐（tuó）：口袋的总称（general reference to all bags）。
⑩ 徐徐焉：慢吞吞地（slowly）。
⑪ 实：装（load）。
⑫ 虞：担忧（worry）。
⑬ 跋：践踏（tread on）。
⑭ 胡：颔下的垂肉（hanging muscle under the chin）。
⑮ 疐（zhì）：碰到障碍（encounter obstacles）。
⑯ 克：成功（succeed）。
⑰ 容与：动作缓慢（slow in action）。
⑱ 揖逊：打恭作揖（make a deep bow）。
⑲ 銮：马身上的铃铛（horse bell）。
⑳ 惟：希望（wish）。速图：赶快想办法（try to find a solution at once）。
㉑ 踽跼（jú jí）：蜷曲（curl）。

have no intention to avoid it." He immediately took out the books to empty his bag and slowly placed the wolf in it. For fear that its chin would be kicked at and its tail trod on, he rearranged the wolf's posture again and again but was unsuccessful. The chasers were approaching but he had not finished his work. The wolf became impatient and said: "It's urgent. Is it really necessary that you bow deeply while saving a man from burning or drowning or that you ring horse bells for avoiding robbers? I want you to move quickly." The wolf bent its four legs and gave Mr. Dongguo a rope to bind them. It buried its head in its hind legs, with head and tail touching each other. It curled its whole body like a hedgehog or a looper, and held its breath like a tortoise. Being motionless as a coiled snake, the wolf put itself at the mercy of Mr. Dongguo. The good man did what he was told to help the wolf huddle nicely in the bag, then tied the opening of the bag and shouldered it up to the back of the donkey. After that, he led his donkey out of the way, waiting for Zhao's hunting contingent to pass by.

Soon Jianzi arrived. Seeing that the wolf was nowhere, he became furious and cut the end of a shaft off his carriage. He showed the cut-off to Mr. Dongguo, yelling at him: "Who dares to cover up the direction in which the wolf has escaped? I will cut off his head as I did to the shaft!" Mr. Dongguo immediately lay down on the ground, crawled forward and then knelt to say:

胡①，猬缩蝼屈②，蛇盘龟息，以听命先生。先生如其指③内④狼于囊，遂括⑤囊口，肩举驴上，引避道左⑥以待赵人之过。

　　已而简子至，求狼弗得，盛怒，拔剑斩辕⑦端示先生，骂曰："敢讳⑧狼方向者，有如此辕！"先生伏踬⑨就地，匍匐以进，跽⑩而言曰："鄙人不慧⑪，将有志于世，奔走遐⑫方，自迷正途，又安能发狼踪以指示夫子之鹰犬也？然尝闻之，'大道以多歧⑬亡⑭羊'。夫羊，一童子可制之，如是其驯⑮也，尚以多歧而亡；狼非羊比，而中山之歧可以亡羊者何限？乃区区⑯循大道以求之，不几于⑰守

---

① 曲脊掩胡：弓着脊梁，遮住垂肉（bend its back and cover its hanging muscle）。
② 猬缩蝼屈：蜷缩像刺猬，弯曲像尺蝼（curl up like a hedgehog, bend like a looper）。尺蝼（huò），桑树上的一种虫子（mulberry looper）。
③ 如其指：依照它的意思（according to his idea）。指：旨（aim）。
④ 内：纳（put into）。
⑤ 括：结，扎上（tie, knit）。
⑥ 道左：路旁（wayside）。
⑦ 辕：车前驾牲口的部分（shafts of a cart or carriage）。
⑧ 讳：隐瞒（conceal）。
⑨ 伏踬（zhì）：趴下（lie on one's stomach）。
⑩ 跽（jì）：跪（kneel）。
⑪ 不慧：不才（without capability）。
⑫ 遐：远（far）。
⑬ 歧：岔道（branch road）。
⑭ 亡：丢失（lose）。
⑮ 如是其驯：像这样的温驯（tame like this）。
⑯ 区区：仅仅（only）。
⑰ 几于：近似于（similar to）。

"Though I'm not intelligent, I'm determined to do something good for the nation. Now I am travelling far away from home and at the moment I have lost my way to the destination. How can a lost man give a hint to your falcons and hounds on how to find the wolf? I have heard that when a main road branches, sheep easily go astray. Sheep are tame and a young boy is able to control them, but they also go astray at the fork in the road. Sheep cannot be compared with wolves. Here in Zhong Shan, the road often divides into sideways and there are so many labyrinths to lead sheep toward the wrong way. You are searching for the wolf only on the main road. I am afraid that you are doing things by the wrong methods just like someone who stands by a tree stump waiting for a hare to dash itself against it or like another who climbs a tree to catch fish. Besides, the officials in charge of mountains and rivers have something to do with hunting. Please ask them about the trace of the wolf. Why should you blame a passerby like me? Although I am not clever, I still know what wolves are like. They are greedy and cruel and often do wicked things together with jackals. Now that you are determined to get rid of the wolf, it is my duty to offer you some help. Why should I cover up something and not tell you the truth?" Without saying anything, Jianzi returned to his carriage to continue his hunting, while Mr. Dongguo drove his donkey to hurry on his journey.

株①缘木②乎？况田猎，虞人之所事也，君请问诸③皮冠④。行道之人何罪哉？且鄙人虽愚，独不知夫狼乎：性贪而狠，党豺为虐⑤，君能除之，固当窥左足⑥以效微劳，又肯讳之而不言哉？"简子默然，回车就道，先生亦驱驴兼程而进。

良久，羽旄⑦之影渐没，车马之音不闻。狼度⑧简子之去远，而作声囊中曰："先生可留意矣。出我囊⑨，解我缚，拔矢我臂⑩，我将逝矣。"先生举手出狼，狼咆哮谓先生曰："适为虞人逐，其来甚速，幸先生生我⑪。我馁⑫甚，馁不得食，亦终必亡而已。与其饥死道路，为群兽食，毋宁⑬毙于虞人，以俎豆于贵家⑭。先生

---

① 守株：守株待兔（wait every day under the tree, in the hope that a hare would kill itself by crashing into a tree trunk）。
② 缘木：缘木求鱼（climb trees to catch fish）。
③ 问诸：向……打听（ask about ... from）。
④ 皮冠：打猎时所戴的帽子，这里代表管狩猎的专官（a kind of hat that's put on while hunting, here referring to the officials in charge of hunting）。
⑤ 党豺为虐：跟豺结伙为虐（team up to do wicked deeds with jackals）。
⑥ 窥左足：举步之劳（by stepping forward）。窥：跬（kuǐ），半步（half step）。
⑦ 羽旄：旗帜上的装饰（ornaments on flags）。
⑧ 度（duó）：估计（estimate）。
⑨ 出我囊：把我从口袋里放出来（let me out of the bag）。
⑩ 拔矢我臂：把我胳膊上的箭拔去（pull out the arrow from my arm）。
⑪ 生我：救活了我（save me）。
⑫ 馁（něi）：饿（hungry）。
⑬ 毋宁：不如（would rather）。
⑭ 俎豆于贵家：供贵族作食品（as food for noblemen）。俎（zǔ）豆，都是古代盛食品的器皿（household utensils for containing food）。

Gradually the flags and banners of the contingent were out of sight and the sound of horses and carriages was no longer heard. Estimating that Zhao Jianzi had gone far away, the wolf said from inside the bag: "It's time for you to consider me, sir. Let me get out of the bag. Untie the rope and pull out the arrow from my arm. Then I will go away." As soon as Mr. Dongguo had released it, the wolf roared fiercely and uttered: "Just now I was chased by the hunters who ran after me very quickly. Fortunately I was saved by you. Now I am hungry. If I have nothing to eat, I'm certain to die. I would rather be killed by the huntsmen so that my meat could be served to the noblemen than die on the road to have my body eaten by other beasts. You are a Mohist and believe in the theory that we should wear ourselves out from head to foot to help others. So I don't think you value your body so much that you would not allow me to eat you." Then the wolf opened its mouth and brandished its claws to attack the good man.

Mr. Dongguo rapidly used his hands to fight the beast. Drawing back while fighting, he dodged behind the donkey and vigorously ran around it. The wolf could not do any harm to the man who did not stop his resisting. Finally they were both completely exhausted, gasping for breath on either side of the donkey. Then the man uttered, "Wolf, you betray me, you betray me!" The wolf said: "Originally I did not intend to betray you, but

既墨者，摩顶放踵，思一利天下①，又何吝②一躯啖我③而全微命乎？"遂鼓吻奋爪，以向先生。

先生仓卒以手搏之，且搏且却，引蔽驴后，便旋④而走，狼终不得有加于先生，先生亦竭力拒，彼此俱倦，隔驴喘息。先生曰："狼负我，狼负我！"狼曰："吾非固欲负汝，天生汝辈，固需吾辈食也。"相持既久，日晷⑤渐移。

……

遥望老子杖藜⑥而来……先生且喜且愕⑦。舍狼而前，拜跪啼泣，致辞曰："乞丈人一言而生。"丈人问故，先生曰："是狼为虞人所窘⑧求救于我，我实生之。今反欲咥⑨我，力求不免，我又当死之⑩。……今逢丈人，岂天之未丧斯文也⑪！敢乞一言而生。"因顿首杖下，俯伏听命。丈人闻之，欷歔⑫再三，以杖叩狼曰："汝误矣。

---

① 摩顶放踵，思一利天下：这是孟子评论墨者的话，意为自我刻苦，以利天下（this is Mencius' comment on Master Mo; Mencius said, "He would brave all difficulties, having no regard for physical discomfort from head to toe, for the benefit of the country"）。摩顶放踵：从头到脚受尽劳苦（suffer from head to foot）。
② 何吝：为何舍不得（why hate to part with）。
③ 啖（dàn）我：给我吃（let me eat you）。
④ 便旋（pián xuán）：回旋（round and round）。
⑤ 日晷（guǐ）：日影（shadow of the sun）。
⑥ 杖藜（lí）：拄着藜做的拐杖。藜，一种野生的植物，茎老可以作杖（lean on a stick made of goosefoots, a kind of wild plant）。
⑦ 愕（è）：惊（scare）。
⑧ 窘：困（be hard pressed）。
⑨ 咥（dié）：吃（eat）。
⑩ 死之：为此而死（die of this）。
⑪ 岂天之未丧斯文也：莫非天不绝我这书生的命（can it be that God does not want my life？）。斯文：指读书人（intellectuals）。
⑫ 欷歔（xī xū）：叹息（sigh）。

you people were born to be eaten by us." For quite some time they were locked in a stalemate while the shadow of the sun was gradually moving.

...

All of a sudden, Mr. Dongguo saw in a little distance an old man, leaning on a wooden stick, approaching... It was a pleasant surprise and he ran away from the wolf and knelt down before the old man. He sobbed, "Could you please say something to save my life?" The old man asked what had happened. He answered: "This wolf was being chased by hunters and found no way to escape. I have saved his life but now he wants to eat me. I have begged for mercy in vain and I will be killed by the beast. ... Now you have unexpectedly come to this site and it seems that Heaven does not want me at this time. Could you say something for me to save my life?" After saying this, he knelt down, with his head touching the ground near the end of the old man's stick, waiting for his words. On hearing this, the old man repeatedly heaved deep sighs. Then he knocked the wolf with his stick, saying: "You are wrong. You return evil for good and nothing is more ominous than this. Confucianism held that if a person did not betray others who had bestowed a benefit on him, he would be a filial son to his parents. Confucianism also said that between father and son even tigers or wolves have love. Now you have betrayed your benefactor, even

夫人有恩而背之，不详莫大焉①，儒谓受人恩而不忍背者，其为子必孝，又谓虎狼知父子②。今汝背恩如是，则并父子亦无矣。"乃厉声曰："狼，速去，不然，将杖杀汝。"

狼曰："丈人知其一，未知其二。请诉之。愿丈人垂听③。初，先生救我时，束缚我足，闭我囊中，压以诗书，我鞠躬不敢息，又蔓词④以说⑤简子，其意盖将死我囊而独窃其利也。是安可不咥？"丈人顾先生曰："果如是，是羿亦有罪焉⑥。"先生不平，具状⑦其囊狼怜惜之意。狼亦巧辩不已以求胜。丈人曰："是皆不足以执信⑧也。试再囊之，吾观其状果困苦否。"狼欣然从之，信⑨足先生。先生复缚置囊中，肩举驴上，而狼未知也。丈人附耳谓

---

① 不祥莫大焉：再没有比这更不吉利的事了（nothing more ominous than this）。
② 虎狼知父子：即使是虎狼，也懂得父子之爱（even a tiger or a wolf knows love between father and son）。
③ 垂听：请求别人倾听自己诉说的谦辞（self-depreciatory expression of asking others to let one recount one's worries）。
④ 蔓词：无谓的话（nonsense）。
⑤ 说（shuì）：劝说（persuade）。
⑥ 是羿亦有罪焉：这是孟子批评羿传授技艺不知道择人的话。羿是古代善射的人，他教会了逢蒙射箭。后来，逢蒙就把他射死了（Mencius criticized Yi for not knowing how to select suitable apprentices whom he would teach how to shoot; Yi taught Pang Meng to shoot but he was later shot by Pang Meng）。
⑦ 具状：原原本本说明（explain from the very beginning to the end）。
⑧ 执信：取信（enjoy the trust of）。
⑨ 信：伸（stretch）。

those who have ignored love between father and son would not have done so." Having finished his words, the old man shouted angrily: "Wolf, get away from here. Otherwise I'll beat you to death with my stick."

The wolf said: "Old man, you are aware of one side of the matter but not the other. Please listen and let me clarify. In the beginning, while rescuing me from the hunters, this man bound my feet and placed me in the bag. He tied the opening and put books on its top. Inside the bag, I bent my body and did not dare to gasp for breath. Then he talked some nonsense to Jianzi in an attempt to make me die in the bag so that he could take the benefit for himself. Why should I have pity for him and not eat him?" Looking at Mr. Dongguo, the old man said, "If that's the case, even the legendary Yu would be considered guilty." Mr. Dongguo held this unfair and explained in detail how he had pity for the wolf when putting it into the bag. The wolf kept quibbling in order to win the case. The old man said: "All these reasons are not convincing. Let's try to put the wolf into the bag again to see whether he really suffers." The wolf readily accepted this idea and stretched its legs toward Mr. Dongguo. Once again the good man bound its legs and put it into the bag. Then he used his shoulder to lift the whole thing up to the donkey's back. The wolf inside was unaware what was happening outside. The old man whispered to

先生曰:"有匕首否?"先生曰:"有。"于是出匕,丈人目①先生使引匕刺狼。先生曰:"不害狼乎?"丈人笑曰:"禽兽负恩如是,而犹不忍杀,子固仁者,然愚亦甚矣!……仁陷于愚,固君子之所不与②也。"言已大笑……遂举手助先生操刃,共殪③狼,弃道上而去。

---

① 目:以目示意(give a hint through a glance)。
② 不与:不赞成(not approve of)。
③ 殪(yì):杀死(kill)。

Mr. Dongguo, "Have you got a dagger?" The latter answered "Yes" and took out his dagger. Indicating by a wink, the old man hinted to him to stab the wolf with the dagger. Mr. Dongguo asked, "Will it hurt the wolf?" The old man laughed and said: "This beast has betrayed your act of mercy but you do not have the heart to kill it. You are very kind indeed, but you are stupid as well. Having too much benevolence in heart but acting stupidly is not a gentleman's behavior." He burst into laughter when he finished his words and then helped the kind-hearted man hold the dagger to kill the wolf. After that they left, forsaking the wolf on the road.

记王忠肃公翱事

崔铣

公①一女，嫁为畿辅②某官某③妻。公夫人甚爱女，每迎女，婿固④不遣⑤，恚⑥而语⑦女曰："而翁⑧长铨⑨，迁⑩我京职⑪，则汝朝

---

① 公：王翱（1384—1467），字九皋，盐山（今河北盐山）人，明代名臣。历事成祖、宣宗、英宗、代宗、宪宗五帝，擢任吏部尚书（Wang Ao, styled himself Jiugao, from Yanshan, Hebei Province; a famous minister in the Ming Dynasty, and respectively served five emperors: Chengzu, Xuanzong, Yingzong, Daizong and Xianzong. He was promoted minister in charge of the Ministry of Official Personnel Affairs）。
② 畿（jī）辅：京城周围一带。明代自1403年改以北京为都，所以这里是指北京附近的州县（area around the capital. The Ming Dynasty moved its capital to Beijing in 1403, so here refers to prefectures and counties near Beijing）。
③ 某官某：做某官的某人（a certain person holding a certain official position）。
④ 固：必（be bound to）。
⑤ 遣：遣归，指送妻子回娘家（send back, referring to sending one's wife back to her parents' home）。
⑥ 恚（huì）：怨恨，愤怒（hate, anger）。
⑦ 语（yù）：动词，对……说（as a verb, say to sb.）。
⑧ 而翁：你的父亲（your father）。
⑨ 铨（quán）：铨选。量才授官。吏部执掌铨选，所以吏部长官为长铨（select. Appoint officials on the basis of their abilities. The Ministry of Official Personnel Affairs was in control of selecting officials, so its director was called 长铨）。
⑩ 迁：调（transfer）。
⑪ 京职：京官（officials working in the capital）。

THE NOBLE DEEDS OF THE REVERED MR. WANG AO

Cui Xian

Mr. Wang Ao had a daughter, whose husband held an official position in an area near the capital. Wang's wife loved her daughter but each time she asked her daughter to come to visit, her son-in-law always prevented his wife from going to see her parents. The son-in-law was not happy and said to his wife: "Your father is in charge of selecting officials. If he transfers me to work in the capital, you can visit your mother every day. To your father, to transfer me to the capital will be just as easy as shaking down withered tree leaves. Why is he so mean as not to help me?" The daughter sent a message to her mother. One evening, Mrs. Wang

夕①侍母；且迁②我如振落叶③耳，而固吝者何④？"女寄言⑤于母。夫人一夕置酒⑥，跪白公⑦。公大怒，取案⑧上器击伤夫人，出，驾⑨而宿于朝房⑩，旬⑪乃还第⑫。婿竟不调⑬。

公为都御史⑭，与太监某守辽东⑮。某亦守法，与公甚相得⑯也。后公改两广⑰，太监泣别，赠大珠四枚。公固辞⑱。太监泣曰："是

① 朝夕：早晚（in the morning and evening）。
② 迁：这里的"迁"有提拔的意思（here meaning "promote"）。
③ 如振落叶：如同摇掉将落的树叶（as easy as shaking down withered tree leaves）。
④ 固吝者何：硬是吝惜到如此地步，是什么原因呢（why is he so mean as to refuse doing something for me）？
⑤ 寄言：托人捎话（ask sb. to take a message to）。
⑥ 置酒：置办酒席（make a feast）。
⑦ 跪白公：欠身告诉丈夫（bend her body slightly and tell her husband）。
⑧ 案：桌子（table）。
⑨ 驾：坐车（take a cart）。
⑩ 朝房：办公室（office）。
⑪ 旬：十日（ten days）。
⑫ 还第：自朝房回家（go home from the office）。
⑬ 竟不调：终究没有迁调官职（finally fail to be transferred to the capital）。
⑭ 都御史：监察机关都察院的长官（senior official of the top-level supervisory agency in the Ming Dynasty）。
⑮ 辽东：明军镇名，今辽宁省（name of a strategic post in the Ming Dynasty, today's Liaoning Province）。
⑯ 相得：情投意合（be closely allied in opinion and feelings）。
⑰ 改两广：调任两广总督（be transferred to be governor of the two provinces of Guangdong and Guangxi）。
⑱ 固辞：坚决辞谢（refuse firmly）。

arranged a feast. She kneeled before her husband, asking him to help their son-in-law. Mr. Wang got furious at what she had said and picked up an item from the table and threw it to injure her. Then he left by carriage and stayed at the guest house of the imperial court for more than ten days before returning home. His son-in-law was not transferred in the end.

When serving as the chief procurator, Mr. Wang guarded Liaoning together with a eunuch. The eunuch was a law-abiding person, as well as a close friend of Mr. Wang. Later on, Mr. Wang was transferred to be the governor of Guangdong and Guangxi provinces. On his departure, the eunuch cried and presented to him a gift of four big pearls. He firmly refused the gift. The eunuch

非贿得之①。昔先皇②颁③僧保④所货⑤西洋珠于侍臣,某得八焉,今以半别公⑥,公固知某不贪也。"公受珠,内⑦所著⑧披袄⑨中,纫⑩之。后还朝,求⑪太监后⑫,得二从子⑬。公劳⑭之曰:"若⑮翁廉⑯,若辈⑰得无⑱苦⑲贫乎?"皆曰:"然。"公曰:"如有营⑳,予佐㉑尔贾㉒。"

---

① 是非贿得之:这不是受贿赂得来的珍珠(these pearls have not been obtained from accepting bribes)。
② 先皇:已经亡故的皇帝(a certain deceased emperor)。
③ 颁:赏赐(award)。
④ 僧保:明英宗时的太监(name of a eunuch in the age of Emperor Yingzong of the Ming Dynasty)。
⑤ 货:买(buy)。
⑥ 以半别公:拿一半作为分别时赠送与你的礼物(give half of the pearls to you as a departure gift)。
⑦ 内:纳,放入(put inside)。
⑧ 著:穿(wear)。
⑨ 袄:穿在外面的上衣(upper outer garment)。
⑩ 纫:缝(sew)。
⑪ 求:寻访(look for)。
⑫ 后:后代。这里指太监的后嗣。宦官多以侄辈承嗣(later generations, posterity. Here referring to descendants of an eunuch. Most eunuchs had their nephews succeed them)。
⑬ 从子:侄子(nephew)。
⑭ 劳(lào):慰问(express sympathy and solicitude for)。
⑮ 若:你们的(your)。
⑯ 廉:廉洁(honest, with clean hands)。
⑰ 若辈:你们(you)。
⑱ 无:莫非,岂不是(can it be that; is it possible that)。
⑲ 苦:苦于(suffer from)。
⑳ 营:经营(manage, engage in)。
㉑ 佐:助(help)。
㉒ 贾:价,钱(money)。

sobbed: "I did not get them from bribery. The late emperor once awarded his subjects some pearls which Special Envoy Sengbao had bought from the West, and I received eight. Now I give half of them to you as a gift on your departure. You certainly know I am not a corrupt person." Mr. Wang accepted the pearls, and sewed them inside his garment. On returning to the imperial court some years later, he looked for the eunuch's descendants and found his two nephews. Mr. Wang expressed sympathy for them: "Your uncle was an honest man. Do you have any financial difficulty?" They answered, "Yes." Mr. Wang said, "If you want to go into business, I will help you with money." Thinking that he was unable to help them, but only being kind to them, the two

二子心计①，公无从办②，特③示④故人⑤意耳。皆阳⑥应曰："诺⑦。"公屡促⑧之，必如约⑨。乃伪为屋券⑩，列贾⑪五百金，告公。公拆袄，出珠授之，封识宛然⑫。

---

① 心计：心里盘算（calculate）。
② 无从办：无法办到（unable to get sth. done）。
③ 特：只是，不过（only, just）。
④ 示：表示（show）。
⑤ 故人：老朋友（old friend）。
⑥ 阳：通"佯"，假装（pretend）。
⑦ 诺：答应声，犹曰"是"（answer, meaning "yes"）。
⑧ 屡促：多次催促（urge many times）。
⑨ 必如约：一定要按照说定的办（be sure to do sth. according to what's agreed on）。
⑩ 乃伪为屋券：便伪造了一张买房契（then forge a title deed for a house）。
⑪ 列贾：开列的价格（the asking price）。
⑫ 封识（zhì）宛然：封好的记号如初封时一样（the mark remains the same as when it was originally sealed）。识：同"志"（be equal to "sign"）。

pretended to believe him and answered "All right." Many times Mr. Wang assured them that he was certain to do what was agreed. They forged the title deed for a house with an asking price of five hundred *liang* of silver and informed him of this. He tore open his garment and took out the pearls for them, with the sealing strip still intact.

说　琴

何景明

何子①有琴,三年不张②。从其游者戴仲鹖③,取而绳以弦④,进而求操⑤焉。何子御⑥之,三叩⑦其弦,弦不服指⑧,声不成文⑨。徐察其音,莫知病端⑩。仲鹖曰:"是病于材⑪也。予观其黟然⑫黑,衺然⑬腐也。其质⑭不任弦⑮,故鼓⑯之弗扬⑰。"

---

① 何子:作者自称(the author calls himself)。
② 不张:没有上弦(without string)。
③ 戴仲鹖(hé):名冠,字仲鹖,信阳人。曾从何景明学诗。正德年间(1506—1521)进士,以为官清介闻名(Dai Guan styled himself Zhonghe, from Xinyang. He used to learn poetry from He Jingming. He was a successful candidate for the imperial examination in the period of the Zhengde Reign and became famous for being an upright official)。
④ 绳以弦:装上弦(fit / furnish strings)。
⑤ 操:弹奏(play)。
⑥ 御:用,这里指弹奏(here referring to "play")。
⑦ 叩:用指弹(pluck with fingers)。
⑧ 不服指:不顺从手指(not obedient to the fingers)。
⑨ 文:曲调(tune, melody)。
⑩ 端:原由(reason)。
⑪ 病于材:做琴的材料不好(the musical instrument was made of bad material)。
⑫ 黟(yī)然:深黑色(dark black)。
⑬ 衺(xié)然:歪邪不正的样子(deflection, skew)。衺:同"邪"。
⑭ 其质:琴的木质(quality of *qin*)。
⑮ 不任弦:经不起弦的力量(can't stand the force of strings)。
⑯ 鼓:弹(pluck)。
⑰ 弗扬:不响亮(not loud and clear)。

THE SECRET OF THE MUSICAL INSTRUMENT, QIN

He Jingming

Master He possesses a *qin* (a kind of seven-stringed pluck musical instrument popular in ancient China) but he has not played it for three years. One of his followers named Dai Zhonghe took it out from where it had been shelved and fixed strings on it. Then he presented it to Master He and asked him to play. The latter started to play by plucking the strings three times but the strings, resistive to his finger movement, did not make any melodious sound. On examining the sound carefully, what made it so discordant could not be found. Zhonghe said: "The problem comes from the material of which the instrument was made. I find dark black, askew and rotten. Because of its bad quality, the wood, unable to stand the force of the strings, does not vibrate properly to produce a good sound."

Master He said: "Alas! There is nothing wrong with the material. I will blame the *qin* maker. What a *qin* maker should do

何子曰："噫①！非材之罪②也。吾将尤③夫攻④之者也。凡攻琴者，首选材，审⑤制器⑥，其器有四：弦、轸⑦、徽⑧、越⑨。弦以被音⑩，轸以机弦⑪，徽以比度⑫，越以亮节⑬。被音则清浊见⑭，机弦则高下⑮张⑯，比度则细大弗逾⑰，亮节则声应不伏⑱。故弦取其韧密⑲也，轸取其栝⑳圆㉑也，徽取其数㉒次㉓也，越取其中疏㉔也。今是琴弦之韧疏，轸

---

① 噫（yī）：叹词（interjection）。
② 罪：毛病（fault）。
③ 尤：怨（blame, complain）。
④ 攻：制造（make）。
⑤ 审：精心考虑（consider carefully）。
⑥ 制器：指制琴（referring to making the musical instrument）。
⑦ 轸（zhěn）：系琴弦的轴，可以转动，控制松紧（pegs used for winding the strings to adjust the tension of each string）。
⑧ 徽：琴面上所标出的用手指按弦的部位记号（marks indicated on the surface of a qin for pressing strings）。
⑨ 越（huó）：琴瑟底下的小孔（a special hole in the underside of the *qin*）。
⑩ 被音：发出声音（produce sound）。
⑪ 机弦：调整琴弦（adjust strings）。
⑫ 比度：调节音节高低的度数（finger position scales which enable the player to keep the accuracy of the tone）。
⑬ 亮节：加大音量（to amplify the sound volume）。
⑭ 见：现（appear）。
⑮ 高下：指声音的高低（referring to the pitch of a sound, high or low）。
⑯ 张：展开，引申为显出（unfold, the extended meaning is to reveal）。
⑰ 逾：超越（surmount）。
⑱ 伏：低沉（low and deep）。
⑲ 韧密：坚韧细密（tenacious and fine）。
⑳ 栝（guā）：琴轸的栝（插入琴内的一端）（the end of a peg inserted into the qin）。
㉑ 圆：滚圆易转（so round that it is easy to turn）。
㉒ 数：指琴徽的度数（readings of the whole tone scale on the *qin*）。
㉓ 次：准确，合乎次序（accurate; in the right order）。
㉔ 中疏：中空（hollow and cavernous）。

before anything else is to select the material and then carefully design how to make a *qin* out of this material. A *qin* has four components: strings, tune pegs, *hui* (finger position scales) and *huo* (a special hole in its underside). Strings are used for making sound; tune pegs for adjusting strings; *hui* for keeping tone accuracy and *huo* for amplifying sound volume. Plucked by the player, the strings can produce either clear or raucous sound. Wound by the pegs, the strings can be made tight or loose for pitching the sound. Indicated by *hui*, the qin player plucks out exactly the right tone, neither too high nor too low. Modified by *huo*, the sound coming through the hole becomes intensively resonant. To be a good *qin*, it should be furnished with tenacious and delicate strings. The instrument should have round notched pegs for winding the strings. It should have accurate scales (*hui*) to indicate the finger position for the player and the hole in its underside (*huo*) should be cavernous and hollow. Look at this *qin*! Its strings are stiff, the notch of each peg is rough, the scales to indicate the pitch are inaccurate and the hole for producing a resonant sound effect is too shallow and narrow. Therefore, this *qin*, with stiff strings, is unable to produce a variety of sound. The rough notch makes each peg fail to properly regulate the volume of sound and

之栝滞①，徽之数失钧②，越之中浅以隘③。疏故清浊弗能具④，滞故高下弗能通⑤，失钧故细大相逾，浅以隘故声应沉伏。是以宫商⑥不诚职⑦，而律吕⑧叛度⑨。虽使伶伦⑩钩弦而柱指⑪，伯牙⑫按节而临操⑬，亦未知其所谐⑭也。

"夫是⑮琴之材，桐之为也。始桐之生邃谷⑯，据盘石⑰，风雨之所化，云烟之所蒸，蟠纡⑱轮囷⑲，璀璨⑳岪郁㉑，文炳彪凤㉒，质㉓

---

① 滞：不流动（not flowing）。
② 失钧：失调，不准确（lose balance, inaccurate）。
③ 隘（ài）：狭窄（narrow）。
④ 具：完备（complete, perfect）。
⑤ 通：流通，交换，引申为调节（circulate, exchange, here meaning "to regulate" by extension）。
⑥ 宫商：此泛指音阶（referring here to musical scale in general）。
⑦ 诚职：忠诚地尽职（fulfill one's duty faithfully）。
⑧ 律吕：音律（temperament）。
⑨ 叛度：违背了标准（violate the standard）。
⑩ 伶伦：传说中黄帝时代的大音乐家（a great musician in time of the Yellow Emperor according to legend）。
⑪ 钩弦柱指：用指头弹琴（play qin with fingers）。
⑫ 伯牙：春秋时人，以善于弹琴著名（a man living in the Spring and Autumn Period, famous for being skillful in playing qin）。
⑬ 按节临操：按节奏演奏（play in rhythm）。
⑭ 谐：和谐（harmony）。
⑮ 是：这，此（this）。
⑯ 邃（suì）谷：深谷（deep valley）。
⑰ 盘石：巨石（huge rock）。
⑱ 蟠（pán）纡（yū）：屈曲回旋的样子（buckling and circling）。
⑲ 轮囷（qūn）：屈曲盘绕的样子（buckling）。
⑳ 璀璨：此处意为色彩鲜明（bright-colored）。
㉑ 岪（fú）郁：山高险的样子（of mountain: high and dangerous）。
㉒ 文炳彪凤：木质上闪现出虎、凤一样的纹理（texture of the wood looks like tiger's stripes or phoenix's patterns）。彪：虎身上的斑纹，这里指虎（tiger stripe, here referring to tiger）。
㉓ 质：指木材的质料（material of wood）。

inaccuracy of the scales has mixed up the pitch. Its high and low sound trespasses each other for its scales are inaccurate while the shallow and narrow hole in its underside makes the instrument unable to sound resonantly. Therefore, if the instrument is unable to perform its duty and fails to reach the standard, even when we had Linglun (a great musician during the reign of the Yellow Emperor) or Boya (a musical giant during the Spring and Autumn Period) play it with their dexterous fingers and masterful minds, they would not be able to make any harmonious melody.

"This instrument is made from the wood of a phoenix tree. This phoenix tree grew in a deep valley, occupying a huge rock. Having been combed by the wind, washed by the rain, as well as bathed in clouds and mists, it had grown into a huge and tall tree, buckled but bright in color. We cannot say that the wood of this tree is not wonderful. Its quality is as fine as gold and jade and its grain looks like the stripes on a tiger or the pattern on a phoenix. Let's say that an artisan uses this wood to make a *qin*. He starts his work by strictly following the specifications for making a good *qin*. He is planning to make an instrument and then keep it for future use. He chops the wood from which to shape a *qin* and then polishes the unfinished product until a perfect *qin* comes

参①金玉，不为不良也。使攻者制之中其制②，修③之畜④其用⑤，斫⑥以成之，饰以出之。上而君得之，可以荐⑦清庙⑧，设⑨大廷⑩，合神纳宾⑪，赞实⑫出伏⑬，畅民洁物；下而士人得之，可以宣⑭气养⑮德，道⑯情和志。何至默然邪然，为腐材置物⑰耶？

"吾观天下之不罪材者寡⑱矣。如常以求固执⑲，缚柱⑳以求张

---

① 参：比（comparable to）。
② 中其制：符合规格标准（meet a criterion）。
③ 修：加工打磨（processing, polishing）。
④ 畜：蓄，储蓄（deposit）。
⑤ 用：功用（function）。
⑥ 斫（zhuó）：砍，削（chop, pare with a knife）。
⑦ 荐：指供献（sacrifice）。
⑧ 清庙：宗庙（ancestral temple of a ruling house）。
⑨ 设：陈设（furnish）。
⑩ 大廷：朝廷（royal court）。
⑪ 合神纳宾：祭祀神灵，招待宾客（offer sacrifices to gods and entertain guests）。
⑫ 赞实：有助于万物的生长结果（help all plants grow and bear fruits）。赞：助（help）。实：结果实（bear fruits）。
⑬ 出伏：使蛰虫由地下出动（to call hibernating animals and insects to awake and come out from underground）。
⑭ 宣：疏散，疏通（evacuate, unclog）。
⑮ 养：修养，陶冶（cultivate, mould）。
⑯ 道：导（lead, guide）。
⑰ 置物：被弃置的东西（discarded things）。
⑱ 寡：少（few）。
⑲ 如常以求固执：对一个平常的材料，勉强要求它是最好的材料（force an ordinary material to be the best one）。
⑳ 缚柱：犹言"胶柱"，即把柱（轸）固定死（fix the peg）。

into being. The beautiful instrument can be presented to the top level — the monarch. Then it will be played at the ceremonies to offer sacrifices in the ancestral temple of the royal family or at the celebrations in the imperial court. The music accompanies the activities of worshiping God and entertaining guests which are carried out in the attempt to help all plants grow well and bear fruits and to call all the hibernating animals and insects to awake. As a result, all the people under heaven feel happy and everything on earth becomes clean. If this instrument is in the possession of a scholar, it will be used to express aspirations and cultivate morals, guiding emotions and harmonizing will. How come my qin looks awful, so black like useless rotten wood?

"I have noticed that very few people in the world do not blame the material when something goes wrong. Ordinary materials are expected to be exactly like the best one. The tune pegs which have been attached to the instrument with glue are forced to turn for adjusting the tension of the strings. The qin maker is confused himself but he tries to distinguish the confusing tones. His vision is as tiny as a bean but he attempts to make big gains. Giant timber is used for making rafters while thin wood for pillars. In doing so, can anybody expect a good outcome from

弛①，自混②而欲别③物，自褊④而欲求多⑤。直木轮⑥，屈木辐⑦，巨木节⑧，细木㮡⑨，几何⑩不为材之病也？是故君子慎焉⑪，操⑫之以劲⑬，动之以时，明之以序⑭，藏之以虚⑮。劲则能弗挠⑯也，时则能应变也，序则能辨方也，虚则能受益也。劲者信也，时者知⑰也，序者义也，虚者谦也。信以居⑱之，知以行之，义以制⑲之，谦以保之。朴其中，文⑳其外。见㉑则用世㉒，不见则用身㉓。故曰虽愚必明，虽柔必强。

---

① 张弛：松紧（degree of tightness）。
② 混：混淆（confound, confuse）。
③ 别：分辨（distinguish）。
④ 褊（biǎn）：狭小。这里指度量不大（narrow; here referring to narrow-minded）。
⑤ 求多：想多得（want to get more）。
⑥ 直木轮：以直木作轮，这里的"轮"用作动词（use straight wood to make wheels）。
⑦ 屈木辐：以曲木作车轮中车毂和轮圈的连接物（use bent wood to make spokes）。
⑧ 节：柱头上承接房梁的木块，这里用作动词（joint, knob, node; here used as a verb）。
⑨ 㮡（lì）：最中间的房梁。这里是支柱的意思（the central beam; here meaning support）。
⑩ 几何：多少（how many）。
⑪ 焉：于此（here）。
⑫ 操：掌握，指选材（master, referring to selecting material）。
⑬ 劲：坚强有力（strong）。
⑭ 序：次序（order）。
⑮ 虚：不自满（not self-satisfied）。
⑯ 挠：弯曲（crooked）。
⑰ 知：同"智"（wisdom）。
⑱ 居：处于（be in a certain condition）。
⑲ 制：控制（control）。
⑳ 文：文饰（decorate）。
㉑ 见：现，被发现（be discovered）。
㉒ 用世：为世所用（work for the world）。
㉓ 用身：独善其身（to seek one's personal edification only）。

the material? Therefore, a real gentleman is cautious in making a judgment on the material. In practice, one should put forth his strength while operating an instrument, seek an opportunity before taking action, establish an order of priority in the process of observation and find ample room to store his instrument. Through strength, he cannot be prevented from reaching his goal. Being on the alert for an opportunity, he is ready to cope with any change. Observing the situation in the order of priority, he can easily find the direction in which to head. Having an ample capacity, he is able to take in benefits. Strength can be seen as one's credit, opportunity as his wisdom, order as his moral principles and capacity as his modesty. Credit is his nest to live in; wisdom can direct his operations; moral principles have been drawn up for self-discipline and modesty is good for self-protection. Though his appearance is full of rich and bright colors, simplicity always accompanies his inner world. If he is known by other people, he will do something for the world. If nobody knows him, he will concentrate on self-cultivation. So it is said: when someone looks silly, he may be wise; when he appears soft, he is probably tough. Why should we blame the material?"

材何罪焉!"

仲鹞怃然①离席曰:"信取于弦乎?知取于轸乎?义取于徽乎?谦取于越乎?一物而众理备焉。予不敏,愿改弦更张②,敬服斯说。"

---

① 怃(wǔ)然:茫然自失的样子(utterly ignorant, be in the dark)。
② 改弦更张:改换、调整琴弦,使声音和谐(change and adjust string to make the music sound harmonious)。

As soon as Master He finished his talk, Zhonghe left his seat, saying emotionally: "Now I have come to realize: credit comes from the string, wisdom from the peg, morality from the scale and modesty from the hole. How marvelous it is that one object contains so many principles! I am not as sensible as I should be. I admire your theory and I am willing to change over to new ways in my study, just like changing the string of a musical instrument to make the music more melodious."

项脊轩志

归有光

项脊轩①,旧②南阁子也。室仅方丈③,可容一人居。百年老屋,尘泥渗漉④,雨泽⑤下注⑥;每移案⑦,顾视⑧无可置⑨者。又北向⑩,不能得日,日过午已昏⑪。余稍为⑫修葺⑬,使不上漏。前辟⑭四窗,垣墙周庭⑮,以当南日⑯,日影反照,室始洞然⑰。又杂植兰桂竹木于庭,旧

---

① 项脊:项脊泾,地名(name of a place)。轩:有窗的小屋子(a small room with windows)。
② 旧:原来的(original)。
③ 方丈:一丈见方(one square *zhang*)。
④ 渗(shèn)漉(lù):渗(ooze);漏(leak)。
⑤ 雨泽:雨水(rainwater)。
⑥ 下注:向下流(flow down)。
⑦ 案:桌子(table)。
⑧ 顾视:环看四周(look around)。
⑨ 置:安放(put)。
⑩ 北向:方向朝北(in the northern direction)。
⑪ 昏:黑暗(dark)。
⑫ 稍为:稍微(a little, slightly)。
⑬ 修葺(qì):修缮(repair)。
⑭ 辟:开(open)。
⑮ 垣墙周庭:砌上围墙,环绕庭院(build an enclosure around the yard)。这里的"垣"与"周"皆用作动词(here 垣 and 周 are used as verbs)。
⑯ 当:挡(cover)。
⑰ 洞然:敞亮(bright and spacious)。

THE HUT CALLED XIANGJIXUAN

Gui Youguang

Xiangjixuan, originally called Nangezi, is a hut in the yard of my house. Being a square *zhang* (11 square meters) in size, it can house one person. This one hundred-year old building used to have a leaking roof and mud could not be prevented from oozing and rain from pouring into it. Every time I move a table, I look around but find no place to put it elsewhere. Also, it faces north and no sunshine enters, so after noontime the inside was already dark. I had it repaired a little, making its roof leak-proof and opening four windows in front. An enclosure to block the southern exposure of the sun has also been built. The reflected sunlight makes the room look bright and spacious. In the yard I have grown orchids, cinnamon and bamboos which have shed luster on the ancient railings. With books accumulated on the shelf, sometimes I lie on my back whistling songs, sometimes I sit still listening to all the sounds coming from outside. Birds often come to the quiet yard to peck at food and will not fly away even when people come near. On the fifteenth evening of the month, when the

时栏楯①，亦遂增胜②。借③书满架，偃仰④啸歌⑤，冥然兀坐⑥，万籁⑦有声；而庭阶寂寂，小鸟时来啄食，人至不去。三五之夜⑧，明月半墙，桂影斑驳⑨，风移影动，珊珊⑩可爱。

然予居于此，多可喜，亦多可悲。先是，庭中通南北为一。迨⑪诸父⑫异爨⑬，内外多置小门，墙往往⑭而是。东犬西吠⑮，客逾庖而宴⑯，鸡栖于厅。庭中始为篱，已⑰为墙，凡⑱再⑲变矣。家有老

---

① 栏楯（shǔn）：栏杆。纵的叫栏，横的叫楯（railing. The vertical one is called 栏；the horizontal one is called 楯）。
② 增胜：增添了光彩（shed lustre on）。胜：光彩（lustre radiance）。
③ 借：积（accumulate）。
④ 偃（yǎn）仰：仰卧（lie on one's back and face upward）。
⑤ 啸歌：长啸或吟唱（whistling and chanting）。
⑥ 冥然兀坐：静静地端坐着（sit upright in silence）。
⑦ 籁：从孔穴里发出的声音；泛指声音（sound coming from any hole or cavity）。
⑧ 三五之夜：农历每月十五的夜晚（evening of the 15th day in each lunar month）。
⑨ 斑驳（bó）：色彩相杂状（motley, mixed colours）。
⑩ 珊珊（shān）：环佩的声音，引申为美好的样子（sound of a jade ring or pendant; here the meaning has been extended to a lovely manner）。
⑪ 迨（dài）：等到（by the time）。
⑫ 诸父：伯叔们（uncles）。
⑬ 异爨（cuàn）：分灶做饭，意思是分了家（cooking on separate stoves, meaning live apart）。
⑭ 往往：到处（everywhere）。
⑮ 东犬西吠：东边的狗对着西边叫。分家后，狗把原住同一庭院的人当作陌生人（dogs in the east bark to the west. After the family has been divided into two, the dogs regard the original family members as strangers）。
⑯ 逾庖（páo）而宴：越过厨房去吃饭。庖，厨房（going through kitchens to have dinner. 庖, kitchen）。
⑰ 已：已而，随后不久（soon after）。
⑱ 凡：总共（in all）。
⑲ 再：两次（twice）。

moon shines upon half the wall, the cinnamon trees strew motley shadows on it and one can see a lovely picture of moving shadows driven by the wind.

However, when I lived in this dwelling place, I experienced many things, happy and sad. At first, the northern and southern ends of the yard were open to each other, forming a natural path. Later on, my father and his brothers decided to have their families live apart. Therefore quite a few small doors were set up and walls added everywhere, to separate their households. As a result, dogs started to bark at the originally acquainted people, visitors had to walk through the kitchens to attend feasts and chickens dared to perch in the living rooms. At first the yard was divided by fences and later by walls and it has undergone two big changes like this. Here once lived an old woman, a maidservant of my late grandmother. She had suckled two generations and my mother, when she was alive, treated her very well. The western side of the hut was linked to the bedrooms and my mother had been there once. The old woman said to me, "Your mother used to stand here outside your study for quite a while." She also said: "When your elder sister was a baby and one day was crying in my arms, your mother knocked on the door with her fingers and asked: 'Is the baby feeling cold or is she hungry?' I answered from the other side of the door." She did not finish her words before I

妪①，尝居于此。妪，先大母②婢也，乳二世③，先妣④抚⑤之甚厚。室西连于中闺⑥，先妣尝一至。妪每谓余曰："某所⑦，而⑧母立于兹。"妪又曰："汝姊⑨在吾怀，呱呱⑩而泣；娘以指叩门扉曰：'儿寒乎？欲食乎？'吾从板外相为应答。"语未毕，余泣，妪亦泣。余自束发⑪，读书轩中，一日，大母过⑫余曰："吾儿，久不见若影，何竟日⑬默默在此，大类⑭女郎也？"比去⑮，以手阖⑯门，自语曰："吾家读书久不效⑰，儿之成，则可待乎！"顷之⑱，持一象笏⑲至，曰："此吾祖太

---

① 老妪（yù）：老太婆（old woman）。
② 先大母：已死的祖母（one's late grandmother）。
③ 乳二世：给两代人喂奶（suckle two generations）。
④ 先妣（bǐ）：已死的母亲（one's late mother）。
⑤ 抚：待（treat）。
⑥ 中闺：内室（inner chamber）。
⑦ 某所：某某地方（a certain place）。
⑧ 而：尔，你的（your）。
⑨ 汝姊（zǐ）：你的姐姐（your elder sister）。
⑩ 呱呱（gū）：小儿哭声（the cry of a baby）。
⑪ 束发：古代男孩成年时把头发挽到头顶上（while growing up, a boy's hair will be coiled on the top of his head）。
⑫ 过：经过（go by）。
⑬ 竟日：整天（all day long）。
⑭ 大类：很像（be very similar to）。
⑮ 比去：等到离开（when she left）。
⑯ 阖（hé）：通"合"，合上（equal to 合，close）。
⑰ 效：奏效，这里指得到功名（get the desired result, here meaning getting an official rank）。
⑱ 顷之：一会儿（after a while）。
⑲ 笏（hù）：古代君臣在朝廷上相见时臣子手中所拿的用玉、象牙或竹子制成的狭长板子，上面可以记事（a tablet held before the chest by officials when received in audience by the emperor）。

cried and she cried too. Since the age of fifteen, I had been doing my reading in this room. One day my grandmother came to see me and said: "My boy, I haven't seen you for a long time. Why do you stay here from morning till night as quiet as a girl?" She closed the door while leaving and said to herself: "It has been a long time since anyone in my family has succeeded in obtaining an official rank. The day when my grandson succeeds in getting this can be expected!" After a while, she came back holding an ivory tablet, saying: "This is what my grandfather, the revered Chamberlain for Ceremonial held during the Xuande Reign (1426–1435) when received in audience by the Emperor. You will need it in the future." Looking at this old item, its history seemed to have just happened yesterday and I could not help bursting into tears for a long time.

To the east of my study was once a kitchen. When people were going there, they would pass by. I had been staying in this small hut day and night with the windows closed all the time. Gradually, I became able to judge from their steps who was walking past. Perhaps it's protected by God as this hut has survived four fires in all.

常公宣德①间执此以朝,他日汝当用之!"瞻顾②遗迹,如在昨日,令人长号③不自禁。

轩东,故④尝为厨,人往,从轩前过。余扃牖⑤而居,久之,能以足音辨人。轩凡四遭火,得不焚,殆⑥有神护者。

余既为此志,后五年,吾妻来归⑦,时至轩中,从余问古事,或凭几学书。吾妻归宁⑧,述诸小妹语曰:"闻姊家有阁子,且何谓阁子也?"其后六年,吾妻死,室坏不修。其后二年,余久卧病无聊,乃使人复葺南阁子,其制⑨稍异于前。然自后余多在外,不常居。

庭有枇杷树,吾妻死之年所手植也,今已亭亭如盖矣。

---

① 宣德:明宣宗年号(the reign title of Emperor Xuanzong of the Ming Dynasty)。
② 瞻顾:瞻仰、回忆(look at with reverence and recall)。
③ 长号(háo):大哭(cry long and bitterly)。
④ 故:过去(in the past)。
⑤ 扃(jiōng)牖(yǒu):关着窗户(close the window)。扃,门窗上的插销(bolt on a window)。牖,窗户(window)。
⑥ 殆:恐怕,大概(maybe or probably)。
⑦ 来归:嫁到我家来(married to my family)。归,古代女子出嫁(a woman marries)。
⑧ 归宁:出嫁的女儿回娘家省亲(a married woman goes back to her parents' home for a visit)。
⑨ 制:格式和样子(shape and style)。

Five years after I wrote this note, I married and my wife moved to this place. She often visited my study, sometimes asking me about old stories, sometimes sitting at the table learning how to write. When she came back from her visit to her parents, she told us her younger sister's query. Her sister had said: "I heard that your home has a unique hut. How unique is it?" Six years after that, my wife passed away and the hut fell into disrepair. Two years later, I fell ill and was confined to bed. I had nothing to do and decided to have the hut renovated and its structure has changed slightly after the renovation. However, since then I have often lived elsewhere and seldom came back to stay here.

In the yard there's a loquat tree which was planted by my wife in the year she passed away. Now it has become a big tree, standing straight with dense leaves like a canopy.

任光禄①竹溪记

唐顺之

余尝游于京师侯家富人之园,见其所蓄②,自绝徼③海外奇花石无所不致④,而所不能致者唯竹。吾江南人斩竹而薪⑤之,其为园⑥,亦必购求海外奇花石,或千钱买一石、百钱买一花,不自惜。然有竹据⑦其间,或芟⑧而去⑨焉,曰:"毋以是占我花石地!"而京师人苟⑩可致一竹,辄⑪不惜数千钱;然才遇霜雪,又槁⑫以死。以其难致而又多槁死,则人益贵⑬之。而江南人甚或笑之曰:"京师人乃⑭宝吾之所薪!"

---

① 光禄:官名(official title)。
② 蓄:蓄藏(collection)。
③ 绝徼(jiào):边远地区(remote area)。
④ 致:买到(got)。
⑤ 薪:此处用作动词,当柴烧(used as a verb, meaning: burn as firewood)。
⑥ 园:花园(park)。
⑦ 据:占据(occupy)。
⑧ 芟(shān):锄除(to chant poems and sing songs loudly)。
⑨ 去:去除(get rid of)。
⑩ 苟:假如(if)。
⑪ 辄(zhé):每每(often)。
⑫ 槁:枯干(withered)。
⑬ 贵:珍贵(to treasure; to value)。
⑭ 乃:竟然(go so far as to)。

GUANGLU REN'S BAMBOO-STREAM GARDEN

Tang Shunzhi

I have visited some gardens of the noble and rich families in the capital. What I saw were collections of all sorts of unique objects such as exotic flowers and rare stones from remote areas and abroad. The only thing they are unable to add to their collections is bamboo. We, people living in the area south of the Yangtze River, chop bamboo to use as firewood. When we build a garden, we want to obtain rare flowers and stones from abroad. We never hesitate to spend a thousand pieces of gold on a stone and a hundred on a flower tree. If we see bamboo occupying a space in the garden, we will cut it, saying, "Do not let it occupy the place where I am going to grow flowers and lay out stones." However, people of the capital would be willing to pay a lot of money if they could have bamboo, even a single one, transplanted into their gardens. Unfortunately, bamboo will wither and die as soon as it comes across the first frost or snow. The people of the capital value bamboo highly because it is so hard to get and so easy to die in the north. Some southerners even sneered at them,

呜呼！奇花石诚为京师与江南人所贵，然穷①其所生之地，则绝徼海外之人视之，吾意其亦无以②甚异于竹之在江以南。而绝徼海外，或素不产竹之地，然使其人一旦见竹，吾意其必又有甚于京师人之宝之者。是将不胜③笑也。语云④："人去乡⑤则益贱，物去乡则益贵。"以此言之，世之好丑，亦何常之有⑥乎！

余舅光禄任君治园于荆溪⑦之上，遍植以竹，不植他木。竹间作一小楼，暇则与客吟啸⑧其中。而间⑨谓余曰："吾不能与有力者争⑩池亭花石之胜，独此取诸土⑪之所有，可以不劳力而蓊然⑫满园，亦足适也。因自谓竹溪主人。甥其为我记之。"

---

① 穷：追究（look into, investigate）。
② 无以：没有什么（nothing the matter）。
③ 不胜：经不起（cannot stand）。
④ 语云：俗语说（common saying）。
⑤ 去乡：离开本土（leave one's native land）。
⑥ 何常之有：有何固定的看法（what fixed idea do they have？）。
⑦ 荆溪：在今江苏省宜兴市南，注入太湖（a stream in the south of today's Yixing, Jiangsu Province, flowing into the Taihu Lake）。
⑧ 吟啸：吟诗高歌（to chant poems and sing songs loudly）。
⑨ 间：间或，偶然（occasionally, now and then）。
⑩ 争：比赛（compete）。
⑪ 土：土生土长（be born and brought up in one's native land）。
⑫ 蓊（wěng）然：草木茂盛的样子（luxuriant）。

saying, "How funny it is that the people of the capital see our firewood as a precious object."

Alas! Strange flowers and stones are loved dearly by not only the people of the capital but also those living in the regions south of the Yangtze River. Ironically, if we trace back to the areas where the flowers and stones have come from, we will find that, in the eyes of the people living in those remote areas or outside our country, the flowers and stones we treasure are nothing special, just as the people of the south regard bamboo. Some remote areas or overseas land may not produce bamboo. If the people living there have a chance to see bamboo, I think they may love it more dearly than those who live in the capital. How funny it is that people have such different attitudes towards bamboo! As the saying goes, "Away from his hometown, a man will lose his value; whereas the value of an object will increase outside the producing area." If this is the case, is there any fixed criterion for distinguishing beautiful from ugly and good from bad?

My uncle Mr. Ren, who is the director of the banqueting court, has built a garden by the Jing Stream. Bamboo has been planted everywhere and no other trees can be seen in the garden. A small building has been built in the bamboo grove. My uncle often goes there in his spare-time, chanting poems and singing songs with his guests. Once he said to me: "I cannot afford to contend with those

余以谓君岂真不能与有力者争,而漫然①取诸其土之所有者;无乃独有所深好②于竹,而不欲以告人欤?昔人论竹,以为绝无声色臭③味可好④。故其巧怪不如石,其妖艳绰约⑤不如花,孑孑然⑥有似乎偃蹇⑦孤特⑧之士,不可以谐⑨于俗。是以自古以来,知好⑩竹者绝少。且彼京师人亦岂能知而贵之,不过欲以此斗富,与奇花石等耳。故京师人之贵竹,与江南人之不贵竹,其为不知竹一⑪也。君生长于纷华⑫,而能不溺⑬乎其中,裘⑭马⑮、僮奴⑯、歌舞,凡诸富人所酣嗜⑰,一切斥⑱去。尤挺挺不⑲妄⑳与人交,凛然有偃蹇孤特之气,此其于竹必有自得焉。而举凡㉑万物,可喜可玩,

---

① 漫然:漫不经心(pay no heed to; totally unconcerned)。
② 有所深好:有深厚的喜爱之情(have a deep love in)。
③ 臭(xiù)味:气味(smell, odour)。
④ 可好:值得喜爱(be worth loving)。
⑤ 妖艳绰约:颜色艳丽,姿态柔美(bright-colored and gently beautiful)。
⑥ 孑孑然:孤独的样子(lonely)。
⑦ 偃蹇(yǎn jiǎn):高傲(arrogant, haughty)。
⑧ 孤特:孤高独立(lonely and independent)。
⑨ 谐:协调(coordinate, cohere with)。
⑩ 好:喜好(like, be fond of)。
⑪ 一:一样的(same)。
⑫ 纷华:富贵豪华(rich, honourable and luxurious)。
⑬ 溺:沉溺(indulge, wallow)。
⑭ 裘:皮衣(fur clothing)。
⑮ 马:马车(carriage)。
⑯ 僮奴:奴仆(servant)。
⑰ 酣嗜:尽情爱好(love / like heartily)。
⑱ 斥:排除(get rid of)。
⑲ 挺挺:正直(honest, upright)。
⑳ 妄:胡乱(carelessly, causally)。
㉑ 举凡:大凡(generally, in most cases)。

powerful people for the beautiful pools, pavilions, flowers and stones. What I can do is to make use of the advantages which my land can provide. In this way, I have been able to make my garden luxuriant and beautiful, thus giving myself a lot of enjoyment and satisfaction. So I call myself 'Master of the Bamboo-Stream Garden.' May I ask you, my nephew, to write something about it for me?"

I do not think my uncle is really unable to compete with those powerful people and that he has to gain advantage from his land. I wonder if he is very fond of bamboo but unwilling to let others know about his affection. People of the past, while commenting on bamboo, often said that this plant did not have any charm or fragrance which was worth loving. As a matter of fact, bamboo is neither as unique as strange stones, nor as graceful and colorful as exotic flowers. Individually, an erect bamboo looks like an arrogant and lonely man who does not cohere with other people. Therefore since ancient times, there have been very few people who know the merits of bamboo and love it. Do the people of the capital really treasure bamboo because they know how good it is? No, what they want is to show off their fortune by adding bamboo to their collections of rare stones and flowers. So the people of the capital who love bamboo dearly and those living in the south who do not care for it as much have something in common: neither of

固有不能间①也欤？然则②虽使竹非其土之所有，君犹将极其力以致之，而后快乎其心。君之力虽使能尽致奇花石，而其好固有不存也。

嗟乎③！竹固可以不出江南而取贵④也哉！吾重⑤有所感矣！

① 间：割舍（give up, part with）。
② 然则：既然这样，那么（since it is so, then）。
③ 嗟乎：唉（alas）。
④ 取贵：被人珍贵（be valued）。
⑤ 重：深，甚（deeply, extremely）。

them know the merits of bamboo. Having been brought up in a noble and rich family, Mr. Ren has never wallowed in luxury and extravagance. He rejects anything that rich people love to enjoy such as fur coats, horse-drawn carriages, child servants, song and dance. Being upright in character and stern in manner, he has never carelessly associated with other people, thus in always looking arrogant and lonely he resembled the disposition of a self-complacent individual bamboo. Among the numerous objects in the world, is there anything so lovely and amusing that it is impossible to be taken away from somebody? Yes, bamboo is so special to Mr. Ren that even if it were not a native plant in our region, Mr. Ren would spare no effort to collect it and in the future it would give him a lot of pleasure. Though his financial capacity could have helped him obtain all kinds of rare flowers and stones, he is not interested in doing so.

Alas! Even in the south, bamboo, a native plant, can also be loved dearly by some local people. I have been deeply moved by this finding.

题《海天落照图》后

王世贞

《海天落照图》，相传小李将军昭道①作，宣和②秘藏，不知何年为常熟刘以则③所收，转落吴城④汤氏。嘉靖⑤中，有郡守，不欲言其名，以分宜⑥子大符⑦意迫得⑧之。汤见消息非常，乃延⑨仇英实父⑩别室⑪，摹一本，将欲为米颠⑫狡狯⑬，而为怨

---

① 小李将军昭道：唐代著名画家李思训之子李昭道。李思训曾任右武卫大将军，因此人们称李昭道为小李将军（son of the famous painter of the Tang Dynasty Li Sixun, named Li Zhaodao. Li Sixun was appointed to the position of Right Defending General, so people called Li Zhaodao Young General Li）。
② 宣和：宋徽宗的年号（the reign title of Emperor Huizong of the Song Dynasty）。
③ 刘以则：明代收藏家（an art collector of the Ming Dynasty）。
④ 吴城：苏州（today's Suzhou City）。
⑤ 嘉靖：明世宗的年号（the reign title of Emperor Shizong of the Ming Dynasty）。
⑥ 分宜：明代奸臣严嵩，因其是江西分宜人，故称为分宜（a treacherous court official of the Ming Dynasty, Yan Song, who was from Fenyi County in Jiangxi and so called by the public）。
⑦ 大符：严世蕃，字大符，明嘉靖年间奸相严嵩之子（Yan Shifan styled himself Dafu, son of Yan Song, the traitor minister in the Ming Dynasty）。
⑧ 迫得：逼迫取得（obtain by force）。
⑨ 延：请（ask）。
⑩ 仇英实父：仇英，字实父，号十洲，明代著名画家（Qiu Ying styled himself Shifu, alternatively named Shizhou, a famous painter of the Ming Dynasty）。
⑪ 别室：密室（a room used for a secret purpose）。
⑫ 米颠：米芾（fú），宋代著名画家，为人癫狂，世人称之为"米颠"（Mi Fu, a famous painter of the Song Dynasty, who often acted like a madman, hence "Crazy Mi"）。
⑬ 狡狯（kuài）：米芾善仿古以乱真，故文中称其"狡狯"（Mi Fu was good at modeling after an antique and his replica looked genuine）。

THE INSCRIPTION ON *THE SEA AND SKY IN THE GLOW OF THE SETTING SUN*

Wang Shizhen

Legend has it that the painting of *The Sea and Sky in the Glow of the Setting Sun* was painted by Li Zhaodao whose nick name was Young General Li. This painting was secretly collected by the imperial palace during the Xuanhe Reign of the Song Dynasty. It is unknown in what year this painting was obtained by Liu Yize who was a native of Changshu. Then it fell into the hands of an art collector named Tang from Suzhou. During the Jiajing Reign of the Ming Dynasty, a prefecture chief (I don't want to mention his name) demanded the painting on behalf of Yan Song's son, Yan Shifan (Yan Song was a wicked prime minister of the Ming Dynasty). Considering this was an unusual matter, Mr. Tang asked Qiu Ying (a famous painter of the Ming Dynasty) to make a copy of the painting within a secret room. Qiu Ying's imitation of the rare painting was so good that it seemed as if it were Mi Fu (a famous painter of the Song Dynasty) who had used his cunning workmanship to make the counterfeit look exactly like the original painting. Unfortunately, this secret was exposed by

家①所发②，守怒甚，将致③叵测④。汤不获已⑤，因割⑥陈缉熙⑦等三诗于仇本后，而出真迹，邀所善彭孔嘉⑧辈，置酒泣别，摩挲三日后归守，守以归大符。大符家名画近千卷，皆出其下。寻⑨坐法⑩，籍⑪入天府⑫。隆庆初，一中贵⑬携出，不甚爱赏，其位下小珰⑭窃之。时朱忠僖⑮领缇骑⑯，密⑰以重赀⑱购，中贵诘责甚急，小珰惧而投诸火。此癸酉⑲秋事也。

余自燕中闻之拾遗人⑳，相与慨叹妙迹永绝。今年春，归息弇

---

① 怨家：仇家（foe）。
② 发：揭发（expose）。
③ 致：加（put）。
④ 叵测：灾祸（disaster）。
⑤ 不获已：不得已（be forced to）。
⑥ 割：裁去（cut down）。
⑦ 陈缉熙：陈鉴，字缉熙，明代收藏家（Chen Jian styled himself Jixi, an art collector of the Ming Dynasty）。
⑧ 彭孔嘉：彭年，字孔嘉，明代书画家文徵明的学生（Peng Nian styled himself Kongjia, student of Wen Zhengming, a painter of the Ming Dynasty）。
⑨ 寻：不久（before long）。
⑩ 坐法：受法律制裁。指嘉靖末严嵩革职，严世蕃被处死（punished by law. Here referring to the fact that at the end of Jiajing Reign, Yan Song was removed from office and Yan Shifan was put to death）。
⑪ 籍：登记没收（be registered and confiscated）。
⑫ 天府：宫中（palace）。
⑬ 中贵：受皇帝宠幸的大太监（senior eunuch favored by emperor）。
⑭ 小珰（dāng）：小宦官（junior eunuch）。
⑮ 朱忠僖（xī）：朱希孝，谥忠僖（Zhu Xixiao, whose posthumous title was Zhongxi）。
⑯ 缇（tí）骑：明代的缉捕人员（hounds of law in the Ming Dynasty）。
⑰ 密：暗地里（secretly）。
⑱ 重赀（zī）：重金（in high price）。
⑲ 癸酉：明神宗万历元年（the first year of the Wanli Reign of the Ming Dynasty, AD 1573）。
⑳ 拾遗人：旧货商（junk man）。

Tang's foe. On hearing about the trick, the prefect was so furious that it was hard to predict what misfortune Tang was going to incur. Tang could do nothing but hand over the genuine painting to the prefect. Before doing so, Tang cut off the three poems written by Chen Jixi (an art collector of the Ming Dynasty) and two others and attached them to Qiu Ying's imitation. Then he invited his good friend Peng Kongjia and some others to his residence. A ceremony was held and drinking wine amid tears, they bade farewell to the extraordinary painting. Having been touched emotionally and viewed again and again for three days, the painting was given to the prefect who soon presented it to Dafu (Yan Shifan styled himself Dafu). In his home, Dafu had a large collection of nearly one thousand famous paintings but none of them was as good as this one. Before long he was executed for his evil doings. This painting was then confiscated by the imperial court and became a registered property of the royal palace. In the first year of the Longqing Reign (1567), a senior eunuch who was the emperor's favourite took the painting out of the palace but did not treasure it. One of his subordinates, a junior eunuch, stole it. At that time, Zhu Zhongxi, commander of the hounds of law, was secretly tracing the whereabouts of this painting and intended to offer a high price for it. As the senior eunuch was desperately conducting an interrogation to find out who had stolen the painting, the junior eunuch, for fear that his theft would be discovered, threw it into a fire. This happened in the first autumn of the Wanli Reign (1573).

园①，汤氏偶以仇本见售，为惊喜，不论直收之。

按《宣和画谱》②称昭道有《落照》《海岸》二图，不言所谓《海天落照》者。其图之有御题③、有瘦金④、瓢印⑤与否亦无从辨证，第⑥睹此临迹之妙乃尔，因以想见隆准公⑦之惊世也。实父十指如叶玉人⑧，即临本亦何必减逸少⑨宣示⑩、信本⑪《兰亭》⑫哉！老人馋眼，今日饱矣！为题其后。

---

① 弇（yǎn）园：王世贞家花园名（name of Wang Shizhen's garden）。
② 宣和画谱：宋徽宗时记载宫内名画的册子（books on painting recording famous paintings in the palace when Huizong was in power in the Song Dynasty）。
③ 御题：指宋徽宗的题字（an inscription of Emperor Huizong of the Song Dynasty）。
④ 瘦金：徽宗所创的一种字体（style of calligraphy created by Huizong）。
⑤ 瓢印：徽宗在其所藏古画上所用的瓢形印鉴（the gourd-ladle-shaped seal used by Emperor Huizong to affix on the ancient paintings he collected）。
⑥ 第：只（only）。
⑦ 隆准公：隆准，高鼻梁，帝王之相。李昭道为唐宗室，故称（high bridge of the nose, kingly appearance. Li Zhaodao was so called because he belonged to the imperial clan）。
⑧ 叶玉人：将玉雕成叶状的高手匠人（a master craftsman who can carve out thin leaves from a piece of jade）。
⑨ 逸少：王羲之，字逸少，晋代书法家（Wang Xizhi styled himself Yishao, a calligrapher of the Jin Dynasty）。
⑩ 宣示：王羲之曾临三国魏钟繇所书《宣示表》（Wang Xizhi copied Zhong You's "The Memorial of Proclamation" [Zhong You was an official of the State of Wei in the age of the Three Kingdoms Period]）。
⑪ 信本：欧阳询，字信本，唐代书法家（Ouyang Xun styled himself Xinben, a calligrapher of the Tang Dynasty）。
⑫ 兰亭：王羲之《兰亭序》，传世之兰亭帖为欧阳询所临（Wang Xizhi's "Lanting Xu [Preface to the Poems Collected from the Orchid Pavillion]". The Lanting model of calligraphy handed down from the Jin Dynasty was copied by Ouyang Xun）。

When I was In the Area of Yan, I heard antique dealers talking about the tragedy and sighing over the great loss that such a wonderful painting had vanished for ever. This spring I came back to the Yan Garden for recuperation. It so happened that the Tangs was selling Qiu Ying's imitation of the rare painting. I was so surprised and happy that I bought it immediately without considering the price.

According to *The Book of the Model Paintings* published during the Xuanhe Reign, Li Zhaodao had left to posterity two pictures — *The Setting Sun* and *The Sea Shore*, but *The Sea and Sky in the Glow of the Setting Sun* was not mentioned. It was said that there was to be found on the rare painting Emperor Huizong's inscription. However, it is now impossible to put it to textual research as to whether the inscription was written in the Emperor's special style of calligraphy and whether his gourd-ladle-shaped seal was affixed. Only by viewing the marvelous imitation, could we imagine how the original, drawn by a gentleman with a majestic bearing (Li Zhaodao belonged to the imperial clan, hence such a description of his appearance), had left people on earth gasping with wonder. Qiu Ying had the dexterous fingers of the master craftsman who is able to carve out thin leaves from a piece of jade and the imitation he made can be said as competent as Wang Xizhi's copy of "The Memorial of Proclamation" and Ouyang Xun's copy of "Lanting Xu." An old man like me always desires to see more beautiful things. Today, I feel quite satisfied after I have seen such a beautiful painting, thus writing these words about it.

题孔子像于芝佛院①

李贽

人皆以孔子为大圣，吾亦以为大圣；皆以老、佛②为异端，吾亦以为异端。人人非真知大圣与异端也，以所闻于父师之教者熟也；父师非真知大圣与异端也，以所闻于儒先③之教者熟也；儒先亦非真知大圣与异端也，以孔子有是言也。其曰"圣则吾不能④"，是居⑤谦也。其曰"攻乎异端⑥"，是必为老与佛也。

儒先臆度⑦而言之，父师沿袭而诵之，小子⑧蒙聋⑨而听之。万口一词，不可破也；千年一律，不自知也。不曰"徒诵其言"，而

---

① 芝佛院：佛院名，在今湖北省麻城市龙潭湖畔。公元1584年，58岁的李贽孑然一身来到这里，开始十余年的著书讲学活动（name of a temple, on the bank of the Dragon-Pool Lake in Macheng City, Hubei Province. In 1584, Li Zhi, at the age of 58, came here and began his writing and lecturing activities for more than ten years）。
② 老、佛：指道教与佛教（referring to Taoism and Buddhism）。
③ 儒先：儒学先辈（the forerunners of Confucianism）。
④ 圣则吾不能：意谓我当不了圣人。见《孟子·公孙丑上》（see chapter "Gongsun Chou" of *Mencius*, meaning I cannot be a sage）。
⑤ 居：为（be）。
⑥ 异端：指儒家以外的其他思想学说（other thoughts and theories beyond Confucianism）。
⑦ 臆度：主观猜测（guess）。
⑧ 小子：晚辈（the younger generation）。
⑨ 蒙聋：同朦胧（not bright and clear）。

PAYING TRIBUTE TO CONFUCIUS IN THE ZHIFO TEMPLE

Li Zhi

Everybody regards Confucius as a great sage and I think so too. Everybody regards Taoism and Buddhism as heterodoxy and I also see them like that. Actually, people do not really understand what a great sage is or what heterodoxy is. What they know about them has come from their fathers and teachers. However, their fathers and teachers are not real experts in this regard. They have obtained their knowledge when they were taught by the late Confucianism specialists. Even those specialists did not fully understand the difference between the great sage and heterodoxy. They only surmised from what Confucius himself said. "I do not deserve to be a sage," it was in his modesty he said this. "Let's attack heterodoxy," he must have been referring to Taoism and Buddhism by saying so.

The late Confucianism specialists talked about the doctrines of Confucius according to their conjecture. Our fathers and teachers followed them and repeated their statements and the

曰"己知其人";不曰"强不知以为知",而曰"知之为知之"。至今日,虽有目①,无所用矣。

余何人也,敢谓有目?亦从众耳。既从而圣之②,亦从众而事之③,是故吾从众事孔子于芝佛之院。

---

① 目:这里指眼力,即正确判断是非的能力(here referring to judgment, i.e. ability to distinguish right from wrong)。
② 圣之:把他当作圣人(regard him as a sage)。
③ 事之:侍奉他(attend upon him)。

younger generation listened to what they were taught without any understanding. Everybody echoed the views of others without exception and the same pattern has appeared again and again for thousands of years without being noticed. We heard someone say that he knew the great sage very well but actually he only knew how to recite Confucius' sayings. He would not say that he pretended to know what he did not know but he would let others know anything that he really knew. Now what is the use of our eyes if they cannot see all these problems?

What am I? Do I dare to say my vision is sharp? No, I just follow other people in considering Confucius as a great sage and also honour him. That is why I have come to the Zhifo Temple with many other people to pay tribute to Confucius.

极乐寺纪游

袁宗道

高梁桥①水,从西山②深涧③中来,道④此入玉河⑤。白练⑥千匹,微风行⑦水上,若罗纹纸⑧。堤在水中,两波相夹,绿柳四行,树古叶繁⑨,一树之荫⑩,可覆⑪数席,垂线⑫长丈余。

---

① 高梁桥:北京西直门外高粱河上所架设的桥(a bridge erected across the Gaoliang River outside the Xizhi Gate in Beijing)。
② 西山:北京西郊名胜,是太行山的支脉,众山连接,山名很多,总名为西山(a scenic spot in the western suburb of Beijing, branch range of the Taihang Mountain. It has many names and is generally called the West Mountain)。
③ 涧:夹在两山间的流水(flowing water between two peaks)。
④ 道:取道,流经(by way of)。
⑤ 玉河:水源出自北京西北玉泉山下,流为玉河,汇成昆明湖,出而东南流,环绕紫禁城,注入大通河(originating from the foot of the Jade-Spring Mountain northwest of Beijing and converging as the Jade River which ran into the Kunming Lake. Then it flowed southeastward, around the Forbidden City, and emptied into the Datong River)。
⑥ 练:白色的熟绢(white silk)。
⑦ 行:经历,引申为吹过(blow past)。
⑧ 罗纹纸:一种表面有像质地轻软的罗那样的椒眼纹的纸(a kind of paper with silk-like quality and fine lines on its surface)。
⑨ 叶繁:枝叶茂盛(flourishing branches and leaves)。
⑩ 荫(yīn):树荫(shade)。
⑪ 覆:遮盖,掩蔽(cover)。
⑫ 垂线:下垂的柳丝(willow branches drooping down)。

VISITING THE HAPPY TEMPLE

Yuan Zongdao

The stream under the Gaoliang Bridge originates from the deep ravine of the West Mountain and flows past here into the Jade River, appearing as a thousand bolts of white silk. When a faint breeze blows, the ripples on the surface of the water look like silken paper. The dyke was built in the water between two rivers. On the dyke are four lines of green willows. Leaves are still flourishing on the old trees. The shade from one tree can cover several mats and the branches hang down over one *zhang* (1 *zhang* = 3.3 metres) long.

On the northern shore there are many Buddhist and Taoist temples with red gates and dark purple halls, which extend for dozens of *li* (1 *li* = 0.5 km). The distant trees on the opposite shore, either tall or short, are crowded together in clumps, separated by paddy fields. The West Mountain, like a conch-shaped hair bun, towers between forest and water.

The Happy Temple is about three *li* from the bridge. The road is good. Riding through the green shade on horseback is like

岸北佛庐①道院②甚众，朱门绀③殿，亘④数十里。对面远树，高下攒⑤簇⑥，间⑦以水田。西山如螺髻⑧，出⑨于林水之间。

极乐寺去⑩桥可⑪三里，路径亦佳，马行绿荫中若张盖⑫。殿前剔牙松⑬数株，树身鲜翠微黄，班剥⑭若大鱼鳞，大可七八围⑮许⑯。

暇日曾与黄思立诸公游此。予弟中郎⑰云："此地小似钱塘⑱苏堤⑲。"余因叹西湖胜境入梦已久，何日挂进贤冠⑳，作六桥下客子㉑，了此山水一段情障㉒乎！

是日分韵各赋一诗而别。

---

① 佛庐：佛寺（the Buddhist Temple）。
② 道院：道教的庙宇（Taoist Temple）。
③ 绀（gàn）：深青透红之色（dark purple）。
④ 亘（gèn）：延续不断（extend; stretch）。
⑤ 攒（cuán）：聚集（collect together）。
⑥ 簇（cù）：丛聚（crowd together）。
⑦ 间（jiàn）：隔（separate）。
⑧ 螺髻：螺壳状的发髻（conch-like hair bun）。
⑨ 出：显露（appear）。
⑩ 去：距离（be apart / away from）。
⑪ 可：大约（about）。
⑫ 张盖：打伞（spread an umbrella）。
⑬ 剔牙松：针叶像牙签一样的松树（a kind of pine tree, with toothpick-like leaves）。
⑭ 班剥：斑驳（mottled）。
⑮ 围：计圆周的量词（a word used to calculate the measurement of a circle）。
⑯ 许：表示约略估计之词（about）。
⑰ 中郎：作者的弟弟袁宏道，字中郎，明代著名散文家（the author's younger brother Yuan Hongdao, a famous prose writer of the Ming Dynasty）。
⑱ 钱塘：古县名，即今日杭州（today's Hangzhou）。
⑲ 苏堤：在杭州西湖，宋苏轼任杭州知府时所筑，横截湖面（a famous dam across the West Lake, built while Su Shi governed Hangzhou）。
⑳ 挂进贤冠：进贤冠，古代儒者所戴的缁布冠（a kind of black hat worn by a Confucianist scholar in ancient China）。挂冠：弃官而去（give up one's official position）。
㉑ 客子：旅居异乡的人（visitor, traveler）。
㉒ 情障：情怀（feelings）。

being under the spread of an umbrella. In front of the hall there are several pine trees with toothpick-like leaves. Their trunks are coloured fresh green and light yellow, mottling like large fish scales and each tree is about seven or eight *wei* (7 or 8 arm spans) thick.

On one leisure day, I traveled here together with Huang Sili and some others. My younger brother, Zhonglang said: "This place looks a little like the Su Dam in Qiantang." On hearing his words, I sighed: Long have I dreamed of touring the wonderful scenery of the West Lake; when may I resign from my office and, like a traveler under the Six Bridges, fulfil my dream to see those sights!

That day each wrote a poem in different rhymes and then we said good-bye to each other.

满井①游记

袁宏道②

燕③地寒,花朝节④后,余寒犹厉。冻风⑤时作,作则飞沙走砾,局促⑥一室之内,欲出不得。每冒风驰行,未百步,辄返。

廿二日,天稍和,偕数友出东直⑦,至满井。高柳夹堤,土膏⑧微润,一望空阔,若脱笼之鹄。于时冰皮⑨始解,波色乍明,

---

① 满井:北京郊区景点(a scenic spot in the suburb of Beijing)。
② 袁宏道:晚明著名散文家,字中郎,与其兄袁宗道、弟袁中道并称"三袁"。他反对"文必秦汉,诗必盛唐"的风气,提倡"独抒性灵,不拘格套"的性灵说,对推动文体解放作出了重要贡献(a famous prose-writer in the later Ming Dynasty, alternatively named "Mid-Son," one of the "Three Yuans" [together with his elder brother Zongdao and younger brother Zhongdao]. He opposed "returning to the past and copying books of ancient sages." He advocated writing one's own natural disposition and intelligence. With his fresh and active style, he contributed greatly to the development of prose-writing)。
③ 燕:旧时河北省的别称。北京古称燕京(another name of Hebei Province. Beijing was called Yanjing in the old days)。
④ 花朝节:百花的生日(阴历二月十二或十五)(Birthday of Flowers, on the 12th or 15th in the second lunar month)。
⑤ 冻风:冷风(freezing wind, also cold wind)。
⑥ 局促:狭窄,拘束(narrow; confined in a small room)。
⑦ 东直:东直门(the Dongzhi Gate)。
⑧ 膏:肥沃(fertile)。
⑨ 冰皮:冰覆水面,如水有皮(ice covering water like skin)。

TRAVELLING TO THE SCENIC SPOT MANJING

Yuan Hongdao

The area of Yan was cold and even colder after the Birthday of Flowers. Freezing winds often blow, carrying flying sand and rolling gravel. Confined in a small room, I was unable to go out. When I did brave the wind, I failed to stride one hundred steps and had to return.

On the 22nd, it was a little warmer. Together with some of my friends, I went out of the Dongzhi Gate and arrived at Manjing, where high willows lined a dam and the soil was fertile and slightly moist. A vast expanse of fields stretched before me and I felt as if I were a swan which had just escaped from its cage. The thin ice had just begun to thaw and the waves immediately brightened. Layers of fish-scale-like waves, so clear that you could see to the bottom, were glittering like a mirror box newly opened and suddenly letting out a crystal light. The mountain ranges, washed by sunny snow, were beautiful and graceful. Appearing gaily-coloured and radiant enchanting as if having been wiped clean, they looked like lovely girls who had just washed their faces and brushed and

鳞浪层层，清澈见底，晶晶然如镜之新开，而冷光①之乍出于匣也。山峦为晴雪所洗，娟然②如拭，鲜妍明媚，如倩女③之靧面④而髻鬟之始掠也。柳条将舒未舒，柔梢披风，麦田浅鬣⑤寸许。游人虽未盛，泉而茗者⑥，罍⑦而歌者，红装而蹇⑧者，亦时时有。风力虽尚劲，然徒步则汗出浃背。凡曝沙之鸟，呷浪之鳞，悠然自得，毛羽鳞鬣⑨之间，皆有喜气。始知郊田之外，未始无春，而城居者未之知也。

夫能不以游堕事⑩，而潇然⑪于山石草木之间者，惟此官⑫也。而此地适与余近，余之游将自此始，恶⑬能无纪⑭？己亥⑮之二月也。

---

① 冷光：清亮的光（crystal light）。
② 娟然：美好的样子（beautiful and graceful appearance）。
③ 倩女：妩媚的女子（charming girl）。
④ 靧（huì）面：洗脸（wash face）。
⑤ 浅鬣（liè）：像鬃毛一样的麦苗（mane-like wheat seedlings）。
⑥ 泉而茗者：喝着用泉水烹制的茶（drink tea brewed in spring water）。
⑦ 罍（léi）：盛酒器，这里用作动词，指喝酒（an ancient urn-shaped wooden wine-vessel; here used as a verb, meaning drink wine）。
⑧ 红装而蹇：穿着华丽却骑的是驴（be gaily dressed but ride donkeys）。蹇：驴，这里亦用作动词（donkey, here also used as a verb）。
⑨ 鬣：鱼鳍（fish fin, similar to a beast's mane）。
⑩ 堕（huī）事：误事（causing delay in business）。堕：同"隳"。
⑪ 潇然：舒畅、轻快的样子（happy and lively manner）。
⑫ 此官：作者当时任顺天府教授，公事清闲，所以有余暇出游（the author was then a professor of Shuntian Prefecture [today's Beijing area]. At that time he was not busy with his work, thus having leisure to travel）。
⑬ 恶（wū）：怎（how）。
⑭ 纪：记述（writing）。
⑮ 己亥：明万历二十七年（1599）（the 27th year of the Wanli Reign of the Ming Dynasty）。

coiled their hair into buns. The willow twigs were almost about to unfold, with their supple tips splitting in the wind. The mane-like wheat seedlings in the fields were over an inch long. Although sightseers were not many, there were often those who drank tea brewed in spring water, who sang while drinking and who were gaily dressed and rode donkeys. In spite of the cold wind, we were soaked with sweat while walking. All the birds sunbathing in the sands and the fish sipping the waves, carefree and content, expressed joy through their feathers or fins. I soon realised that anytime during the year there was always spring in the suburbs but the town dwellers were not aware.

The reason why I could wander happily and lightheartedly among mountains and rocks, grass and trees without causing any delay in business was only because of my less important position. What is more, this location is nearby. Therefore, from this place I will commence more sightseeing. How could I not record my thoughts? In the second month of the 27th year of the Wanli Reign (1599).

虎丘①记

袁宏道

虎丘去②城可③七八里。其山无高岩邃④壑⑤,独以近城故,箫鼓⑥楼船,无日无之。凡月之夜,花之晨,雪之夕,游人往来,纷错如织⑦,而中秋节为尤胜。

每至是日⑧,倾城⑨阖户⑩,连臂而至⑪。衣冠士女⑫,下迨⑬蔀

---

① 虎丘:位于江苏苏州郊外(Tiger Hill, situated in the suburb of Suzhou, Jiangsu Province)。
② 去:距离(away from)。
③ 可:大约(about)。
④ 邃:深邃(deep)。
⑤ 壑:山谷(gully; ravine)。
⑥ 箫鼓:吹箫打鼓(playing Xiao and beating drum)。箫,管乐器名(a vertical bamboo flute)。
⑦ 纷错如织:指游客纷乱,来往如织([tourists] weave in and out in disorderly fashion)。
⑧ 是日:指中秋节这天(referring to the Mid-autumn Festival)。
⑨ 倾城:全城(the whole city)。
⑩ 阖户:关上门,指全家出动(close the door, here referring to the whole family)。
⑪ 连臂而至:连续不断到来(come continuously)。
⑫ 衣冠士女:打扮整齐的男男女女(men and women who were magnificently decked out)。
⑬ 迨:及(to; till)。

THE TIGER HILL

Yuan Hongdao

The Tiger Hill is situated about seven or eight *li* from the city. It has no high cliffs or deep ravines. As it is close to the city, luxurious pleasure-boats, from which beautiful music and songs issue, can be seen daily on the nearby canal. On each moonlit night, on each flowery morning or snowy evening, tourists weave in and out in disorderly fashion, especially during the Mid-autumn Festival.

Whenever this festival occurs, all families go out from the city and a crowd of people, jostling each other, continuously arrive. Men and women whether from official or poor families are all beautifully dressed up. Many people sit by the roadside on mats, with wine. From the Rock of Holding Thousands of People to the Hill Gate, numerous tourists are closely packed side by side, resembling fish scales. Hardwood musical clappers pile up like a hill and wine contained in cups or pots is being poured like flying clouds. From afar, people appear like many wild geese which have landed on level sand, or similar to rosy clouds spreading over a

屋①，莫不靓妆②丽服，重茵累席③，置酒交衢④间。从千人石⑤上至山门，栉比⑥如鳞⑦，檀板⑧丘积⑨，樽罍⑩云泻，远而望之，如雁落平沙，霞铺江上，雷辊⑪电霍⑫，无得而状⑬。

布席⑭之初，唱者千百，声若聚蚊，不可辨识。分曹⑮部署⑯，竞以歌喉相斗，雅俗既陈，妍媸⑰自别。未几而摇头顿足⑱者，得数十人而已。已而明月浮空，石光如练，一切瓦釜⑲，寂然停声，属而和者，才三四辈；一箫，一寸管⑳，一人缓板而歌，竹肉㉑相发，清

---

① 蔀（bù）屋：贫民所居之屋（cottages in which poor people live）。
② 靓妆：涂脂抹粉（paint and powder oneself）。
③ 重、累：重叠（overlapping）；茵、席：坐垫（mattress）。
④ 交衢：四通八达的大路（highroad leading in all directions）。
⑤ 千人石：虎丘的巨石名（name of a big rock on Tiger Hill）。
⑥ 栉比：如梳齿一样拢在一起（placed closely side by side like the teeth of a comb）。
⑦ 鳞：鱼鳞（fish scale）。
⑧ 檀板：檀木所制打节拍的板子（hardwood clappers）。
⑨ 丘积：堆积如山（piled together like a hill）。
⑩ 樽罍（léi）：酒器（cups and urns containing wine）。
⑪ 雷辊（gǔn）：雷声般的车轮声（wheels rolling like thunder）。
⑫ 电霍：电闪（lightening flash）。
⑬ 无得而状：无法形容（can't be described）。
⑭ 席：聚会（gathering）。
⑮ 分曹：分批（in groups）。
⑯ 部署：安排（arrange）。
⑰ 妍媸（chī）：美丑（beautiful and ugly）。
⑱ 摇头顿足：手舞足蹈（shake one's head and stamp one's feet. Here referring to the winners）。
⑲ 瓦釜：瓦缶，瓦器，这里指粗陋的音乐（originally meaning earthen jar, here referring to vulgar music）。
⑳ 管：管乐器（pipe instrument）。
㉑ 竹肉：竹，指箫管（referring to pipe instruments made of bamboo）；肉，指歌喉（referring to singing voice）。

river. To use the image of lightening and thunder would not be strong enough in describing the scene of bustle and excitement.

At the commencement of the gathering, there were thousands of singers, whose voices sounded like swarming mosquitoes, difficult to distinguish. Then they were divided into groups which contested against each other. This naturally separated the elegant and beautiful from the vulgar and ugly. Soon only dozens of winners remained, shaking their heads and stamping their feet. Then the moon rose and seemed to float in the sky. The rocks of the hill reflecting the moonlight looked like white silk. All the unrefined songs and music suddenly stopped. Only three or four singers still performed. Accompanied by a vertical bamboo flute and a short pipe, one was singing a slow song whilst beating a hardwood clapper. The singer's voice, coming together with the sound of musical pipes, was melodious and loud, overwhelming the audience with joy. It was now deep into the night. In the moonlight, the trees cast interlacing shadows resembling straggly water plants upon the ground. At this moment flutes and clappers were no longer in use. A singer appeared on the stage and the audience held their breath to listen to the extraordinary voice which was as thin as a girl's long hair but so strong that it reached the clouds and echoed in the sky. Every word coming from this singing voice lingered in the air for quite some time. On hearing

声亮彻，听者魂销。比至夜深，月影横斜，荇藻①凌乱，则箫板亦不复用；一夫登场，四座屏息，音若细发，响彻云际，每度一字，几尽一刻②，飞鸟为之徘徊，壮士听而下泪矣。

剑泉③深不可测，飞岩如削。千顷云④得天池⑤诸山作案⑥，峦壑竞秀，最可觞⑦客。但过午则日光射人，不堪久坐耳。文昌阁亦佳，晚树犹可观。面北为平远堂旧址，空旷无际，仅虞山⑧一点在望。堂废久矣，余与江进之⑨谋所以复之，欲祠⑩韦苏州⑪、白乐天⑫诸

---

① 荇（xìng）藻：水中植物（plants in water）。
② 刻：古代分一昼夜为一百刻（in ancient china, a day and a night was divided into a hundred *ke*）。
③ 剑泉：又名剑池（pond for quenching swords）。
④ 千顷云：虎丘山最高处的一个景点（Sea of Clouds, name of a scenic spot on top of the Tiger Hill）。
⑤ 天池：天池山，又名华山，在苏州郊外（the Tianchi [the Heavenly Pond] Mountain, alternatively named Huashan, is situated on the outskirts of Suzhou）。
⑥ 案：几桌（table）。
⑦ 觞（shāng）：酒器，这里用作动词，饮酒助兴（drinking vessels, here used as a verb）。
⑧ 虞山：在江苏常熟市西北（situated northwest of Changshu City, Jiangsu Province）。
⑨ 江进之：名盈科，字进之。万历年间进士，曾任长洲县令（named Yingke, styled himself Jinzhi, a successful candidate for the highest imperial examination in the age of the Wanli Reign of the Ming Dynasty; he once held the position of the magistrate of Changzhou County in today's Jiangsu Province）。
⑩ 祠：祠堂，这里用作动词（ancestral temple, here used as a verb, meaning enshrine and worship）。
⑪ 韦苏州：唐代诗人韦应物，曾任苏州刺史（a poet of the Tang Dynasty; he once held the position of the prefectural governor of Suzhou）。
⑫ 白乐天：唐代诗人白居易，曾任苏州刺史（a poet of the Tang Dynasty; he once held the position of the prefectural governor of Suzhou）。

it flying birds slowed down to hover overhead and even a warrior could not hold back his tears.

The Sword Pond is too deep to be fathomed and the steep and rocky cliff is as sharp as a knife. The mountains around the Sea of Clouds have the appearance of tables of various sizes and one of them has the nick name of the Heavenly Pond. The high rocks and the deep ravine, in their beauty, vie with each other to create an ideal place for tourists to wine and dine. However, after midday, sunshine enters and it is too hot to stay here for long. The scenery around the Tower of Prosperous Culture is also pretty with trees worth watching when night has fallen. Situated to the north is the former site of the Pingyuan Hall. It occupies a vast expanse of fields and the only thing that can be seen here is Mount Yu in the distance. The hall was ruined long ago. Mr. Jiang Jinzhi and I planned to restore it and also to establish a temple to honour the great poets Wei Suzhou and Bai Letian and some others. However, not long afterwards I fell ill and had to resign from office and return to my hometown. I am afraid that Jinzhi has lost interest in doing so. It is its fate that a natural or man-made landscape should be either well looked after or ruined.

When I was the county magistrate of Wu for two years, I visited the Tiger Hill six times. On the sixth visit, I went there together with Jiang Jinzhi and Fang Zigong. We sat on the

公于其中，而病寻作；余既乞归，恐进之之兴亦阑①矣。山川兴废，信有时②哉！

吏③吴④两载，登虎丘者六。最后与江进之、方子公同登，迟⑤月生公石⑥上。歌者闻令来，皆避匿去。余因谓进之曰："甚矣，乌纱⑦之横⑧，皂隶⑨之俗⑩哉！他日去官，有不听曲此石上者，如月⑪！"今余幸得解官称吴客矣。虎丘之月，不知尚识余言否耶？

---

① 阑：尽（end）。
② 时：机会（chance）。
③ 吏：做官，这里用作动词（be an official, here used as a verb）。
④ 吴：苏州。
⑤ 迟：等候（wait for）。
⑥ 生公石：虎丘大石名（name of a big rock on Tiger Hill）。
⑦ 乌纱：指官宦（referring to officials）。
⑧ 横：骄横（arrogant and imperious）。
⑨ 皂隶：衙门的差役（runners in a feudal government）。
⑩ 俗：粗俗（vulgar, coarse）。
⑪ 如月：对月发誓（swear to the moon）。

Shengong Rock, waiting for the moon to rise. On hearing that the magistrate was coming, all the singers fled to hide. I said to Jinzhi: "It is beyond understanding why all our officials are arrogant and overbearing and their attendants always behave badly. Under the moon, I vow that one day when I no longer hold any official position I will come and sit on the Shengong Rock to listen to the Music." I am now fortunate to be able to resign from office and I am here as a visitor to Wu. Moon over the Tiger Hill, do you still remember my words?

与丘长孺①书

袁宏道

闻长孺病甚，念念。若长孺死，东南风雅②尽矣，能无念耶？弟作令③备极丑态，不可名状。大约遇上官则奴，候过客则妓，治钱谷则仓老人④，谕百姓则保山婆⑤。一日之间，百暖百寒，乍阴乍阳，人间恶趣，令一身尝尽矣。苦哉！毒哉！

家弟秋间欲过吴⑥。虽过吴，亦只好冷坐衙斋，看诗读书，不得如往时，携胡孙⑦登虎丘山⑧故事也。

---

① 丘长孺：名坦，字坦之，号长孺，湖北麻城人，公安派作家，与三袁兄弟相友善（Qiu Tan styled himself Tanzhi, alternatively named Changru and was from Macheng, Hubei, a writer of Gong'an school, friendly with the Three Yuan brothers）。
② 风雅：泛指诗文方面的事（generally referring to literary pursuits）。
③ 令：县令（county magistrate）。
④ 仓老人：管理官仓的老吏（old clerk in charge of public granary）。
⑤ 保山婆：媒婆（woman matchmaker）。
⑥ 吴：吴县，即今江苏苏州（Wu county, i.e. today's Suzhou）。
⑦ 胡孙：即"猢狲"，猴子，喻小孩（monkey, referring to children figuratively）。
⑧ 虎丘山：苏州著名的景点，在市郊（a famous scenic spot on the outskirts of Suzhou）。

A LETTER TO QIU CHANGRU

Yuan Hongdao

I have been extremely worried since I heard that you, Changru, were seriously ill. If you were to abandon the world, there would not be any further literary pursuits in the Southeast. How can I not be worried?

Holding the position of a county magistrate, I have been unable to behave myself properly and words cannot describe the ugliness of some of my behaviours. For instance, I look like a slave while attending those higher-ups. I resemble a streetwalker while greeting passing officials. I am not better than a doddering old clerk while managing the public granary and I sound like a woman matchmaker while giving explicit instructions to ordinary people. In a single day, I experience all sorts of happenings of the human world which are similar to the changeable weather: now warm, now cold; cloudy one moment and sunny the next. What miserable experiences and what harmful behaviour!

This autumn my younger brother will come to Wu County for a visit. When he comes, he will have to sit alone in the study of the

近日游兴发不？茂苑①主人虽无钱可赠客子，然尚有酒可醉，茶可饮，太湖一勺水可游，洞庭一块石②可登，不大落莫也。如何？

---

① 茂苑：苏州的代称（another name for Suzhou）。
② 洞庭一块石：指太湖中的东西洞庭山（referring to the Eastern and Western Dongting Hills in the Tai Lake）。

government office, reading books and poems. He will not be able to take some children to climb the Tiger Hill as he used to do.

Do you have any recent interest in coming here for sightseeing? I cannot afford to give money to my guest but I have wine for you to drink your fill and tea to taste. We have the expanse of water of the Tai Lake on which boat-riding is enjoyable. Also, the rocky Dongting Hill is nice for climbing. Once you are here, you will not have the slightest loneliness in your heart. Do you want to come?

晚游六桥^① 待月记

袁宏道

西湖最盛,为春为月。一日之盛,为朝烟,为夕岚^②。今岁春雪甚盛,梅花为寒所勒^③,与杏桃相次开发^④,尤为奇观。

石篑^⑤数为余言:"傅金吾^⑥园中梅,张功甫玉照堂^⑦故物也,急往观之!"余时为桃花所恋,竟不忍去。湖上由断桥至苏堤

---

① 六桥:在杭州西湖苏堤上,依次为映波桥、锁澜桥、望山桥、压堤桥、东浦桥、跨虹桥(six bridges on the Su Dam of the West Lake in Hangzhou. They are in turn, Wave-Reflected Bridge, Billow-Locking Bridge, Mountain-Seeing Bridge, Dyke-Pressing Bridge, East-Riverside Bridge and Striding-Rainbow Bridge)。
② 岚:雾霭(mist)。
③ 勒:制约(restrict)。
④ 相次开发:依次开放(bloom in turn, almost at the same time)。
⑤ 石篑:即陶望龄,字周望,号石篑,会稽(今浙江绍兴)人,公安派作家(named Tao Wangling, styled himself Zhouwang, alternatively named Shikui, from Shaoxing in Zhejiang, a writer of the Gong'an School)。
⑥ 傅金吾:不详(unknown about his identity)。金吾:官名,掌宫廷宿卫(name of an official position, in charge of palace defence)。
⑦ 张功甫玉照堂:名镃,南宋将领张俊之孙。玉照堂是他的园林,传说有400株名贵的梅花(Zhang Gongfu's real name was Zi who was the grandson of Zhang Jun, a general in the Southern Song Dynasty. It is said that the Jade-Shining Hall, the name of his garden, had 400 rare plum trees)。

VISITING THE SIX BRIDGES AT NIGHT TO AWAIT THE MOON

Yuan Hongdao

The most beautiful scenery of the West Lake comes in spring and from the moon. During the day, the most spectacular view is either the morning haze or the evening mist. This year, the spring snow was so heavy that the blooming of the plum trees has been delayed by the cold weather. It is amazing to see their blossoms coming together with that of the apricot and peach trees.

My friend Shikui said to me several times: "The plum trees in Fu Jinwu's garden used to grow in Zhang Gongfu's Jade-Shining Hall. Let's hurry to have a look." I was then so attracted by those peach blossoms that I declined to go. From the Broken Bridge to the Su Dam, green haze and red fog permeated over the West Lake for more than twenty *li* (10 km). The sound of music carried by the wind came to our ears and the fragrant sweat from the female sightseers was dripping like rain. The tourists, dressed in silk and satin, outnumbered the grass growing along the dam. What a pretty and coquettish picture it was!

一带，绿烟红雾①，弥漫二十余里。歌吹②为风，粉汗③为雨，罗纨④之盛，多于堤畔之草，艳冶极矣。

然杭人游湖，止⑤午、未、申三时，其实湖光染翠之工，山岚设色之妙，皆在朝日始出，夕舂⑥未下，始极其浓媚。月景尤不可言，花态柳情，山容水意，别是一种趣味。此乐留与山僧、游客受用，安可为俗士道哉！

---

① 绿烟红雾：绿叶如烟，红花似雾（green smoke of leaves and red fog of flowers）。
② 歌吹：音乐（music）。
③ 粉汗：女人身上流的汗（fragrant sweat from women）。
④ 罗纨：身穿绸缎衣服的游客（tourists in silks and satins）。
⑤ 止：只（only）。
⑥ 夕舂（chōng）：夕阳（the setting sun）。

However, people of Hangzhou tour the West Lake only at the three time periods during the day: *Wushi* (11:00–13:00), *Weishi* (13:00–15:00) and *Shenshi* (15:00–17:00). Actually the lake looks extremely beautiful at the time when the morning sun has just risen to tint the lake jade green. It also looks marvellous at dusk when the setting sun paints the mist floating about the lakeside hills with varied colours. The view on a moonlit night is particularly superb: the flowers' postures are more graceful in the moonlight and the willow trees seem to disclose their sentiments at night; the hills are faintly visible in the darkness and the waters murmur emotionally to the moon. This kind of pleasure can only be enjoyed by the monks and tourists. How can a philistine explain this enjoyment!

山居①斗鸡记

袁宏道

余向在山居,南邻一姓金氏,隐于掾②,爱畜美鸡。一姓蒋氏,隐于商③,从燕地归,得一巨鸡。燕地种原巨,而此巨特甚,足高尺许,粗毛厉嘴,行迟迟有野鹳④状,婆娑可人⑤。群鸡见之,辄避去。独掾隐家一鸡,纵步饮啄如常。玉羽金冠,娟然⑥又更可人。然其体状,较之巨鸡,止⑦可五之一。巨鸡遇之,侮其小,随意加啄,美鸡体状虽小,气不肯下,便跃然起斗。巨鸡张翅雄视,时

---

① 山居:住在山区,此指作者的故乡湖北公安县(living in a mountainous area. Here referring to the author's hometown, Gong'an County, Hubei)。
② 掾(yuàn):官府的属员。旧时恭维官职低微而心志清高的人为"吏隐",意谓虽居官位而与隐者相似(a minor official. In old days people complimented minor officials who were aloof from politics and material pursuits by calling them "hermit official," meaning that although they are minor officials, they resemble hermits)。
③ 隐于商:用法与隐于掾相同。即虽是商人,但与隐者相似(the same as hermit official, meaning although he is a merchant, he resembles a hermit)。
④ 鹳:鸟类的一属。大型涉禽,形似鹤鹭(stork, a large wading bird, like a crane or egret)。
⑤ 婆娑可人:盘旋、徘徊的样子,令人爱看(lovely when circling and lingering about)。
⑥ 娟然:姿态美好的样子(beautiful posture)。
⑦ 止:只(only)。

WATCHING COCKFIGHTING IN THE MOUNTAIN

Yuan Hongdao

I used to live in a mountainous area. My neighbour on the southern side of my home was a man named Jin. A minor official living in this secluded place, he was fond of raising attractive cockerels. Another neighbour Mr. Jiang, though a merchant, preferred to live as a hermit. He had just returned from the Yan Region with a giant rooster. Yan's roosters were usually large but this one was exceptionally huge. With legs over one *chi* (one-third of a metre) long, it had very thick feathers and a sharp beak. It moved slowly with the elegant gait of a stork and looked lovely while strolling about. At the sight of the giant, all the other fowls fled. The only exception was the handsome cock raised by the secluded official. As usual, it strode up and pecked at food. With jade-like feathers and a golden cockscomb, it really was a beautiful creature. However, its size was only one-fifth of that of the giant. Seeing it small in size, the giant tried to bully the small one by pecking at it. Though small, the handsome cock was unwilling

欲即下，美鸡惟凝意①抵防，不敢轻发。于是各张武勇，且前且后，两两相持，每费余刻②。巨鸡或逗雄一下，美鸡自分③不能当，即乘来势，从匿巨鸡跨下，避其冲甚巧。巨鸡一时不知美鸡置身何所，美鸡从巨鸡尾后腾起，乘其不意，亦得一加于④巨鸡。巨鸡才一受毒⑤，便怒张扑来。美鸡巧⑥不及避，乃大受荼毒⑦。

余自初观斗至止，大抵见美鸡或得一捷，则大生欢喜，且睁睁盼美鸡或再捷而卒不可得。而亦终不想及为之所⑧，美鸡将不堪⑨。

余正在烦恼间，有童子从东来，停足凝眸。既而抱不平，乃手搏巨鸡，容美鸡恣意数啄，复大挥巨鸡几掌。巨鸡失势遁去，美鸡乘势蹑⑩其后，直抵其家。须臾⑪，巨鸡复还追美鸡至斗所。童子仍前如是。如是再四。适两书生见童子谆谆⑫用意为此，乃笑曰："我未见人而乃与畜类相搏以为事也。"童子曰："较之读书带

---

① 凝意：集中注意力（concentrate its attention）。
② 余刻：刻，计时单位。古代分一昼夜为一百刻。余刻，即一刻有余（ke, timing unit. In ancient China, a day and night is divided into 100 ke. 余刻 meaning more than 1 ke of time）。
③ 自分：自己料想（anticipate）。
④ 一加于：施以一击（give sb. a strike）。
⑤ 毒：害（halm）。
⑥ 巧：碰巧（by chance）。
⑦ 荼毒：残害（brutally injure or kill）。
⑧ 为之所：为之安排蔽身之所（arrange a shelter for it）。
⑨ 不堪：受不了（cannot stand it）。
⑩ 蹑：追逐（follow along behind, track）。
⑪ 须臾（yú）：片刻（moment, instant）。
⑫ 谆谆：这里意谓反复不倦（here meaning: again and again）。

to give in and jumped to fight against the opponent. The large one immediately spread its wings, glaring at the enemy, ready to attack. While the other one, keeping to the defensive, did not want to take the initiative in launching an attack. Thus the two valiant fighters, now face to face, now one behind the other, were locked in a stalemate for quite some time. Then the large cock attempted to throw its weight about. The handsome one, knowing that it was impossible to resist the mighty force, found an opening into which to rush and hide under the hip of the enemy. This technique to avoid an attack was so clever that the giant did not know where to find its opponent. The hiding one, without being noticed, suddenly jumped from behind the tail of the enemy and gave it an unexpected strike. The giant was hurt and sprang furiously at the attacker. The latter did not have time to avoid the swoop and suffered a great deal.

Watching the entire fight, I felt very happy when I saw the handsome cock getting the upper hand. I eagerly anticipated that it would happen once more but I failed to see it again. Now I had come to realise that the handsome cock badly needed a shelter otherwise it would be tortured to death.

No sooner had I begun to worry about the fate of my favourite than a young boy approached from the east. He halted to attentively watch the fighting and soon decided to take up the

乌纱帽，与豪家横族①共搏小民，不犹愈耶？"两书生愧出。

　　余久病，未尝出里许②，世间锄强扶弱豪行快举，了③不得见；见此以为奇，逢人便说。说而人笑，余亦笑；人不笑，余亦笑。说而笑，笑而跳，竟以此了④一日也。

---

① 豪家横（hèng）族：仗势横行的豪门大族（rich and powerful family acting against law and reason）。
② 里许：居住的地方（living place）。
③ 了：完全（completely）。
④ 了：了结，结束（end）。

cudgels for the weaker one. He combated the large cock with his hands to allow the small one to wilfully peck it. Then he gave the bully several big slaps. Being powerless, the giant bird could do nothing but run away. The handsome one leapt at the chance to track the enemy to its home. Not long afterwards the giant turned back to follow its opponent to their battlefield. The boy repeated what he had done previously and then he had to do it again twice. Two passing scholars, seeing the young boy did not tire of doing the same thing again and again, laughed and said, "We have never seen anybody take animal-fighting so seriously." The boy replied, "Compared with those scholar-officials who help the rich and powerful families suppress common people, am I not better?" On hearing this remark, the two scholars walked away, ashamed.

An illness had long kept me to my house, thus I had never seen the munificent acts of eliminating bullies and helping the downtrodden that had happened in the human world. What I saw on that day was really amazing. I told this story to whoever I met. When the listener laughed, I also laughed. If the listener was not amused by my story, I still laughed. Laughing after talking and jumping while laughing, thus I spent a happy day.

江行日记二则

袁中道

其一

夜雪大作。时欲登舟至沙市①,竟②为雨雪所阻。然万竹中雪子③敲戛④,铮铮⑤有声,暗窗红火,任意⑥看数卷书,亦复有少趣。

自叹每有欲往,辄⑦复不遂。然流行坎止⑧,任之⑨而已。鲁直⑩所谓"无处不可寄一梦"也。

---

① 沙市:在湖北江陵县东南十五里长江北岸(situated on the northern shore of the Yangtze River, 15 *li* southeast of Jiangling County, Hubei Province)。
② 竟:终于(in the end)。
③ 雪子:即霰(graupel, snowball)。
④ 敲戛:敲打(beat, strike)。
⑤ 铮铮:象声词(clank, clang)。
⑥ 任意:随便(at will)。
⑦ 辄:总是(always, usually)。
⑧ 流行坎止:比喻在顺利情况下就行动,碰到困难就停止(act in favourable circumstances and stop in difficult ones)。
⑨ 任之:听之任之(let nature take its course)。
⑩ 鲁直:黄庭坚,字鲁直,北宋诗人(Huang Tingjian, styled himself Luzhi, a famous poet of the Northern Song Dynasty [960–1127])。

TWO DIARY ENTRIES ABOUT MY VOYAGE ON THE YANGTZE RIVER

Yuan Zhongdao

The First

It had snowed heavily during the night when I was to sail to Shashi and in the end I was stopped by the rain and snow. Snowballs were thudding among thousands of bamboos. The windows were dark and the stove was glowing red. I chose some books at random and felt quite satisfied with reading.

Then I sighed, why did I often fail to start on my journey every time I planned to go somewhere? I soon came to realise that it is a good idea to start a journey when circumstances are favourable and to stay home when they become difficult and let nature take its course. The famous writer Huang Luzhi said, "We can have a good dream wherever we are."

其二

　　天霁①。晨起登舟，入沙市。午间，黑云满江，斜风细雨大作。予推篷四顾②：天然一幅烟江幛子③。

---

① 霁（jì）：雨雪止（cease raining or snowing）。
② 顾：看（look）。
③ 烟江幛子：画着烟雨江景的屏幛（a screen painted with a scene of misty rain on a river）。

The Second

It had stopped snowing. Arising in the morning, I intended to go to Shashi by boat. By noon black clouds had collected over the river, bringing wild wind and drizzling rain. On opening the boat covering, I looked around. What a screen painted by nature!

夏 梅 说

钟惺

　　梅之冷，易知也。然亦有极热之候①。冬春冰雪，繁花灿灿②，雅俗③争赴④，此其极热时也。三、四、五月，累累其实⑤，和风甘雨之所加，而梅始冷矣。花实俱往⑥，时维⑦朱夏⑧。叶干相守，与烈日争，而梅之极冷矣！故夫看梅与咏梅者，未有于无花之时者也。

　　张渭⑨《官舍早梅》诗所咏者，花之终，实之始也。咏梅而及于实，斯已难矣，况叶乎！梅至于叶，而过时久矣。廷尉⑩董崇

---

① 候：时（time）。
② 灿灿：花盛开的样子（appearance of flowers in full bloom）。
③ 雅俗：文人雅士与普通人（refined scholars and ordinary people）。
④ 赴：去（go to）。
⑤ 累累其实：果实累累（fruit hanging in clusters; fruit hanging heavy）。
⑥ 往：消失（disappear）。
⑦ 时维：正当……之时（just when ... ）。
⑧ 朱夏：即夏天，引自《尔雅》："夏为朱明。"（i.e. summer, from a word in an ancient Chinese dictionary, "Summer is red and bright"）。
⑨ 张渭：字正言，唐代诗人。大历间曾官礼部侍郎（Zhang Wei, styled himself Zhengyan, a poet of the Tang Dynasty; once appointed to the position of vice-minister of the Ministry of Rites）。
⑩ 廷尉：秦汉掌司法的官员，明代称为大理寺卿（official in charge of judicature in the Qin and Han dynasties; minister of the highest Judiciary in the Ming Dynasty）。

THE SUMMER PLUM

Zhong Xing

It is common knowledge that the plum blooms in cold weather. However, there is also a period of time in very hot weather when the plum demonstrates its other strong point. When winter is changing into spring, the plum trees, with flowers in full bloom, looking bright and splendid amid ice and snow, attract all sorts of people, both highbrows and lowbrows who fall over each other to see the blossoms. This is the hottest moment for the plum during the year. While in the third, fourth and fifth month of the year, the plum trees, clustered with fruits and bathed in gentle breeze and sweet rain, begin to be given the cold shoulder. No sooner have the plum trees lost all their flowers and fruit than it is already summer. Their leaves and trunks, clenching each other, fight against the scorching sun. It is at this time when the plum is left out in the cold. That is why people never go to view and extol the plum at the time when it does not have any flowers.

What Zhang Wei wrote in his poem *The Early Plum Blossom by My Official Residence* was about the plum blossom when it was

相①,官南都②,在告③。有夏梅诗,始及于叶。何者?舍叶无所为夏梅也。予为梅感此情谊,属④同志者⑤和⑥焉,而为图卷以赠之。

夫世固有处极冷之时之地,而名实之权在焉。巧者乘间⑦赴之,有名实之得,而又无赴热之讥,此趋梅于冬春冰雪者之人也,乃真附热者⑧也。苟真为热之所在,虽与地之极冷,而有所必辨焉。此咏夏梅意也。

①董崇相:名应举,福建人,时任南京大理寺丞(named Yingju, from Fujian Province, was then appointed assistant minister of the highest Judiciary in Nanjing)。
②南都:今江苏省南京市,明成祖迁都北京后,以南京为南都(Nanjing. After the third emperor of the Ming Dynasty moved his capital to Beijing, Nanjing was called the south capital)。
③在告:古代官员在家休假(officials go on a vacation at home)。
④属:同"嘱"(tell, enjoin)。
⑤同志者:观点相同的朋友(friends sharing the same views)。
⑥和:和诗(write a poem in reply)。
⑦乘间:钻空子(take advantage of loopholes)。
⑧附热者:巴结权贵的人(those who curry favor with the powerful)。

changing into fruits. It is difficult to write a poem involving its fruits, let alone its leaves. When leaves appear on a plum tree, it is already long past its blooming season. Dong Chongxiang, the head of the highest Judiciary in the south capital (Nanjing), wrote a poem about the summer plum while he was having a vacation at home. In his poem, leaves were involved for the first time. Why? The answer is that the summer plum does not exist without leaves. Touched by his love for the plum, I asked my friends, who shared the same views with me, to write poems on the same theme and of the same rhyme scheme as Mr. Dong's poem. Then I drew a painting and presented it to him.

In the world, there are certainly some people who hold power to enjoy both fame and fortune though living in a freezing area where frigid weather prevails. Some crafty people acted when a good chance was available to get close to the powerful. By doing so, they gained fame and wealth without being derided by others for the conduct of attaching themselves to bigwigs. These people are similar to those flower-viewers who attach themselves to plum blossoms amid ice and snow when the season is changing from winter to spring. If it is where power is located, even though a powerful man lives in an extremely cold area, he should be clearly identified. This is my concept in writing the ode to the summer plum.

浣花溪记

钟惺

出成都南门，左为万里桥①，西折纤秀长曲，所见如连环、如玦②、如带、如规、如钩，色如鉴③、如琅玕④、如绿沉瓜⑤，窈然深碧，潆回城下者，皆浣花溪委⑥也。然必至草堂，而浣花有专名，则以少陵⑦浣花居在焉耳。

① 万里桥：在成都南门外，原名长星桥。传说三国蜀费祎出使吴国，诸葛亮在桥边践行，说："万里之行始于此。"因改称万里桥（outside the southern gate of Chengdu, originally named the Changxing Bridge. It is said that Fei Yi from the Kingdom of Shu in the Three Kingdoms Period was sent on a mission to the State of Wu; Zhuge Liang, while giving him a farewell dinner by this bridge, said to him: "A ten thousand *li* journey begins with the first step." After that the name of the bridge was changed into the Ten-Thousand-Li Bridge）。
② 玦（jué）：环状有缺口的玉佩（penannular jade ring, worn as an ornament in ancient China）。
③ 鉴：镜（mirror）。
④ 琅玕（láng gān）：似玉的美石（a jade-like stone）。
⑤ 绿沉瓜：颜色深绿的一种瓜（a kind of dark green melon）。
⑥ 委：水的下流（end, lower reaches of a river）。
⑦ 少陵：杜甫曾在少陵（旧址在今陕西西安南）居住过，自称少陵野老（name of a place south of Xi'an, Shaanxi where Du Fu once lived and called himself "Wild Old Man of Shao Ling"）。

THE FLOWER-WASHING STREAM

Zhong Xing

Going out of the southern gate of Chengdu, I saw on the left the Ten-Thousand-*Li* Bridge. A narrow and long stream was flowing gracefully in a zigzag way toward the west. All the way along, it demonstrated varied shapes, with one section resembling a chain of rings and another being similar to a penannular jade bracelet. There were also sections in the shape of a belt, or a pair of compasses and even a hook. The water of the stream also differed from one section to another. It was as clear as a mirror in one section but became green in all other sections — here tinted with jade-like light green and there with dark green like a watermelon. This green water also circled the city wall and all in all what I had seen was the Flower-Washing Stream. However, this stream had earned this special name only because it flowed past a cottage with the nick name of the Flower-Washing Residence in which Du Fu (712–770, a great poet of the Tang Dynasty) used to live.

After walking for three or four *li*, I arrived at a Temple called Qingyang Gong. On my way coming here, the stream was always in my sight, sometimes at a distance, sometimes within arm's reach. Bamboo and cypress trees could be seen everywhere. I looked at

行三四里为青羊宫①,溪时远时近,竹柏苍然,隔岸阴森者尽溪,平望如荠②,水木清华,神肤洞达③。自宫以西,流汇而桥者三,相距各不半里,舁夫④云通灌县,或所云"江从灌口来"是也。

人家住溪左,则溪蔽不时见,稍断则复见溪,如是者数处,缚柴编竹,颇见次第。桥尽,一亭树道左,署曰"缘江路"。过此则武侯祠,祠前跨溪为板桥一,覆以水槛⑤,乃睹"浣花溪"题榜⑥。过桥,一小洲横斜插水间如梭,溪周之,非桥不通,置亭其上,题曰"百花潭水"。由此亭还度桥,过梵安寺,始为杜工部⑦祠。像颇清古⑧,不必求肖⑨,想当尔尔⑩。石刻像一。附以本传,何仁仲别驾署华阳⑪时所为也。碑皆不堪读。

---

① 青羊宫:又称青羊观,在成都西南浣花溪附近,是一座著名的道教宫观,相传为老子和关尹喜会见之处(the Qingyang Temple, near Flower-Washing Stream southwest of Chengdu, a famous Taoist temple; it is said to be where Lao Zi met with Yin Xi)。
② 荠:荠菜(shepherd's purse)。
③ 神肤洞达:神清气爽(in clear and crisp spirit)。
④ 舁(yú)夫:抬轿的人(sedan chair carrier)。
⑤ 水槛:建于桥上像走廊一样的亭子(corridor-like pavilion on a bridge)。
⑥ 题榜:匾额(horizontal inscribed board)。
⑦ 杜工部:杜甫曾被任命为工部员外郎,故称(Du Fu was once appointed councilor of the Ministry of Public Works)。
⑧ 清古:古朴而高雅(simple but elegant)。
⑨ 肖:像(resemble)。
⑩ 尔尔:如此(like this)。
⑪ 别驾:明清州府副长官通判的别称(another name for assistant to prefecture magistrate in the Ming and Qing dynasties)。署华阳:代理华阳县令(act on behalf of the magistrate of Huayang County)。

the other side of the stream and saw a wild profusion of vegetation stretching to the end of the stream. This lush green field looked like a huge vegetable plot of shepherd's purse. The combination of beautiful stream and verdant plants made the viewers feel refreshed in mind and heart. West of the temple was where branches joined to form a wide stream and three bridges had to be built. They were only less than half a *li* apart. Sedan carriers said it led to Guan County. This echoed the saying of which I was already aware — "The river comes from a place called Guan."

The villagers lived on the left bank. The stream was sometimes invisible as cottages often blocked my view and it reappeared again and again through the gaps. Not only from one spot did I see such a peculiar view. The cottages had their doors made of neatly woven firewood or bamboo. Having passed by the three bridges, I saw a pavilion on the left side of the road with a sign of "Road alongside the River." The pavilion was followed by Wuhou Ci — a memorial hall to Zhuge Liang (181–234, an outstanding statesman and strategist in the Three Kingdoms Period). In front of the temple was a wooden bridge across the stream and railings had been set up on its sides. There I saw a board inscribed with "Flower-Washing Stream." After crossing the bridge, I saw a slanting islet like a shuttle inserted into the water. Surrounded by water, it was accessible only by bridge. A pavilion stood there and it had an inscription of "Hundred-Flower Pond." From this pavilion I returned to the bridge and crossed it. Having passed the Fan'an Temple, I finally arrived at Du Gongbu Ci — a temple to honour Du Fu. In his portrait, he looked thin and old. It might not resemble Du Fu himself as it must have been a product

钟子曰:杜老二居①,浣花清远,东屯②险奥③,各不相袭④。严公⑤不死,浣溪可老⑥,患难之于朋友大矣哉!然天遣此翁增夔门一段奇耳。穷愁奔走,犹能择胜⑦,胸中暇整⑧,可以应世,如孔子微服⑨主司城贞子⑩时也。

时万历辛亥十月十七日,出城欲雨,顷之霁。使客游者,多由监司郡邑招饮,冠盖稠浊⑪,磬折⑫喧溢⑬,迫暮⑭促归。是日清晨,偶然独往。楚人⑮钟惺记。

---

① 居:居所(dwelling place)。
② 东屯:夔州(今重庆奉节)东瀼溪,据说后汉时公孙述在这里屯过田,所以叫东屯。766 年四月,杜甫从成都迁移到这里居住(name of a place in Kuizhou [today's Fengjie County, Chongqing], where Du Fu once lived)。
③ 险奥:形势险要,地方僻远(out-of-the-way)。
④ 各不相袭:各不相同(be different from each other)。
⑤ 严公:严武,曾任剑南节度使,杜甫的友人(Yan Wu was then Governor of Sichuan, Du Fu's friend)。
⑥ 可老:可供养老(could provide for his old age)。
⑦ 择胜:选择一个好地方居住(select a good place to live)。
⑧ 暇整:安详(calm and carefree)。
⑨ 微服:身穿便装(in plain clothes)。
⑩ 司城贞子:春秋时陈国大夫,姓名不详,死后尊为司城贞子。孔子流亡到陈国时,曾住在他家里(a senior official of the State of Chen in the Spring and Autumn Period. His name being unknown, he was so called respectfully after his death. Confucius once lived in his home when he was exiled to the State of Chen)。
⑪ 冠盖稠浊:形容官员来往,车马繁乱(used to describe officials coming and going with many cabs and horses)。
⑫ 磬折:形容打躬作揖,弯腰如磬(used to describe people making a bow like qing [a kind of ancient musical instrument, like a zigzag ruler made of jade or stone])。
⑬ 喧溢:声音嘈杂(noisy sound)。
⑭ 迫暮:傍晚(at nightfall)。
⑮ 楚人:钟惺是湖北竟陵人,竟陵古属楚国,故自称楚人(Zhong Xing was from Jingling, Hubei Province, belonging to the State Chu in ancient times)。

of imagination. There's also a stone-engraving portrait of him, with his biography attached written by He Renzhong when he was the acting magistrate of Huayang County. Unfortunately, the inscription on the stone tablet was no longer legible.

Master Zhong said: "Of Du Fu's two former residences, the one by the Flower-Washing Stream is a peaceful and secluded dwelling place; the one in Dongtun is located in a remote and dangerous area. They are different from each other." If the Revered Mr. Yan had not passed away so early, Du Fu would have been able to live longer in the cottage by the Flower-Washing Stream and spend the last years of his life peacefully. It is true that a friend is best found in adversity! However, it was God's will that Du Fu should experience unusual times in Kuizhou. When he was poor and depressed, he was still able to find a place with nice surroundings in which to live. In whatever circumstances, he could always keep calm and carefree and was able to cope with the difficult situation. His behavior was similar to what Confucius did when he was exiled to the State of Chen, wearing plain clothes and living in the house of a senior official named Sicheng Zhenzi.

I travelled to this historical site on the 17th day of the 10th month in the 39th year of the Wanli Reign (1611). When I was walking out of the city, it was going to rain but soon fined up. The tourists from the royal court were mainly entertained with good wine by local officials. I saw an endless stream of horses and carriages and heard uproarious talk and laughter. It was not until the evening gloom began to fall that the tourists started to leave. Strangely enough, I went there by myself in the early morning. This was written by Zhong Xing from Chu.

避风岩记

张明弼

避风岩在端州①之北三十里许，或曰与砚坑②相近。古未有是名，余避风其下，故赠以是名也。余何以避风其下？崇祯③己卯④仲秋，余供役粤帷⑤。二十五日既竣事⑥，则遍谒粤之大吏⑦。大吏者，非三鸣鼓吹不启户，非启户则令长⑧不敢入。余东驰西鹜⑨，左诇⑩

---

① 端州：在今广东肇庆市端州区，出产端砚（in today's Duanzhou District, Zhaoqing City, Guangdong, famous for producing the Duan ink-stone）。
② 砚坑：端州境内有柯烂山，中有砚坑（the Ink-Stone Pit: a historical site, located in the Kelan Mountain within Duanzhou Prefecture）。
③ 崇祯：明思宗年号（the reign title of Emperor Sizong of the Ming Dynasty）。
④ 己卯：崇祯十二年（1639）。
⑤ 供役粤帷：在广东某地任职（hold a post in a certain place in Guangdong Province）。
⑥ 竣事：了事，完事（finish the job）。
⑦ 大吏：高官（high official）。
⑧ 令长：指县令、县长（county magistrate）。
⑨ 东驰西鹜：东跑西颠（run about busily）。
⑩ 诇（xiòng）：探询（inquire about）。

THE WIND-SHELTER CLIFF

Zhang Mingbi

The Wind-Shelter Cliff is about thirty *li* (15 km) north of Duanzhou and it is said this cliff is close to the famous Ink-Stone Pit. There was not such a name in the past and I have so called it as I once took shelter from the wind at this cliff. Why did I take shelter from the wind over there? In mid-autumn of the 12th year of the Chongzhen Reign (1639), I took up a post in Guangdong Province. On the 25th of the month, having finished all the preparation for my new position, I started to make a courtesy call on every high-ranking official in the province. I soon found that their houses would not have the front doors opened unless visitors had beaten the drums and blown the horns at least thrice. If their doors were not opened, even the county magistrate did not dare to enter. I rushed about busily, waiting for someone and asking for more information. My eyes were tired as they had seen so many doorkeepers, official attendants, crimson flags carried by the guards of some high officials and red caps worn by the officials' bailiffs. My ears were almost deafened as they had been disturbed by the noise of gongs and drums being beaten to clear the way for some officials in the streets and the loud voices complimenting, flattering and even yelling in the big halls.

右需①，目厌于阍②驺③卤簿④绛旗⑤朱帽⑥之状，耳厌于笳鼓引赞殿喝之声，手足筋骨疲于伏谒拜跽⑦以头抢地之事。眩瞀⑧车上，至不择店肆而解衣卧之。凡六日而毕，则又买舟过肇，谒制府⑨。制府官厌贵，礼愈绝，控拜数四，颔之而已。见毕即登舟，将返杨山。

九月朏⑩，宿三十里外。力引数步，偶得一岩。江回峰抱，风力稍损，乃息焉。及旦而视之，则断崖千尺，上侈下弇⑪，状如檐牙。仰而睨⑫之，若层衡之列烟上，崩峦倾返，颓石矗⑬突，时有欲落之势，栗⑭乎不可以久留焉。狂飙不息，竟日⑮居其下。胥仆相扶，上舟一步，得坐于石隙草际。听怒涛声，若奔走败马；望沸波，若一群白鹅鼓翼江心；及跳沫山足，又若千百素鳞⑯跃上岸。

---

① 需：等待（await）。
② 阍（hūn）：司阍，看门人（doorkeeper）。
③ 驺（zōu）：驺从，大官的侍从人员（high officials' attendants）。
④ 卤簿：帝王和官员们出行时的仪仗（flags, weapons, etc. while kings and officials go on a journey）。
⑤ 绛旗：深红色的旗帜（crimson flags）。
⑥ 朱帽：指衙役（referring to yamen runner）。
⑦ 跽（jì）：长跪（kneel for a long time）。
⑧ 眩瞀（mào）：眼睛昏花，视物不明（dim-sighted）。
⑨ 制府：总督（governor）。
⑩ 朏（fěi）：新月开始发光，亦用于农历每月初三日的代称（translucent light of a nascent moon, also refers to the third day of every lunar month）。
⑪ 上侈（chǐ）下弇（yǎn）：上面宽大，下面收缩（the above is wide and the below is narrow）。
⑫ 睨（nì）：斜着眼看（look askance）。
⑬ 矗：直立，高耸（stand tall and upright）。
⑭ 栗：害怕得发抖（shiver with fear）。
⑮ 竟日：整天（all day long）。
⑯ 素鳞：白色的鱼儿（white fish）。

My arms, legs, muscles and bones were exhausted as I had done so much kneeling, bending and even lying prostrate for all sorts of social formalities. While getting onto the carriage, I felt so dizzy from fatigue that I immediately lay down in it. I did not have energy left to find a hotel so I slept in the carriage in my formal clothing. It took me six days to finish all the visits and then I went to Zhaoqing by boat. There I visited the prefecture magistrate who, for showing off his posting and power, required ridiculous formalities from his visitors. I was told to kowtow four times to him (usually three times would be enough toward a high official) and he only nodded to me in reply. Having visited him, I soon went back to my boat and sailed to Yangshan County.

It was the third day in the ninth month of that year (1639). In the gleam of the crescent moon, my boat had stopped sailing at a spot thirty *li* north of Zhaoqing. Then, it drifted a short distance to the foot of a cliff where the river took a sharp turn. Surrounded by mountains, it was not so windy at the cliff and I decided to spend the night there. The next morning when I looked around, I found an isolate cliff one thousand *chi* (3 *chi* = 1 metre) high. With its upper part being wider than the lower, the cliff was in the shape of a palace's eaves. Looking up, there seemed to be one row of railings behind another above the haze. Around the cliff, the mountain peaks, appearing unstable, seemed in immediate danger of collapse. A bare rock, imposingly projecting from the cliff above us, looked most likely to fall down at any time. It made us shiver with fear and we did not want to stay here for long. However, the wild whirlwind did not cease and we had to stay under this the whole day. Supported by each other, I, together

石崖磔磔①,不沾土壤。而紫茎缠带,青芜数尺,一偃②一立,若青狮奋迅③而不得去,又若怒毛之兽,风过毛竖,不能自休。身住江坳,目力相界,不能数里,而阴氛④交作,如处黑帷。从者皆惨容而相告曰:"日复夕矣,将奈何?"余笑而语之曰:

"第⑤安之,第安之。吾视夫复嶂重峦⑥,缭青纬碧⑦,犹胜于院署之严丽也;吾视夫崩崖倾石,怒涛沸波,犹胜于贵人之颐颊心腑也⑧;吾视夫青芜紫茎,怀烟孕露,犹胜于大吏之绛骑彤驺⑨也;吾视夫谷响山啸,激壑鸣川,犹胜于高衙之呵殿赞唱也;吾视夫藉草⑩坐石,仰瞩云气,俯视重泉,犹胜于拳跽伏谒⑪于尊宦之阶下也。天或者见吾出则伛偻,入则簿书,已积两载矣,无以抒吾胸中之浩浩者,故令风涛阻滞,使此孤岩以恣吾数刻之探讨⑫乎?

---

① 磔(zhé)磔:原指古代分裂肢体的刑法,这里形容山石棱角分明(dismemberment, originally a form of punishment in ancient China, here used to describe pointed cliffs)。
② 偃:倒伏(get flattened)。
③ 奋迅:急速奔跑(run rapidly)。
④ 阴氛:阴云(dark clouds)。
⑤ 第:但(just)。
⑥ 复嶂重峦:崇山峻岭(high mountains and lofty peaks)。
⑦ 缭青纬碧:青白的云团缭绕在碧绿的山峰间(blue or white clouds swirling among the green mountains)。
⑧ 颐颊心腑:面容和内心(facial expression and inner heart)。
⑨ 绛骑彤驺:穿红衫骑绛马的随从(official attendants in red garments and astride red horses)。
⑩ 藉草:以草为垫(use grass as a mat)。
⑪ 拳跽伏谒:磕头跪拜(worship on bended knees; kowtow)。
⑫ 恣吾数刻之探讨:让我有几刻时间纵情地探讨(give me some time to probe as deep as I like into this subject)。

with my attendants and servants, left the boat and walked a few steps to find a space to sit between two rocks on the edge of a grassland. The roaring billows sounded like galloping horses and the surging waves looked like a flock of white geese flapping their wings over the water surface at the centre of the river. The foam, made by the waves breaking on the foot of the mountain, resembled thousands of fish jumping onto the shore. The rocky cliff with craggy edges did not have any soil attached to it. At its foot, the purple vines, similar to ribbons twining on the ground and the dark green weeds several *chi* tall, one creeping on the ground and the other standing erect, combined to resemble a green lion which desperately attempted to make a dash but had failed to do so. It also appeared as a furious beast whose fur, in a strong wind, stood up and remained erect for a long time. In the col by the river, we were unable to see far and dark clouds like black curtains shrouded us. My attendants looked miserable, saying to each other: "What shall we do if the strong wind keeps blowing from morning till night?" I smiled and said to them:

"Calm down and don't worry! In my eyes, the undulating high mountains veiled in white clouds and green fogs are more magnificent than the imposing governmental office buildings; the unsafe cliff and dangerous rocks together with the violent waves are more beautiful than the facial expressions and behavior of powerful people; the green weeds and purple vines bathed in the mist and dew are more attractive than the high officials' entourages dressed in purple and riding red horses. To my ears, the howling of the wind echoing through the valley and in the mountain accompanied by the sound of waterfalls in the gullies and rushing torrents of the river are

或兹岩壁立路绝，猿徒鼯党，犹难托寄，若非习金丹火龙之术①，腾空蹑虚，不能一到。虽处大江之中，飞帆如织，而终无一人肯一泊其下，以发其奇气而著其姓字；天亦哀山灵之寂寞，伤水伯之孤清，故特牵柅②余舟，与彼结一日之缘耶？余年少有志，养二龙于水壑，调一鹤于中峰，与羽服思玄之徒③，上烟驾，登月馆，以望四海三山，如聚米萦带；而心为时夺，至堕俗网，往返数千里，徒以充厮养之役，有才无时，甘于下人。今日见此水石，若见好友，犹恐谆芒、卢敖④诸君，诋余以井甃之识⑤，而又何事愁苦于兹岩之下乎？"

---

① 金丹火龙之术：指道家炼丹飞升的法术（referring to Taoists' magic art of making pills of immortality and becoming a flying celestial being）。
② 柅（nǐ）：止（stop）。
③ 羽服思玄之徒：穿着羽毛制的衣服，思想玄秘深奥的人，即学道求仙的人（people who wear clothes made of feathers and whose thought secretly deep, i.e. those who want to become immortals by learning Taoism）。
④ 谆芒：《庄子·天地》里虚拟的寓言人物。卢敖：秦始皇时方士，曾怂恿始皇求仙（Zhun Mang, a fictional character in *Zhuangzi*. Lu Ao, an alchemist in the reign of the First Emperor of the Qin Dynasty, who used to urge the emperor to try to become an immortal）。
⑤ 井甃（zhòu）之识：指井蛙之见，即平庸短浅的见识（knowledge of a frog at the bottom of well, i.e. limited and shortsighted knowledge）。井甃：砖砌的井（well made of bricks）。

more pleasant than the noise of complimenting, flattering and yelling in a big hall. I have also found that looking up to watch clouds and fogs or looking down to view a stream of spring water while leaning on the grass or sitting on a rock are much more comfortable than kneeling and kowtowing while paying a visit to a high official at his house. Already for two years, I have never been able to stretch my back while walking out from home or to put down document files and books while staying at home, thus I did not have any chance to give expression to my aspiration and determination. Heaven might have seen all this and have decided to arrange gusts of strong wind and high waves to hinder my journey and force my boat to anchor at this isolated cliff so that I can have this opportunity to see such extraordinary scenes and create many marvellous feelings and thoughts. Being high, upright and inaccessible from land, there were no signs of apes and weasels around the cliff. Only those people, who had learnt, through the process of making elixirs, the magic arts of jumping high into the air and riding the mists, could have reached this place. Situated at the centre of the river and having so many boats passing by, the cliff did not have anybody else anchor his boat at its foot. Nobody was interested in expressing his impressions and leaving his name here. Feeling pity for the loneliness of mountains and rivers, Heaven had purposely retained my boat from sailing on, thus bringing me to a one-day close contact with them. When I was young, I entertained the high ambition of keeping a pair of dragons in a ravine and taming a crane amid mountain peaks. Together with those people who had intended to become immortals by learning Taoism, I climbed up to some sacrificial altars veiled in incense smoke, or mounted the moon halls in order to get a glimpse of the

从者皆笑,余乃纳以兹名。

岩顶有一石,望之如立人,或曰飞来之塔顶也;或曰当是好奇者,跻是崖之巅,如昌黎不得下[①],乃化而为石云。岩侧有二崩石,一大一小,仅可束两缆。小吏程缨曰:"当黑夜暴风中,舟人安能择此,神引维以奉明府[②]耳。"语皆不可信,并记之。

[①] 如昌黎不得下:相传韩愈登华山顶峰,见山势奇险,惊恐而哭(it is said that when having reached the summit of Mount Huashan, Han Yu, a poet of the Tang Dynasty, was so frightened to find himself standing on top of a dangerously steep and high mountain that he cried in fear)。
[②] 明府:唐代以后多用以尊称县令(used to respectfully address a county magistrate after the Tang Dynasty)。

Four Seas and Three Hills which were said to be the dwelling places of immortals. In the distance, they looked like piles of rice and twists of ribbon. Later, I was bewildered by the conventional views and fell into the worldly net of an official career. I had to travel thousands of *li* for a position which was as lowly as the tasks of raising horses and cooking food for rich families. Possessing unrecognised talents, I had to take a humble job which has made me resemble a subservient servant. Today when I came across this river cliff, I felt like I was seeing a good friend. For fear that people like Zhun Mang and Lu Ao would tease me by saying: 'You are a man with narrow vision similar to a frog at the bottom of a well. Why should you be so distressed at the foot of a cliff?'"

On hearing what I had said, all my attendants laughed. I have therefore found a name for the cliff.

A rock rests on top of the cliff and looks like a man standing there. It is said that this rock, resembling the top of a pagoda, has come from nowhere. As another saying goes: A man with curiosity climbed up the top of the cliff but was unable to come down, just as Han Yu (a famous writer of the Tang Dynasty) had difficulty in descending Mount Huashan and that man later turned into a rock. Two fallen rocks, one big and one small, lie on one side of the cliff and they are just large enough to tie onto them two ropes for mooring a boat. My assistant Cheng Ying said: "On this stormy dark night, how could a boatman find such a good anchoring pole? It is Heaven's will that has led your Excellency here." Though his remark was an exaggeration, I still included it in my writing.

再游乌龙潭记

谭元春

潭宜澄,林映潭者宜静,筏宜稳,亭阁宜朗,七夕①宜星河,七夕之宾客宜幽适无累。然造物者②岂以予为此拘拘者③乎!

茅子越中④人,家童善篙⑤楫⑥。至中流,风妒之,不得至荷荡,旋近钓矶,系筏垂柳下,雨霏霏⑦湿幔⑧,犹无上岸意。已而雨注下,客七人,姬六人,各持盖⑨立幔中,湿透衣表。风雨一时至,潭不

---

① 七夕:夏历七月七日晚上,传说喜鹊在天河搭桥,让牛郎织女渡河相会(the evening of the seventh day of the seventh lunar month. It is said that in this evening magpies span a bridge for the Cowherd and the Weaving Maid to cross the Milky Way to meet)。
② 造物者:指天(Heaven)。
③ 拘拘者:拘泥的人(stickler)。
④ 茅子:茅元仪,字止生,归安(今浙江湖州吴兴区)人。越中:明代绍兴府,古称越州。而归安属湖州府(Mao Yuanyi, styled himself Zhisheng, from Gui'an, today's Wuxing District, Huzhou City, Zhejiang Province. The Shaoxing Prefecture in the Ming Dynasty was called Yuezhou. Gui'an belonged to Huzhou Prefecture in ancient China)。
⑤ 篙:撑船的长竹竿(boat-pole)。
⑥ 楫:划船的桨(oar)。
⑦ 霏霏:形容雨雪密集(describing dense rain or snow)。
⑧ 幔:帷幔(curtain hangings)。
⑨ 盖:雨具(rain gear)。

REVISITING THE BLACK-DRAGON LAKE

Tan Yuanchun

A lake should have clear water and the wood which is reflected in the lake should present a tranquil scene. A raft should be able to drift steady on the lake and the pavilion and tower on the lakeside should have a brilliant appearance. On the seventh evening of the seventh month of the year, the sky should be clear to reveal the wonder of the Milky Way and the sightseers should feel relaxed and comfortable. However, will Mother Nature see me as a fussy person and do something to taunt me?

Mr. Mao Yuanyi was a native of the Yuezhou district and his servant was a good helmsman. While sailing somewhere near the centre of the lake, our raft was prevented by the wind from reaching the lotus marsh, so we tied it at the nearby fishing rock. It began drizzling and the screens on the raft were soon wet but we did not intend to go ashore. Soon the rain became torrential. The seven male pleasure-seekers and six female singers, standing inside the screens and each holding rain gear, were all soaking wet. Then a wild storm hit the lake which was suddenly out of control. Frightened, the girls asked to go ashore, regardless of their delicate silk stockings. We had to move our feast to a newly built veranda. No sooner had we sat down than the rain started to hover overhead and seemed to fly from the tops of the trees. The

能主①。姬惶恐求上，罗袜无所惜。客乃移席新轩，坐未定，雨飞自林端，盘旋不去，声落水上，不尽入潭，而如与潭击。雷忽震，姬人皆掩耳欲匿至深处。电与雷相后先，电尤奇幻，光煜煜②入水中，深入丈尺，而吸其波光以上于雨，作金银珠贝影，良久乃已。潭龙窟宅之内，危疑未释。

是时风物倏忽，耳不及于谈笑，视不及于阴森，咫尺③相乱；而客之有致者反以为极畅，乃张灯行酒，稍敌风雨雷电之气。忽一姬昏黑来赴，始知苍茫历乱，已尽为潭所有，亦或即为潭所生；而问之女郎来路，曰"不尽然"，不亦异乎？

招客者为洞庭吴子凝甫，而冒子伯麟、许子无念、宋子献孺、洪子仲伟，及予与止生为六客，合凝甫而七。

---

① 潭不能主：潭惊慌失措，不知如何是好（being panicked, the lake can't act on its own）。
② 煜煜（yù）：明亮耀眼的样子（dazzlingly bright）。
③ 咫尺：很近（very near）。

falling rain made a noise on the surface of the lake as though it would rather beat the water than immerse into the lake. Suddenly thunder roared and the girls, all covering their ears, wanted to hide deep in a shelter. The lightening flashed alternately with rumbling thunder. The lightening was particularly fantastic and its dazzling light went deep into the water for several meters. The rain, drawing light from the waves over the lake, became like phantoms of gold, silver, pearls and shells and they lasted for quite some time before disappearing. All these had disturbed the palace of the Black Dragon in the lake and the Dragon King was frightened and felt puzzled at what had happened.

Now the scene greatly changed. Our ears could not hear other people talking and laughing and our eyes could not see in the darkness. Within a foot away from us there was a sight of chaos. Those who were in high spirits were exhilarated by this atmosphere. We lit the lanterns and began to drink and by doing so our fears abated and we became relaxed. All of a sudden, a new girl, appearing from the darkness, came to attend the party. I came to realize that this kind of extraordinary and unexpected thing caused by a thunderstorm could only have happened here or it was created by the Black-Dragon Lake. When asked what she had seen on her way coming here, the girl said that it was not quite like this. It is really unusual, isn't it?

The host was Mr. Wu Ningfu from Dongting and the six guests were Mao Boling, Xu Wunian, Song Xianru, Hong Zhongwei, Zhisheng (Yuanyi) and me. If Ningfu was added in, there were seven altogether.

游黄山日记（后）（节选）

徐宏祖

初四日①。十五里，至汤口②。五里，至汤寺③，浴于汤池④。扶杖望硃砂庵⑤而登。十里，上黄泥冈。向时云里诸峰，渐渐透出，亦渐渐落吾杖底。转入石门⑥，越天都⑦之胁⑧而下，则天都、莲

---

① 初四日：明万历四十六年（1618）农历九月初四（on the fourth day in the ninth month of the lunar calendar in the 46th year of the Wanli Reign of the Ming Dynasty）。
② 汤口：镇名，在黄山脚下，为上山必经之路（name of a town, at the foot of Mount Huangshan, the only way to ascend the mountain）。
③ 汤寺：原名祥符寺，创建于唐开元十八年（730），因靠近汤泉，故俗称汤寺（originally named Xiangfu Temple, founded in the 18th year of the Kaiyuan Reign of the Tang Dynasty, so called because of being near to the hot spring）。
④ 汤池：即汤泉，池深三尺，长丈许，池水朱红色，有朱砂，可治病（a hot spring with its pool three *chi* deep and more than one *zhang* long; the spring water is bright red and contains cinnabar, can be used to cure some illnesses）。
⑤ 硃砂庵：本名慈光寺，创建于明嘉靖年间。庵在朱砂峰下，其右为天都等峰，左为莲花等峰（originally named Ciguang Temple, founded during the Jiajing Reign of the Ming Dynasty, under the Cinnabar Peak. On its right are Tiandu Peak, etc; on its left are the Lotus Peak, etc）。
⑥ 石门：峰名，两壁夹峙如门，故名（name of a peak, its two cliffs standing as if pressing from both sides）。
⑦ 天都：黄山主峰，高约1900米，峭岩绝壁，险峻难登（the highest peak of Mount Huangshan, about 1900 metres high, too precipitous to ascend）。
⑧ 胁：两边（both sides）。

A DIARY ENTRY ABOUT TOURING MOUNT HUANGSHAN (SECOND VISIT) (EXCERPTS)

Xu Hongzu

On the fourth day (of the ninth month of the 46th year of the Wanly Reign, 1618), having travelled fifteen *li* (1 *li* = 0.5 km), I arrived at a small town called Tangkou. Then I travelled another five *li* and came to the Hot-Spring Temple where I bathed in the hot spring pool. Leaning on a stick, I began to climb the mountain heading for the Cinnabar Temple. After walking another ten *li*, I found myself on the Yellow-Mud Ridge. The hidden peaks gradually appeared from behind the clouds and little by little these peaks dropped below my walking stick. Turning into the Rock Gate, I walked downhill via the waist of the Tiandu Peak and saw the two peaks, Tiandu and Lotus, towering beautifully into the sky. On the wayside, an uphill branch road stretched eastward. It was a road unknown to me. I immediately walked onto it and via this mountain path I almost reached the side of the Tiandu Peak. Once again I ascended northward and soon I was walking through a rock rift. The mountain path zigzagged between one pair of rocky ridges after another. This road had been built in such a way that where it was blocked, the obstacle was dug through; where it

花^①二顶，俱秀出天半^②。路旁一岐^③东上，乃昔所未至者，遂前趋直上，几达天都侧。复北上，行石罅^④中。石峰片片夹起；路宛转石间，塞者凿之，陡者级^⑤之，断者架木通之，悬者植梯^⑥接之。下瞰峭壑阴森，枫松相间，五色纷披^⑦，灿若图绣^⑧。因念黄山当生平奇览，而有奇若此，前未一探，兹游快且愧矣！

时夫仆俱阻险行后，余亦停弗上；乃一路奇景，不觉引余独往。既登峰头，一庵翼然^⑨，为文殊院^⑩，亦余昔年欲登未登者。左天都，右莲花，背倚玉屏风，两峰秀色，俱可手揽^⑪。四顾奇峰错列，众壑纵横，真黄山绝胜处！非再至，焉知^⑫其奇若此？

① 莲花：与天都并称黄山两大峰，山峰形似莲花瓣，故名（one of the two highest peaks of Mount Huangshan, side by side with Tiandu Peak, so called because of its lotus-like shape）。
② 天半：半空（in mid-air）。
③ 岐：岔道（branch road）。
④ 罅（xià）：裂缝（crevice）。
⑤ 级：用作动词，凿石级（as a verb, to make a stone step by chiseling）。
⑥ 植梯：竖起梯子（erect a ladder）。
⑦ 五色纷披：五彩斑斓（a riot of colors）。
⑧ 图绣：图画刺绣（pictures and embroidery）。
⑨ 翼然：如鸟儿张翼一样（as a bird opens its wings）。
⑩ 文殊院：寺名，在天都、莲花两峰之间（name of a temple, between the two peaks, Tiandu and Lotus）。
⑪ 揽：持或握（clasp or hold）。
⑫ 焉知：哪里知道（how could I know）。

was too steep, the rocky slope was chiseled to make steps; where there was a gap, a wooden bridge was built across it; and where the upper section of the road suspended in midair, a ladder was erected to link it with the lower section of the road. Looking down I saw a deep and dark gully where maple trees alternated with pine. They demonstrated such a colorful and brilliant view that it resembled a painting or an embroidered needlework. I was aware that Mount Huangshan had the most peculiar scenery I had ever seen in my life. Whereas on my previous trip, I had not explored such a superb view and this experience made me feel not only excited but also regretful.

Hindered by the hazardous situation on the road, all my servants lagged behind. I also stopped climbing for a while. However, the view in front of me was so special that I was impelled to move along alone. On the top of the ridge, I saw a temple built in the shape of a bird opening its wings. It was the Wenshu Temple. This was a spot which I had intended to ascend on my previous visit but had failed to reach. To the left of the temple was the Tiandu Peak and to the right was the Lotus Peak. The Jade Screen Peak towered behind me and the two peaks in front me were so close that it seemed as if I could grab and hold their beauty. Looking around, I saw spectacular peaks interlock like jigsaws, ravines and gullies crisscrossing each other like a chessboard. Here was the beauty of beauties among Mount Huangshan's various scenes. If I had not come here for the second time, could I have known there was such a spectacular spot as

遇游僧①澄源②至，兴甚涌。时已过午，奴辈适至。立庵前，指点两峰。庵僧谓："天都虽近而无路，莲花可登而路遥。只宜近盼天都，明日登莲顶。"余不从，决意游天都，挟③澄源、奴子④仍下峡路。至天都侧，从流石⑤蛇行⑥而上。攀草牵棘，石块丛起则历⑦块，石崖侧削则援崖⑧。每至手足无可着处，澄源必先登垂接。每念上既如此，下何以堪？终亦不顾。历险数次，遂达峰顶。惟一石顶壁起犹数十丈，澄源寻视其侧，得级，挟⑨予以登。万峰无不下伏，独莲花与抗⑩耳。时浓雾半作半止⑪，每一阵至，则

① 游僧：云游和尚（a roaming monk）。
② 澄源：和尚名（name of a monk）。
③ 挟：携同（bring sb. along）。
④ 奴子：僮仆（servant）。
⑤ 流石：溜滑的山石（skidding stones）。
⑥ 蛇行：伏地爬行（crawling on the ground）。
⑦ 历：越过（surmount）。
⑧ 援崖：攀登悬崖（climb a cliff）。
⑨ 挟：这里作扶持讲（here meaning support with the hand）。
⑩ 抗：抗衡（match, compete）。
⑪ 半作半止：忽兴忽止（now appear, now disappear）。

this? Encountering a roaming monk named Chengyuan, my interest in sightseeing increased even further. It was not until after mid-day that my servants arrived. We stood in front of the temple, pointing at the two peaks. A monk from the temple said: "The Tiandu is near but there is no road to go there. The Lotus Peak can be ascended but it's a long way to get there. We can only view Tiandu from somewhere around here and tomorrow we will climb to the top of Lotus." I did not listen to him and I made up my mind to tour Tiandu. Together with Chengyuan and my servants, I took the valley way to go down to the side of Tiandu. Then I began to go uphill by crawling like a snake on slippery rocks. While climbing a cliff, we had to hold and pull on weeds, brambles and thorns. When confronted by a clump of rocks, we surmounted them. When facing a steep cliff, we clambered step by step. Each time I was unable to hold onto anything to continue climbing, Chengyuan would scale ahead of me and then lend me his hand to pull me up. I was wondering what descending would be like if ascending the peak was so difficult but finally I stopped being so apprehensive. Having overcome one danger after another, we reached the top of the peak. There was only one stony ridge, two or three scores of *zhang* (1 *zhang* = 3.3 metres) high, which we had not climbed. Chengyuan searched from one side to another and found steps. Supported by him, I climbed to the top. Standing on the apex, numerous peaks were below its height and only the Lotus Peak could rival this height. Around here the fogs were unpredictable — one moment gathering and the next dispersing.

对面不见。眺莲花诸峰,多在雾中。独上天都,予至其前,则雾徙①于后;予趆②其右,则雾出于左。其松犹有曲挺纵横者;柏虽大干如臂,无不平贴石上,如苔藓然。山高风巨,雾气去来无定。下盼诸峰,时出为碧峤③,时没为银海④。再眺山下,则日光晶晶,别一区宇也。日渐暮,遂前其足⑤,手向后据地,坐而下脱。至险绝处,澄源并⑥肩手相接。度险,下至山坳⑦,暝色已合。复从峡度栈⑧以上,止⑨文殊院。

① 徙:移动(move)。
② 趆(dī):小步快跑(run with short steps)。
③ 峤(jiào):尖而高的山(a high pointed mountain)。
④ 银海:雾气如白色波涛(fog-like white waves)。
⑤ 前其足:把足伸向前(put his foot forward)。
⑥ 并:同时应用(use two different objects simultaneously for the same purpose)。
⑦ 山坳:山下低洼处(flat land or lowland between mountains/hills)。
⑧ 栈:栈道(a plank road built along the face of a cliff)。
⑨ 止:住宿(to stay; put up)。

Every time a puff of dense fog came, people standing face to face could not see each other. Looking into the distance, I saw the Lotus and other peaks were mostly enveloped in fog. I alone ascended the top of Tiandu where the fog was playing a hide-and-seek game with me: when I walked forward to approach the fog in front of me, it shifted further backward; when I ran to the right side, it built up on the left. In contrast with the pine trees whose trunks were upright with horizontally growing branches, the cypress, though their boughs were as thick as our arms, all bent to touch the rocks. Viewed from the heights they looked like patches of green moss. It was very windy on the top of the high mountain and the fogs were difficult to ascertain when they would come or go. Overlooked from where I stood, all those peaks were now showing their pointed green tops, now sinking into the sea of silvery white clouds. Then looking down to the foot of the mountain, I saw another world which was bathed in glittering sunshine. As the sun was setting, we started descending the mountain by sliding down in a sitting position with our legs stretching forward and our hands touching the ground behind us. Every time when we were at a very dangerous spot, Chengyuan would support me with both his shoulders and hands. Having overcome all sorts of dangers, we came to a low-lying area at the foot of the mountain where we found the surroundings were already shrouded in the curtain of darkness. We went up from the valley and via the plank road to end our journey at the Wenshu Temple.

核 舟 记

魏学洢

明有奇巧①人曰王叔远,能以径寸之木②为③宫室、器皿④、人物,以至鸟兽、木⑤石,罔不⑥因势象形,各具情态。尝贻⑦余核舟一,盖大苏⑧泛⑨赤壁云。

舟首尾长约八分有奇⑩,高可⑪二黍许⑫。中轩敞⑬者为舱⑭,箬篷⑮覆之。旁开小窗,左右各四,共八扇。启窗而观,雕栏相望焉。

---

① 奇巧:奇妙精巧(wonderful and exquisite)。
② 径寸之木:直径一寸的木头(wood whose diameter is a *cun* across)。
③ 为:做(make)。
④ 器皿:指器具(utensil)。
⑤ 木:树木(trees)。
⑥ 罔不:无不,都(all without exception)。
⑦ 贻:赠(present as a gift)。
⑧ 大苏:苏轼,人们称他和他的弟弟苏辙为"大苏""小苏"(Su Shi, a famous poet of the Song Dynasty. People usually call him and his younger brother Su Zhe the Elder Su and the Younger Su)。
⑨ 泛:泛舟,坐着船在水上游览(go boating, go sightseeing on a river or lake)。
⑩ 有奇:有余(more than ...)。
⑪ 可:大约(about)。
⑫ 许:上下(about, or so)。
⑬ 轩敞:宽敞明亮(spacious and bright)。
⑭ 中轩敞者为舱:中间高起而开敞的部分是船舱(in the centre the wide open part is the boat's cabin)。
⑮ 箬(ruò)篷:用箬竹叶做成的篷(covering made from bamboo leaves)。

A MINIATURE BOAT CARVED FROM A PEACH STONE

Wei Xueyi

During the Ming Dynasty there lived a man named Wang Shuyuan who was an ingenious artisan of excellent workmanship. He was able to carve, out of a tiny piece of wood with a diameter of one *cun* (1.3 inches) only, a mansion, or utensils and human figures. He could also make birds, beasts, trees and rocks. All his handicraft works were done in such a way that the veins of the wood were cleverly used in the formation of various shapes and each of his works possessed distinctive artistic appeal. Once he presented me with a tiny boat carved from a peach-stone. This handicraft article depicts a scene of the boat ride taken by Su Shi (a famous poet of the Song Dynasty) when he travelled by water to visit Chibi (a historical site which became famous after it had witnessed a large-scale battle on the river in AD 208).

The tiny boat is around 8 *fen* (about 3 cm) or more long from stem to stern and about 2 millet grains high. In the middle, the bulging high and wide part is the cabin, which is covered by a

闭之，则右刻"山高月小，水落石出①"，左刻"清风徐来，水波不兴②"，石青③糁④之。

船头坐三人，中峨冠⑤而多髯⑥者为东坡，佛印⑦居右，鲁直⑧居左。苏、黄共阅一手卷⑨。东坡右手执卷端⑩，左手抚鲁直背。鲁直左手执卷末⑪，右手指卷，如有所语⑫。东坡现右足，鲁直现左足，各微侧⑬，其两膝相比⑭者，各隐卷底衣褶中。佛印绝⑮类⑯弥勒⑰，袒胸露乳，矫⑱首昂视，神情与苏黄不属⑲。卧右膝⑳，诎㉑右臂支船，而竖其左膝，左臂挂念珠倚之，珠可历

---

① 山高月小，水落石出：苏轼《后赤壁赋》中的句子（words cited from Su Shi's "The Second Ode to Chibi"）。
② 清风徐来，水波不兴：苏轼《前赤壁赋》中的句子（words cited from Su Shi's "The First Ode to Chibi"）。徐：缓缓地（slowly）。兴：起（rise）。
③ 石青：一种青色颜料（a kind of azure pigment）。
④ 糁（sǎn）：涂（smear）。
⑤ 峨冠：高高的帽子（a high hat）。
⑥ 髯：腮须（whiskers）。
⑦ 佛印：即佛印禅师，苏轼的朋友（a Buddhist monk, Su Shi's friend）。
⑧ 鲁直：黄庭坚，字鲁直（Huang Tingjian styled himself Luzhi）。
⑨ 手卷：横幅的画卷（a horizontal picture scroll）。
⑩ 卷端：指画卷的右端（right end of a picture scroll）。
⑪ 卷末：指画卷的左端（left end of a picture scroll）。
⑫ 如有所语：好像在说什么似的（seem to say something）。
⑬ 微侧：略微侧转（slightly turning）。
⑭ 比：靠近（close to）。
⑮ 绝：极（extremely）。
⑯ 类：像（similar to）。
⑰ 弥勒：佛教菩萨之一（Maitreya, a Bodhisattva）。
⑱ 矫：举（raise）。
⑲ 不属：不相关连（not related to）。
⑳ 卧右膝：右膝卧倒（lay down the right knee）。
㉑ 诎（qū）：屈，弯曲（bend）。

roof made of bamboo splints and leaves. Four little windows are set on each side of the cabin, eight in all. When they are opened, beautifully carved symmetrical railings can be seen outside them. When they are closed, I can see on the right inscriptions of Su Shi's lines: "The mountain is high but the moon looks small; when the water subsides, the rocks emerge." While on the left side of the windows the lines read: "The cool breeze is blowing gently; it is not stirring even a ripple on the waters." The inscriptions were painted with azurite (a blue pigment made of azure stone).

Three men are sitting on the bow of the boat. The one In the middle, with thick beard and moustache and wearing a high hat, is Dongpo (Su Shi's alias). Sitting on his right is Foyin (a monk who was Su Shi's friend) and on his left is Huang Luzhi. Su and Huang are viewing a hand scroll. Su has his right hand holding one end of the scroll and his left hand caressing Huang's back. While Huang, with his left hand holding the other end, is pointing at the scroll with his right hand as if saying something. Dongpo's right foot and Luzhi's left foot can be seen. Both of them stand slightly sideways. Each has one knee close to that of the other man, and below the hand scroll these two knees seem to be visible through the creases of their clothes. Foyin looks extremely like Maitreya, stripped to the waist with his breasts exposed. Holding his head up and looking into the sky, his expression is dissimilar to that of the

历①数也。

舟尾横卧一楫②。楫左右舟子③各一人。居右者椎髻④仰面,左手倚一衡⑤木,右手攀右趾,若啸呼状。居左者右手执蒲葵扇,左手抚炉,炉上有壶,其人视端容寂⑥,若听茶声然。

其船背稍夷⑦,则题名其上,文曰"天启壬戌⑧秋日,虞山⑨王毅叔远甫刻",细若蚊足,钩画了了⑩,其色墨⑪。又用篆章⑫一,文曰"初平山人",其色丹⑬。

通计一舟,为⑭人五,为窗八;为箬篷,为楫,为炉,为壶,为手卷,为念珠各一;对联、题名并篆文,为字共三十有四。而

---

① 历历:清清楚楚(absolutely clear)。
② 楫:桨(paddle)。
③ 舟子:划船的人(paddler)。
④ 椎髻:椎形发髻(vertebra-shaped bun)。
⑤ 衡:横(horizontal)。
⑥ 视端容寂:眼睛正视,神色平静(not look sideways, with a quiet expression)。
⑦ 夷:平(level)。
⑧ 天启壬戌:天启壬戌年(1622)。天启,明熹宗年号(the reign title of Emperor Xizong of the Ming Dynasty)。
⑨ 虞山:山名,在江苏常熟西北,这里代指常熟(name of a mountain, situated to the northwest of Changshu, Jiangsu, here taking the place of Changshu)。
⑩ 了了:清清楚楚(be absolutely clear)。
⑪ 墨:黑(black)。
⑫ 篆章:篆字图章(a seal engraved with seal characters)。
⑬ 丹:红色(red)。
⑭ 为:刻成(carve into)。

other two men. Laying his right knee down and getting support from his bent right arm which is holding the deck, he stretches his left knee and has beads on his left arm which leans on this knee. Each individual bead of the string can be easily counted.

Horizontally on the stern lies a paddle, on each side of which, a paddler is resting. The one on the right wears his hair in a vertebra-shaped bun and faces upward. With his left hand leaning on a horizontal log and his right hand pulling his right toes, he seems to be whistling. The one on the left, with his right hand holding a cattail-leaf fan and his left hand stroking a stove with a pot on it, is gazing straight ahead with a calm expression as if listening to the sound coming from inside the tea pot.

The bottom of the boat is quite level and the name of the artisan was inscribed on it: "Carved by Wang Yi, styled with the name of Shuyuan from Yushan in autumn of the 2nd year of the Tianqi Reign." The strokes of the characters in this inscription are as thin as a mosquito's legs. All the strokes, either vertical or horizontal, even the hooks, are neat and distinctive and painted black. There is also a red seal affixed and the seal script reads: "Chuping Shanren."

Counting how many objects there are on the boat, I saw five people, eight windows, a bamboo awning, a paddle, a stove, a pot, a hand scroll and a string of beads. In addition, there are altogether

计其长,曾①不盈②寸。盖简③桃核修狭④者为之。嘻,技亦灵怪⑤矣哉⑥!

---

① 曾:尚,还(still, yet)。
② 盈:满(full)。
③ 简:拣(select, choose)。
④ 修狭:长而窄(long and narrow)。
⑤ 灵怪:奇妙(wonderful)。
⑥ 矣哉:表示感叹语气词,相当于"了啊"(modal particle expressing a sigh)。

thirty four characters which are respectively contained on the antithetical couple, the inscription of date and name as well as the seal. How long is the boat? It is less than one *cun*. The artisan selected a long and narrow peach-stone for making the boat. Oh, his skill is absolutely superb!

西湖七月半

张岱

西湖七月半,一无可看,止可看看七月半之人。看七月半之人,以五类看之:其一,楼船①箫鼓②,峨冠③盛筵,灯火优④傒⑤,声光相乱,名为看月而实不见月者,看之;其一,亦船亦楼,名娃⑥闺秀⑦,携及童娈⑧,笑啼杂之,环坐露台⑨,左右盼望,身在月下而实不看月者,看之;其一,亦船亦声歌,名妓闲僧,浅斟⑩低唱⑪,弱管轻丝⑫,竹

---

① 楼船:舱作楼形的大船(a big ship with a building-like cabin)。
② 箫鼓:这里用作动词,吹箫击鼓(here used as verbs: play xiao, a vertical bamboo flute and beat a drum)。
③ 峨冠:高高的帽子(high hats)。
④ 优:优伶,演戏的人(actor or actress)。
⑤ 傒(xī):通"奚",仆人(servants)。
⑥ 娃:美女,这里指歌妓之类(beautiful girls, here referring to prostitutes good at singing and dancing)。
⑦ 闺秀:大家女子(girls from respectable families)。
⑧ 童娈(luán):娈童,俊美的男童(handsome boys)。
⑨ 露台:楼船上的阳台(balcony on the building-like ship)。
⑩ 浅斟:慢慢饮酒(drink slowly)。
⑪ 低唱:低回宛转地唱(sing in a low but sweet voice)。
⑫ 弱管轻丝:轻柔的管弦音乐(gentle music played with pipe and string instruments)。

THE WEST LAKE IN THE MIDDLE OF THE SEVENTH MONTH

Zhang Dai

In the middle of the seventh month of the year, nothing but people can be seen on the West Lake. At this time of the year, there are five distinct categories of people on the lake. The first category is attributed to the powerful men who, wearing high hats, dine and wine at a lavish dinner served on a big towered boat where, under bright lights, musical instruments such as *xiao* and drums are played, actors, actresses and servants are here and there ... The host has come here for the purpose of enjoying a full moon but with his attention being attracted to something else, he does not actually see the moon. There are others who also enjoy themselves on a big towered boat together with professional female singers, graceful girls from rich families and handsome boys. The host, surrounded by his laughing and yelling companions who sit in a circle on the flat roof of the boat, looks to his right and left but not to the sky to see the moon overhead. These rich men fall into the second category. The people in the third one, also on a boat with

肉相发①，亦在月下，亦看月而欲人看其看月者，看之；其一，不舟不车，不衫不帻②，酒醉饭饱，呼群三五③，跻④入人丛，昭庆⑤断桥⑥，嚣呼⑦嘈杂，装假醉，唱无腔曲⑧，月亦看，看月者亦看，不看月者亦看，而实无一看者，看之；其一，小船轻幌⑨，净几暖炉，茶铛⑩旋⑪煮，素瓷⑫静递⑬，好友佳人，邀月同坐⑭，或匿影⑮树下，或逃嚣⑯里湖⑰，看月而人不见其看月之态，亦不作意⑱看月者，看之。

---

① 竹肉相发：竹，指管乐器，如箫、笛、笙之类（pipe musical instruments made of bamboo, like *xiao*, flute and *sheng*）。肉，指歌喉（singer's voice）。相发，相互协和（harmonize with each other）。

② 不衫不帻（zé）：不穿长衫，不戴头巾，指放荡随便（do not wear long gown and kerchief, referring to being dissipated or informal）。帻：头巾（kerchief）。

③ 呼群三五：呼朋唤友，三五成群（youngsters walked together in threes and fours, calling each other）。

④ 跻：挤（crowd）。

⑤ 昭庆：昭庆寺，又名菩提院，在西湖东北岸（Zhaoqing Temple, also named Bodhi Yard, on the northeastern bank of the West Lake）。

⑥ 断桥：原叫宝祐桥，唐代称为断桥，在西湖白堤东端，靠近昭庆寺（originally named Baoyou Bridge, called the Broken Bridge during the Tang Dynasty; it is located at the eastern end of Bai Dyke, near Zhaoqing Temple）。

⑦ 嚣呼："嚣"，同"叫"（shout in a loud voice）。

⑧ 无腔曲：不成腔调的曲子（tuneless song）。

⑨ 轻幌：轻细的帐幔（light and fine curtains）。

⑩ 茶铛（chēng）：烧茶的小锅（little pot for cooking tea water）。

⑪ 旋：随即（presently）。

⑫ 素瓷：白净的瓷（fair and clear china）。

⑬ 静递：静静地传递（pass on silently）。

⑭ 邀月同坐：邀请来在月下同坐（ask friends to sit under the moon）。

⑮ 匿影：藏身（hide oneself）。

⑯ 逃嚣：躲避喧闹（avoid noise）。

⑰ 里湖：西湖以苏堤为界，分为外湖和里湖两部分，苏堤以西为里湖（the West Lake is divided into two parts — the inner lake and outer lake by the Su Dyke and the part to the west of the Su Dyke is inner lake）。

⑱ 作意：着意，用心（act with care）。

music, are accompanied by courtesans and monks. They drink wine while enjoying the harmonious sounds of the singers' voice and pipe and string musical instruments' tone. Under the moon, the host is viewing it but actually he wants others to see how he enjoys the moon. There are also small groups of people who take neither boats nor carriages, wear neither long gowns nor head-coverings but dine and wine to satiety. In threes and fours, these people elbow themselves into the crowd, making a lot of noise, pretending to be drunken and sing tunelessly while passing the Zhaoqing Temple and crossing the Broken Bridge. These people watch the moon and also the moon-viewers, even the passers-by who are not enjoying the moon. In reality, they do not see anything and they fall into the fourth category. The fifth are those moon-viewers who hire a small boat covered by light and fine curtains to entertain their close friends and some beautiful women in the moonlight. They sit at a clean table. Tea is being made in a teakettle over the fire of a stove and is served in fine porcelain cups. The boat sometimes hides in the shade of a tree, sometimes shifts to the inner lake away from the noise of the crowd.

The people of Hangzhou usually start to tour the West Lake soon after daybreak and finish their tour at dusk. They seem to avoid the moon as they would a foe. However, people loved the honours in celebration of Ghosts' Festival this evening, therefore

杭人游湖，巳①出酉②归，避月如仇。是夕好名③，逐队争出，多犒④门军⑤酒钱。轿夫擎燎⑥，列俟⑦岸上。一入舟，速⑧舟子⑨急放⑩断桥，赶入胜会⑪。以故⑫二鼓⑬以前，人声鼓吹⑭，如沸如撼⑮，如魇⑯如呓⑰，如聋如哑⑱。大船小船一齐凑岸，一无所见，止见篙⑲击篙，舟触舟，肩摩肩，面看面而已。少刻⑳兴尽，官府席散，

---

① 巳（sì）：巳时，约为上午9时至11时（the period of the day from 9 a.m. to 11 a.m.）。
② 酉：酉时，约为下午5时至7时（the period of the day from 5 p.m. to 7 p.m.）。
③ 是夕好名：七月半是鬼节，又叫"中元节"，这天夜晚要祭祀鬼魂。这里是说人们喜好虚名（the 15th of the 7th month is the spirit festival; in the evening people usually offer sacrifices to ghosts. Here referring to that people are fond of honours）。
④ 犒（kào）：用酒食或财物慰劳（bring food and drink or gifts to sb. to express one's appreciation for service rendered）。
⑤ 门军：守城门的军士（the soldiers who were guarding the city gate）。
⑥ 擎（qíng）燎：举着火把（hold high torches）。
⑦ 列俟（sì）：排着队等候（wait by lining up）。
⑧ 速：催促（hasten）。
⑨ 舟子：船夫（boatman）。
⑩ 放：行（船）（sailing）。
⑪ 胜会：热闹的集会（bustling gathering）。
⑫ 以故：因此（so, therefore）。
⑬ 二鼓：二更，约为夜里11点左右（about 11 p.m.）。
⑭ 鼓吹：各种乐器奏出的音乐声（music played by all kinds of musical instruments）。
⑮ 撼：摇动（shaking）。
⑯ 魇（yǎn）：梦魇，做噩梦时发出的呻吟或惊叫（groan or scream in a nightmare）。
⑰ 呓：说梦话（utterance in one's dream）。
⑱ 如聋如哑：指喧闹声震耳欲聋，人们说话互相听不见（in a deafening noise people cannot hear each other）。
⑲ 篙：撑船用的竹竿（boat pole）。
⑳ 少刻：片刻，不一会儿（a moment, a short while）。

crowds of people swarmed to the lake outside the city. While going through the city gate, many of them gave handsome tips to the guards. After their passengers had alighted from the chairs, the sedan-chair carriers holding high torches lined up on the bank of the lake to wait. As soon as they embarked, the pleasure-seekers urged the boatmen to sail immediately to the Broken Bridge in order to arrive at the centre of the festival activities in time. Before midnight, loud voices, mixed with musical instruments' noisy tones, created deafening sounds which were similar to those of water-boiling or earthshaking and to the screaming in a nightmare or the utterances in someone's sleep. While big and small boats were drawing near the lake side simultaneously, all that could be seen were poles hitting each other, boats touching one another as well as people rubbing elbows with each other, hence everybody kept finding himself face-to-face with another. Not long afterwards, as no one had any enthusiasm left, the feasts of the local authorities had come to an end. The yamen runners soon cleared the way for the officials by shouting at the top of their voices. The sedan-chair carriers called out to warn the passengers on the boats that the city gate would soon be shut. Then in the darkness, lanterns and torches, resembling numerous stars in the sky, gathered and moved away. Groups of people on the shore were also hastening to leave, trying to get through the

皂隶①喝道②去。轿夫叫,船上人怖③以关门,灯笼火把如列星④,一一簇拥而去。岸上人亦逐队赶门⑤,渐稀渐薄,顷刻散尽矣。

吾辈始舣舟⑥近岸,断桥石磴⑦始凉,席⑧其上,呼客纵饮。此时月如镜新磨⑨,山复整妆,湖复颒面⑩,向⑪之浅斟低唱者出,匿影树下者亦出。吾辈往通声气⑫,拉与同坐。韵友⑬来,名妓至,杯箸⑭安⑮,竹肉发。月色苍凉⑯,东方将白,客方散去。吾辈纵舟,酣睡于十里荷花之中,香气拍人⑰,清梦甚惬⑱。

---

① 皂隶:衙役(yamen runner)。
② 喝道:官员外出,衙役们在前面开路,喝令行人散开(when an official went out, yamen runners would clear the way for him by shouting an order for pedestrians to spread apart)。
③ 怖:吓唬(scare)。
④ 列星:罗列在天空的星(stars spreading out in the sky)。
⑤ 赶门:急忙赶路进城门(hurry on to enter the city gate)。
⑥ 舣(yǐ)舟:拢船靠岸(move the boat close to the shore)。
⑦ 石磴:石阶(stone stairs)。
⑧ 席:用作动词,摆开宴席(arrange a feast)。
⑨ 如镜新磨:月亮好像刚刚磨过的铜镜一样明亮(the moon is as bright as a bronze mirror which has just been polished)。
⑩ 颒(huì)面:洗脸(face-washing)。
⑪ 向:刚才(just now)。
⑫ 往通声气:过去打招呼(go to say hello)。
⑬ 韵友:风雅的朋友(elegant friends)。
⑭ 箸:筷子(chopsticks)。
⑮ 安:摆好(set in order)。
⑯ 苍凉:凄凉(dreary)。
⑰ 拍人:扑人([of an odor] to assail someone's nostrils)。
⑱ 惬(qiè):心满意足(be fully satisfied and content)。

city gate before it was shut. There were less and less people on the shore and then all had gone.

Now we began to move our boat toward the shore. The stone stairs at Broken Bridge had cooled and we sat there to have a picnic. I encouraged my friends to drink to their hearts' content. At this moment the moon looked like a bronze mirror which had just been polished. In the bright moonlight the hills had taken on a new look and the surface of the lake was as fresh as a beautiful girl's countenance. Those who had been drinking lightly and singing in a low voice were now turning up and those who had been hiding in the shade of trees were emerging. We went over to say hello to them and invite them to come to sit on the stone stairs with us. Hence graceful scholars had come to join us, followed by social butterflies. Cups and chopsticks were laid on the table, music and song began. When the moon turned pale and bleak and the first whitish ray appeared on the eastern horizon, our guests began to leave. Whereas, my friend and I soon slept soundly on our boat which was drifting freely within the vast expanse of lotus leaves and flowers. Amid the overwhelming fragrance of the flowers, each one of us was having a beautiful dream.

湖心亭看雪

张岱

崇祯五年①十二月,余住西湖。大雪三日,湖中人、鸟声俱绝。

是日,更定②矣,余拏③一小舟,拥毳衣④炉火,独往湖心亭看雪。雾凇沆砀⑤,天与云与山与水,上下一白;湖上影子,惟长堤一痕、湖心亭一点与余舟一芥⑥、舟中人两三粒而已!

到亭上,有两人铺毡对坐,一童子烧酒,炉正沸。见余,大喜曰:"湖中焉得⑦更有此人!"拉余同饮。余强饮⑧三大白⑨而别。问其姓氏,是金陵人,客此。

---

① 崇祯五年:1632 年。崇祯:明思宗年号(the reign title of Emperor Sizong of the Ming Dynasty)。
② 更(gēng)定:更深人静,更阑人静(all is quiet in the dead of night)。更,一夜分为五更(one of the five two-hour periods into which the night was divided)。定,人声静谧(voices calm down)。
③ 拏:牵引(tow; drag)。
④ 毳(cuì)衣:皮衣(fur clothing)。
⑤ 雾凇(sōng):像雾一样的寒气(cold air similar to fog)。沆砀(hàng dàng):白气弥漫的样子(white air permeating)。
⑥ 芥(jiè):小草;细小的东西(small grass; something tiny and trivial)。
⑦ 焉得:哪能(how can)。
⑧ 强饮:强迫自己喝下去(force oneself to drink)。
⑨ 大白:酒盏名(name of a wine cup)。

VIEWING THE SNOW SCENE FROM THE MID-LAKE PAVILION

Zhang Dai

In the twelfth month of the fifth year of the Chongzhen Reign (1632), while staying by the West Lake, I saw snow falling continuously for three days. After that, there were no signs of human beings nor sounds of birds on the lake.

In the dead of night when all was quiet, I towed a small boat. Wearing fur clothes and carrying a burning stove, I went alone to the Mid-Lake Pavilion to see snow. Over the lake, the curling mist and fogs mixed with the fluttering flakes made the sky, the clouds, the hills and the waters all white, high and low. The only shadows I could see in the lake were that of the long causeway which was reflected in the shape of a belt, that of the Mid-lake Pavilion in the shape of a dot, my boat — a leaf and the men in the boat — a couple of rice grains.

Walking into the pavilion, I saw two men sitting face to face on a felt carpet. A boy servant was heating wine on a stove over a roaring fire. The two men were overjoyed to see me and said

及下船,舟子①喃喃②曰:"莫说相公③痴④,更有痴似相公者!"

---

① 舟子:船夫(boatman)。
② 喃喃:低声含糊地说(murmur)。
③ 相公:对年轻人的一种称呼(a form of address used to call a young man)。
④ 痴:痴迷(infatuated)。

merrily: "Good heavens! How could we expect to see someone else on the lake!" They invited me to drink together. I forced myself to drink three cups of wine and then said good-bye to them. While asking their names, I was also told that they were natives of Jinling and had come here for a visit.

As soon as I came back to the boat, I heard the boatman murmuring: "Don't say you are crazy. There are people even crazier than you."

五人墓碑记

张溥

五人者,盖当蓼洲周公①之被逮,激于义而死焉者也。至于今,郡之贤士大夫请于当道②,即除③魏阉④废祠⑤之址以葬之;且立石于其墓之门,以旌⑥其所为。呜呼,亦盛矣哉!

夫五人之死,去今之墓而葬⑦焉,其为时止十有一月耳。夫十有一月之中,凡富贵之子,慷慨得志之徒,其疾病而死,死而湮

---

① 蓼(liǎo)洲周公:周顺昌,字景文,号蓼洲,吴县(今苏州)人,万历年间进士,曾官福州推官、吏部员外郎等职,因反对宦官魏忠贤专权被捕下狱,死于狱中(Zhou Shunchang styled himself Jingwen and was alternatively named Liaozhou, from Wu County — today's Suzhou. He was a successful candidate for the highest imperial examination during the Wanli Reign [1573–1620] and held the position of assistant governor of Fuzhou and then was appointed to the position of councilor of the Ministry of Civil Personnel. He was put in prison and died there because he opposed the notorious eunuch Wei Zhongxian who attempted to grab all the power)。
② 当道:当权者,这里指当地长官(people in authority, here referring to the local official)。
③ 除:修治(repair)。
④ 魏阉:魏忠贤(Wei Zhongxian)。
⑤ 废祠:魏忠贤专权时,其党羽在各地为他建立生祠,事败后,这些祠堂均被废弃(when Wei Zhongxian was in power, his henchmen built many memorial halls for him; but when he collapsed, these halls were all discarded)。
⑥ 旌(jīng):表扬,赞扬(praise)。
⑦ 墓而葬:修墓安葬,这里的墓用作动词(build a tomb and bury, here 墓 is used as a verb)。

THE EPITAPH INSCRIBED ON THE FIVE-MEN'S TOMB

Zhang Pu

The five men were those who, inspired by the arrest of the revered Mr. Zhou Shunchang (Liaozhou was his literary name), had each died a martyr. Now some virtuous scholar-officials of the prefecture have asked the local authority to bury them at the site of the former memorial hall in memory of Wei Zhongxian (a notorious eunuch of the Ming Dynasty who seized the power by killing virtuous and able officials one after another) and to have a tombstone erected which will extol their heroic deeds. Oh! How wonderful it is to have this great thing done!

It is only 11 months from the death of the five men to their burial within this tomb. During these 11 months, many people have died of illness. Even the descendants of wealthy and influential families or those who proudly achieved their ambitions are among the dead, swept towards oblivion, let alone ordinary people who were never known to the public. What is the reason why only these five men have become illustrious after their death?

没①不足道者，亦已众矣；况草野之无闻者欤？独五人之皦皦②，何也？

予犹记周公之被逮，在丁卯三月之望③。吾社④之行为士先者⑤，为之声义⑥，敛赀财以送其行，哭声震动天地。缇骑⑦按剑而前，问："谁为哀者？"众不能堪，抶而仆之⑧。是时以大中丞⑨抚吴⑩者为魏之私人⑪，周公之逮所由使也；吴之民方痛心焉，于是乘其厉声以呵，则噪而相逐。中丞匿于溷藩⑫以免。既而以吴民之乱请于朝，按诛⑬五人，曰颜佩韦、杨念如、马杰、沈扬、周文元，即

---

① 湮没：埋没（fall into oblivion）。
② 皦（jiǎo）皦：同"皎皎"，这里指显赫（very clear and bright, here meaning illustrious, celebrated）。
③ 丁卯三月之望：指明熹宗天启七年（1627）三月十五日（the 15th of the 3rd month in the 7th year of the Tianqi Reign, 1627）。
④ 吾社：指复社。张溥等组织复社，以继承东林党为号召（referring to the Fu Association, organized by Zhang Pu, etc. to carry on the cause of the Donglin Party）。
⑤ 行为士先者：行为能够成为士人表率的人（the one whose behavior has set an example for scholars）。
⑥ 声义：伸张正义（let justice prevail）。
⑦ 缇骑（tí jì）：本是汉代京城中逮捕人犯的马队，这里指明代锦衣卫，当时为魏忠贤掌握（this is originally the cavalry in the capital of the Han Dynasty that arrested criminals. Here referring to the Guards in Red, controlled by Wei Zhongxian at that time）。
⑧ 抶（chì）而仆（pū）之：将其打倒在地（knock sb. down）。抶：击（hit）。仆：使仆倒（make somebody fall on the ground）。
⑨ 大中丞：官职名（name of an official position）。
⑩ 抚吴：做吴地的巡抚（act as an imperial inspector to the Area of Wu）。
⑪ 魏之私人：魏忠贤的党徒（one of Wei Zhongxian's henchmen）。
⑫ 溷（hùn）藩：厕所（a toilet）。
⑬ 按诛：追究案情判定死罪（look into the case and sentence somebody to death）。按：审查（investigate）。

I still remember that it was on the 15th day of the 3rd month in the 7th year of the Tianqi Reign (1627) when the revered Mr. Zhou was arrested. Those in our association, who had set an example for others to follow, stepped forward to uphold justice for him. They collected money for him along the way to see him off, with the sound of their wailing shaking heaven and earth. The commander of the local Guards in Embroidered Coats (a secret service of the Ming Dynasty), holding the sheath of his sword, walked towards the crowd and asked sternly, "For whom are you grieving?" Unable to control their anger, the demonstrators whipped him and pushed him to the ground. At that time, the official who acted as the imperial inspector to the area of Wu was one of Wei Zhongxian's henchmen. He was the one who had precipitated the arrest of the revered Mr. Zhou. The people of Wu hated him very much. When he screamed a rebuke at them, the demonstrators shouted at the top of their voices while chasing him. He hid himself in a toilet covered by a fence in order to avoid being killed. Not long afterwards, on the accusation of leading the uprising of the Wu people, he appealed to the throne for the execution of five men. The five men were Yan Peiwei, Yang Nianru, Ma Jie, Shen Yang and Zhou Wenyuan. They are the five who have just been buried together in this tomb.

On the execution ground, with grand airs on their faces, they

今之傫然①在墓者也。

然五人之当刑也，意气扬扬②，呼中丞之名而詈③之，谈笑以死。断头置城上，颜色不少变。有贤士大夫发五十金，买五人之脰④而函⑤之，卒与尸合。故今之墓中全乎为五人也。

嗟乎！大阉⑥之乱，缙绅⑦而能不易其志者，四海之大，有几人欤？而五人生于编伍⑧之间，素不闻诗书之训，激昂大义，蹈死不顾，亦曷⑨故哉？且矫诏⑩纷出，钩党⑪之捕遍于天下，卒以吾郡之发愤一击，不敢复有株治⑫；大阉亦逡⑬巡畏义⑭，非常之谋⑮难

---

① 傫（lěi）然：聚集的样子（the scene of gathering）。
② 扬扬：昂扬（或自若）（triumphantly or to appear calm and at ease）。
③ 詈（lì）：骂（curse）。
④ 脰（dòu）：颈项，头（neck; head）。
⑤ 函：匣子（box）。这里是用棺材收敛的意思（put a dead body in a coffin）。
⑥ 大阉：指魏忠贤（referring to Wei Zhongxian）。
⑦ 缙绅：即士大夫（literati and officialdom）。缙：搢，插（tuck in, i.e. a man who tucks a tablet 笏 in his girdle）。绅：大带，垂着衣带的人（a big band, i.e. a man who lets his band hanging down）。
⑧ 编伍：指平民（the common people）。古代编制平民户口，五家为一"伍"（in the old days every five families were organized into a unit）。
⑨ 曷：何（what）。
⑩ 矫诏：假托皇帝的名义颁发的诏书（a counterfeit imperial edict）。
⑪ 钩党：被指为有牵连的同党（the person who was accused of being a member of the same party）。
⑫ 株治：株连惩治（involve others in a criminal case and punish them）。
⑬ 逡（qūn）巡：欲进不进、迟疑不决的样子（hesitate to move forward）。
⑭ 畏义：害怕群众的正义斗争（be afraid of the just struggle of the masses）。
⑮ 非常之谋：指篡夺帝位的阴谋（scheme to usurp the throne）。

appeared immensely proud. They cursed the wicked official and called him by his name. Remaining calm in the face of death, they went on talking as cheerfully as ever. Hanging on the city wall, their heads still kept nearly the same facial expression as before they were severed. A virtuous scholar-official spent fifty *liang* of silver to buy the five men's heads and placed them in five coffins. Later the five heads were put together with the bodies to make the whole corpses to be buried in this tomb.

Alas! How many officials were there throughout the nation who could keep their aspirations unchanged when the evil eunuch Wei Zhongxian had seized all the power? The five men were born to common families and they had never been taught the *Book of Songs* and the *Collection of Ancient Texts* but they were firm and stern in upholding justice and faced death unflinchingly. How did they become heroes? At the time when counterfeit imperial edicts kept appearing and the arrest of upright officials on the charge of implicated offences happened everywhere, a sudden and strong resistance took place in our city Suzhou. As a result, Wei Zhongxian and his henchmen did not dare to continue the implicating punishment of innocent people. Wei himself, being afraid of the just struggle of the people, hesitated to take any action and found it difficult to fulfill his plan to usurp the throne at one swoop. Finally he came to a bad end when a wise

于猝①发，待圣人②之出而投缳道路③，不可谓非五人之力也。

由是观之，则今之高爵显位，一旦抵罪④，或脱身以逃，不能容于远近，而又有剪发杜门⑤，佯狂不知所之者，其辱人贱行⑥，视⑦五人之死，轻重固何如哉？是以蓼洲周公忠义暴⑧于朝廷，赠谥褒美⑨，显荣于身后；而五人亦得以加其土封⑩，列其姓名于大堤之上，凡四方之士，无有不过而拜且泣者，斯固百世之遇也。不然，令五人者保其首领，以老于户牖⑪之下，则尽其天年，人皆得以隶

---

① 猝（cù）：突然（suddenly）。
② 圣人：指崇祯皇帝朱由检（referring to Emperor Chongzhen whose name was Zhu Youjian）。
③ 投缳（huán）道路：天启七年，崇祯即位，将魏忠贤放逐到凤阳去守陵，不久又派人去逮捕他。魏得知消息后，畏罪吊死在路上（in the 7th year of the Tianqi Reign, Chongzhen ascended the throne and exiled Wei Zhongxian to Fengyang County in Anhui Province to guard the tombs but soon sent his man to arrest him. Hearing the news, Wei hanged himself on his way to Fengyang County）。缳：绳索（rope）。投：扔（throw）。
④ 抵罪：因犯罪而受相应惩罚（be punished for committing a crime）。
⑤ 剪发杜门：剃发为僧，闭门索居（shave one's head to become a monk and live alone by shutting one's door）。
⑥ 辱人贱行：可耻的人格，卑贱的行为（shameful character, humble behavior）。
⑦ 视：比较（compare）。
⑧ 暴（pù）：显露（manifest himself）。
⑨ 赠谥（shì）褒美：赠以谥号，表彰美行（give sb. a posthumous title in praise of his good behavior）。指崇祯追赠周顺昌"忠介"的谥号（the Emperor Chongzhen gave Zhou Shunchang a posthumous title "Zhongjie", meaning "loyal and righteous"）。
⑩ 加其土封：增修他们的坟墓（to repair and consolidate the tomb）。
⑪ 户牖（yǒu）：门和窗。这里指居家（door and window, here referring to living an ordinary life）。

man succeeded to the throne. He was sent into exile by the new emperor and had to hang himself when he came to the end of his tether. Can't we say that the tragic death of the evil eunuch was the result of the five men's great efforts?

Having reviewed this event, let's look at the following occurrences: When high officials have committed a crime and will be punished, some try to escape but wherever they go, nobody wants them; some others either shave their hair to become monks and shut themselves up to live in seclusion, or feign madness and pretend not to know where to go. How disgraceful and shameless are those people! Compared with the heroic death of the five men, the shameful life of those escaped officials is too awful to be mentioned. When the revered Mr. Zhou's loyalty and righteousness finally reached the imperial ears, he was given a posthumous title for his good deeds, thus enjoying a great honor after his death. As a result, the five men's tomb was given more earth for consolidation and their names were listed on the dyke. Visitors from all over the country, while passing by and without exception, would pay their respects to the five men with tears in their eyes. "Leaving a good name for a hundred generations" is really something great. If all this had not happened, if, say, their heads had remained on their shoulders and they had died a natural death at home, others might have pushed them around

使之，安能屈①豪杰之流，扼腕②墓道，发其志士之悲哉？故予与同社诸君子，哀斯墓之徒有其石也，而为之记，亦以明死生之大，匹夫③之有重于社稷④也。

贤士大夫者，冏卿⑤因之吴公⑥，太史⑦文起文公⑧、孟长姚公⑨也。

①屈：使屈身，倾倒（make sb. greatly admire）。
②扼腕：一只手扼住另一只手的手腕，表示悲愤（clutch one wrist with the other hand to express grief and indignation）。
③匹夫：平民，这里指五义士（common people, here referring to the five chivalrous persons）。
④社稷：国家（nation）。
⑤冏（jiǒng）卿：太仆卿，官职名（name of an official position）。
⑥因之吴公：吴默，字因之（Wu Mo styled himself Yinzhi）。
⑦太史：指翰林院修撰（a writer and editor in the imperial academy）。
⑧文起文公：文震孟，字文起（Wen Zhenmeng styled himself Wenqi）。
⑨孟长姚公：姚希孟，字孟长（Yao Ximeng styled himself Mengchang）。

like treating their servants. In this case, how could they have made outstanding people bow to them and wring their hands to express their sorrow in front of their tomb? Therefore I, together with my comrades of the same association, feeling disappointed over the blankness on the tombstone, have written an epitaph to elaborate on the significance of life and death and to express our view that even an ordinary man can make a great contribution to his country.

The above-mentioned virtuous scholar-officials are Mr. Wu Mo (styled Yinzhi), a high official; Mr. Wen Zhenmeng (styled Wenqi) and Mr. Yao Ximeng (styled Mengchang), both members of the Imperial Academy.

海 市 记

吴伟业

余常之中州①,与吾友张石平相见于大梁②。大梁为天下饶③,其城郭险以固④,宫观崇以峻⑤。士女之所杂沓⑥,车马之所辐辏⑦,五方⑧百货罗布⑨而错列⑩。乃置酒登繁台,北望黄河从天上来,屈

---

① 中州:古豫州(今河南省一带),居九州之中(an administrative area, located at the centre of the nine administrative divisions in ancient China; also called Yuzhou, equivalent to today's Henan Province)。
② 大梁:古地名,即今开封市(an ancient name of today's Kaifeng City in Henan Province)。
③ 饶:富足之地(a richly endowed area)。
④ 险以固:险要而牢固(occupying a strategic position to become difficult of access and easily defended)。
⑤ 崇以峻:高而陡峭(high and steep; here used to describe a tall and upright building)。
⑥ 杂沓(zá tà):纷杂繁多貌(numerous and disorderly; here used to describe people's movement — come in a continuous stream)。
⑦ 辐辏(fú còu):形容人或物聚集像车辐集中于车毂一样(people or objects converging from all around as spokes of a wheel on the hub)。
⑧ 五方:指东、西、南、北、中(five directions, i.e. east, west, south, north and centre)。
⑨ 罗布:罗列分布(spread out; lay out)。
⑩ 错列:交错地陈列(staggered arrangement; be laid out disorderly)。

THE CASTLES IN THE AIR

Wu Weiye

I often visit Zhongzhou. This time while journeying there, I met my friend Zhang Shiping in Daliang. The city of Daliang is located in one of the most richly endowed areas under heaven. Its city wall, occupying a strategic position, is difficult of access and easily defended. In the city, the famous Taoist temple stands tall and upright. Men and women bustle about and jostle against each other. Constant streams of horses and carriages flow through the streets. General merchandise from different parts of the country are laid out disorderly here and there. So I bought wine and carried it up to the natural platform called Fantai. Standing there and looking to the north, I saw the Yellow River coming from the sky. It seemed as if a huge reservoir with winding sides had overturned and was pouring its water from the sky. The turbulent river was rushing to Yique and from there it would prepare to run through the Longmen Gorge. It is gorgeous to see how magnificent scenes are created.

I have been parted from Shiping for more than ten years.

潢①倒注，汹汹②乎奔伊阙③以走龙门④。岂不壮哉！

别去十余年，石平官两浙观察，余访之湖上，握手话旧事，叹息久之。酒酣耳热，石平曰："子乃言大梁哉！予过盐官观海市矣。始登楼望海，见海中有浮图⑤长三十仞，白云滃滃⑥从之。初谓绝岛所未有之奇也。已而石塘阗沸⑦，盐官人皆走且呼曰，海市矣！海市矣！未几，赤壁矗起，甃城⑧剥落，若堵墙。少间，色变白，危楼⑨数十间涌出其际。窗棂⑩玲珑，金碧如画。忽苍烟飞来，复阁尽没，而修竹万丛，松柏槎枒⑪，层城睥睨⑫，横亘异状。烟尽，楼脊渐出，顿还旧观。乃有长桥出于水上，隐隐历历⑬，车马无声

---

① 屈潢（huáng）：潢，积水池（pond; pool; reservoir）。这里指黄河像个弯弯曲曲的大积水池（here the Yellow River is described as a huge reservoir with winding sides）。
② 汹汹：水腾涌的样子（surging; turbulent）。
③ 伊阙：地名。在今洛阳市南（a scenic spot, located to the south of today's Luoyang City）。
④ 龙门：即禹门口。在山西河津市西北和陕西韩城市东北。黄河至此，两岸峭壁对峙，形如门阙，故名（Longmen — the Dragon Gate, located to the northwest of Hejin City, Shanxi Province and to the northeast of Hancheng City, Shaanxi Province. At this point, sheer precipices rise on either side of the Yellow River like one gate after another, hence its name）。
⑤ 浮图：佛塔（Buddhist pagoda）。
⑥ 滃（wěng）滃：形容云气涌起（rise of clouds）。
⑦ 阗（tián）：声音很大（noisy）；沸：沸腾（boiling）。
⑧ 甃城（zhòu qī）：砖砌的台阶（brick stairs）。甃：砖砌的（brick）；城：台阶的梯级（flight of stairs）。
⑨ 危楼：高楼（tall building）。
⑩ 窗棂（líng）：窗格（window lattice）。
⑪ 槎枒（chá yā）：槎牙，树木枝杈歧出（interlaced branches of a tree）。
⑫ 睥睨（pì nì）：斜眼傲视（look sideways in an arrogant manner）。
⑬ 隐隐历历：有的模糊，有的清楚（some are blurred and some are distinctly visible）。隐隐：不清楚（blurred）；历历：鲜明（distinctly, clearly）。

Now he has been promoted to the position of the governor of both the eastern and western parts of Zhejiang Province. I met him on the lake. Having shaken hands, we recalled our common past experiences which made us sigh again and again for quite some time. Warmed with wine, Shiping said: "You have been speaking highly of Daliang. Now I am going to tell you something about the castles in the air which I saw while passing Yanguan. On that day, no sooner had I climbed to the top of a tower to view the sea than I saw in the distance a Buddhist pagoda, thirty *ren* (about fifty metres) tall, surrounded by rolling white clouds. At first I thought this might be a peculiar scene which had never been seen before on this isolated island. Soon the hubbub of voices burst out and this sounded like water boiling in a cauldron. The local people of Yanguan rushed about calling out: 'Castles in the air! Castles in the air!' Not long afterwards, a red cliff appeared, towering aloft. It looked like a big wall with some of its bricks missing. A moment later, the colour turned white and dozens of tall buildings emerged from the site of the wall. With exquisite window lattices, the buildings looked as splendid as pictures. Suddenly dark mists came from nowhere and all the multiple buildings immediately disappeared. Instead of these, dense bushes of tall and slender bamboos, pine and cypress with interlocking branches came into being. The fairytale city arrogantly overlooked from high and strange happenings seemed to be everywhere. When all the

楼船旗帜，似有人队介^①而立。其余若鼎者、铛^②者、幡盖者、盘盂杯鎗^③者，目之所接，手之所指者，盖不可胜数矣，而又倏忽^④尽矣。"石平之述海市如此。

嗟乎！黄河决，汴城陷，畴昔^⑤之游所登临而肆眺^⑥者，尽荡为洪流、堙^⑦为鱼鳖；乃东海巨浸中顾有宫阙、城市、舟车、百物，俨然一都会焉。嘻，此不可解也！余与石平复相视笑，遂握笔为之记。

---

① 介：处在中间（in between）。
② 铛（chēng）：平底浅锅（pan）。
③ 鎗（chēng）：酒器（wine vessel）。
④ 倏忽（shū hū）：忽然（suddenly）。
⑤ 畴（chóu）昔：往昔（in former times; in the past）。
⑥ 肆眺：纵目远看（look as far as the eye can see; gaze into the distance）。
⑦ 堙（yīn）：埋没（bury; cover up with earth, snow, rocks, etc.）。

mists had dispersed, the roofs of the tall buildings reappeared and the original scene immediately came back. Then a long bridge emerged from the water and some parts could be seen clearly and some were blurred. Carriages and horses did not make any noise. On a towered ship decorated with flags, there seemed to be people standing in lines between the flags. There were many others. Some looked like cauldrons or pans and some were similar to imperial canopies. We also saw table wares such as plates, jars, cups and wine vessels. Countless as they were, all the objects which were seen or pointed at by the crowd suddenly disappeared." This was what Shiping had said about the castles in the air.

Alas! The city of Bian (another name for Daliang) had been flooded and the whole city was immersed in water when the embankment of the Yellow River was breached. What I saw last time while overlooking the city from a height have been wiped out by the powerful current of the flood and all have become fish and turtles' companions. Whereas over the vast expanse of waters of the Eastern Sea, there appeared palace buildings, urban streets, boats, carriages and many other things — all these seemed to be parts of a metropolis. Oh, how can we explain this peculiar phenomenon? Shiping and I smiled into each other's eyes. Then, holding my pen I wrote these notes.

《奇零草》自序

张煌言

余自舞象①,辄②好为诗歌。先大夫③虑④废⑤经史⑥,屡以为戒,遂辍⑦笔不谈,然犹时时窃⑧为之。及登第⑨后,与四方贤豪交益广,往来赠答,岁久⑩盈箧⑪。会⑫国难频仍⑬,余倡大义于江东⑭,敕甲敵

---

① 舞象:古代儿童成年时(15岁)跳的一种武舞。因此舞象即指成年(a kind of military dance for a child more than fifteen years old in ancient times. So it refers to a child more than fifteen)。
② 辄(zhé):经常,总是(often, always)。
③ 先大夫:作者死去的父亲(the author's late father)。
④ 虑:担心(worry)。
⑤ 废:妨碍(hinder)。
⑥ 经史:儒家经典和历史(Confucian classics and history books)。
⑦ 辍(chuò):停止(stop)。
⑧ 窃:私下(in secret)。
⑨ 登第:考中(pass the imperial examination)。
⑩ 岁久:时间长了(for a long time)。
⑪ 箧(qiè):小箱(a little box)。
⑫ 会:适逢(just when)。
⑬ 频仍:连续多次(frequent)。
⑭ 倡大义于江东:1645年南明王朝垮台后,清军南下,作者被派去浙东支持朱以海号召人民抗清(in 1645, after the Southern Ming Dynasty collapsed and the Qing troops moved southward, in the eastern part of Zhejiang, the author was sent to support Zhu Yihai to call on people to fight against the Qing invaders)。

PREFACE TO *SPARSE WITHERED GRASS*

Zhang Huangyan

Since the age of fifteen, I have been fond of writing poetry. My late father, fearing this would hinder my study of Confucian classics and history, often dissuaded me. So I stopped but still wrote poems secretly from time to time. After passing the imperial examination, I made friends with more and more celebrities and famous scholars from far and near and we often wrote poems to present or reply to each other. As time passed by, my file container became full of our writings. At the time when frequent national calamities were occurring, I initiated an anti-Qing movement in the east of Zhejiang. While preparing for the war, I found that nearly all my past poetry writings were lost. From then on, whether going out for military affairs or drafting imperial decrees in the court, I still wrote poems in my spare time to express my

干①，凡从前雕虫之技②，散亡③几尽矣。于是出筹④军旅⑤，入典⑥制诰⑦，尚得于余闲吟咏性情。及胡马渡江，而长篇短什⑧，与疏草⑨代言⑩，一切皆付之兵燹⑪中，是诚笔墨之不幸也。

余于丙戌⑫始浮海⑬，经今十有七年⑭矣。其间忧国思家，悲穷⑮悯⑯乱，无时无事不足以响动心脾⑰。或提师⑱北伐，慷慨长歌；或避虏⑲南征，寂寥⑳短唱。即当风雨飘摇㉑，波涛震荡㉒，愈能令孤

---

① 敹（liáo）甲敿（jiǎo）干：指做战斗的准备（prepare for fighting）。敹，缝（sew）。敹甲，把甲胄缝合起来（sew armour）。敿，系，连（tie）。干，盾牌（shield）。敿干，把盾牌上的绳子系好（tie the ropes on the shield）。
② 雕虫之技：指诗歌创作活动（referring to the poetry writing）。
③ 散亡：散失（be lost）。
④ 筹：筹划（prepare, plan）。
⑤ 军旅：军队（army troops）。
⑥ 入：入朝做官（to become an official in the imperial court）；典：主管（be in charge of sth.）。
⑦ 制诰：替皇帝起草诏令（draft imperial decrees for the king）。
⑧ 什（shí）：篇什（referring to poems and writings in general）。
⑨ 疏草：指自己给鲁王上书的底稿（drafts of memorials to the throne）。
⑩ 代言：指替鲁王起草的诏令（drafted decrees for the king）。
⑪ 兵燹（xiǎn）：战火（flames of war）。
⑫ 丙戌：清顺治三年（1646）。当时清兵占领浙东，鲁王奔台州，作者随后东行（in the third year of the Shunzhi Reign of the Qing Dynasty [1646] when the Qing troops occupied the eastern part of Zhejiang, King Lu rushed to Taizhou [today's Linhai County]; the author also went there afterwards）。
⑬ 浮海：泛海（floating on the sea）。
⑭ 十有七年：17年（for seventeen years）。
⑮ 穷：困厄，处境困难（difficult situation）。
⑯ 悯（mǐn）：忧虑（be worried）。
⑰ 响动心脾：触动内心（move one's heart）。
⑱ 提师：领兵（lead troops）。
⑲ 虏：指清兵（referring to the Qing troops）。
⑳ 寂寥：指心境的寂寞、抑郁（here meaning depressed, in low spirits）。
㉑ 风雨飘摇：喻动荡不安（figuratively meaning turbulent）。
㉒ 波涛震荡：喻局势动乱（figuratively meaning turmoil situation）。

thoughts and feelings. By the time the enemy crossed the Yangtze River, all my writings, long and short, drafts of memorials to the emperor and imperial edicts were lost in the flames of war. That is the real bad luck of writings.

Since the third year of the Shunzhi Reign (1646), I had been at sea for 17 years. During this period, I often worried about the fate of my country and the safety of my family, feeling saddened by the difficult circumstances and the turbulent situation which constantly made a great impact on me. When leading my troops on an expedition northward, in high and vigorous spirits I would compose long poems. However, while taking the troops southward to avoid the enemy's attack, I would feel depressed in spirit and write short ones. By doing so, I was able, amongst the political turmoil and maritime turbulence, to express my loyalty to the royal court and my affection towards my family. Do people think that my poetry is as pessimistic as the demoralized writings written for mourning a fallen nation or lamenting the miserable

臣恋主，游子怀亲。岂曰亡国之音①，庶几②哀世③之意。

乃丁亥④春，舟覆于江，而丙戌所作亡矣。戊子⑤秋，节移于山⑥，而丁亥所作亡矣。庚寅⑦夏，率旅复入于海⑧，而戊子、己丑所作又亡矣。然残编断简⑨，什存三四⑩。迨⑪辛卯⑫昌国⑬陷⑭，而笥⑮中草⑯竟靡有孑遗⑰。何笔墨之不幸，一至于此⑱哉。

---

① 亡国之音：反映国家危亡的音乐（music presaging the fallen state）。
② 庶几：几乎（almost）。
③ 哀世：哀叹世事（lament world affairs）。
④ 丁亥：清顺治四年（1647）四月，作者行军至崇明，大风覆舟，被俘，后乘机逃归（in the fourth year of the Shunzhi Reign [1647]. In April, when the author marched to Chongming, his boat was overturned by strong wind and he was captured; later he managed to escape）。
⑤ 戊子：清顺治五年（1648）（the fifth year of the Shunzhi Reign）。
⑥ 节移于山：主将移驻山上（chief commander moved onto a mountain）。节：符节，代指主将。是年作者到上虞招集义兵，入平冈山下寨（symbol standing for chief commander. That year the author went to Shangyu County and recruited soldiers for the establishment of a stronghold in Pinggang Mountain）。
⑦ 庚寅：清顺治七年（1650）（the seventh year of the Shunzhi Reign）。
⑧ 复入于海：这年鲁王驻舟山，作者率兵到舟山护卫（that year King Lu encamped in Zhoushan, Zhejiang. The author led his troop to Zhoushan to defend him）。
⑨ 残编断简：指残缺不全的文字（incomplete writings）。编、简：书籍（books）。
⑩ 什存三四：只有十分之三四留存（only three or four out of ten remain）。什：十（ten）。
⑪ 迨（dài）：等到（till）。
⑫ 辛卯：顺治八年（1651）（the eighth year of the Shunzhi Reign）。
⑬ 昌国：舟山（Zhoushan islands）。
⑭ 陷：失陷（fall into enemy hands）。
⑮ 笥（sì）：用竹编的装东西的方形器（square bamboo-plaited basket or suitcase）。
⑯ 草：草稿（drafts）。
⑰ 靡（mǐ）有孑（jié）遗：一个也没剩下（not a single one remained）。
⑱ 一至于此：竟到了这样的地步（unexpectedly to such a degree）。

world?

In spring of the 4th year of the Shunzhi Reign (1647), my boat capsized on the Yangtze River and all my manuscripts written in the previous year were lost. Then in autumn of the following year, I went with the chief commander to a station in a mountainous area and on the way lost what I had previously written. In summer of the 7th year of the Shunzhi Reign (1650), I led my troops to sail on the sea again. During the transference, all my writings of the previous two years went missing. On collecting my incomplete writings, only one-third of them still remained. One year later, Zhoushan Islands fell into enemy hands and my drafts stored in a bamboo case were all gone. Why did my writings have such misfortune?

After that I began to compile my old and new writings, and they gradually became a book. In the 13th year of the Shunzhi Reign (1656), the Kingdom of Chang was again conquered by the enemy and I lost one-third of my file. Two years later, my

嗣是①缀辑②新旧篇章，稍稍③成帙④，丙申⑤，昌国再陷，而亡什之三。戊戌⑥，覆舟于羊山⑦，而亡什之七。己亥，长江之役⑧，同仇⑨兵燹⑩，予以间行⑪得归，凡留供覆瓿⑫者，尽同石头书邮⑬，始知文字亦有阳九之厄⑭也。

年来叹天步⑮之未夷⑯，虑河清之难俟⑰，思借声诗⑱以代

---

① 嗣是：此后（after that）。
② 缀辑：编辑（compile, edit）。
③ 稍稍：渐渐（gradually）。
④ 帙（zhì）：卷册（volume）。
⑤ 丙申：清顺治十三年（1656）（the 13th year of the Shunzhi Reign）。
⑥ 戊戌：清顺治十五年（1658）（the 15th year of the Shunzhi Reign）。
⑦ 羊山：地名（name of a mountain north of Zhoushan, Zhejiang）。
⑧ 长江之役：这年夏作者会合郑成功的部队，再从长江西上攻镇江，直趋芜湖（in summer that year, the author, together with Zheng Chenggong's troop, moved westward along the Yangtze River to attack Zhenjiang, Jiangsu and then hastened to Wuhu, Anhui）。
⑨ 同仇：战友，这里指郑成功（battle companion, here referring to Zheng Chenggong）。
⑩ 兵燹（jiān）：兵败（defeated in the war）。
⑪ 间行：从小路走（walking on pathway）。
⑫ 覆瓿（bù）：盖罐子（covering a little jar）。瓿：小瓦罐（jar, pot）。
⑬ 石头书邮：石头是地名，在江西省新建县西北贡水西岸，又称石头渚。晋代殷羡曾为豫章太守，当他行至石头渚时，将朋友托他带回家的信全部投进水中。这里借指自己的全部文稿全部沉水（name of a place, also called Stone Islet, on the west shore of the Gongshui River northwest of Xinjian County in Jiangxi. During the Jin Dynasty, Yin Xian who was once the chief of Yuzhang Prefecture, on arriving at the Stone Islet, threw into the river all the letters which his friends had asked him to take to their homes. Here this allusion is borrowed to mean all his drafts sink into water）。
⑭ 阳九之厄：据说106年中要有灾荒9次，即所谓"百六阳九"（it's said that there are nine droughts in 106 years）。厄：灾难（disaster）。
⑮ 天步：国家的命运（fate of a country）。
⑯ 夷：平，安定（smooth）。
⑰ 河清之难俟：古人认为等待黄河澄清是不可能的（people in ancient times thought that it's impossible to wait for a clear Yellow River）。俟：等到（wait until）。
⑱ 声诗：古代诗歌多半能伴乐歌唱（many poems in ancient times could be sung accompanied with music）。

boat overturned near the Sheep Mountain and two-thirds of the collection of my poems vanished. In the following year, my battle companion was defeated in the battle on the Yangtze River but I managed to return home by a secret pathway. The manuscripts which could have been used for covering a pottery jar as its lid had all sunk to the bottom of the river. I began to know that writings, like human beings, were subject to calamities.

These years I have often sighed over the unsettled situation of my country and I know that to ease the social unrest would be as difficult as to turn the Yellow River into a clear river. I have been trying to make poetry perform the same function as a chronicle. Therefore I have asked my relatives and friends to give me what they have in their records. What's more, I have also collected from my guests' attendants what they can provide from their notebooks. One by one I write down what I have obtained from these two sources. Having a retentive mind, I recall what are still memorised and write them down on pieces of paper. Quite a

年谱。遂索友朋所录，宾从所抄，次第①之。而余性颇强记②，又忆其可忆者，载诸楮③端，共得若干首，不过如全鼎一脔④耳。独从前乐府歌行，不可复考⑤，故所订几若"广陵散⑥"。

嗟乎！国破家亡，余谬膺节钺⑦，既不能讨贼复仇，岂欲以有韵之词⑧，求知⑨于后世哉！但少陵⑩当天宝之乱⑪，流离蜀道，不废风骚⑫，

---

① 次第：编排次序（make up orders）。
② 强记：记忆力强（have a good memory）。
③ 楮（chǔ）：桑类的树，皮可制桑皮纸，因以代指纸（a kind of tree, belonging to the mulberry, can be used as the material of paper. Here referring to paper）。
④ 全鼎一脔（luán）：尝一脔肉而知一镬（huò）之味。这里意指他全部作品的一部分（by eating one piece of meat, you know the taste of the whole cooking vessel. Here meaning only part of all his writings）。
⑤ 考：查找，追忆（seek and recall）。
⑥ 广陵散：古曲名，晋代嵇康善弹此曲。后为司马昭所害，临刑前索琴弹之，曰："广陵散于今绝矣。"这里意指作者的部分诗歌像广陵散曲一样失去了（name of an old tune. Ji Kang of the Jin Dynasty was good at playing it. When put to death by Sima Zhao, he asked for a *qin* to play, saying, "The tune of Guangling no longer exists from now on." Here meaning part of the author's poems were lost like the Tune of Guangling）。
⑦ 谬膺节钺（yuè）：谦说自己受任为军事统帅（a modest way of saying "I have been appointed the commander of the army"）。膺：受（receive）。节：符节（commander's seal and tally）。钺：古时的斧头（a battle-axe used in ancient China）。任命大将时，皇帝给受任者象征权力的符节和斧钺（When appointing someone commander, the emperor gives him a seal and a battle-axe symbolizing power）。
⑧ 有韵之词：押韵的作品（rhymed verse）。
⑨ 求知：求得了解（make oneself understand）。
⑩ 少陵：杜甫（Du Fu）。
⑪ 天宝之乱：指唐玄宗天宝十四年（755）安禄山发动的叛乱（a rebellion initiated by An Lushan in the 14th year of the Tianbao Reign of Emperor Xuanzong in the Tang Dynasty）。
⑫ 不废风骚：没有停止诗歌创作（did not stop writing poems）。

few poems have been collected but all these are just like a piece of meat picked up from a stewpot. The only thing that cannot be traced are folk songs and ballads. To collect these would be as hard as to collect the no longer existing Tune of Guangling.

Oh! My country has fallen and my family has shattered but I have been wrongly appointed to be the military commander. Do I still dream of making myself famous for my poetry to later generations when I am unable to take revenge on the enemy and defeat them? Nearly 1000 years ago during the Tang Dynasty, Du Shaoling (Du Fu) did not cease to give full play to his talent for poetry writing when he was forced to leave home and wander about in Sichuan Province to avoid the rebellion headed by An Lushan. What he wrote has been labeled as historical poetry ever since. About 400 years before that, during the Jin Dynasty, Tao Jingjie (Tao Yuanming), having experienced the disasters of war, resigned from office. He never stopped writing while leading an idyllic life. Whatever he wrote, he would date it with the reign

后世至今，名为诗史。陶靖节①躬②丁③晋乱，解组④归来，著书必题义熙⑤。宋室既亡，郑所南⑥尚以铁匣投史⑦窑井⑧，至三百年而后出。夫亦其志⑨可哀，其情诚可念⑩也已。然则何以⑪名《奇零草》？是帙零落凋⑫亡，已非全豹⑬，譬犹兵家握奇⑭之余，亦云余行间⑮之作也。

时在永历十六年⑯，岁在壬寅端阳⑰后五日，张煌言自识⑱。

① 陶靖节：陶渊明（Tao Yuanming）。
② 躬：亲身（personally）。
③ 丁：当，遇（meet with; run into）。
④ 解组：解去系在身上的印带，指辞官（untie one's seal and its ribbon from one's body. Here meaning resigning from one's office）。
⑤ 义熙：晋安帝年号。相传陶渊明不肯臣服于刘裕，所以在作品中保存晋帝年号（the reign title of Emperor Andi of the Jin Dynasty. Tao Yuanming was said to refuse to submit to the rule of Liu Yu and kept using in his works the reign title of the emperor whom he used to serve during the Jin Dynasty）。
⑥ 郑所南：南宋诗人、画家（a poet and painter of the Southern Song Dynasty）。
⑦ 铁匣投史：宋亡后，郑所南隐居乡间，著诗文集《心史》，装在铁匣里，投在枯井中，到明末才被发现，世称"铁函心史"（after the downfall of the Song Dynasty, Zheng Suonan retired to the countryside where he composed an anthology entitled *The History of Heart*; he put it in an iron box and threw the box into a dried well. The iron box was not discovered until the end of the Ming Dynasty, and it has been called by later generations "The History of Heart in an Iron Box"）。
⑧ 窑（yuān）井：枯井（dried well）。
⑨ 志：心志（will）。
⑩ 念：思念（long for）。
⑪ 何以：因何，为什么（why）。
⑫ 凋：草木枯败，这里比喻作品散失（grasses and trees wither. Here figuratively meaning the loss of writings）。
⑬ 全豹：全体（the whole picture）。
⑭ 握奇：即《握奇经》，古代的一部兵书（a book on the art of war）。
⑮ 行（háng）间：军旅之间（intervals between battles）。
⑯ 永历十六年：清康熙元年（1662）（the first year of the Kangxi Reign of the Qing Dynasty）。永历：明桂王朱由榔建国年号（the reign title of King Gui of the Ming Dynasty）。
⑰ 端阳：端午节（the Dragon Boat Festival — the 5th day of the 5th lunar month）。
⑱ 识：志（make notes, record）。

title of Yixi to express his loyalty to the emperor whom he used to serve. Zheng Suonan placed, in an iron box, a collection of his poems which he had written while leading a secluded life after the fall of the Song Dynasty. He dropped the iron box into a dry well and it appeared 300 years later. It was sad that he had to do so but his aspirations have roused our admiration. Why did I use the words "Sparse Withered Grass" as the title of my book? I want to tell readers that it is an incomplete collection since so many poems and essays have scattered and disappeared during the chaotic wartime. I also intend to present a wartime literature containing most of my writings written in the intervals between battles.

Zhang Huangyan himself made this note on the 10th day of the 5th month in the 16th year of the Yongli Reign (1662).

狱中上母书

夏完淳

不孝①完淳今日死矣,以身殉父,不得以身报母矣。

痛自严君②见背③,两易春秋④,冤酷⑤日深,艰辛历⑥尽。本图⑦复见天日⑧,以报大仇,恤死⑨荣生,告成黄土⑩;奈⑪天不佑⑫我,钟⑬虐⑭先朝⑮,一旅⑯才兴⑰,便成齑粉⑱。去年之

---

① 不孝:儿女对父母的自称(a term which is often used by a son or a daughter to humbly call himself or herself while addressing his or her parents)。
② 严君:对父亲的敬称(respectful form of address for someone to call his father)。
③ 见背:去世(die)。
④ 两易春秋:即过了两年(two years passed)。
⑤ 酷:惨痛(deeply grieved, bitter)。
⑥ 历:经历(undergo, experience)。
⑦ 图:图谋(plot, scheme)。
⑧ 复见天日:指恢复明朝(return to the Ming Dynasty)。
⑨ 恤死:使死去的人得到安慰(comfort the dead)。
⑩ 告成黄土:向九泉之下的父亲报告我们的成功(report our success to my father in the tomb / the nether world)。黄土:坟墓(grave, tomb)。
⑪ 奈:无奈(cannot help but; have no choice but)。
⑫ 佑:帮助(help)。
⑬ 钟:聚集(gather)。
⑭ 虐:灾祸(disaster, calamity)。
⑮ 先朝:指明朝(referring to the Ming Dynasty)。
⑯ 一旅:古代兵制,五百人为一旅(the organisational system in the olden days: 500 soldiers make up a brigade)。
⑰ 兴:起(rise)。
⑱ 齑(jī)粉:碎屑,粉末。这里比喻崩溃(powder; here figuratively meaning breakdown)。

A LETTER WRITTEN IN JAIL TO MY MOTHER

Xia Wanchun

Your son, Wanchun, will die today. I will sacrifice my life for my father and I do not have anything left to repay to you, Mother.

Two years have elapsed since Father passed away. I have experienced all kinds of hardships in my life, with hatred and sorrow deepening in my heart day by day. Originally I attempted to regain freedom so that I would be able to take a great revenge in order to comfort the dead, bring honor to the living and report our success to my father in the tomb. Unfortunately, Heaven did not help me. Disasters were heaped upon the previous dynasty. No sooner had a troop been organised than it was broken down. Last year, while defeated in the launching of an armed revolt, I thought that I was certain to die. Who knows why I did not die that time but I will die today. Though my life has been prolonged

举①,淳已自分②必死,谁知不死③,死于今日也。斤斤④延此二年之命,菽水之养⑤无一日焉。致慈君⑥托迹于空门⑦,生母⑧寄生⑨于别姓,一门漂泊,生不得相依,死不得相闻;淳今日又溘然⑩先从⑪九京⑫:不孝之罪,上通于天⑬。

呜呼!双慈⑭在堂,下有妹女,门祚⑮衰薄,终鲜⑯兄弟。淳一死不足惜,哀哀⑰八口,何以为生?虽然,已矣⑱!淳之身,父之所遗;淳之身,君之所用。为父为君,死亦何负⑲于双慈!但慈君推干

---

① 去年之举:指 1646 年起兵抗清失败事(referring to his defeat when launching an armed revolt against the Qing troops in 1646)。
② 分:料想(expect)。
③ 不死:指当年没有死(referring to not die that year)。
④ 斤斤:仅仅(only)。
⑤ 菽(shū)水之养:贫家对父母的供养(a poor family provides for their parents)。菽:豆(beans)。
⑥ 慈君:指作者的嫡母盛氏(referring to the author's legal mother whose family name is Sheng)。
⑦ 托迹于空门:做了尼姑(be a Buddhist nun)。托迹:藏身(hide oneself)。空门:佛门,佛寺(Buddhist temple)。
⑧ 生母:指作者的生母陆氏,其父夏允彝之妾(referring to the author's own mother named Lu, his father's concubine)。
⑨ 寄生:寄居(live away from home)。
⑩ 溘(kè)然:忽然(all of a sudden)。
⑪ 从:追随(follow)。
⑫ 九京:亦称"九原",指墓地(referring to a graveyard)。
⑬ 上通于天:连上天都知道了(even known to Heaven)。
⑭ 双慈:指嫡母和生母(referring to his legal mother and own mother)。
⑮ 门祚:家门的福分(good fortune of one's own family)。
⑯ 鲜:少,这里指没有(few, here meaning no)。
⑰ 哀哀:可怜的样子(pitiful manner)。
⑱ 虽然,已矣:尽管如此,那也只好算了(even so, leave it at that)。
⑲ 负:对不起(let sb. down; be unworthy of)。

by two years, I have failed to fulfill my duty to look after you even for one day. Because of my negligence, my legal mother became a Buddhist nun and my own mother had to live away from home. Our whole family has been leading a wandering life and we cannot rely on each other when we are alive nor can we ask about each other after death. Suddenly I have to go to the graveyard, carrying my sin of filial impiety known to Heaven.

Alas! My two mothers are still in good health and I have a younger sister and a daughter at home but our family has been so unlucky that I do not have any male sibling. I will die without any regrets for myself but I am worried about the eight helpless people of our family — How will you make a living after my death? Even so, leave it at that! My life was given to me by my father but it belongs to the monarch. To die for my father and the monarch, I will not let you down, my two mothers! Over the past fifteen years, my respected legal mother has always given me every attention and taught me how to learn Confucian classics and poetry. Tremendous kindness like this is rare to be seen in the world.

就湿①,教礼习诗,十五年如一日。嫡母慈惠,千古所难②,大恩未酬③,令人痛绝。——慈君托之义融女兄④,生母托之昭南女弟⑤。

淳死之后,新妇⑥遗腹⑦得雄⑧,便以为家门之幸。如其不然,万勿置后⑨!会稽大望⑩,至今而零极⑪矣!节义文章如我父子者几人哉?立一不肖⑫后如西铭先生⑬,为人所诟笑⑭,何如不立之为愈⑮耶!呜呼!大造⑯茫茫⑰,总归无后。有一日中兴再造⑱,则庙

---

① 推干就湿:把床上干处让给幼儿,自己睡在湿处。指母亲养育子女的辛劳(when the bed gets wet, the mother places her baby on the dry spot while she herself sleeps on the wet side. That is referring to a mother's pains in bringing up her children)。
② 难:罕见(seldom seen)。
③ 酬:报答(repay)。
④ 义融女兄:作者的姐姐夏淑吉,字美南,号荆隐。义融当是她又一名字(the author's elder sister Xia Shuji, styled Meinan, alternatively named Jingyin. Yirong is another name for her)。
⑤ 昭南女弟:作者的妹妹夏惠吉,字昭南,号兰隐(the author's younger sister Xia Huiji, styled Zhaonan, alternatively named Lanyin)。
⑥ 新妇:作者结婚两年的妻子钱秦篆(the author's wife Qian Qinzhuan, who married him two years ago)。
⑦ 遗腹:即遗腹子(posthumous child)。
⑧ 雄:男孩(boy)。
⑨ 置后:抱养别人的孩子为后嗣(adopt a child to act as one's descendant)。
⑩ 会稽大望:会稽郡的大族。这里即指夏姓大族。会稽:郡名,作者的故乡松江县属会稽郡(a big family in Kuaiji Prefecture; here referring to the big family named Xia. The author's hometown Songjiang County belonged to Kuaiji Prefecture)。
⑪ 零极:零落衰败到极点(extremely decayed)。
⑫ 不肖:品行不好(unworthy, worthless)。
⑬ 西铭先生:张溥,别号西铭,生前无子,死后由钱谦益代为立嗣,名永锡(Zhang Pu, alternatively named Ximing, having no son during his lifetime; after his death, an heir named Yongxi was appointed to him, arranged by Qian Qianyi)。
⑭ 诟笑:诟骂,耻笑(abuse and sneer)。
⑮ 愈:好(good)。
⑯ 大造:造化,指天(the Creator, Nature)。
⑰ 茫茫:不明(boundless and indistinct)。
⑱ 中兴再造:指明朝恢复(referring to the recovery of the Ming Dynasty)。中兴:衰而复兴(reviving, coming back to activity)。再造:重新创造(create again)。

Being unable to repay your kindness has made me feel great pain. Now I have to entrust you, my legal mother, to my elder sister Yirong and my own mother to my younger sister Zhaonan.

If, after my death, my pregnant wife gives birth to a son, it will bring good fortune to our family. If this is not the case, never adopt a boy to be my descendant. A prominent family in Kuaiji Prefecture has now gone into decline. How many fathers and sons can maintain moral integrity as my father and myself did? If I, like Mr. Ximing, adopted an unworthy son and consequently we were sneered at by others, it would be better not to adopt any one. Alas! The universe is boundless and it is impossible to eternally keep the family line alive. If one day our dynasty is restored, we will be able to enjoy sacrifices in our ancestral temples for thousands of years. We will be served very well there, not like hungry ghosts being fed only with wheaten rice and pig's feet. If there is one who dares to talk nonsense about adopting heirs, I will from the nether world, together with my father, whose posthumous title is Wenzhong, kill that stupid and stubborn person and never forgive him.

食①千秋，岂止麦饭②豚蹄③，不为馁鬼④而已哉！若有妄言⑤立后者，淳且与先文忠⑥在冥冥诛殛⑦顽嚚⑧，决不肯舍！

兵戈天地⑨，淳死后，乱且未有定期⑩。双慈善保玉体⑪，无以淳为念。二十年后，淳且与先文忠为北塞之举⑫矣！勿悲勿悲！相托之言，慎勿⑬相负！武功甥⑭将来大器⑮，家事尽以委⑯之。寒食⑰盂兰⑱，一杯清酒，一盏寒灯，不至作若敖之鬼⑲，则吾愿毕矣！

① 庙食：指鬼神在祠庙里享受祭祀（referring to ghosts and gods enjoying sacrifice in ancestral temples）。
② 麦饭：磨麦连皮做成的面食（cooked wheaten food with its skin）。
③ 豚蹄：猪蹄（pig's feet）。
④ 馁鬼：饿鬼（hungry ghost）。
⑤ 妄言：乱说（talk nonsense）。
⑥ 先文忠：作者的父亲夏允彝死后，谥号文忠（the posthumous title of the author's father Xia Yunyi was Wenzhong）。
⑦ 诛殛（jí）：杀死（kill）。
⑧ 顽嚚（yín）：愚顽之人（an ignorant and stubborn man）。
⑨ 兵戈天地：遍地战乱（chaos everywhere caused by war）。
⑩ 定期：终止的时候（time to stop）。
⑪ 玉体：身体，敬词（body, a respectful word）。
⑫ 北塞之举：出师北伐，将清人赶出北方的边界（lead a troop to drive the Qing invaders out from the northern border）。
⑬ 慎勿：千万不要（be sure not to）。
⑭ 武功甥：作者姐姐夏淑吉的儿子侯檠（qíng），字武功（son of the author's elder sister Xia Shuji, who styled himself Wugong）。
⑮ 大器：大材（a great talent）。
⑯ 委：托付（entrust）。
⑰ 寒食：节名，冬至后105天。古时从这天起三天内不生火做饭，所以叫寒食（name of a festival, the 105th day after the Winter Solstice. In olden days, from that day on, people would not make a fire to cook for three days）。
⑱ 盂兰：即盂兰盆会或节，佛教的鬼节（the Buddhist name for the Ghost Festival, on the 15th day of the seventh lunar month）。
⑲ 若敖之鬼：没有后代的饿鬼。若敖为楚国一大氏族名，后被灭（hungry ghosts without descendants. Ruoao was the name of a big family from the State of Chu, later destroyed）。

Now everywhere is in chaos caused by the war and it will be hard to predict when the war will cease after my death. My two mothers, please take good care of yourselves and do not worry about me. In twenty years, I will, together with my father, lead a troop to drive the invaders out of the northern border! Do not cry, do not be sad! Be sure not to forget what I said! My nephew Wugong is a great future talent and he is the right person to be designated to take care of all our family affairs. If, on the Cold-Food Festival and the Ghost Festival I am served a cup of good wine, lit by a dim lantern, so that I will not become a hungry ghost, I will be quite satisfied!

My wife has been married to me for two years and she has

新妇结褵①二年，贤孝素著②。武功甥好为我善待之，亦武功渭阳情③也。语无伦次④，将死言善⑤，痛哉痛哉！

人生孰无死？贵得死所⑥耳！父得为忠臣，子得为孝子。含笑归太虚⑦，了我分内事。大道本无生⑧，视身若敝屣⑨。但⑩为气⑪所激⑫，缘⑬悟天人理⑭。恶梦十七年，报仇在来世。神游天地间，可以无愧矣！

① 结褵（lí）：女子出嫁。褵是古代女子的佩巾，出嫁时由母亲亲自为她结褵（in ancient times when a girl got married, her mother would tie a kind of kerchief for her）。
② 素著：一向是很显著的（always remarkable）。
③ 渭阳情：甥舅之间的情谊。春秋时晋国公子重耳曾在秦国避难。他是秦太子的舅舅。后来秦王帮助重耳回国为君，太子送他到渭水之阳，并作诗赠别（friendship between a nephew and his uncle. During the Spring and Autumn Period, the prince of the State of Jin named Chong'er once took refuge in the State of Qin. He was the brother of the crown prince's mother of the State of Qin. Later when the king of Qin helped Chonger to return to his motherland, the crown prince saw him off to the north of the Wei River and presented him with a poem at departure）。
④ 语无伦次：说话没有条理次序（ramble in one's statement）。
⑤ 将死言善：人快死的时候，他所说的话是善意的（when a man is dying, what he says is out of goodwill）。
⑥ 得死所：即死得其所（die a worthy death）。
⑦ 归太虚：归天或回到天堂（pass away, return to heaven）。
⑧ 大道本无生：按道家的说法，人从无而生，死后又归于无（as Taoists say, a man is born out of nil and will return to nil after death）。
⑨ 敝屣（xǐ）：破鞋子（worn-out shoes）。
⑩ 但：只（only）。
⑪ 气：刚正之气（moral integrity）。
⑫ 激：激发（arouse, stimulate）。
⑬ 缘：因（because of, as a result of）。
⑭ 天人理：天意与人事的道理（truth about God's will and human affairs）。

been remarkably virtuous and filial. If Wugong can take good care of her for me, he can be praised as a good nephew like the Crown Prince of the State of Qin (a historical personage of the Spring and Autumn Period). Although my statement is rambling, the words of a dying man are sincere. How painful it is! Really painful! Who will not die? It's a valuable death if a man dies for a worthy cause! As a father, my father was a royal official faithful to the imperial court. As a son, I am a devoted off-spring filial to my parents. Having finished my duty, I will go to Heaven with a smile. According to an ancient philosophy, nothing has ever existed in the world, so a human body can be belittled as a pair of shoes. Inspired by the unyielding integrity coming from the past, l have come to realize God's will and human behavior. It is like a nightmare when I recall the seventeen years I have spent. I will take revenge in my next life. No regrets will remain in my heart when I travel up to Heaven and back down to earth.

原　君

黄宗羲

有生①之初，人各自私②也，人各自利③也；天下有公利而莫或④兴之，有公害而莫或除之。有人者出⑤，不以一己之利为利，而使天下受其利；不以一己之害为害，而使天下释⑥其害；此其人之勤劳必千万于天下之人。夫以千万倍之勤劳，而己又不享其利，必非天下之人情所欲居⑦也。故古之人君，量⑧而不欲入⑨者，许由、务光⑩是也；入而又去之者⑪，尧、舜是也；初不欲入而不得去者，

---

① 有生：有生命，指有人类（when life or mankind began）。
② 自私：只管自己（only think of oneself）。
③ 自利：同"自私"（same as 自私）。
④ 莫或：没有什么人（no one）。
⑤ 有人者出：有这么一个人出来（there comes one）。
⑥ 释：免除（weed out）。
⑦ 居：居其位，处于那个地位，引申为接受（hold that post, meaning by extension: accept）。
⑧ 量：考虑（think over, consider）。
⑨ 入：就其位，即为君（hold that post, i.e. be the monarch）。
⑩ 许由、务光：传说中的高士。唐尧让天下于许由，许由认为是对自己的侮辱，就隐居箕山中。商汤让天下于务光，务光负石投水而死（men of noble character from legend. When Tang Yao handed over the crown to Xu You, Xu regarded it as an insult and retired into Mount Ji. When Shang Tang handed over the crown to Wu Guang, he committed suicide by carrying a big stone to drown himself in a river）。
⑪ 入而又去之者：尧以天下禅舜，舜以天下禅禹，所以说去之。（Yao handed over his crown to Shun and Shun handed his crown to Yu, so they gave up their posts）。去：放弃（give up）。

ON THE OBLIGATION OF MONARCHS

Huang Zongxi

When mankind came into being, everybody was selfish, caring only about himself and paying attention only to his own interests. There was nobody in the world who would do something good toward the public cause and no one would step forward to get rid of public nuisances. Then, an unusual man emerged. He did not regard his own interests as something he should enjoy for himself, whereas he allowed all other people to benefit from him. He did not regard his own sufferings as something that tortured only him and he was willing to relieve all other people of these sufferings. The effort he made must have been one-hundred times more than that of other people. His effort was so great but he did not grab anything for his own enjoyment. This was not what other people wanted to do. Therefore in ancient times, there were different attitudes towards the obligation of being a monarch. Xu You and Wu Guang, after careful consideration, did not want to take the throne while Yao and Shun first took the throne and then gave it up. Different from them, Da Yu at first rejected the offer but later he had to take it up. Were ancient people different

禹是也。岂古之人有所异哉？好逸恶劳，亦犹夫①人之情也。

后之为人君者不然。以为天下利害之权皆出于我，我以天下之利尽归于己，以天下之害尽归于人，亦无不可；使天下之人，不敢自私，不敢自利，以我之大私为天下之大公。始而惭焉，久而安焉。视天下为莫大之产业，传之子孙，受享无穷；汉高帝所谓"某业所就，孰与仲多②"者，其逐利之情，不觉溢之于辞③矣。

此无他，古者以天下为主，君为客，凡君之所毕世④而经营者，为天下也。今也以君为主，天下为客，凡天下之无地而得安宁者，为君也。是以其未得之也，屠毒天下之肝脑⑤，离散天下之子女，以博⑥我一人之产业，曾⑦不惨然。曰："我固为子孙创业也。"其既得之也，敲剥天下之骨髓，离散天下之子女，以奉⑧我一人之淫乐，视为当然。曰："此我产业之花息⑨也。"然则，为天下之大

---

① 犹夫：好似（be like）。
② 某业所就，孰与仲多：汉高祖刘邦登帝位后，曾对其父说："始大人常以臣无赖，不能治产业，不如仲（其兄刘仲）力，今某之业所就，孰与仲多？"（the founder of the Han Dynasty Liu Bang once said to his father after he came to power: "You often regarded me as a rascal because I could not manage property and could not do better than Zhong. Now compare what I am engaged in with Zhong, whose is more？"）
③ 溢之于辞：流露在言语里（revealing in his words）。
④ 毕世：一辈子（all one's life）。
⑤ 屠毒天下之肝脑：为自己争夺帝位，不惜使天下人民肝脑涂地，悲惨地死去（to scramble for one's throne, one forces the people all over the country to dash their brains out on the ground and die the cruelest death）。屠毒：宰割毒害（cut up and poison）。
⑥ 博：求得，换取（gain, get in return）。
⑦ 曾：竟然（go so far as to）。
⑧ 奉：供（supply for）。
⑨ 花息：利息（interest）。

from people of our time? No, this is not the case. It is human nature that they also loved ease and comfort but hated to work.

Monarchs of later generations were not like that. They thought that they had the power to decide who should enjoy the benefits and who should suffer the troubles. They never felt guilty for grabbing all the good things for themselves and making other people have the bad ones. Under their rule, nobody in the whole nation dared to be self-centred, to care about only his own interests or to blend his own major interests with the public ones. In the beginning, the monarchs felt a little ashamed of themselves for doing so. Not long afterwards, they started to take this for granted. They felt at ease in regarding the whole nation as their own property and to pass it down to their descendants from generation to generation. Emperor Gao of the Han Dynasty once said to his father: "Compared with my second brother, have I engendered greater achievement of property than he?" He did not realize that his aspiration for personal gain was revealed through his words.

There was only one reason for this. In ancient times, monarchs saw the nation as the principal factor and themselves as the subordinate. Therefore, they believed that when they were on the throne whatever they did was for the whole nation. However, nowadays a monarch always regards himself as the owner of the nation. Because of him, no peaceful land has ever existed on earth. Before seizing the state power, in order to gain something for

害者，君而已矣，向使①无君，人各得自私也，人各得自利也。呜呼！岂设君之道②固如是乎？

古者天下之人爱戴其君，比之如父，拟之如天，诚不为过也。今也天下之人怨恶其君，视之如寇雠③，名之为独夫④，固其所也⑤。而小儒⑥规规焉⑦以⑧君臣之义⑨无所逃于天地之间，至桀⑩、纣⑪之暴，犹谓汤、武不当诛之，而妄传伯夷、叔齐无稽之事⑫，乃兆人万姓⑬崩溃之血肉，曾不异夫腐鼠⑭。岂天地之大，于兆人万姓之

---

① 向使：当初假使（if at the beginning）。
② 设君之道：设立君主的道理（the reason for setting up a monarch）。
③ 寇雠（chóu）：强盗，仇敌（robber, foe）。
④ 名之为独夫：称他为独夫（call him a tyrant spurned by the people）。
⑤ 固其所也：原是应得的结果（well-deserved result）。
⑥ 小儒：眼光狭小的读书人（narrow-sighted scholar）。
⑦ 规规焉：拘谨地，死板地（overcautious, inflexible）。
⑧ 以：认为（think, hold）。
⑨ 君臣之义：君与臣之间的伦理关系（moral relationship between a monarch and his subjects）。
⑩ 桀（jié）：夏朝最后一位国君，以残暴著名（the name of the last ruler of the Xia Dynasty, traditionally considered as a tyrant）。
⑪ 纣（zhòu）：商朝最后一位统治者，暴君（the last ruler of the Shang Dynasty, a tyrant too）。
⑫ 伯夷、叔齐无稽之事：伯夷、叔齐是商朝的二位王子。武王伐纣时，伯夷、叔齐曾拦住他的马头，极力劝阻，认为臣不能伐君。商亡以后，他们不食周粟，饿死于首阳山（Boyi and Shuqi were two princes of the Shang Dynasty. When King Wu of the Zhou Dynasty attacked King Zhou of the Shang Dynasty, they held back his horse's head and tried hard to dissuade him from attacking, thinking that a subject should not attack his monarch. After the Shang Dynasty fell, they did not eat food from Zhou and died of hunger in the Shouyang Mountain）。无稽：无从查考（cannot be ascertained）。
⑬ 兆人万姓：千千万万的老百姓（thousands on thousands of common people）。
⑭ 腐鼠：腐烂的死鼠，比喻毫无价值的东西（rot mouse, figuratively referring to a thing of no worth）。

himself, he tragically manipulated the people to die for him and thus tearing families apart. He did not feel sorry for this and said: "I have been doing so to establish an undertaking for my children and grandchildren." Having conquered the country, he began to exploit the people like a bloodsucker, causing families to be separated and scattered so that he could lead a life of luxury and debauchery. He never felt ashamed for doing so and said: "I am enjoying the interests coming from my property." So we can say that the monarch has been the source of the greatest disasters. If from the very beginning monarchs had never existed, the people might have been able to care for themselves and protect their own interests. Alas! Was this the ancient idea of having a monarch to rule the people?

In ancient times, the people of the whole nation adored their monarch so much that it is not an overstatement to say that they loved him as much as they did to their fathers and they respected him as much as they did to Heaven. Nowadays the people hate their monarch. They see him as their enemy and call him "tyrant." This is currently the monarch's well-deserved treatment. However some dogmatic scholars, adhering to the old doctrine, hold that the relationship between a monarch and his ministers (such as: the monarch treats his ministers with propriety, so the ministers serve the monarch with loyalty) has for ever existed under heaven and cannot be avoided. In their mind, though King Jie and King Zhou were cruel and heartless, they should not have been killed

中，独私①其一人一姓乎！是故武王圣人也，孟子之言，圣人之言也；后世之君，欲以如父如天之空名，禁人之窥伺②者，皆不便于其言③，至废孟子④而不立，非导源于小儒乎？

虽然，使⑤后之为君者，果能保此产业，传之无穷，亦无怪乎其私之⑥也。既以产业视之，人之欲得产业，谁不如我？摄缄滕，固扃鐍⑦，一人之智力，不能胜天下欲得之者之众，远者数世，近者及身，其血肉之崩溃在其子孙矣。昔人⑧愿世世无生帝王家，而

---

① 私：偏爱（be partial to, love one more than another）。
② 窥伺：暗中找机会夺取君位（secretly try to find a chance to seize the throne）。
③ 不便于其言："其言"即前文"孟子之言"——"民为贵，社稷次之，君为轻"。感到他的话对自己不利（regarding Mencius' words as disadvantageous to him as the sage said: "The people occupy the noblest place, the state comes second and the monarch last"）。
④ 废孟子：明太祖曾一度下诏废除祭祀孟子（the founder of the Ming Dynasty issued an order to cease the offering of sacrifices to Mencius）。
⑤ 使：如果（if）。
⑥ 私之：据天下为己有（take land under heaven as one's own）。
⑦ 摄缄（jiān）滕（téng），固扃（jiōng）鐍（jué）：紧紧地捆好，牢牢地锁好（bind it tight and lock it fast）。摄：收紧（tighten up）。缄：封固（close）。滕：绳子（rope）。扃：关钮（a bolt or hook for fastening a door）。鐍：锁钥（lock）。
⑧ 昔人：指南朝宋顺帝，被逼出宫讲了这番话（referring to Emperor Shun of the Song Dynasty, one of the four dynasties of the Southern Dynasties, who said so when forced to go out from his palace）。

by Tang (founder of the Shang Dynasty) and Ji Fa (founder of the Zhou Dynasty). These scholars also fabricated the unascertainable story of Boyi and Shuqi (two princes of the Shang Dynasty who tried to dissuade Ji Fa from launching a military attack on their father — King Zhou). In the eyes of these scholars, there was no difference between the flesh and blood of thousands upon thousands of sacrificed ordinary people and the rotten dead bodies of rats. Among the millions upon millions of people on earth, is the monarch the only favorite of God? If this was not the case, then Ji Fa could be regarded as a sage and the saying of Mencius (372 BC – 289 BC) was what a sage uttered. Monarchs from later generations have continuously attempted to use their empty title of "Father" or "Heaven" to forbid others from secretly trying to find an opportunity to seize their thrones. Finding Mencius' saying so disadvantageous to them, they issued instructions to abandon the practice of worshiping Mencius. Did not this wrongdoing come from the ridiculous idea of the dogmatic scholars?

If monarchs in later generations could successfully keep their own properties and pass them on from generation to generation, it is not hard to understand why they considered the properties as their own. Since they regarded the throne as their own property, it is natural for them to suspect that other people had as much desire as they for the throne. Therefore, they bound it tight and locked it fast. However, a single man's wit was outnumbered by the

毅宗①之语公主②，亦曰："若何为生我家！"痛哉斯言！回思创业时，其欲得天下之心，有不废然③摧沮④者乎！

是故明乎为君之职分，则唐、虞之世，人人能让，许由、务光非绝尘⑤也；不明乎为君之职分，则市井之间，人人可欲，许由、务光所以旷⑥后世而不闻也。然君之职分难明，以俄顷淫乐⑦不易无穷之悲，虽愚者亦明之矣。

---

① 毅宗：即明朝崇祯皇帝朱由检（Emperor Chongzhen of the Ming Dynasty, Zhu Youjian; he was called Sizong by the Southern Ming Dynasty, later it was changed to Yizong）。
② 公主：指崇祯之女长平公主。李自成进京，崇祯自缢前，用剑砍自己女儿，叹息说："你为什么生在我家？"（referring to Princess Changping, Emperor Chongzhen's daughter. When Li Zicheng entered Beijing, before Chongzhen hanged himself, he cut his daughter with a sword, sighing: "Why were you born to my family?"）
③ 废然：颓丧的样子（in the dumps）。
④ 摧沮：灰心气馁（lose heart, become dejected）。
⑤ 绝尘：超绝尘世，高出一切世上的人（extraordinary）。
⑥ 旷：空，绝（never occur again）。
⑦ 俄顷淫乐：片刻的荒淫行乐（indulge in a moment of pleasure）。

ambition of all those people under heaven who wished to seize the throne. This situation would occur, at most, several generations later but sometimes it would happen as early as the time when the monarch was still on the throne. Most of the time, the descendants of a monarch incurred the consequences and died tragically amid the bloodshed of many other people. While being expelled from his palace, Emperor Shun of Song in the Southern Dynasties said that he wished that in later generations no one would be born to a royal family. Before trying to kill Princess Changping with a sword and then hanging himself, Emperor Chongzhen said to his daughter, "Why were you born into my family?" How sad was this remark! Looking back to the old days when the undertaking was being established, was the monarch's ambition to seize the state power mingled with downheartedness and frustration?

Only in the era of Tang Yao and Yu Shun, was everyone who had the opportunity to become a monarch willing to give up his chance to somebody better qualified. Xu You and Wu Guang were not immortals. They also lived in the human world where, without understanding the duty of a monarch, even ordinary people could have an ambition for the throne. Therefore people without ambition, like Xu You and Wu Guang have never since their era come into being. Even without the knowledge of the duty of a monarch a fool could see clearly that it was not worthwhile to enjoy one moment's luxurious pleasure at the cost of suffering endless disasters afterwards.

芙蕖（节选）

李渔

芙蕖①之可人②，其事不一而足，请备③述之。

群葩④当令⑤时，只在花开之数日，前此后此皆在过⑥而不问⑦之秋⑧矣。芙蕖则不然⑨：自荷钱⑩出水之日，便为点缀⑪绿波；及其茎⑫叶既生，则又日高日上⑬，日上日妍⑭。有风既作飘摇⑮之态，无风亦呈袅娜⑯之姿，是我于花之未开，先享无穷逸致⑰矣。迨

---

① 芙蕖：即荷花，又名莲花，芙蓉（lotus）。
② 可人：合人心意（satisfactory; satisfying）。
③ 备：全，尽（all, fully）。
④ 群葩：百花（all the flowers）。
⑤ 当令：合乎时节（in season）。
⑥ 过：过时，不当令（not in season）。
⑦ 不问：无人问及（no one asks about it）。
⑧ 秋：时候（time）。
⑨ 然：如此（like this）。
⑩ 荷钱：初生的荷叶，小如铜钱（newborn lotus leaf, the size of a coin）。
⑪ 点缀：装饰，点涂（embellish）。
⑫ 茎：指荷梗（stem）。
⑬ 日高日上：一天天高起来，一天天往上长（keep growing upwards and become taller and taller day by day）。
⑭ 妍：美（beautiful）。
⑮ 飘摇：飘拂摇曳（drift about in the wind; sway; shake; totter）。
⑯ 袅娜：细长柔美的样子（slender and graceful; willowy）。
⑰ 逸致：悠闲的情趣（a leisurely, carefree mood）。

LOTUS (EXCERPTS)

Li Yu

Lotus endears itself to us in many ways. Let me tell you in detail.

Other flowers attract people's attention for several days only when they are in blossom. Before or after these days, they are unnoticed as they are not in season. Lotus is different: from the time its coin-like, newborn leaves emerge from the water, it starts to embellish the green water; when its stems and leaves grow, it becomes taller and more beautiful each day. In the wind, it drifts about; when there is no wind, it looks so slender and graceful that I begin to enjoy its endless beauty even before it blooms. When the lotus finally comes to flower, it is so tender that water seems to drip from its petal. It produces flowers continuously from summer to autumn. That is lotus's duty and man derives the benefits from

至①菡萏②成花,娇姿欲滴③,后先相继,自夏徂④秋,此则在花为分⑤内之事,在人为应得之资⑥者也。及花之既谢⑦,亦可告无罪于主人矣;乃复蒂⑧下生蓬⑨,蓬中结实⑩,亭亭⑪独立,犹似未开之花,与翠叶并擎⑫,不至白露为霜⑬而能事⑭不已⑮。此皆言其可目⑯者也。

可鼻,则有荷叶之清香,荷花之异馥⑰,避暑而暑为之退⑱,纳凉⑲而凉逐⑳之生。

至其可人之口者,则莲实与藕皆并列盘餐而互芬㉑齿颊㉒者也。

---

① 迨至:等到(until)。
② 菡萏(hàn dàn):荷花的别称,未开曰菡萏,已开曰芙蕖(another name for lotus when it is not in bloom)。
③ 欲滴:形容花的娇嫩(used to describe the delicacy and tenderness of a flower)。
④ 徂(cú):到(up to)。
⑤ 分:名分,本分(one's job / duty)。
⑥ 应得之资:这里指应得到的收获与报偿(deserved harvest or recompense)。
⑦ 谢:花叶凋落(flowers or leaves wither)。
⑧ 蒂:花托(the base of a flower or fruit)。
⑨ 蓬:即莲房,莲蓬(lotus pod)。
⑩ 实:指莲子(lotus seed)。
⑪ 亭亭:耸立的样子(appearance of towering aloft)。
⑫ 擎:高举,这里指耸立(hold high, here meaning to tower aloft)。
⑬ 白露为霜:指到了秋天霜降的时候(when the first frost comes in autumn)。
⑭ 能事:擅长的本事(one's skillful ability)。
⑮ 已:止(stop)。
⑯ 可目:适宜于观赏(suitable for viewing)。
⑰ 异馥:特殊的香气(special fragrance)。
⑱ 退:减退(decrease, reduce)。
⑲ 纳凉:乘凉(enjoy the cool)。
⑳ 逐:随(follow)。
㉑ 芬:香。这里用作动词(sweet, fragrant; here used as a verb meaning to produce fragrance)。
㉒ 齿颊:指口中和嘴边(here meaning teeth and lips)。

it. As the lotus withers, it can say without any regret that it has never betrayed its owner: pods containing seeds grow from the stems of the withered flowers. Each lotus pod, similar to a bud ready to burst, pokes out from the water among the green leaves. Not until late autumn when the first frost comes does it stop presenting these abilities. All these are able to be seen.

The delicate fragrance of lotus leaves can be smelt. When its special fragrance is used to drive away summer heat, the heat will decrease; when used to bring coolness, the cool immediately exists.

Both the lotus seeds and the roots are edible and can be served at the dinner table and give fragrance to our teeth and lips.

Only the withered leaves at the time of frost resemble ugly and useless waste materials. However, if collected and stored they can be used to wrap items in the following year.

只有霜中败叶,零落难堪,似成弃物①矣;乃摘而藏之,又备经年裹②物之用。

是芙蕖也者,无一时一刻不适耳目之观,无一物一丝不备家常之用者也。有五谷③之实而不有其名,兼百花之长而各去其短,种植之利④有大于此者乎?

---

① 弃物:废物(waste material)。
② 裹:包扎(wrap up)。
③ 五谷:指稻、黍、稷、麦、菽五种谷物(grain such as rice, two kinds of millet, wheat and bean)。
④ 种植之利:指种花植树的收益(income from growing flowers and planting trees)。

So lotus suits the eye and ear and every part is useful in our daily life. Though not named as such, it is a grain. It possesses the good attributes of other flowers but it is free from their weaknesses. Is there any other plant more beneficial to mankind than the lotus?

与 人 书

顾炎武

人之为学,不日进①则日退。独学无友②,则孤陋③而难成;久处一方,则习染④而不自觉。不幸而在穷僻之域⑤,无车马之资⑥,犹当博学审问,"古人与稽⑦",以求其是非之所在,庶几⑧可得十之五六。若既不出户,又不读书,则是面墙之士⑨,虽子羔、原宪⑩之贤,终无济于天下。子曰:"十室之邑⑪,必有忠信如丘者焉,不如丘之好学也。"夫以孔子之圣,犹须好学,今人可不勉乎?

---

① 日进:每天进步(progress every day)。
② 独学无友:独自学习,没人陪伴(study alone without companion)。
③ 孤陋(lòu):孤陋寡闻(with very limited knowledge and scanty information)。
④ 习染:沾染某种坏习惯(contract / fall into a bad habit)。
⑤ 穷僻之域:穷乡僻壤(district shut off from the outside world)。
⑥ 资:费用(expense)。
⑦ 稽(jī):计较,争论(find fault with)。
⑧ 庶几:差不多(almost)。
⑨ 面墙之士:人不学习,就像面向墙壁,一无所见(if one does not study, he is like facing a wall and sees nothing)。
⑩ 子羔、原宪:二人皆为孔门弟子。子羔,姓高,名柴,字子羔;原宪,又名原思,字子思(two disciples of Confucius. Zigao, also named Gao Chai, styled himself Zigao; Yuan Xian also named Yuan Si, styled himself Zisi)。
⑪ 邑:城市(city or town)。

A LETTER TO AN ANONYMOUS PERSON

Gu Yanwu

If a person does not make any progress every day in his studies, he is sure to fall behind day by day. If one studies alone without any companion, he can hardly be successful owing to the lack of discussion and information. If one lives in one place for a long time, he will unknowingly be influenced by a bad local habit. A man has unluckily settled down in an out-of-the-way place and there are not horses and carriages for him to go out from this place and return. This person, by reading widely and thinking deeply as well as "consulting the ancient wise men" to find out what the answer to major issues of principle are, may be able to find out half or more than half the answers. Whereas, another person who always stays at home without reading any books can be given the nickname of "Facing the Wall Man." Even if he were as virtuous as Zigao or Yuan Xian, he will never make any contribution to the nation. Confucius said, "Even in a tiny town with only ten households, there must be someone who is as loyal and honest as I but there might not be anybody who is as diligent in study as myself." As a sage, Confucius still needed to study diligently. How can modern people not study hard?

李姬传

侯方域

李姬①者名香②,母曰贞丽③。贞丽有侠气,尝一夜博④,输千金立尽。所交接皆当世豪杰,尤与阳羡⑤陈贞慧⑥善也。姬为其养女,亦侠而慧,略知书,能辨别士大夫贤否⑦,张学士溥⑧、夏吏部允

---

① 姬:古代常用作对妇女的美称,但有时也指侍妾(a form of address often used in ancient China for a lady but sometimes was used to refer to a concubine)。
② 李香:秦淮名妓。后来孔尚任《桃花扇》塑造她为剧中女主角(a courtesan in the Qinhuai Area in Nanjing. Later Kong Shangren in his *Peach-Flower Fan* portrayed her in a female leading role)。
③ 贞丽:姓李,字淡如,秦淮名妓,香君的义母(her family name was Li; she styled herself Danru, a courtesan in the Qinhuai area in Nanjing, Li Xiangjun's adoptive mother)。
④ 博:赌博(gamble)。
⑤ 阳羡:古县名,此处指宜兴(name of a county in ancient China, here referring to Yixing)。
⑥ 陈贞慧(1604—1656):字定生,与侯方域、冒襄、方以智同称为四公子,为明末爱国社团复社领导人之一(styled himself Dingsheng; one of the Four Young Masters along with Hou Fangyu, Mao Xiang and Fang Yizhi and one of the leaders of the Fu Association, a patriotic association at the end of the Ming Dynasty)。
⑦ 贤否(pǐ):好坏(good or bad)。
⑧ 张学士溥:张溥(1602—1641),字天如,江苏太仓人,曾联合江南若干文士建立复社,继承了东林党人评议时政的传统。因曾中崇祯四年进士,故称"学士"(Zhang Pu styled himself Tianru, from Taicang, Jiangsu; he set up the Fu Association with several intellectuals from regions south of the Yangtze River, which carried forward the tradition of the Donglin Party: discussing politics. As he had passed the imperial examination in the 4th year of the Chongzhen Reign, he was called "Scholar")。

THE STORY OF LADY LI

Hou Fangyu

The real name of Lady Li was Li Xiang and her mother was Zhenli. Being generous and chivalrous, Zhenli had once, only on one night gambled away 1000 pieces of gold. All those with whom she associated were people of exceptional ability. She was on particularly good terms with Chen Zhenhui from Yangxian. As Zhenli's adoptive daughter, Lady Li was gallant and intelligent. Being literate to some extent, she knew how to distinguish good officials from bad ones. She was highly praised by Zhang Pu, a scholar and Xia Yunyi, an official of the Ministry of Civil Personnel Affairs. When young, she had been graceful, open-minded and straightforward, thus outshining all others. At the age of 13, she learnt from Zhou Rusong of Suzhou the four long poetic dramas written by Tang Xianzu (a famous dramatist of the Ming Dynasty).

彝①亟②称之③。少，风调④皎爽⑤不群⑥。十三岁，从吴⑦人周如松⑧受歌玉茗堂⑨四传奇⑩，皆能尽其音节⑪。尤工琵琶词，然不轻发⑫也。

雪苑⑬侯生⑭，己卯⑮来金陵，与相识。姬尝邀侯生为诗，而自歌

① 夏吏部允彝（？—1646）：字彝仲，江苏松江（今属上海）人，博学善文，与陈子龙等创建几社，与复社相呼应。明亡，起兵抗清，兵败投水自沉。因曾在吏部供职，故称"吏部"（Xia Yunyi styled himself Yizhong, from Songjiang County [now in Shanghai], Jiangsu. He was learned and good at writing and set up the Ji Association with Chen Zilong, etc. which acted in cooperation with the Fu Association. After the Ming Dynasty fell, he led a military troop to resist the Qing army. After failure, he drowned himself in a river. He was called "the Ministry of Official Personnel Affairs," because he had worked there）。
② 亟（jí）：屡屡，频频（often）。
③ 称之：称许她，赞美她（praise her）。
④ 风调：风韵（graceful bearing, charm）。
⑤ 皎爽：爽朗豪迈（open-minded and generous）。
⑥ 不群：超尘拔俗，不同于一般人（tower above the rest, outshine all the others）。
⑦ 吴：这里指无锡（here referred to Wuxi）。
⑧ 周如松：即明末清初著名曲艺家苏昆生（a famous ballad singer of the late Ming and early Qing dynasties）。
⑨ 玉茗堂：明代戏曲家汤显祖（1550—1617）书室，在江西临川（famous dramatist of the Ming Dynasty — Tang Xianzu's office, in Linchuan, Jiangxi）。
⑩ 四传奇：汤显祖所著四部戏曲（four plays written by Tang Xianzu）。
⑪ 尽其音节：尽数掌握《牡丹亭》等曲词演唱难度很大的音律节奏（completely master the tonality and rhythm of the verses of the plays such as *The Peony Pavilion* etc. which were very difficult to sing）。
⑫ 发：发声，唱歌（sounding, singing）。
⑬ 雪苑：侯方域的别号（Hou Fangyu's alternative name）。
⑭ 侯生：作者自称（a self-styled name used by the author）。
⑮ 己卯：崇祯十二年（1639）（the 12th year of the Chongzhen Reign, 1639）。

She had a good grasp of the rhyme and rhythm of the four dramas. She was especially good at singing the ballad *The Tale of Pipa* but seldom performed it.

Mr. Hou Fangyu came to Jinling (today's Nanjing) in the 12th year of the Chongzhen Reign and made the acquaintance of Lady Li. She once asked Mr. Hou to write poetry for her and in return she sang songs for him. Earlier on, Ruan Dacheng from Anhui was sentenced to hard labor for attaching himself to Wei Zhongxian and later he went into hiding in Nanjing. He was condemned and rejected by the upright local people. The strong and consistent resistance was initiated and led by Chen Zhenhui from Yangxian and Wu Yingji from Guichi. Ruan had to seek help and he hoped that Mr. Hou could do something for him. He had his good friend General Wang take good wine and delicious food to Hou's house every day to dine and wine together. Feeling strange, Lady Li said to Hou: "General Wang is not rich and he cannot afford expensive social activities. Why don't you ask him what is behind the

以偿之。初,皖人阮大铖①者,以阿附魏忠贤②论③城旦④,屏居⑤金陵,为清议⑥所斥。阳羡陈贞慧、贵池吴应箕⑦实首其事⑧,持之力⑨。大铖不得已,欲侯生为解之,乃假⑩所善王将军⑪,日载酒食与侯生游。姬曰:"王将军贫,非结客者,公子盍叩之⑫?"侯生三问,将军乃屏人⑬述大铖意。姬私语侯生曰:"妾少从假母⑭识阳羡君⑮,其人有高义,闻

---

① 阮大铖(1587—1646):字集之,号圆海,安徽怀宁人,明末奸臣(Ruan Dacheng styled himself Jizhi, alternatively named Yuanhai, from Huaining, Anhui, a treacherous court official at the end of the Ming Dynasty)。
② 魏忠贤(1568—1627):河北肃宁人,明朝大监,曾勾结皇帝乳母结党专权,杀害忠良。崇祯时被贬,途中自杀(from Suning County, Hebei Province, a eunuch in the Ming Dynasty. He colluded with the emperor's wet nurse to grab all the power by ganging up and killing officials loyal to their sovereign. When Chongzhen came to power, Wei was demoted and committed suicide on the exile way)。
③ 论:定罪处理(convict sb. of a crime)。
④ 城旦:秦汉时徒刑名称,白天防寇,夜间筑城。此处作苦役代称(name of sentence: guard against bandits during the day and construct city wall at night; here meaning hard labor)。
⑤ 屏居:隐藏行踪而居(live by concealing one's whereabouts)。
⑥ 清议:公正的舆论(fair-minded public opinion)。
⑦ 吴应箕(1594—1645):字次尾,安徽贵池人。复社领导人之一。清兵破南京后,起兵抗清,兵败被执,不屈就义(Wu Yingji styled himself Ciwei, from Guichi, Anhui, one of the leaders of the Fu Association. When Nanjing fell to the Qing army, he led a troop to resist the Qing army. After defeat he was captured and died a hero's death)。
⑧ 首其事:首先揭发、声讨阮大铖的罪恶事迹(be the first one to expose and denounce Ruan Dacheng's criminal deeds)。
⑨ 持之力:竭力坚持这件事(spare no effort to persist in this thing)。
⑩ 假:委托(trust)。
⑪ 王将军:阮之门客(a hanger-on of Ruan Dacheng)。
⑫ 盍叩之:何不请问他(why not ask him)。
⑬ 屏人:屏退外人(dismiss outsiders)。
⑭ 假母:养母,指李贞丽(adoptive mother, referring to Li Zhenli)。
⑮ 阳羡君:指陈贞慧(referring to Chen Zhenhui)。

feasts?" When they met again, Hou asked Wang that question and kept asking until the latter, having dismissed the people around, told Hou what was Dacheng's intention. After that, Lady Li said to Hou in private: "When I was young, I already knew Mr. Zhenhui because of my adoptive mother. He is a noble-minded man. I heard that Mr. Wu Yingji is also an upright and reputable man. You are on good terms with both of them. Why are you going to betray your best friends because of Ruan? Besides, you are from a notable family and a great clan. Why are you so humble that you are going to do something for this notorious man? Can you, a knowledgeable man, be more politically short-sighted than I, a humble woman?" Hou applauded her remark and when General Wang came to see him, he pretended to lie drunk in bed. The general was very upset and soon left. Then he severed ties with the scholar.

Before long, Hou failed to pass the imperial examination. Lady Li gave him a farewell dinner at the Peach-Leaf Ferry and sang the ballad *The Tale of Pipa* for him. After singing, she said to

吴君①尤铮铮②，今皆与公子善，奈何以阮公负至交乎！且以公子之世望③，安事④阮公！公子读万卷书，所见岂后于贱妾⑤耶？"侯生大呼称善，醉而卧⑥。王将军者殊怏怏，因辞去，不复通⑦。

未几，侯生下第⑧。姬置酒桃叶渡⑨，歌琵琶词以送之，曰："公子才名文藻，雅⑩不减中郎。中郎⑪学不补行⑫，今琵琶所传词⑬固

---

① 吴君：指吴应箕（referring to Wu Yingji）。
② 铮铮：刚正不阿的姿态（attitude of being upright and tenacious）。
③ 世望：世家望族（a family holding high official positions over generations）。
④ 安事：何必侍奉（why wait upon）。
⑤ 贱妾：古代女子自谦之称（a term which, in ancient times, was often used by a lady to address herself）。
⑥ 醉而卧：沉醉而酣卧（get drunk and sleep soundly）。
⑦ 不复通：绝交（break off relations）。通：交通，往来（exchange of friendly visits）。
⑧ 下第：应考而未中（fail to pass the imperial examination）。
⑨ 桃叶渡：金陵名胜之一，在今南京城内秦淮河与清溪合流处。相传晋王献之送其妾桃叶于此渡河，后人遂名其渡为桃叶渡（one of the scenic spots where the Qinhuai River and the Clear Stream meet in Nanjing. According to legend, Wang Xianzhi once saw off his concubine Peach-Leaf to cross the river here. Later generations call it Peach-Leaf Ferry）。
⑩ 雅：向来（always, all along）。
⑪ 中郎：东汉蔡邕（133—192）曾官左中郎将，故称"中郎"。《琵琶记》即以蔡邕与赵五娘的故事为题材（Cai Yong was a historical figure of the Eastern Han Dynasty. He was once appointed the left "Zhonglang" and so called. The Tale of Pipa was based on the story of Cai Yong and Zhao Wuniang）。
⑫ 学不补行：学识的渊博不能弥补德行的缺陷（one's broad and profound knowledge cannot make up for his moral fault）。
⑬ 琵琶所传词：指《琵琶记》中蔡邕抛亲弃妻、赴考入赘等情节（referring to the story of The Tale of Pipa: Cai Yong forsook his wife and parents to marry and live with his bride's rich and powerful family after he had passed the imperial examination）。

him: "Your literary talent and fame compare well with that of Cai Yong's (a famous writer of the Eastern Han Dynasty). It is a pity that Cai Yong's scholarly attainments could not gloss over his moral blemishes. Although the story of *The Tale of Pipa* is fictional, the fact that Cai was too close to Dong Zhuo cannot be concealed. You are unconventional and unrestrained by nature. Now that you have been frustrated in the examination, I wonder when we will meet again after you have left. Please cherish your good name for ever and don't forget *The Tale of Pipa* I have sung for you. I will never sing it for anybody else."

妄①,然尝昵②董卓③,不可掩④也。公子豪迈不羁,又失意,此去相见未可期,愿终自爱,无忘妾所歌琵琶词也!妾亦不复歌矣!"

侯生去后,而故开府⑤田仰⑥者,以金三百锾⑦,邀姬一见。姬固却之。开府惭且怒,且有以中伤姬。姬叹曰:"田公宁⑧异于阮公乎?吾向⑨之所赞⑩于侯公子者谓何?今乃利其金而赴之,是妾卖⑪公子矣!"卒不往。

---

① 固妄:诚然是虚诞的(it is indeed false)。
② 昵:亲近(be close to)。
③ 董卓(?—192):字仲颖,汉临洮(今甘肃岷县)人。汉献帝时专权乱政,祸国殃民。后为吕布、王允所诛。曾重用蔡邕。被诛后,人皆庆贺,独蔡邕叹息色变,因此下狱而死(Dong Zhuo styled himself Zhongying, from Lintao [today's Minxian County, Gansu]. In the time of Emperor Xiandi of the Han Dynasty, he grabbed all the power and disturbed administration and brought calamity to the country and to the people. Later he was killed by Lü Bu and Wang Yun. Dong used to put Cai Yong in an important position. After Dong was killed, everybody celebrated this event; Cai Yong was the only one who was upset and sighed and because of this he was put in jail and died there)。
④ 掩:掩盖(conceal)。
⑤ 开府:原指开建府署、辟置僚属,明、清时则督抚也称开府(originally meaning: setting up government offices and disposing of an official. In the Ming and Qing dynasties, a civil and military governor was also so called)。
⑥ 田仰:字百源,贵州贵阳人。马士英亲戚,南明弘光时为淮扬巡抚(Tian Yang styled himself Baiyuan, from Guiyang, Guizhou, Ma Shiying's relative. During the Hongguang Reign of the Southern Ming Dynasty, he was appointed patrolling supervisor in the area of Huaiyang)。
⑦ 锾(huán):古代重量单位,此处为货币单位(weight unit in ancient China, but here is monetary unit)。"三百锾"即白银三百两(300 liang of silver)。
⑧ 宁:岂,难道(isn't that ... ?)。
⑨ 向:往昔,过去(in the past, in former times)。
⑩ 赞:评述(commentary)。
⑪ 卖:叛卖,负心(betray, fail to be loyal to one's love)。

After Hou had left, Tian Yang, the former imperial inspector in the Huaiyang District, invited Lady Li to his place and promised to give her 300 *huan* of silver if she came. She sternly refused the invitation. Feeling ashamed and resentful, Tian spread calumnious rumors about Lady Li. She sighed and said: "Is this Mr. Tian any different from the notorious Mr. Ruan? Why did I admire Mr. Hou? If I accept the invitation because of the money he promised to give me, I would be blamed for betraying Mr. Hou." She never went to see Tian.

就 亭 记

施闰章

地有乐乎游观①,事不烦②乎人力,二者常难兼之③;取之官舍,又在左右,则尤难。临江④地故⑤硗⑥啬⑦,官署坏陋,无陂⑧台亭观⑨之美。予至则构⑩数楹⑪为阁山草堂,言近乎阁皂⑫也。而登望无所,意常怏怏⑬。一日,积雪初霁⑭,得轩⑮侧高阜⑯,引领⑰南望,

---

① 游观:游览,观赏(go sight-seeing; view and admire)。
② 烦:烦劳(trouble)。
③ 之:代上文"二者"(referring to the two things above)。
④ 临江:今江西清江(today's Qingjiang County, Jiangxi Province)。
⑤ 故:原来,本来(original)。
⑥ 硗(qiāo):土地不肥(not fertile)。
⑦ 啬:土地出产少(produce little)。
⑧ 陂(bēi):山坡(hillside)。
⑨ 观(guàn):楼台(tower, a high building)。
⑩ 构:建屋(build houses)。
⑪ 数楹(yíng):几间(several rooms)。楹:原指堂屋前的明柱(originally referring to a pillar in front of the central room)。
⑫ 阁皂:阁皂山,在清江县东40里,形如阁,色如皂(黑色)(the Black-Pavilion Mountain, situated 40 li east of Qingjiang County, looks like a black pavilion)。
⑬ 怏(yàng)怏:闷闷不乐(feeling depressed)。
⑭ 霁(jì):雨或雪停止,放晴(clear up after rain or snow)。
⑮ 轩:有窗的廊子或小屋子(a small room or veranda with windows)。
⑯ 阜(fù):土山(mound)。
⑰ 引领:伸长脖子,翘首远望(crane one's neck to look into the distance)。

THE READY-MADE PAVILION

Shi Runzhang

It is always difficult to find a spot which is good for sightseeing but does not need repair and renovation and it is even harder to find such a spot set amid the official residences where we live. Linjiang has been noted for its infertile soil and poor farm produce. The official residences here are simple and crude and all look dilapidated. Among the surroundings, no beautiful things such as terraces, pavilions and towers could be seen. Since I came to Linjiang, I have built several small buildings. I call them the Pavilion-Mountain Cottages, giving to them the meaning of being close to the Black-Pavilion Mountain. However, here I could not ascend a height to enjoy a distant view so I often felt upset about this. One day when the weather cleared after a long snow, I climbed up the mound near one of the cottages and looked southward to see green mountains and white snow. Their bright colours made me feel relaxed and happy. After that I had all the weeds and rubbish removed from the mound and then built a bamboo pavilion on it. I grew flowers and trees around the

山青雪白，粲然①可喜。遂治其芜秽②，作③竹亭其上，列植花木，又视其屋角之障④吾目者去之，命⑤曰就亭，谓就其地而不劳也。

古之士大夫出官于外，类⑥得引⑦山水自娱。然或逼⑧处都会⑨，讼狱⑩烦嚣⑪，舟车旁午⑫，内外酬应不给⑬。虽仆仆⑭于陂台亭观之间，日餍⑮酒食，进丝竹⑯，而胸中之丘壑⑰盖⑱已寡⑲矣。何者？形⑳怠㉑意㉒烦，而神㉓为之累㉔也。

---

① 粲（càn）然：颜色鲜明（bright-coloured）。
② 治其芜秽：清除杂草（wipe out weeds）。治：进行某种工作（engage in a certain job）。
③ 作：建（build）。
④ 障：遮住（cover, hide from view）。
⑤ 命：起名（give name to）。
⑥ 类：大都（for the most part, mostly）。
⑦ 引：招致，求（seek, go in quest of）。
⑧ 逼：临近（close to, near）。
⑨ 都会：大都市（city, metropolis）。
⑩ 讼狱：诉讼的案件（lawsuit）。
⑪ 嚣（xiāo）：声音杂乱（clamour, hubbub）。
⑫ 旁午：纵横，引申为事物纷杂（crisscross, extended to mean: disorderly）。
⑬ 不给：忙不过来（too busy to）。
⑭ 仆仆：劳苦（travel-worn and weary, toil）。
⑮ 餍（yàn）：吃饱（have enough food）。
⑯ 丝竹：弦乐器和管乐器，泛指音乐（string and wind musical instruments, referring to music in general）。
⑰ 胸中之丘壑：寄情山水的兴致（interest of abandoning oneself to nature）。
⑱ 盖：大概（probably, most likely）。
⑲ 寡：少（few, little）。
⑳ 形：身体（body）。
㉑ 怠：倦（tired, weary）。
㉒ 意：心情（mood, feeling）。
㉓ 神：精神（spirit, mind）。
㉔ 累：妨碍（hinder）。

pavilion and one of its four eaves had to be cut off as it blocked my view. I named it the Ready-Made Pavilion, meaning that everything is ready on the spot and no work needs to be done.

In ancient times, nearly every scholar who held an official position which was away from home would find a way for self-amusement by enjoying the beauty of mountains and rivers. Nowadays when we happen to place ourselves near a big city, we are often disturbed by the hustle and bustle of lawsuits and trial proceedings. Boats and carriages keep coming and going and we have too many social engagements on our hands. Though our social activities are often carried out inside pavilions, terraces and towers where we dine and wine while listening to string and wind music, we seldom pay attention to the beauty of the surroundings. Why? Energy-exhaustion and mind-bending make us insensitive to everything.

As a prefecture seat, Linjiang is located in a remote area by the Ganjiang River. This quiet area looks like a vast expanse of hilly wilderness. I have pity for the people who live in such a poor area and in return they receive well the measures I have taken to govern the prefecture, thus we have been living in harmony with each other. The local customs are thrifty and simple, lawsuits seldom happen and visitors are rarely seen here. Every day as soon as my subordinates get off work, I shut the door of my office

临①之为郡②,越③在江曲④,阒⑤焉若穷山荒野。予方愍⑥其凋敝⑦,而其民亦安予之拙⑧,相与休息。俗俭讼简,宾客罕,吏散⑨则闭门,解衣槃礴⑩移日⑪,山水之意,未尝不落落焉⑫在予胸中也。顷岁⑬军兴⑭,征求⑮络绎⑯,去阁皂四十里,未能舍职事一往游。聊⑰试登斯亭焉,悠然⑱户庭,凭陵⑲雉堞⑳,厥㉑位东南,日月先至。碧嶂㉒清流㉓,江帆汀㉔鸟,烟雨之出没,橘柚之青葱㉕,莫不变

---

① 临：临江府（Linjiang Prefecture）。
② 郡：府的别称（another name for prefecture）。
③ 越：远（far, distant）。
④ 江曲：靠赣江的偏僻地方（a remote place near Ganjiang River）。
⑤ 阒（qù）：寂静（quiet, still）。
⑥ 愍（mǐn）：怜（be sympathetic to）。
⑦ 凋敝：衰败（decline, wane）。
⑧ 拙：政务宽减（be lenient in government administration）。
⑨ 吏散：属员散去（a superior official is deserted by his subordinates）。
⑩ 槃礴（pán bó）：箕坐，伸腿坐地（sit on the ground with one's two legs stretched, like a dustpan）。
⑪ 移日：日影移动，指经过一段时间（the sun moves, meaning after a period of time）。
⑫ 落落焉：明显的样子（obvious）。
⑬ 顷岁：近年（in recent years）。
⑭ 军兴：打仗（fight, make war）。
⑮ 征求：征调军用财物（requisition military supplies）。
⑯ 络绎：接连不断（in an endless stream）。
⑰ 聊：姑且（tentatively, for the moment）。
⑱ 悠然：闲静的样子（carefree and leisurely）。
⑲ 凭陵：凭临，靠近（near, close to）。
⑳ 雉堞（dié）：城上的女墙（parapet wall of the city; crenellation; battlement）。
㉑ 厥：其（his or her or its）。
㉒ 碧嶂：青绿色的山（dark green mountain）。
㉓ 清流：清澈的流水（limpid flowing water）。
㉔ 汀（tīng）：江中或水边的平地（a shallow islet on a stream）。
㉕ 青葱（cōng）：鲜绿（vivid green）。

and then take off my official robe to sit on the floor for some time with my legs stretched. Posing like a dustpan, the desire to enjoy the beautiful landscape never fails to vividly come to my mind. In recent years, the requisition for military supplies has never ended owing to the non-stop warfares. Though the Black-Pavilion Mountain is only 40 *li* (1 *li* = 0.5 km) away, I have been unable to put aside my work to go there for sightseeing. What I can do is to ascend the Ready-Made Pavilion. It sits quietly among the houses, close to the city wall. Located in the southeast, it is always the first to embrace the rising sun or the up-moving moon. From here I can see dark green mountains, limpid flowing water, white sails on the river and perching birds on the islets. Rain may come at any time and will stop all of a sudden. Tangerine and pomelo, having been washed by the rain, appear a lush green. In such changeable weather, there is nothing that does not keep altering its appearance. Time and again unique and beautiful scenes come into my sight. The pavilion is a collector of all the beautiful views around it. Staying in It, I have a feeling that the river, the mountains and clouds, by touching my heart and caressing my eyelash, try to please me and have intimate contact with me.

气象①、穷②妍③巧,戛④胸拂⑤睫,辐辏⑥于栏槛之内,盖若江山云物有悦我而昵就⑦者。

夫君子居则有宴息⑧之所,游必有高明之具⑨。将以宣气⑩节情⑪,进于⑫广大疏通⑬之域⑭,非独⑮游观云尔也。予窃有志⑯,未之逮⑰,姑⑱与客把酒咏歌,陶然⑲以就醉⑳焉。

---

① 变气象:变化外貌,形态多样(changing appearance, various shape)。
② 穷:尽,极(to the greatest extent; extremely)。
③ 妍:美(beautiful)。
④ 戛(jiá):触击(touch, contact)。
⑤ 拂:掠过(caress, stroke)。
⑥ 辐辏(còu):聚集(converge)。
⑦ 昵就:来亲近(come to be on intimate terms with)。
⑧ 宴息:安息(rest)。
⑨ 高明之具:美好的佐游之物(fine things to assist sb. in sightseeing)。
⑩ 宣气:发泄胸中郁结之气(give vent to one's pent-up spirit)。
⑪ 节情:调节情绪(regulate one's mood)。
⑫ 进于:达到(reach)。
⑬ 广大疏通:开朗舒畅(open-minded and happy)。
⑭ 域:境地(condition, circumstances)。
⑮ 非独:不只是(not only)。
⑯ 窃有志:私自想这样做(want to do so privately)。
⑰ 逮:达到(achieve, attain)。
⑱ 姑:暂且(for the moment)。
⑲ 陶然:喜悦的样子(happily)。
⑳ 就醉:趋向于醉,归于醉(tend to be drunk)。

A gentleman, while staying at home, can always find a spot in his residence for entertainment. While travelling, he always carries something special that will help him give vent to his pent-up emotion and regulate his mood so that he can enjoy not only the landscape but also an elated and blissful mind. Unable to follow their example, I have found my own way to enjoy myself by holding a wine cup and reciting poetry with my friends. What pleasure I feel as I gradually become drunk!

芋老人传

周容

芋老人者,慈水祝渡①人也。子佣出②,独与妪③居渡口。一日,有书生避雨檐下,衣湿袖单④,影乃益瘦⑤。老人延⑥入坐,知从郡城⑦就⑧童子试⑨归。老人略知书,与语久,命妪煮芋以进⑩。尽一器⑪,再进,生为之饱,笑曰:"他日不忘老人芋也。"雨止,别去。

---

① 慈水祝渡:地名(name of a place)。慈水:今浙江慈溪市(today's Cixi City, Zhejiang)。祝渡:祝家渡(the Zhujia Ferry)。
② 佣出:出外给人做工(go out to work for other people)。佣:受雇(be employed)。
③ 妪(yù):老年妇女(old woman)。
④ 袖单:衣服单薄(in thin clothes)。
⑤ 影乃益瘦:身影显得更加单薄清瘦(one's figure appears thinner and weaker)。
⑥ 延:邀请(invite)。
⑦ 郡城:这里指宁波府(here referring to Ningbo Prefecture)。
⑧ 就:参加(take part in)。
⑨ 童子试:科举中录取秀才的考试(imperial examination to enroll Xiucai)。童子:即童生,未取得秀才资格的读书人都称童生(intellectuals before passing the imperial examination at the county level)。
⑩ 进:进献(provide)。
⑪ 尽一器:吃完一碗(eat one bowl of sth.)。

THE OLD TARO MAN

Zhou Rong

The old taro man lived by the Zhujia Ferry in Cixi County. His son worked far away from home as a hired labourer, thus only he and his old wife lived in his home. One day, a young scholar took shelter from the rain under the eaves of his house. In thin and wet clothes, he looked rather skinny. The old man invited him to come in and found that he had just taken the county-level imperial examination and was on his way to go home. Some knowledge about literature and history enabled him to have a long talk with the young scholar. While chatting, he asked his wife to cook taro. After the young man had finished a full bowl of cooked taro, he was given another one until he was full. With a smile he said to the old man, "I will never forget your taro." He left when the rain stopped.

Ten years later, having passed the top-level imperial examination, the young scholar became the prime minister. One day, he told his chef to cook taro for him but was disappointed by the taste. He put down his chopsticks and sighed, "Why did the

十余年，书生用甲第为相国①，偶命厨者进芋，辍箸②叹曰："何向者③祝渡老人之芋之香而甘也！"使人访其夫妇，载以来。丞、尉④闻之，谓⑤老人与相国有旧，邀见讲钧礼⑥，子不佣矣。

至京，相国慰劳曰："不忘老人芋，今乃烦尔妪一煮芋也。"已而妪煮芋进，相国亦辍箸曰："何向者之香而甘也！"老人前曰："犹是芋也，而向之香且甘者，非调和之有异，时、位之移人也。相公⑦昔自郡城走数十里，困于雨，不择食矣；今者堂有炼珍⑧，朝分尚食⑨，张筵列鼎⑩，尚何芋是甘⑪乎？老人犹喜相公之止于芋⑫也。老人老矣，所闻实多：村南有夫妇守贫者，织纺井臼⑬，佐读

---

① 用甲第为相国：因为科举考取高等当了宰相（become the prime minister as the result of his success in the imperial examination at the highest level）。用：因为（because）。
② 辍箸：放下筷子（lay down his chopsticks）。
③ 向者：从前（in the past）。
④ 丞、尉：县丞、主簿等，都是知县的佐理官（county magistrate's assistants）。
⑤ 谓：以为（think）。
⑥ 讲钧礼：以平等之礼相待（treat them equally）。
⑦ 相公：对宰相的尊称（respectful form of address for prime minister）。
⑧ 炼珍：精美的食品（exquisite food）。
⑨ 朝分尚食：在朝廷分得皇帝赏赐的食物（get imperial food bestowed by the emperor）。
⑩ 张筵列鼎：大摆宴席，列鼎而食（give a banquet with tripods full of delicious food lining up among the guests）。
⑪ 何芋是甘：哪个芋吃起来是甜的呢（which taro tastes sweet）？
⑫ 止于芋：只在食芋一事上忘旧（The only thing that has changed is one's taste for taro）。
⑬ 织纺井臼：勤苦过日子（to live a life of hard work and frugality）。井：汲井水（draw well water）。臼：舂米（husk rice with mortar and pestle）。

taro cooked by the old couple living near the Zhujia Ferry taste so delicious but this one not?" He sent his men to visit the old couple and bring them to the capital. The local civil and military officials heard the news and thought that this couple was the prime minister's old friends and treated them very well. Furthermore, their son no longer needed to do hard and low-paid work.

When the old couple arrived in the capital, the prime minister greeted them by saying: "I cannot forget your taro. May I ask your wife to cook taro for me today?" When the cooked taro was presented to him, he tasted it and soon put down his chopsticks. He asked, "Why was the taro you cooked on that day so nice but not this one?" The old man replied: "That was also taro and it was not cooked in a different way. Nothing but the situation has changed. On that day, you had walked a dozen miles from the town in rain and felt so hungry that you were not choosy about what you were eating. Today you have very good food at home and sometimes you are given super delicacies from the imperial court. You wine and dine so often, can you still recognise the deliciousness when you now eat taro? I'm glad to see that the change you have had is only your taste for taro. I'm old enough to know many things. A poor couple used to live in the southern part of my village. The wife worked very hard day and night, spinning and weaving, drawing water from the well and husking rice by

勤苦，幸获名成①，遂宠妾媵②，弃其妇，致郁郁而死，是芋视③乃④妇也。城东有甲乙同学者，一砚⑤、一灯、一窗、一榻⑥，晨起不辨衣履⑦，乙先得举⑧，登仕⑨路，闻甲落魄⑩，笑不顾，交以绝，是芋视乃友也。更闻谁氏子，读书时，愿他日得志，廉干⑪如古人某，忠孝如古人某，及为吏，以污贿⑫不饬⑬罢⑭，是芋视乃学也。是犹可言也；老人邻有西塾⑮，闻其师为弟子说前代事，有将⑯、相，有卿、尹⑰，有

---

① 名成：功成名就（achieve success and win recognition）。
② 妾媵（yìng）：泛指妾（referring to concubines in general）。
③ 芋视：把……看作芋（regard sth. as taros）。
④ 乃：他的（his）。
⑤ 一砚：合用一砚（use the same inkstone）。
⑥ 榻：床（bed）。
⑦ 不辨衣履：分不清衣服、鞋子是谁的，表示交情非常深（cannot tell whose clothes and shoes, meaning their friendship is deep）。
⑧ 得举：考取举人或进士（pass the imperial examinations）。
⑨ 仕：做官（be an official）。
⑩ 落魄：穷困不得志（poverty-stricken, not self-satisfied）。
⑪ 廉干：廉洁而有才能（honest and able）。
⑫ 污贿：贪污财物（graft money or property）。
⑬ 不饬（chì）：行为不端（behave badly）。
⑭ 罢：被罢官（be dismissed from office）。
⑮ 西塾：过去私人设立的学舍。古礼塾师为宾，位在西（private school in the past. According to the Chinese etiquette, the teacher as a guest, is usually on the west）。
⑯ 将：高级武官（high-ranking military officer）。
⑰ 相、卿、尹：都是京官（officials in the capital）。

mortar. She did so to support her husband who devoted himself to his studies. However, when the husband achieved success and fame, he bestowed favor on his concubines and deserted his wife. The poor lady soon died of grief. In the eyes of the husband, his wife was as cheap as taro. Another story happened in the town. Two young scholars lived together in the eastern part of the town. They shared one ink-stone, one lamp, one window and one bed. In the morning when they got up, very often they put on the wrong clothes and shoes. One of them passed the imperial examination and started his official career. When he heard that his former room-mate was unsuccessful and frustrated, he despised this poor man and did not give him any help. Their friendship broke. This case can be described as a man treating his friend as taro. I also heard a story about a man who, while pursuing his studies, had set a goal. He said that if one day he achieved his ambition, he would be as honest and upright as someone in ancient times and as loyal and filial as another ancient personage. However, when he became an official, he was soon dismissed from his position because of corruption, bribery and bad behaviour. In this case this official abused what he had learned and regarded it as taro. These are not the worst. A family school is very close to my home. I overheard the tutor telling his pupils stories of the previous dynasty. He talked about officials at different levels,

刺史、守、令①，或绾黄纡紫②，或揽辔褰帷③，一旦事变④中起，衅孽外乘⑤，辄屈膝叩首迎款⑥，惟恐或后，竟以宗庙⑦、社稷⑧、身名、君宠，无不同于芋焉。然则世之以今日而忘昔日者，岂独一箸间⑨哉！"

老人语未毕，相国遽⑩惊谢⑪曰："老人知道者⑫！"厚资而遣之。于是，芋老人之名大著。

赞曰：老人能于倾盖不意⑬，作缘⑭相国，奇已！不知相国何似⑮，能不愧老人之言否。然就其不忘一芋，固已贤夫并老人而芋

---

① 刺史、守、令：都是地方官（local officials）。
② 绾（wǎn）黄纡（yū）紫：佩着金印。这里代指高官（carry a golden seal, here referring to high officials）。绾：系（bind up）。黄：金印（golden seal）。纡：系结（tie）。紫：系印的紫色绶带（purple ribbon tying a seal）。
③ 揽辔（pèi）褰（qiān）帷：抓住驾驭马匹的缰绳，揭开遮蔽车子的帷帐（hold the controlling rein and open the vehicle curtains）。
④ 事变：朝中政变（coup d'etat in the court）。
⑤ 衅孽外乘：灾殃和事端从外部乘机侵入（calamities and disturbances from outside the nation seem to seize this opportunity to come）。衅：瑕隙（flaw）。孽：坏事（evils）。
⑥ 迎款：投降归顺（surrender, pay allegiance to）。
⑦ 宗庙：指帝王祭祖先的地方（place where emperors offer a sacrifice to their ancestors）。
⑧ 社稷：帝王祭谷神的地方（place where emperors offer a sacrifice to the god in charge of grain）。宗庙、社稷代指国家（referring to nation or country）。
⑨ 岂独一箸间：意思是，不只是停箸不吃这点事（this issue does not exist only in the phenomenon of stopping to pick up the taro with one's chopsticks）。
⑩ 遽（jù）：赶紧（lose no time）。
⑪ 谢：谢罪（offer an apology）。
⑫ 知道者：懂得高深事理的人（a reasonable man）。
⑬ 倾盖不意：无意之中相遇（meet each other by accident）。盖：形状如伞的车盖（umbrella-like vehicle cover）。倾盖，停车交谈（stop to talk）。
⑭ 作缘：结缘（form ties of friendship）。
⑮ 何似：像哪一种人（similar to what kind of person）。

including generals and ministers at the state level, magistrates and governors at prefectural and county levels. How imposing they appeared when wearing gold ornaments and purple gowns! How proud they looked to have their footmen keep a grip on the bridles of the horses they were riding and lift the curtains of their carriages when they were entering or alighting! However, when the nation was put in turmoil by coup d'états and foreign forces took the opportunity to invade its territory, these officials did nothing but immediately bowed and scraped, surrendering to the invaders. In their mind, the nation, the ancestral temples, their own reputation and the imperial beneficence — all these are insignificant as taro. We live in the world today but if we were to forget what happened in the past, it would become an issue not as petty as the taro between our chopsticks!"

Before the old man had finished his story, the prime minister suddenly interrupted him by saying, "Thank you, my old man, you really know quite a lot." The old man was given a generous gift and sent back home. He became quite famous afterwards.

The eulogy says: It is quite unusual that the old man accidentally met with and then formed ties of friendship with the prime minister. We do not know what kind of person the prime minister was, so we wonder if he had anything of which to be ashamed on hearing the old man's words. Judging from the fact

视之者①。特怪老人虽知书，又何长于言至是，岂果知道者欤？或传闻之过实耶？嗟夫！天下有缙绅②士大夫所不能言，而野老鄙夫能言者，往往而然③。

① 固已贤夫并老人而视芋之者：本来已经好于那些把芋老人也一并看作芋的人（be certainly better than those who even regard the old man as taro）。
② 缙（jìn）绅：插笏于绅，是官宦的装束，指上层人物（with a tablet tucked in the girdle, be dressed like an official, referring to upper circles）。缙：插（insert）。绅：大带（girdle）。
③ 然：如此，这样（so, such like that）。

that he did not forget the old man's taro, he must have been better than those who even regarded the old man as taro. It was amazing that even though the old man had limited knowledge about history and politics, he was so eloquent in relating the truth. Was he really a man of great perception, or is it an untrue story about him? Alas! As it often happens, some truths can be spoken by ordinary people but not by officials or scholars.

大铁椎[1] 传

魏禧

庚戌[2]十一月,予自广陵[3]归,与陈子灿[4]同舟。子灿年二十八,好武事,予授以左氏[5]兵谋兵法,因问:"数游南北,逢异人乎?"子灿为述大铁椎,作《大铁椎传》。

大铁椎,不知何许[6]人,北平陈子灿省兄河南,与遇宋将军家。宋,怀庆[7]青华镇人,工技击[8],七省[9]好事者[10]皆来学,人以其雄健,呼宋将军云。宋弟子高信之,亦怀庆人,多力善射,长子灿

---

① 大铁椎(chuí):兵器名。椎:通"槌"。这里指文中使用该兵器之侠客(name of a kind of weapon, big iron club. Here referring to the chivalrous expert in this article who used the weapon)。
② 庚戌:康熙九年(1670)(the 9th year of the Kangxi Reign, 1670)。
③ 广陵:今江苏扬州(today's Yangzhou, Jiangsu)。
④ 陈子灿:生平不详(unknown about his life)。
⑤ 左氏:指《左传》(*Zuo Zhuan / The Commentary of Zuo*)。
⑥ 何许:何处(what place)。
⑦ 怀庆:府名,今河南沁阳(name of a prefecture, today's Qinyang, Henan)。
⑧ 工技击:擅长武术(be good at martial arts)。
⑨ 七省:指河南及其邻近的河北、山东、山西、陕西、安徽、湖北七省(referring to Henan and six other provinces of Hebei, Shandong, Shanxi, Shaanxi, Anhui and Hubei in its vicinity)。
⑩ 好事者:指喜好技击的人(those who are fond of martial arts)。

THE STORY OF BIG IRON CLUB

Wei Xi

In the 11th month of the 9th year of the Kangxi Reign (1670), I came back from Guangling and took the same boat as Chen Zican. A young man of 28, Zican was fond of martial arts. While teaching him the art of war which I had learnt from *Zuo Zhuan* (the first chronological history covering the period from 722 BC to 464 BC), I asked him, "You have travelled from north to south many times, have you encountered any extraordinary person?" Having heard what Zican narrated to me, I wrote "The Story of Big Iron Club."

Nobody knew from where Big Iron Club came. While visiting his elder brother in Henan, Chen Zican from Peking encountered in General Song's home a man with the nickname of Big Iron Club. Song was a native of Qinghua Town in Huaiqing County and an excellent martial arts expert. Many people who loved martial arts came from seven different provinces to learn his skill. They called him General Song as he was big and tall. Gao Xinzhi, one of Song's followers also from Huaiqing, had great physical strength and was good at shooting. He was seven years older than Zican and used to be his schoolmate when they were

七岁①，少同学，故尝与过②宋将军。

时座上有健啖客③，貌甚寝④，右胁⑤夹大铁椎，重四五十斤，饮食拱揖⑥不暂去⑦。柄铁折叠环复⑧，如锁上练⑨，引⑩之长丈许⑪。与人罕言语，语类楚声⑫。扣⑬其乡及姓字，皆不答。

既同寝，夜半，客曰："吾去矣！"言讫⑭不见。子灿见窗户皆闭，惊问信之。信之曰："客初至，不冠不袜，以蓝手巾裹头，足缠白布，大铁椎外，一物无所持，而腰多白金⑮。吾与将军俱不敢问也。"子灿寐⑯而醒，客则鼾睡⑰炕上矣。

一日，辞宋将军曰："吾始闻汝名，以为豪⑱，然皆不足用。

---

① 长子灿七岁：比子灿大七岁（seven years older than Zican）。
② 过：访问（visit）。
③ 健啖（dàn）客：食量大的人（good eater）。
④ 寝：丑陋（ugly）。
⑤ 右胁：右腋下（under one's right armpit）。
⑥ 拱揖：拱手行礼（salute by cupping one hand in the other before one's chest）。
⑦ 不暂去：一会也不离身（always keep sth. on one's side）。
⑧ 柄铁折叠环复：椎之铁柄可折叠环绕（its iron chain could be folded to encircle the handle of the club）。
⑨ 练：链（chain）。
⑩ 引：拉开（stretch）。
⑪ 丈许：一丈左右（about one *zhang*）。
⑫ 类楚声：说话像湖南、湖北一带口音（speak in the accent of Hunan or Hubei）。
⑬ 扣：通"叩"，询问（inquire about）。
⑭ 言讫（qì）：说完（having spoken）。
⑮ 腰多白金：腰带中裹着很多银子（he carried much silver in his waistband）。
⑯ 寐：睡着（sleep）。
⑰ 鼾（hān）睡：熟睡（sleep soundly）。鼾：打呼噜（snore）。
⑱ 豪：英雄（hero）。

young. So Zican had once accompanied him to visit General Song.

At a feast during that visit, there was a good eater who looked rather ugly. He had a big iron club under his right armpit which weighed 40 or 50 *jin* (20 or 25 kilos) and he never let it go while eating and drinking even as he was bowing and scraping. The iron chain on the handle of the club could be folded to encircle the handle in such a way that it looked as if the chain was locked tightly but when stretched, it could be one *zhang* (about 3.3 metres) long. He seldom talked to others and his accent sounded like that of the Chu people. He kept silent when asked about his real name and from where he came.

The three of them shared one bedroom. At midnight, the mystic man said, "I'll go out!" He disappeared soon after finishing his words. Zican was surprised to see that the door and window were still closed and stared at Xinzhi with a look of inquiry. Xinzhi said: "When this man first arrived, he wore neither a hat nor socks. He had a blue handkerchief to wrap his head and a white cloth for foot-binding. Except for the big iron club, he did not have anything else in his hand but carried a lot of silver ingots inside his waistband. Neither the general nor I dared to ask him any question." When Zican woke up from a sound sleep, he found that mystic man was on the *kang* (heatable brick bed, common in north China), snoring.

One day the mystic man bade farewell to General Song, "When I first heard your name, I thought that you were a hero but you do not use your skill in martial arts and I had to say goodbye to you." The

吾去矣！"将军强留①之，乃曰："吾数②击杀响马③贼，夺其物，故仇我④。久居，祸且⑤及汝。今夜半，方期⑥我决斗某所。"宋将军欣然曰："吾骑马挟矢以助战。"客曰："止！贼能⑦且众，吾欲护汝，则不快吾意⑧。"宋将军故自负⑨，且欲观客所为，力请⑩客。客不得已，与偕行。将至斗处，送将军登空堡上，曰："但观之，慎弗声⑪，令贼知也。"

时鸡鸣月落，星光照旷野，百步见人。客驰下，吹觱篥⑫数声。顷之⑬，贼二十余骑四面集，步行负弓矢从者百许人。一贼提刀突奔客，客大呼挥椎，贼应声落马，马首裂。众贼环而进⑭，客奋椎左右击，人马仆地⑮，杀三十许人。宋将军屏息观之，股⑯栗⑰欲堕。

忽闻客大呼曰："吾去矣。"尘滚滚东向驰去。后遂不复至。

---

① 强留：竭力挽留（try one's best to urge one to stay）。
② 数：屡次（time and again; repeatedly）。
③ 响马：拦路抢劫的土匪（bandits who block the road in order to rob）。
④ 仇我：以我为仇（regard me as an enemy）。
⑤ 且：将（will）。
⑥ 期：约定（arrange, appoint）。
⑦ 能：有本领（able）。
⑧ 不快吾意：不能让我痛快搏斗（I cannot fight to my heart's content）。
⑨ 故自负：素来以为自己很有本领（he always thought of himself as an able man）。
⑩ 力请：恳切请求（ask earnestly）。
⑪ 慎弗声：千万不要发出声音（never make a sound）。
⑫ 觱篥（bì lì）：一种用竹做管、芦苇做嘴的乐器（a kind of musical instrument with its pipe made of bamboo and the mouthpiece made of reed）。
⑬ 顷之：一会儿（after a little while）。
⑭ 环而进：围攻（besiege）。
⑮ 仆地：倒地（fall to the ground）。
⑯ 股：两腿（two legs）。
⑰ 栗：发抖（shaking）。

general insistently urged him to stay but he said: "I have time and again attacked and killed the bandits and grabbed their belongings. So they hate me and see me as their enemy. If I stay here too long you will be involved in the trouble I have incurred. I will fight a duel with them somewhere this midnight." General Song said merrily: "I will ride my horse and carry a bow and arrows with me to help you in the fight." That man retorted: "No, please don't go! They have many people and all of them are capable fighters. I will not be able to fight to my satisfaction if I have to protect you." General Song had always been rather conceited, also he was curious to know what this man was going to do, so he insisted on going with him. Unable to persuade the general not to go, the mystic man had to allow him to follow. Before getting to the site of the combat, the man took Song to a deserted fort and said to him: "Watch only and keep silent! Don't let them know you are here!"

At that moment cocks had begun crowing and the moon was already setting. The open field was lit by starlight and human figures could be recognised one hundred steps away. The mystic man galloped down to the combat-site and then blew a bamboo pipe. Soon a score or more bandits on horseback rushed in from every direction, followed by over one hundred strong men on foot carrying bows and arrows. One horseman carrying a cavalry sword suddenly approached the lone fighter. Shouting at the top of his lungs, the warrior brandished his iron club and the bandit immediately fell down from his horse. The weapon was so powerful that the head of the animal was also smashed.

魏禧论曰：子房①得力士，椎秦皇帝博浪沙中。大铁椎其人欤？天生异人，必有所用之。予读陈同甫②《中兴遗传》③，豪俊侠烈魁奇之士，泯泯然④不见功名于世者，又何多也！岂天之生才不必为人用欤？抑⑤用之自有时欤？子灿遇大铁椎为壬寅岁⑥，视其貌当年三十⑦，然则大铁椎今四十耳。子灿又尝见其写市物帖子⑧，甚工⑨楷书也。

---

① 子房：汉初张良，字子房。他原为韩人，秦灭韩，良欲为韩报仇，得力士，为铁椎重百二十斤。秦始皇东游，良与力士狙击之于博浪沙（Zhang Liang, a historical figure of the early Han Dynasty, styled himself Zifang, and was originally from the State of Han. After Qin destroyed Han, Zhang Liang employed a man of unusual strength who had an iron club weighing 120 *jin* in an attempt to kill the first emperor of the Qin Dynasty. Once the emperor travelled east, Zhang, together with the strong man, made a surprise attack on him in a place called Bolangsha）。
② 陈同甫：南宋陈亮，字同甫，著名思想家、文学家（Chen Liang, styled himself Tongfu, was a famous thinker and writer of the Southern Song Dynasty）。
③《中兴遗传》：书名，陈亮著，20卷，凡南渡前后忠臣名将，下及游侠、剧盗等皆为之立传（name of a book written by Chen Liang, twenty volumes, in which the biographies of all the loyal subjects, famous generals, down to those who were adept in martial arts and who were known for their chivalrous conduct as well as noted robbers were written）。
④ 泯泯然：衰微湮灭的样子（appearance of declination and oblivion）。
⑤ 抑：或者（or）。
⑥ 壬寅岁：康熙元年（1662年）（the first year of the Kangxi Reign, 1662）。
⑦ 当年三十：应该是30岁（should be 30 years old）。
⑧ 市物帖子：购物单（shopping list）。
⑨ 工：整齐美好（tidy and beautiful）。

With the other bandits moving towards him from different directions, the superman wielded his iron club to hit here and there. The riders together with their horses fell to the ground one after another and more than thirty bandits were killed. Holding his breath, General Song watched the fierce battle. He was frightened and his legs were trembling so badly that he almost fell down from the fort. Suddenly, he heard the warrior yelling at him: "I'll go now!" Song saw his horse galloping eastwards, raising a cloud of dust behind him. The hero never returned.

Wei Xi has made a comment as follows: Zhang Liang found a man of extraordinary strength and employed him to carry his weapon (a large iron club weighing 120 *jin*) to ambush the First Emperor of the Qin Dynasty at Bolangsha. Does our superman resemble the historical one? If Heaven has endowed someone with exceptional ability, there must be a use for this. However, when I read the *Anecdotes of the Prominent Personages in the Reviving Period* written by Chen Tongfu, I found that there had been many extraordinary men of ability, courage and chivalry who did not achieve great deeds of any sort and had sunk into oblivion. Were the extraordinary abilities of those supermen received at birth not for use? Or could they bring into play their talents only at the right time when opportunity knocked? It was the first year of the Kangxi Reign (1662) when Chen Zican encountered Big Iron Club and at that time he looked 30 years old. If that was correct, he is 40 now. Zican once saw a shopping list written by him and his handwriting was neat and elegant.

口　技

林嗣环

京中有善口技者。会①宾客大宴，于厅事②之东北角，施③八尺屏障④，口技人坐屏障中，一桌、一椅、一扇、一抚尺⑤而已。众宾团坐。少顷⑥，但闻⑦屏障中抚尺一下，满坐⑧寂然，无敢哗者。

遥闻深巷中犬吠，便有妇人惊觉欠伸⑨，其夫呓语⑩。既而⑪儿醒，大啼。夫亦醒。妇抚⑫儿乳⑬，儿含乳啼，妇拍而呜⑭之。又一大儿醒，狺狺⑮不止。当是时，妇手拍儿声，口中呜声，儿含

---

① 会：适逢（happen to, it so happened that）。
② 厅事：大厅，客厅（hall）。
③ 施：设置，安放（set up, put up）。
④ 屏障：屏风、围帐一类用来隔断视线的东西（such things as a screen or a curtain which can be used to cut off the line of sight）。
⑤ 抚尺：艺人表演用的道具，也叫"醒木"（stage property which an actor uses in a performance, also called "attention-catching block"）。
⑥ 少顷：一会儿（a little while）。
⑦ 但闻：只听见（only hearing）。
⑧ 坐：座（seat）。
⑨ 欠伸：打呵欠，伸懒腰（yawn）。
⑩ 呓语：说梦话（talk in one's sleep）。
⑪ 既而：不久（soon）。
⑫ 抚：抚摸，安慰（fondle, comfort）。
⑬ 乳：喂奶（breast-feed, suckle）。
⑭ 呜：轻轻哼唱（croon）。
⑮ 狺狺（yín yín）：这里指喊叫声（cry; yell）。

THE MAGIC OF VOCAL MIMICRY

Lin Sihuan

In the capital city, there was a man who excelled in vocal mimicry. One day he came across a huge banquet held by a family to entertain many guests and was invited to perform there. An eight *chi* (1 *chi* = 1/3 meter) long curtain was set up in the northeastern corner of the hall. The performer was sitting behind the curtain with a table, a chair, a fan and an attention block. All the guests sat in a semicircle facing the curtain. A moment later, the attention block struck the table and the whole audience became silent and nobody dared make any noise.

Then from a distance was heard the sound of a dog barking in a deep lane. Disturbed by the noise, a woman stretched and yawned and her husband mumbled in his sleep. Their baby son awoke and cried loudly. The husband was awakened by the cry and his wife held the baby to her breast to feed him. While sucking milk, the baby kept crying and his mother, by patting and crooning, tried to make the baby sleep again. The husband got up to pass water and his wife, with the baby in her arms, also arose

乳啼声，大儿初醒声，床声，夫叱大儿声，溺瓶中声，溺桶中声，一时①齐发，众妙毕②备③。满堂宾客，无不伸颈侧目④，微笑默叹⑤，以为妙绝也。

未几⑥，夫齁声起，妇拍儿亦渐拍渐止。微闻有鼠作作索索⑦，盆器倾侧⑧，妇梦中咳嗽。宾客意⑨少⑩舒⑪，稍稍正坐。

忽一人大呼"火起"，夫起大呼，妇亦起大呼。两儿齐哭。俄而⑫百千人大呼，百千儿哭，百千犬吠。中间⑬力拉⑭崩倒⑮之声，火爆声，呼呼风声，百千齐作；又夹百千求救声，曳⑯屋许许⑰声，抢夺声，泼水声。凡所应有，无所不有。虽⑱人有百手，手有百指，不能指⑲其一端⑳；人有百口，口有百舌，不能名㉑其一处也。于是

---

① 一时：同时（at the same time）。
② 毕：全，都（complete, all）。
③ 备：具备（have, possess）。
④ 侧目：偏着头看（look with one's head moved to one side）。
⑤ 默叹：默默地赞叹（gasp in silent admiration）。
⑥ 未几：不多久（before long）。
⑦ 作作索索：老鼠活动的声音（sound of rats moving about）。
⑧ 倾侧：倾斜翻倒（lean to one side and turn over）。
⑨ 意：心情（mood, heart）。
⑩ 少：稍微（a little, slightly）。
⑪ 舒：松弛（relax）。
⑫ 俄而：一会儿（a little while）。
⑬ 间：夹杂（be mixed together）。
⑭ 力拉：象声词（mimetic word）。
⑮ 崩倒：倒塌（collapse）。
⑯ 曳（yè）：拉（pull）。
⑰ 许（hǔ）许：象声词（mimetic word）。
⑱ 虽：即使（even, even if）。
⑲ 指：指明（point out）。
⑳ 一端：这里指"一种"（here meaning one kind）。
㉑ 名：说出（speak out）。

from bed to relieve herself. Their elder son, also having woken up, kept murmuring. Then all these sounds were repeated and they came from behind the curtain almost simultaneously: the woman comforting and humming her baby to sleep; the baby crying while keeping his mother's nipple in his mouth; his elder brother just awaking from a dream; the bed creaking; the father scolding his elder son; the man passing water into a bottle and the woman urinating into a commode. The imitation of all these sounds was so vivid and lifelike that the audience craned their necks and narrowed their eyes, smiling and gasping in admiration for the fantastic imitative skill.

Before long, the husband began to snore and his wife gradually stopped patting her baby. It could be heard the slight rustling sound of rats moving around and causing basins and other utensils to slant or overturn. The woman was coughing in her sleep. The audience began to relax and straightened a little in their sitting position.

Suddenly, someone called out, "There is a fire!" The husband arose from bed and yelled with panic and his wife did the same thing. Their two sons began to cry at the same time. Soon came in chorus the yelling of hundreds of people, the crying of hundreds of children and the barking of hundreds of dogs. Amid the panicky voices could be heard the crashing of houses collapsing onto

宾客无不变色离席，奋①袖出②臂，两股战战③，几④欲先走。

忽然抚尺一下，群响毕绝。撤屏视之，一人、一桌、一椅、一扇、一抚尺而已。

---

① 奋：张开（open）。
② 出：露出（reveal）。
③ 战战：哆嗦的样子（trembling manner）。
④ 几：几乎（almost, nearly）。

the ground mixed with the crackling of objects burning in the fire and the howling of a strong wind. All sorts of sounds burst simultaneously and a lot more were coming: hundreds of people crying for help; fire fighters pooling efforts to pull down burning houses; some people desperately trying to save their belongings from fire and water being sprinkled on fire. Any sound that would occur under such circumstances could be heard here. Even if a person had one hundred hands and each hand had one hundred fingers, he would not be able to point out from where a particular sound was coming. Even if somebody had one hundred mouths and each mouth had one hundred tongues, he would not be able to tell one sound from among hundreds of others. Affected by the sounds, all the guests, without any exception, looked horrified and immediately left their seats. With their legs trembling, they stretched out their arms from their sleeves, anxious to run away from the "scene" as soon as possible.

Suddenly, the attention block struck the table and all the sounds ceased at once. Then the curtain was removed and what the audience could see was one man, one table, one chair, one fan, one attention block and nothing else.

送王进士①之任②扬州序

汪琬

诸曹③失之，一郡得之，此十数州县之庆也。国家得之，交游失之，此又二三士大夫之憾也。吾友王子贻上，年少而才。既举进士，于甲第④当任部主事⑤，而用新令，出为推官扬州，将与吾党别。吾见憾者方在燕市⑥，而庆者已翘足企盼，相望江淮之间矣。王子勉旃⑦！事上宜敬，接下宜诚，莅事⑧宜慎，用刑宜宽。反是⑨罪也。吾告王子止此矣。

---

① 王进士：即王士禛，字贻上，号阮亭，又号渔洋山人，山东新城人。顺治十二年（1655）进士（Wang Shizhen styled himself Yishang, alternatively named Ruanting, also Hermit Yuyang, from Xincheng, Shandong, a successful candidate of the imperial examination in the 12th year of the Shunzhi Reign）。
② 之任：到任（assume a post）。王士禛中进士后，出任扬州推官（when Wang Shizhen passed the imperial examination, he went out of the capital to take up the post of assistant governor of Yangzhou Prefecture）。
③ 诸曹：指朝廷各部门（each department of the imperial court）。
④ 甲第：科举考试的等第（grades in the imperial examination）。
⑤ 主事：各部所属司官的最低一级（the lowest grade of the department officials under each ministry）。
⑥ 燕市：指首都（referring to the capital）。
⑦ 勉旃（zhān）：勉之（work hard）。旃，语助词（auxiliary word）。
⑧ 莅事：临事（when dealing with a matter）。
⑨ 反是：与此相反（contrary to this）。

SEEING OFF PALACE GRADUATE WANG TO HIS POST IN YANGZHOU

Wang Wan

If none of the various departments of the imperial court has succeeded in recruiting a gifted scholar but a certain prefecture has him, this could be regarded as a happy event to a dozen counties under its jurisdiction. If the nation has found a good job for him and his friends are unable to keep him by their side, this would be something unhappy to quite a few scholar-officials. My friend, Mr. Wang Yishang is a talented young scholar. According to the grade with which he passed the imperial examination, he should have held an official position in a department of the central government. However, because of the new rule he has to be assigned a post outside the capital. He will say goodbye to his friends and then set off for Yangzhou to take up the post of an assistant governor. I have seen many people in the capital who feel sorry for his departure. I can imagine that lots of people in the region between the Yangtze River and the Huaihe River are eagerly looking forward to his arrival. Mr. Wang, let me say

朔风①初劲，雨雪载途，摇策②而行，努力自爱。

---
① 朔风：北风（north wind）。
② 策：马鞭（horsewhip）。

something for mutual encouragement: be respectful in attending superiors; be honest in dealing with subordinates; be cautious in handling matters and be lenient in passing sentence. If we fail to do so, we will become sinners. So much for my advice to Mr. Wang.

The north wind has turned strong and rain or snow will hinder your journey. You are to whip your horse all the way to your destination. Please work hard and cherish your good reputation.

地震（节选）

蒲松龄

康熙七年①六月十七日戌时，地大震。余适②客③稷下④，方与表兄李笃之对烛饮。忽闻有声如雷，自东南来，向西北去。众骇异，不解其故。俄而⑤几案摆簸，酒杯倾覆；屋梁椽柱，错折有声。相顾失色。久之，方知地震，各疾趋⑥出。见楼阁房舍，仆⑦而复起；墙倾屋塌之声，与儿啼女号，喧如鼎沸。人眩晕不能立，坐地上，随地转侧。河水倾泼丈余，鸭鸣犬吠

---

① 康熙七年：公元 1668 年（in AD 1668）。
② 适：恰好（happen to be）。
③ 客：客居（to stay somewhere as a visitor）。
④ 稷下：今山东省淄博市临淄附近地区（area near today's Linzi of Zibo City, Shandong Province）。
⑤ 俄而：不久（before long）。
⑥ 疾趋：快走（walk quickly）。
⑦ 仆：倒（fall）。

THE EARTHQUAKE (EXCERPTS)

Pu Songling

On the early evening on the 17th day of the 6th month in the 7th year of the Kangxi Reign (1668), a massive earthquake occurred. I happened to be in Jixia, as a visitor and at that moment was drinking by candlelight with Li Duzhi, my elder male cousin. Suddenly I heard a sound resembling thunder coming from the southeast and then going to the northwest. Everybody was shocked and did not know what was happening. Soon tables and desks began swaying and wine cups fell down. Beams, rafters and pillars of the building started to make cracking noises. People looked at each other, their faces turning pale with fear. It took some time before they realised that it was an earthquake. Then everybody rushed out from their homes. I saw storeyed buildings and single-storey houses fall down one after another. The noises coming from the falling of walls and the collapsing of buildings, mingled with children's screaming and women's crying, formed deafening sounds like boiling water in a giant container. Unable to stand steady because of dizziness, people had to sit on the

满城中。逾一时许,始稍定。视街上,则男女裸聚,竞相告语,并①忘其未衣也。后闻某处井倾侧,不可汲;某家楼台南北易向;栖霞②山裂;沂水③陷穴,广数亩。此真非常之奇变也。

---

① 并:都(all)。
② 栖霞:县名,在山东省东部(name of a county, in the east of Shandong Province)。
③ 沂水:县名,在山东省东南部(name of a county, in the southeast of Shandong Province)。

ground but they could not sit still as the ground continued jolting. The splashing river water surged ten feet high. Everywhere in the city, quacking ducks and barking dogs could be heard. The tension began to ease after an hour. I saw naked men and women gathering on the street, unaware that they did not wear anything, exchanging what they had seen and how they had felt. Later I was told that the quake had deformed a well so badly that water could no longer be drawn. I also heard that in someone's house a tower used to have a southern exposure and the quake had made it face north. After the quake, cracks could be seen on the mountain in Qixia County. While in Yishui County, the ground had caved in to become a pit about one acre in size. Such happenings are extraordinary and beyond imagination.

狱中杂记（节选）

方苞

康熙五十一年①三月，余在刑部②狱，见死而由窦③出者日四三人。有洪洞令④杜君者，作⑤而言曰："此疫作⑥也。今天时顺正⑦，死者尚稀，往岁多至日十数人。"余叩所以⑧，杜君曰："是疾易传染，遘者⑨虽戚属⑩，不敢同卧起。而狱中为老监者四，监五室⑪，禁卒居中央，牖其前⑫以通明，屋极⑬有窗以达气。旁四室则

---

① 康熙五十一年：公元1712年（AD 1712）。
② 刑部：官署名。清朝官制六部之一。掌刑法、讼狱，是最高司法机关（name of a government office. One of the six ministries in the bureaucratic establishment in the Qing Dynasty, in charge of penal code and lawsuit. It was the highest judicial authority）。
③ 窦（dòu）：洞。这里指监牢墙上开的洞（hole; here referring to the open hole on the prison's wall）。
④ 洪洞（tóng）令：洪洞县的县令（magistrate of Hongtong County）。洪洞：今山西省洪洞县（today's Hongtong County in Shanxi Province）。
⑤ 作：站起来（stand up）。
⑥ 作：流行（epidemic）。
⑦ 天时顺正：气候正常（in normal climate）。
⑧ 叩所以：问是什么原因（ask why）。叩：问（ask）。
⑨ 遘（gòu）者：染病者（one who catches an illness）。
⑩ 戚属：亲戚（relative）。
⑪ 监五室：每个老监有五间屋子（each old jail has five rooms）。
⑫ 牖（yǒu）其前：在前方开一个窗户（open a window in the front）。
⑬ 屋极：屋顶（roof, housetop）。

THE EVENTS IN A PRISON (EXCERPTS)

Fang Bao

In the 3rd month of the 51st year of the Kangxi Reign (1712), I was serving a sentence in the prison of the Ministry of Punishments where I saw three or four corpses being pulled out through the opening of the prison's wall every day. Mr. Du, a former magistrate of Hongtong County in Shanxi Province, stood up and said: "An epidemic disease is spreading. Now that we are experiencing normal weather conditions, there are currently not many victims. In previous years when this happened, a dozen prisoners would die every day." I asked why and Mr. Du said: "This contagious illness spreads easily. If someone has caught this disease, even his relatives dare not sleep in the same bedroom with him. This prison consists of four old jailhouses and each has five cells. The prison guards occupy the central ones. They have a window on the front wall of their rooms to let in light from outside and a skylight on the roof to let in fresh air, while the other four cells for prisoners do not have any windows. Over 200 prisoners are often kept in one cell. Every day at twilight the cells are locked. Therefore the prisoners have to pass faeces and urine

无之,而系囚①常二百余。每薄暮②下管键③,矢溺④皆闭其中,与饮食之气相薄⑤。又隆冬,贫者席地而卧,春气动,鲜⑥不疫⑦矣。狱中成法⑧,质明⑨启钥,方夜中,生人与死者并踵顶而卧⑩,无可旋避⑪,此所以染者众也。又可怪者,大盗积贼⑫,杀人重囚⑬,气杰旺⑭,染此者十不一二,或随有瘳⑮,其骈死⑯,皆轻系⑰及牵连佐证

---

① 系囚:关押的囚犯(prisoners put behind bars)。
② 薄暮:傍晚(at night fall, at dusk)。
③ 下管键:落了锁(lock)。管键:锁钥(lock and key)。
④ 矢溺:大小便(human excrement)。矢:屎(stool)。溺:尿(urine)。
⑤ 相薄(bó):相混杂(be mixed with)。
⑥ 鲜:少(few)。
⑦ 疫:害病(fall ill)。
⑧ 成法:老规矩(established rules)。
⑨ 质明:天亮时(daybreak)。
⑩ 并踵顶而卧:并排睡一起(lie side by side)。踵:脚后跟(heel)。顶:头顶(top)。
⑪ 旋避:回避(avoid)。
⑫ 积贼:屡次作案的贼(thief repeatedly committing crimes)。
⑬ 重囚:案情重大的囚犯(prisoner whose case is very serious)。
⑭ 气杰旺:精力特别旺盛(very energetic)。
⑮ 或随有瘳(chōu):有的人染上病随即就痊愈了(recover immediately when one falls ill)。瘳:病愈(recovery)。
⑯ 骈(pián)死:接连死去(die in succession)。
⑰ 轻系:轻罪被囚的犯人(prisoner who commits a misdemeanour)。

anywhere in the small enclosed space, causing the smell of their food to be mixed with the bad odour of human excrement. In midwinter, poor prisoners have to sleep on the floor. Very few of them do not fall ill when spring comes. According to an established rule of the prison, the cells are not unlocked until daybreak. Therefore very often at night, prisons have to sleep side by side with dead bodies. No one can avoid this awful situation. That's why there are so many people who are infected. Strangely, hardened bandits, professional robbers, murders and other major criminals are physically strong and full of vim and vigour. Very few of them — one or two out of ten — catch the disease. These prisoners will soon recover even if they fall ill. Only misdemeanants or those who do not commit any crime but get entangled with a case while serving as witnesses die one after another." I asked again: "In the national capital city, there are the city-level prison of the capital and the district-level prisons under the control of the five districts of the capital. Why does the prison of the Ministry of Punishments hold so many criminals?" Mr. Du answered: "In recent years while dealing with more serious cases, neither the city-level nor the district-level courts dare to make decisions. Besides, all criminals who are put under investigation and taken into custody by the infantry commander in charge of the nine gates of the capital are put into the prison of the Ministry of Punishments. In the fourteen departments under this ministry, all the greedy people among the directors and deputies of the departments as well as other officials

法所不及者①。"余曰:"京师有京兆狱②,有五城御史司坊③,何故刑部系囚之多至此?"杜君曰:"迩年④狱讼,情稍重,京兆、五城即不敢专决,又九门提督⑤所访缉纠诘⑥,皆归刑部;而十四司正副郎⑦好事者⑧及书吏⑨、狱官、禁卒,皆利系者之多⑩,少有

① 牵连佐证法所不及者:被牵连、被捉来当证人的那些并没有犯法的人 (those who did not commit any crime but became entangled with a certain case or one who was caught to serve as a witness)。
② 京兆狱:京城监狱,即当时顺天府监狱 (prison in the capital, i.e. prison in the Shuntian Prefecture)。
③ 五城御史司坊:京城分东、南、西、北、中五区,称五城,设五城兵马司,并设巡城御史,负责治安方面的事情。司坊:管理街坊间的刑事案件。坊:当时京城分为十坊,每司负责二坊 (the capital was divided into five districts such as the eastern, southern, western, northern and the central, called "five-city." The department of the five-city troops and horses was set up and its head was called Commander of the Urban-Patrolling Guards, in charge of public security. Each department had two *Fang* under its command and there were ten *Fang* altogether in the capital. Here referring to the prisons under the department and the *Fang*)。
④ 迩年:近年 (recent years)。
⑤ 九门提督:掌管京城九门的步兵统领 (infantry commander in charge of the nine gates of the capital)。九门,指正阳门、崇文门、宣武门、安定门、德胜门、东直门、西直门、朝阳门、阜成门诸门 (the nine gates include Zhengyang, Xuanwu, Chongwen, Anding, Desheng, Dongzhi, Xizhi, Chaoyang and Fucheng)。
⑥ 所访缉纠诘:所访查缉捕来的犯人 (prisoners caught to be investigated)。
⑦ 十四司正副郎:清初刑部设十四司,每司正职为郎中,副职为员外郎 (at the beginning of the Qing Dynasty, under the Ministry of Punishments there were 14 departments. The principal of each department was called Langzhong and the deputy Yuanwailang)。
⑧ 好事者:喜欢多事的人 (busybody)。
⑨ 书吏:掌管文牍的小吏 (clerks in charge of official documents)。
⑩ 利系者之多:以关押的人越多越有利 (benefit from more prisoners)。

such as law secretaries, prison wardens and guards collect benefits from obtaining more prisoners. Therefore, they will do whatever they can to catch anybody who is slightly involved in a case. Once in jail, whether guilty or not, this person will be put in the old jailhouse, with his hands and feet in irons to suffer unbearable pain. Then he will be induced to pay money to be bailed out. Based on his family property, the amount of money they are going to extort from him is estimated. The money obtained in this way will be shared between the officials and clerks. A middle-class family will use up its assets to pay the bail. What a criminal from a family below the middle class can get is to have the handcuffs and shackles removed and to be relocated to a plank house outside the prison. Even this will cost his family a few dozen *liang* of silver. Only those who are from a very poor family with nothing to rely on cannot have their handcuffs and shackles loosened. They are treated in such a way that can be used as an example to warn other inmates. Among the accomplices, those who have been deeply involved in the case may not be in jail. While the others who are minor offenders or innocents may be tortured. Having suffered from piled-up anxiety and anger, bad sleep and awful food, these poor inmates have their health so deteriorated that they get sick and then without any medical treatment, most of them die." ... Old Man Zhu and Young Scholar Yu who had been put in jail together with me and another man named Seng from Tongchuan County who was also in this prison have all died of an illness. Actually, none of them should

连,必多方钩致①。苟入狱,不问罪之有无,必械手足②,置老监,俾③困苦不可忍。然后导以取保④,出居于外,量其家之所有以为剂⑤,而官与吏剖焉。中家⑥以上皆竭资取保,其次⑦求脱械居监外板屋,费亦数十金。唯极贫无依,则械系不稍宽,为标准以警其余。或同系⑧,情罪重者,反出在外,而轻者、无罪者罹⑨其毒。积忧愤,寝食违节⑩,及病,又无医药,故往往至死。"……余同系⑪朱翁、余生及在狱同官⑫僧某,遘役⑬死,皆不应重罚。又某氏以不孝讼其子,左右邻械系入老监,号呼达旦。余感焉,以杜君言泛讯⑭之,众言同,于是乎书。

凡死刑狱上⑮,行刑者先俟于门外,使其党入索财物,名曰"斯

---

① 钩致:像用钩子勾东西一样弄来。这里指逮捕(arrest a person just as one catches something with a hook)。
② 械手足:给手脚戴上刑具(put one's hands and feet in irons)。
③ 俾(bǐ):使(make, cause)。
④ 导以取保:诱导犯人花钱保释(induce a prisoner to be bailed out by paying money)。
⑤ 量其家之所有以为剂:估量他们家中财产多少作为敲诈的依据(estimate one's property and extort money from him according to its value)。剂:调剂(adjusting)。
⑥ 中家:中产之家(middle-class family)。
⑦ 其次:那些次于中产人家的(those inferior to the middle-class family)。
⑧ 同系:同案犯(accomplice)。
⑨ 罹(lí):遭遇,遭受(be caught in, suffer from)。
⑩ 违节:不正常,违反正常规律(unnormal, run counter to normal law)。
⑪ 同系:一同被囚禁的人(prisoners locked up at the same time and place)。
⑫ 同官:县名,今陕西铜川市(name of a county, today's Tongchuan County in Shaanxi Province)。
⑬ 遘役:染病(catch an illness)。遘:遇(meet)。役:疫(illness)。
⑭ 泛讯:普遍地问问(ask universally)。
⑮ 死刑狱上:判了死罪的案件已上奏的(the case of capital crime which had been reported to the emperor)。

have been punished severely. A man sued his son for not performing filial duties. His neighbours became involved and were put into the old jailhouse with their hands and feet in irons. They wailed and cried piteously till dawn. I was touched by Du's story and then I talked to the inmates one by one to find out if his story proved true. They told me the same story, so I wrote it down.

After a memorial had been submitted to the throne indicating a death sentence, the executioner would wait outside the prison and let his partners go into the cell to extort money from the prisoner who was to be executed. This step was called "*siluo*" (making arrangements). If the prisoner was from a rich family, they would talk to the family. However, they would talk to a poor prisoner face to face. A prisoner who is to be executed by dismembering the body and ultimately cutting the throat will be told: "If you make me happy, I'll first stab your heart. Otherwise, your heart will not be dead yet and you will feel the great pain when your four limbs are being cut off one by one." A prisoner who is to be hanged will be told: "If you make me happy, you will breathe your last at the very beginning. Otherwise, you will be hanged three times plus tortured by the instrument of punishment before you die." They cannot extort anything from those who are to be beheaded but they will keep these prisoners' decapitated heads as a mortgage. The rich have to pay nearly one hundred *liang* of silver as a bribe. The poor have to sell their clothes to collect money for the bribe. While those who do

罗"。富者就其戚属,贫则面语之。其极刑①,曰:"顺我,即先刺心;否则四肢解尽,心犹不死。"其绞缢②,曰:"顺我,始缢即气绝;否则三缢加别械③,然后得死。"唯大辟④无可要⑤,然犹质其首⑥。用此⑦,富者赂数十百金,贫亦罄⑧衣装;绝无有者,则治之如所言⑨。主缚者⑩亦然,不如所欲,缚时即先折筋骨。每岁大决⑪,勾者⑫十四三,留者十六七,皆缚至西市⑬待命。其伤于缚者,即幸留,

---

① 极刑:凌迟处死的刑罚(put to death by dismembering the body)。
② 绞缢(yì):绞刑(execution by hanging)。
③ 加别械:加别的刑具(add other instruments of torture)。
④ 大辟:斩首(behead)。
⑤ 要:要挟(put pressure on, threaten)。
⑥ 质其首:留下死者的头作抵押,要家属来赎取,以便勒索(keep the head of the dead as a mortgage and ask his family members to ransom in order to extort money)。
⑦ 用此:因此(therefore)。
⑧ 罄(qìng):用尽(use up; exhaust)。
⑨ 治之如所言:按照他们说的那样处理犯人(handle the prisoners in the normal way)。
⑩ 主缚者:执行捆缚犯人的役吏(yamen runner whose task is to tie up prisoners)。
⑪ 大决:即秋决。封建时代规定在秋天大批地杀犯人(put to death in autumn. It was stipulated in the old days in China that a large number of prisoners were executed in autumn)。
⑫ 勾者:每年秋天,刑部先把判死罪者的姓名奏报皇帝,让皇帝用朱笔勾一下,勾着的,立即处死;未勾着的暂缓执行(every autumn the Ministry of Punishments presented to the emperor in advance a name list of the prisoners who were sentenced to death and asked him to tick some off with a brush-pen dipped in red ink. The ticked ones would be put to death at once and the others would be removed from the list of prisoners under death sentence)。
⑬ 西市:清时京城行刑的场所,在今北京菜市口(place for carrying out the death sentence in the capital in the Qing Dynasty, in today's Caishikou in Beijing)。

not have anything will be executed in the most torturous way. The yamen runners who are in charge of tying up the criminals with rope also do the same thing. They will break the criminals' bones while binding him if the latter cannot make them happy. Every year, most executions occur in autumn. On the list of all the criminals who have been sentenced to death, three or four out of ten are ticked off to be executed immediately while six or seven are kept to be tied up with rope and then transferred to Xishi for further judgement. Those who have been injured while being bound and have luckily survived will not recover from their injury for several months. Some of them will become handicapped for the rest of their life.

Once I asked a senior clerk: "Those who are to be executed or who are being tied up with rope are not your personal enemies. You only want to get some money from them. If they cannot give you anything, you should be lenient with them. Isn't this an act of benevolence?" He answered: "This is to establish a rule to warn other criminals and teach the latecomers a lesson. This is an action to prevent people from cherishing the attitude of avoiding disaster by chance." The yamen runners who handle instruments of torture or the cane beaters are also fond of this trick. The three men who were arrested together with me were tortured by wooden instruments of punishment at the interrogation. One of them paid thirty *liang* of silver and then he was slightly injured to the bone and fell ill for more than one month. Another one paid double and as a result only his

病数月乃瘳①，或竟成痼疾②。

余尝就老胥③而问焉："彼于刑者、缚者④，非相仇也，期有得耳；果无有，终亦稍宽之，非仁术⑤乎？"曰："是立法以警其余，且惩后也；不如此，则人有幸心⑥。"主梏扑者⑦亦然。余同逮⑧以木讯⑨者三人：一人予三十金，骨微伤，病间月⑩；一人倍之，伤肤，兼旬⑪愈；一人六倍，即夕行步如平常。或叩之曰："罪人有无不均⑫，既各有得，何必更以多寡为差⑬？"曰："无差，谁为多与者？"孟子曰："术不可不慎⑭。"信夫！

部中老胥，家藏伪章，文书下行直省⑮，多潜易之，增减要语，奉

---

① 瘳：病愈（recover from an illness）。
② 痼（gù）疾：根深蒂固的疾病（deep-rooted illness）。
③ 老胥：多年的老役吏（old clerk, yamen runner for many years）。胥：掌管文案的小吏（a clerk in charge of documents）。
④ 刑者、缚者：受刑的和被捆的（one who is tortured and one who is bound）。
⑤ 仁术：善行，好心（kind conduct, good intention）。
⑥ 幸心：侥幸心理（the idea of leaving things to chance）。
⑦ 主梏扑者：专管上刑具、打板子的人（one who puts instruments of torture on prisoners or canes them）。
⑧ 同逮：同案被捕的人（a prisoner arrested in the same case）。
⑨ 木讯：用板子、夹棍审讯（interrogate with board and other wooden instruments of torture）。
⑩ 病间月：病了一个多月（be ill for more than one month）。间：隔（be at a distance from）。
⑪ 兼旬：两旬，二十天（twenty days）。
⑫ 有无不均：贫富不均（unequal distribution of wealth）。
⑬ 为差：分等级（in grades）。
⑭ 术不可不慎：语出《孟子·公孙丑》，意谓选择职业不可不慎重（from "Gongsunchou" of *Mencius*. Meaning one should be cautious in the choice of one's occupation）。
⑮ 直省：直属朝廷管辖的省份（a province directly under the imperial court）。

skin had some injuries and it took him only twenty days to recover. The third one paid six times and he walked normally in the evening of that day. Someone asked: "The criminals are some rich and some poor. Since you can get money from each of them, why do you treat them differently according to the amount of money they pay you?" The senior clerk answered: "If there is no difference in the way we treat them, who will pay more money?" Mencius said, "We should be very careful in choosing our occupations." How true it is!

A senior law secretary of the Ministry of Punishments kept a fake seal at home. When official documents came from the imperial court to the province, he would secretly falsify them by adding or deleting some important words. While reading them the executive officials did not know they were not the real documents. He did not dare to do the same thing to the documents which were presented to the emperor or those that were coming and going between two government departments of equal rank. The government decree stipulates: If nobody was killed in a big robbery and quite a few accomplices are involved in this case, only one or two chief instigators are put to death immediately and the others, at the autumn trial, will be given the reduced sentence of being exiled to a distant place. If an immediate death-sentence was listed in the court-verdict report which had just been presented to the emperor, the executioner would wait outside the prison in advance. No sooner had the order of action been given than the prisoner concerned was tied up with rope and dragged

行者莫辨也。其上闻①及移关②诸部，犹未敢然。功令③：大盗未杀人，及他犯同谋多人者，止主谋一二人立决④；余经秋审，皆减等发配。狱辞上⑤，中有立决者，行刑人先俟于门外，命下，遂缚以出，不羁晷刻⑥。有某姓兄弟，以把持公仓，法应立决，狱具矣，胥某谓曰："予我千金，吾生若。"叩其术，曰："是无难，别具本章⑦，狱辞无易，取案末⑧独身无亲戚者二人易汝名，俟封奏时潜易之⑨而已。"其同事者曰："是可欺死者，而不能欺主谳者⑩，倘复请之，吾辈无生理矣。"胥某笑曰："复请之，吾辈无生理，而主谳者亦各罢去。彼不能以二人之命易其官，则吾辈终无死道也。"竟行之，案末二人立决。主者口呿舌挢⑪，终不敢诘。余在狱，犹见某姓，狱中人

---

① 上闻：报告皇上的文书（documents presented to the emperor）。
② 移关：平行机关来往的文书（documents coming and going between departments of equal rank）。
③ 功令：朝廷所定法令（government decree）。
④ 立决：立刻处决（不等到秋决）（put to death immediately, not wait till autumn）。
⑤ 狱辞上：审判书呈奏上去（judicial decision presented to the emperor）。
⑥ 不羁晷（guǐ）刻：一刻不停（not stay for any moment）。晷：比喻光阴，时间（time）。晷刻：片刻（a short moment）。
⑦ 别具本章：另外准备了一份奏章（prepare another memorial to the throne）。
⑧ 案末：列案在同案罪人名单后面的从犯（accessories to the crime who were listed at the rear of the court verdict）。
⑨ 俟封奏时潜易之：等加封向皇帝奏请时偷偷地换过（secretly change it just before it was sealed and presented to the emperor）。
⑩ 主谳（yàn）者：负责审判的官员（official in charge of a trial）。谳：审判定罪（put on trial and convict somebody of a crime）。
⑪ 口呿（qū）舌挢（jiǎo）：张口结舌（be agape and tongue-tied）。呿：张口不能说话（open mouth but cannot speak）。舌挢：翘起舌头。形容惊讶的样子（raise one's tongue, in a surprised air）。

out without any lingering. Two brothers were to be put to death immediately, according to the law, for their crime of monopolising a public granary. The judgment had already been given but the clerical official said to them, "Give me one thousand *liang* of silver and I will save your lives." To answer how their lives could be saved, he said: "It is not difficult. I will prepare another memorial to the throne. I will not change the court verdict. What I need to do is to use the names of two accessories to the crime who are bachelors without any relatives and are listed at the rear of the court verdict report. I will secretly replace your names with theirs just before the memorial is sealed and presented to the throne." One of his colleagues said: "This can fool the convicts who will be put to death but not the officials who are in charge of the trial. If the officials in charge make another memorial to report to the throne, we will all be dead." The law secretary said with a smile: "Yes, we would all go to graves if the officials in charge of the trial did report it. Whereas they would be removed from their positions. They won't save the two lives at the cost of their positions. So there is no reason why we should die." He did what he intended to do and the two men at the rear of the court verdict list were executed. The officials in charge of the trial were so surprised that they were at a loss for words when they were informed of the execution. However, they did not dare to make inquiries about it. Once I saw the two brothers in the prison. Pointing at them, quite a few inmates told me, "Their heads have been saved by bartering with the heads of

群指曰："是以某某易其首者。"胥某一夕暴卒，众皆以为冥谪①云。

凡杀人，狱辞无谋、故者②，经秋审入矜疑③，即免死。吏因以巧法④。有郭四者，凡四杀人，复以矜疑减等，随遇赦，将出，日与其徒置酒酣歌达曙。或叩以往事，一一详述之，意色扬扬，若自矜诩⑤。噫！潒⑥恶吏忍于鬻狱⑦，无责也；而道⑧之不明，良吏亦多以脱人于死为功，而不求其情⑨，其枉民⑩也，亦甚矣哉！

奸民久于狱，与胥卒表里⑪，颇有奇羡⑫。山阴李姓以杀人系狱，每岁致数百金。康熙四十八年，以赦出，居数月，漠然无所事。其乡人有杀人者，因代承⑬之。盖以律非故杀，必久系，终无死法也。五十一年，复援赦减等⑭谪戍⑮，叹曰："吾不得复入此矣！"故例：

① 冥谪（zhé）：受到阴曹地府的惩罚（punished by the nether world）。
② 无谋、故者：没有谋杀或故意杀人罪名的（person without a charge of murder or intentional killing）。
③ 入矜疑：归入"矜疑"一类（put ... in the "pitiful or doubtful" group）。矜疑：其情可怜，其罪可疑（a pitiful circumstance and doubtful crime）。
④ 巧法：取巧枉法，玩弄法令（pervert the law by trickery, play with laws and decrees）。
⑤ 若自矜诩（xǔ）：好像自己很得意（he looked proud of himself）。矜诩：炫耀（show off）。
⑥ 潒（xiè）：污浊（dirty, foul）。
⑦ 鬻（yù）狱：卖官司（go to law against sb. through bribery）。
⑧ 道：世道（the manners and morals of the time）。
⑨ 情：真实情况（reality）。
⑩ 枉民：使百姓蒙受冤屈（wrong the common people）。
⑪ 表里：内外勾结（collude with the enemies from inside and outside）。
⑫ 奇（jī）羡：赢余。指勒索所得（surplus, here referring to gains through extorting）。
⑬ 代承：代替他人承担杀人罪名（bear the charge of murder for the killer）。
⑭ 援赦减：根据大赦条例减刑（commute a sentence according to the rules of general pardon）。援：引用（quote）。
⑮ 谪戍：发配充军（be transported to a distant place for penal servitude）。

two others." The law secretary died suddenly one night and all the inmates thought he had been punished by the force from the nether world.

If somebody was killed and the criminal involved has not been charged with murder or intentional killing, this case, at the autumn trial, will be put into the "pitiful or doubtful" category and the criminal concerned will be exempt from the death sentence. The prison officials and clerks make use of the decree to gain advantage by trickery. A criminal named Guo Si had committed murder four times and each time his sentence was reduced through the "pitiful or doubtful" reason. Then he came across a general amnesty. Before leaving the prison, he bought wine everyday to drink and sing with his men throughout the night. Someone asked him about his past experience and he gave minute descriptions. He was so immensely proud that it seemed as if his past experience was a glorious one. Alas! It is not worth reproaching those corrupt officials for their evil conduct of selling favourable treatments in prisons. However, many good officials, being unaware of the real situation in the prison, also regard the wrongdoing of saving real criminals from the death sentence as a charitable act. They did not investigate the facts of those cases and as a result many innocent people have been treated unfairly and unjustly. How wrong it is!

Some wicked convicts, having been kept in prison for a long time, have found a way to gain a lot of money by colluding with

谪戍者移顺天府羁候①。时方冬停遣,李具状求在狱候春发遣②,至再三,不得所请,怅然而出。

---

① 羁候:关着等候遣送(be locked up in prison to wait to be exiled)。
② 具状求在狱候春发遣:呈文请求留在狱中等待春天遣送(present a petition to ask to stay in the prison until spring deportation)。

prison officials and guards. A man named Li from Shanyin County who was imprisoned in a homicide case could obtain several hundred *liang* of silver every year. In the 48th year of the Kangxi Reign, he was released from imprisonment under an amnesty. Having nothing to do for several months after he left the prison, he felt rather bored. One of his fellow villagers had committed a crime of murder and he bore the punishment for the killer. He was not charged with the offence of intentional killing, so according to the law he was not sentenced to death but was given a long-term imprisonment. In the 51th year of the Kangxi Reign, he enjoyed another amnesty and was given the reduced sentence of being exiled to a remote place for penal servitude. He sighed, "I have no chance to get in here any more." The usual practice had the convicts who were listed for exile transferred into the prison of Shuntian Prefecture to wait for transportation. As the transportation of exile convicts was not carried out during winter, Li presented a petition for staying in this prison until the spring deportation. Although he had requested several times, he was not given the permission to stay in this prison and he had to depart with regret.

左忠毅公逸事

方苞

先君子①尝言，乡先辈②左忠毅公③视学京畿④，一日，风雪严寒，从数骑⑤出，微行⑥入古寺。庑下⑦一生⑧伏案卧，文方成

---

① 先君子：作者自称其已死的父亲（the term which was used by the author to address his late father）。
② 乡先辈：同乡的长一辈人（fellow villager of the elder generation）。
③ 左忠毅公：左光斗，字遗直，号浮丘。因上奏弹劾宦官魏忠贤，遭陷害，受酷刑，死于狱中。追谥"忠毅"（Zuo Guangdou, styled himself Yizhi, alternatively named Fuqiu, was framed and persecuted to death in jail for submitting a memorial to the throne as to impeach Wei Zhongxian. Zhongyi was the posthumous title of Zuo Guangdou）。
④ 视学京畿（jī）：任京城地区的学政（be an official in charge of education in the area near the capital）。
⑤ 从数骑（jì）：几个骑马的随从跟着（followed by several attendants on horseback）。
⑥ 微行：古时皇帝或官员外出时身穿平民服装，以隐蔽身份（in the olden days, when an emperor or a high official went out, to hide his status he wore clothes similar to those worn by the common people）。
⑦ 庑（wǔ）下：厢房里（in a wingroom）。
⑧ 生：书生（intellectual）。

ANECDOTES OF THE REVERED MR. ZUO ZHONGYI

Fang Bao

My late father once told us: When the revered Mr. Zuo Zhongyi, who was a fellow villager from the old generation, held an official position in charge of education in the area near the capital, he went out one day in plain clothes. Braving the severe cold wind and snow and accompanied by several attendants on horseback, he went into an old temple. In a wing room of the temple, he saw a young scholar, bending over a desk and sleeping, with a draft just completed, laid on the desk. After reading it, he took off his marten-fur overcoat, covered the young man and closed the door. He went to see the monk and was informed that this young man was Shi Kefa. Then in the examination hall, when Shi's name was called, Mr. Zuo gazed at him in surprise. As his exam paper was submitted, Mr. Zuo immediately put Shi's name in the first place. He also invited Shi to visit his home. He introduced Shi to his wife by saying: "None of my sons have ambition and capability. Only this young man can some day fulfill

草①。公阅毕，即解貂覆生②，为掩户③。叩④之寺僧，则史公可法⑤也。及试，吏呼名至史公，公瞿然⑥注视，呈卷，即面署第一⑦。召入，使拜夫人，曰："吾诸儿碌碌⑧，他日继吾志事⑨，惟此生耳。"

及左公下厂狱⑩，史朝夕狱门外。逆阉⑪防伺⑫甚严，虽家仆不得近。久之，闻左公被炮烙⑬，且夕且⑭死，持五十金⑮，涕泣谋于禁卒，卒感焉。一日，使史更敝衣，草屦⑯，背筐，手长镵⑰，为⑱

---

① 成草：写成草稿（write a draft）。
② 解貂覆生：解下貂皮外衣，盖在书生的身上（take off his marten-fur overcoat to cover the young scholar）。
③ 掩户：关门（close the door）。
④ 叩：问（ask）。
⑤ 史公可法：史可法，字宪之，号道邻，明末祥符（今河南开封）人，崇祯进士。南明福王时以兵部尚书大学士督师扬州抗清，兵败，不屈而死（Shi Kefa, styled himself Xianzhi, alternatively named Daolin, was from Xiangfu—today's Kaifeng, Henan, a successful candidate in the highest imperial examinations during the Chongzhen Reign. In the time of King Fu of the Southern Ming period, he, as a grand secretary in charge of the Ministry of War, supervised the army in fighting against the Qing army in Yangzhou. When defeated, unyielding, he died）。
⑥ 瞿（jù）然：惊视的样子（gazing in alarm）。
⑦ 面署第一：当面书写，定为第一（write his name in his presence as the winner of the first place）。
⑧ 碌碌：平庸无能（mediocre and incapable）。
⑨ 志事：志向事业（ideal and aspiration）。
⑩ 厂狱：明代特务机构东厂所设的监狱，多由太监掌管（prison set up by Dongchang, the secret services in the Ming Dynasty, usually controlled by eunuchs）。
⑪ 逆阉：指魏忠贤（referring to Wei Zhongxian, an eunuch in power）。
⑫ 伺：探察（explore and examine）。
⑬ 炮烙（páo luò）：一种烧灼的酷刑（a kind of cruel torture by burning）。
⑭ 且：将（will, shall）。
⑮ 五十金：五十两银子（fifty liang of silver）。
⑯ 屦（jù）：鞋（shoes）。
⑰ 镵（chán）：一种类似铲子的工具（a kind of tool similar to a spade）。
⑱ 为：装作（pretend to be）。

my aspirations."

When Mr. Zuo was put in a prison which was set up by Dongchang, the secret service controlled by the vicious eunuchs, Shi stayed outside the prison day and night. The prison was guarded strictly and even Mr. Zuo's servants were not allowed to go near him. Some time later, on hearing that Mr. Zuo, having been tortured with burning metal, was close to death, Shi went to the prison with fifty *liang* of silver. He presented the silver to a prison guard and with tears in his eyes, asked the guard to find a way for him to visit Mr. Zuo. The guard was moved. One day, he arranged for Shi to disguise himself as a cleaner, by wearing shabby clothes and straw shoes, carrying a basket on his shoulder and holding a long spade in his hand. He led Shi inside and made a gesture to show him where to locate Mr. Zuo. Shi saw him sitting on the ground leaning against the wall, his face and forehead had been burnt too destructively to be recognized and his muscles and bones below his left knee had been disintegrated. Shi kneeled before him, holding his knee and sobbed. Recognizing Shi's voice, Zuo, who could not open his eyes, put up his arms to open his eye-lids with his fingers. With eyes blazing like a torch, he said angrily: "What in hell has made you come to this place, you idiot? Our nation is dying and I am finished too! You are unaware of the importance of the national interest and make light of your own

除不洁者，引入。微指左公处，则席地①倚墙而坐，面额焦烂不可辨，左膝以下筋骨尽脱矣。史前跪抱公膝而呜咽。公辨其声，而目不可开，乃奋臂以指拨眦②，目光如炬，怒曰："庸奴③！此何地也，而汝来前！国家之事糜烂至此，老夫已矣，汝复轻身而昧大义，天下事谁可支拄者？不速去，无俟奸人④构陷⑤，吾今即扑杀汝！"因摸地上刑械作投击势。史噤⑥不敢发声，趋⑦而出。后常流涕述其事以语⑧人，曰："吾师肺肝，皆铁石所铸造也。"

　　崇祯⑨末，流贼⑩张献忠出没蕲、黄、潜、桐⑪间，史公以凤庐道⑫奉檄⑬守御。每有警，辄数月不就寝，使将士更休，而自

---

① 席地：以地为席（use ground as a mat）。
② 眦（zì）：眼眶（eye socket）。
③ 庸奴：无能的奴才（incapable lackey）。
④ 奸人：指魏忠贤狱中爪牙（referring to Wei Zhongxian's lackeys in prison）。
⑤ 构陷：编造罪名来陷害（fabricate a case to frame sb.）。
⑥ 噤（jìn）：闭口（shut up）。
⑦ 趋：小步紧走（run in half steps）。
⑧ 语：告诉（tell）。
⑨ 崇祯：明思宗的年号（the reign title of Emperor Sizong of the Ming Dynasty）。
⑩ 流贼：明清士大夫对李自成、张献忠起义军的称呼（what the literati and officialdom in the Ming and Qing dynasties call the uprising troops led by Li Zicheng and Zhang Xianzhong）。
⑪ 蕲（qí）：蕲州府，今湖北蕲春县一带（the Qizhou Prefecture, today's Qichun County area in Hubei Province）；黄：黄州府，今湖北黄冈市一带（the Huangzhou Prefecture, today's Huanggang City area in Hubei Province）；潜：安徽潜山县一带（Qianshan County area in Anhui Province）；桐：安徽桐城市一带（Tongcheng City area in Anhui Province）。
⑫ 凤庐道：管辖凤阳府、庐州府一带的官（official administering Fengyang Prefecture and Luzhou Prefecture）。
⑬ 檄（xí）：古代官府用以征召或声讨的文书（governmental documents used to call up or condemn）。

life. Who will then save our nation? Get away from here quickly, otherwise I will kill you before you are framed by the villains!" Then he touched the instrument of torture which was on the ground and pretended that he would throw this item at Shi. Shi kept silent and walked away immediately. Later he often burst into tears while telling this to others, saying, "My teacher's heart and lungs are made of iron and stone."

At the end of the Chongzhen Reign, the roving bandits led by Zhang Xianzhong haunted the areas of Qizhou, Huangzhou, Qianshan and Tongcheng. The revered Mr. Shi, an official administering Fengyang and Luzhou prefectures, was under orders to defend this area. When on alert for enemy attacks, he would not go to his bedroom for months. He allowed his generals and soldiers to take rest in turn, while he himself sat outside their tents. He selected ten strong soldiers and let them squat and lean back to back on each other, in pairs. As the night drums sounded according to the movement of the water clock, they were replaced by another ten, thus taking turns for a rest. On cold nights, ice and frost could clearly be heard falling from his armour whenever he stood up and shook his clothes. Someone persuaded him to have a short rest and he said, "I'm always worried that I will fail to live up to the expectation of the royal court and betray the trust of my teacher."

坐幄^①幕外。择健卒十人，令二人蹲踞而背倚之，漏^②鼓^③移则番代^④。每寒夜起立，振衣裳，甲上冰霜迸落，铿然^⑤有声。或劝以少休，公曰："吾上恐负朝廷，下恐愧吾师也。"

史公治兵^⑥，往来桐城，必躬造^⑦左公第，候太公、太母起居^⑧，拜夫人于堂上。

余宗老涂山^⑨，左公甥也，与先君子善^⑩，谓狱中语乃亲得之于史公云。

---

① 幄（wò）：帐篷（tent）。
② 漏：古代用滴水计时的工具（water clock）。
③ 鼓：打更的鼓（drum used to sound the night watches）。
④ 番代：轮流替代（replace in turn）。番：轮换（take turns）。
⑤ 铿然：清脆响亮的声音（clear and loud sound）。
⑥ 治兵：训练军队，统帅军队（train and command troops）。
⑦ 躬造：亲身造访（visit sb. personally）。
⑧ 候太公、太母起居：向太公、太母问安（pay his respects to great-grandfather and great-grandmother）。太公太母，指左光斗的父母（referring to Zuo Guangdou's parents）。
⑨ 宗老涂山：同族中辈分高，号涂山的（a senior member in the same clan as mine, whose alternative name was Tushan）。
⑩ 与……善：同……交好（be friendly with）。

Every time he led his troop to a battle field and passed by Tongcheng, Mr. Shi would visit the revered Mr. Zuo's house to pay respects to Zuo's parents and call on his wife as well.

My senior, Tushan, the revered Mr. Zuo's nephew, friendly with my father, said that what Zuo said in prison was personally told to him by the revered Mr. Shi.

范县①署②中寄舍弟墨第四书

郑燮

十月二十六日得家书,知新置③田获秋稼④五百斛⑤,甚喜。而今而后,堪为农夫以没世⑥矣!要须制碓⑦制磨,制筛罗簸箕,制大小扫帚,制升斗斛。家中妇女,率诸婢妾,皆令习舂揄蹂簸⑧之事,便是一种靠田园长⑨子孙气象。天寒冰冻时,穷亲戚朋友到门,先泡一大碗炒米送手中,佐以酱姜一小碟,最是暖老⑩温贫之

---

① 范县:1744年作者曾在山东范县(今属河南)任知县(in 1774 the author was appointed magistrate of Fanxian County, Shandong Province [today it belongs to Henan Province])。
② 署:办公处所(government office)。
③ 置:买(buy)。
④ 秋稼:秋天庄稼所获(autumn harvest from crops)。
⑤ 斛(hú):量器名。古代十斗为一斛,后改为五斗(a dry measure used in the olden days, originally equal to 10 dou 斗, later 5 dou)。
⑥ 没世:过一辈子(throughout one's life)。
⑦ 碓(duì):舂米谷用的设备(a treadle-operated tilt hammer for hulling rice)。
⑧ 舂:把东西放在石臼或乳钵里捣以去壳(pound, pestle, e.g. husk rice);揄(yóu):往石臼中放谷、取米(put grain in a stone mortar or take rice from it);蹂:搓(rub with hands);簸:用簸箕扬去糠秕(winnow with a dustpan)。
⑨ 长:养育(bring up)。
⑩ 暖老:给老人温暖(give warmth to an old man)。

THE FOURTH LETTER TO MY YOUNGER BROTHER MO

Zheng Xie

On the 26th of the 10th month (in this lunar year), I received a letter from home and was very pleased to know that 500 *hu* (25,000 litres) autumn grain had been harvested from the land we have lately obtained. From now on we will be able to rely on farming for the rest of our life. Now we need to prepare rice husking devices such as mortars, millstones, sieves, sifts, winnowing baskets, big and small brooms, as well as capacity-measuring devices of various sizes. Let all the women in our family, together with the maidservants, learn how to husk rice with mortar and pestle and winnow the chaff from grain, etc. By doing so, the prospect of bringing up our offspring through farming our land will be able to be opened. In icy weather when poor relatives or friends come to visit us, we can use boiling water to dip puffed rice and give to each of them, before anything else, a big bowl of this instant food together with a small plate of pickled ginger. They are good refreshments to give warmth to poor elderly people in cold weather. On a leisurely day while eating cakes made of crushed rice, we also cook thick porridge. Holding the bowl with both hands, we draw back our necks to sip the hot porridge. Even on a frosty or snowy morning, we feel warm all over our bodies. Alas!

具①。暇日咽碎米饼，煮糊涂粥，双手捧碗，缩颈而啜②之，霜晨雪早③，得此周身俱暖。嗟乎！嗟乎！吾其长为农夫以没世乎！

我想天地问第一等人，只有农夫，而士为四民④之末。农夫上者种地百亩，其次七八十亩，其次五六十亩，皆苦其身，勤其力，耕种收获，以养天下之人。使天下无农夫，举世皆饿死矣。我辈读书人，入则孝，出则弟⑤，守先待后⑥，得志⑦泽⑧加于民，不得志修身⑨见⑩于世，所以又高于农夫一等。今则不然，一捧书本，便想中举、中进士、作官，如何攫⑪取金钱，造大房屋，置多田产。起手便错走了路头，后来越做越坏，总没有个好结果。其不能发达者，乡里作恶，小头锐面⑫，更不可当⑬。夫束⑭修⑮自好⑯者，岂无其人；经济⑰自期，抗怀千古⑱者，亦所在多有。而好人为坏人

① 具：指食物（food）。
② 啜（chuò）：吃（sip or eat）。
③ 雪早：雪天早晨（snowy morning）。
④ 四民：士农工商（scholar, farmer, artisan and merchant）。
⑤ 弟：悌，顺从兄长（be obedient to one's elder brother）。
⑥ 守先待后：保存先人的美德，传给后代（preserve one's ancestors' moral excellence and pass on to later generation）。
⑦ 得志：志愿实现（achieve one's ambition; have a successful career）。
⑧ 泽：恩泽（bounties bestowed by a monarch or an official）。
⑨ 修身：培养自身的道德品质（cultivate one's moral character）。
⑩ 见：现（appear）。
⑪ 攫（jué）：夺取（seize, grab）。
⑫ 小头锐面：善于钻营者（good at securing personal gain）。
⑬ 当：容忍（intolerable）。
⑭ 束：节制（control, be moderate in）。
⑮ 修：修养（training, accomplish, cultivate）。
⑯ 自好：自爱（self-respect）。
⑰ 经济：经世济民（govern and benefit the people）。
⑱ 抗怀千古：与古人媲美（compare favorably with ancient people）。

Alas! If only we could be farmers for the rest of our life.

I reckon farmers are the first-class human beings in the world while scholars should be ranked the last of the four categories of occupation, i.e. scholar, farmer, artisan and merchant. The most capable farmers can each look after 100 *mu* (6.67 hectares) of land from ploughing to harvesting while the second best farmers can each deal with 70 to 80 *mu* and the less capable ones can only manage 50 to 60 *mu*. They all work very hard, devoting themselves to ploughing, sowing and harvesting. It is farmers who feed all people under heaven. Without farmers, the whole world would die of hunger. We scholars, filial to our parents at home and respectful to our elder brothers outside, have maintained our ancestors' moral integrity and passed it to later generations. If we could achieve our ambition, we would bestow our favours on the people. If we did not have a successful career, we would cultivate our moral character and then become noble men. If this is the case, scholars could be higher than farmers in their ranking. However, today's scholars are different. Nowadays as soon as a scholar picks up a book, he will think of becoming a successful candidate in an imperial examination at the provincial or state level. He also dreams of becoming an official after passing the imperial examination and then using his power to grab money, build a big house and buy more farmland. These scholars have taken the wrong way from the very beginning. Afterwards, the more actions they take, the more mistakes they make and they will definitely end up with a bad result. Those, who have failed in pursuing an official career and have not become rich, will do evil things in the countryside. Being too clever at securing personal gains, their odious conduct is intolerable. We cannot say that good people who behave themselves with dignity and self-

所累，遂令我辈开不得口；一开口，人便笑曰："汝辈书生，总是会说，他日居官，便不如此说了。"所以忍气吞声，只得捱人笑骂。工人制器利用，贾人①搬有运无，皆有便民之处。而士独于民大不便，无怪乎居四民之末也！且求居四民之末，而亦不可得也。

愚兄平生最重农夫，新招佃地人②，必须待之以礼。彼称我为主人，我称彼为客户，主客原是对待之义，我何贵而彼何贱乎？要体貌③他，要怜悯他；有所借贷，要周全④他；不能偿还，要宽让⑤他。尝笑唐人《七夕》诗⑥，咏牛郎织女，皆作会别可怜之语，殊失命名本旨。织女，衣之源也，牵牛，食之本也，在天星为最贵；天顾重之，而人反不重乎？其务本⑦勤民，呈象⑧昭昭⑨可鉴矣。吾邑⑩妇人，不能织绸织布，然而主中馈⑪，习针线，犹不失为勤谨。近日颇有听鼓儿词⑫，以斗叶⑬为戏者，风俗荡轶⑭，亟宜戒之。

---

① 贾人：商人（merchant）。
② 佃地人：佃户（tenant farmer）。
③ 体貌：以礼相待（treat sb. with due respect）。
④ 周全：成全帮助（help sb. attain his aim）。
⑤ 宽让：忍让（be tolerant）。
⑥《七夕》诗：写于七月七日晚上歌咏牛郎织女故事的诗（poems written in the evening on the 7th day of the 7th month about the legend "The Cowherd and the Weaving Maid"）。
⑦ 本：指农业（agriculture）。
⑧ 呈象：表现出的形象（vivid image）。
⑨ 昭昭：明白（clear, plain）。
⑩ 邑：县（county）。
⑪ 主中馈（kuì）：指主持家中饮食之事（take charge of food in one's home）。
⑫ 鼓儿词：大鼓书（Dagu, versified story sung to the accompaniment of a small drum and other instruments）。
⑬ 斗叶：玩纸牌（play cards）。
⑭ 荡轶：放荡（dissolute, unconventional）。

respect do not exist. As a matter of fact, we can find quite a few noble men everywhere who regard it as their duty to defend the national interest and who always try to be as good as the ancient sages. However, good people have always been implicated by bad people and it had thus made us unable to speak out. Whenever we started to talk, there would be someone who would tease us by saying: "You scholars like to mouth fine words. Once you become officials, you will talk differently." In meek submission we have to swallow insult and let them wantonly abuse us. Artisans make utensils to meet other people's need. Merchants transport goods to where they are short in the supply. People of other occupations can all do something to benefit other people but scholars cannot do so. No wonder scholars rank last among the four categories of occupation. However, they may not be qualified to bring up the rear even if they were willing to be there.

It has always been my attitude to respect farmers and we should treat newly solicited tenant farmers with due respect. They call us owners and we call them tenants. The owner and the tenant are the two sides of a coin. They are equal and none is above the other. We should honour our tenants and have pity on them. When a farmer asks for a loan, we should let him get it. If later he is unable to pay back the loan, we should give him more time to repay it and not blame him for the delay. I used to mock the poems of the Tang Dynasty written on the 7th evening of the 7th lunar month about the Cowherd and the Weaving Maid (two legendary figures who meet on that evening every year in Heaven). Those poems were composed of lines expressing joys and sorrows for the meeting and parting of the separated lovers. From the poems we cannot see anything related to the real meaning of their titles. Weaving maids are producers of clothing materials while

吾家业地①虽有三百亩,总是典产②,不可久恃。将来须买田二百亩,予兄弟二人,各得百亩足矣,亦古者一夫③受田百亩之义也。若再求多,便是占人产业,莫大罪过。天下无田无业者多矣,我独何人,贪求无厌,穷民将何所措④足乎!或曰:"世上连阡越陌⑤,数百顷有余者,子将奈何?"应之曰:他自做他家事,我自做我家事,世道⑥盛⑦则一德⑧遵王⑨,风俗偷⑩则不同为恶,亦板桥之家法也。哥哥字。

---

① 业地:耕种之地(farming land)。
② 典产:典押的土地(land in pawn)。
③ 夫:成年男子(a grown-up man)。
④ 措:安放(put)。
⑤ 连阡越陌:形容田地广阔,阡陌相连(describing wide fields, whose footpaths are linked to each other)。阡陌:田间小路(crisscross footpaths between fields)。
⑥ 世道:社会(society)。
⑦ 盛:开明(enlightened)。
⑧ 一德:一心一意(heart and soul; wholeheartedly)。
⑨ 遵王:遵守王法(abide by the law)。
⑩ 偷:败坏(ruin, corrupt, debase)。

cowherds are farmhands who help produce food grain. Across the Milky Way, the two stars representing the Cowherd (Altair) and Weaving Maid (Vega) are quite brilliant in the sky. Heaven has put them in a prominent position. Why does man neglect their real value? In real life, a cowherd and a weaving maid are diligent people engaged in the most important undertakings — farming and weaving. Reflected in the configuration of the two stars, their merits are shining bright. The women in our county cannot do any weaving job, either making silk or cloth but they know how to cook and they are also good at needlework, thus they can still be regarded as dutiful and industrious. Recently quite a few people have indulged in listening to Dagu (the local musical story telling show) and playing cards. Such unhealthy hobbies should be abandoned.

Although we have 300 *mu* (about 49 acres) of farming land, this is mortgaged land in pawn and cannot be relied on for long. In the future we need to buy 200 *mu* of land and each of us will get 100 *mu*. That is enough and it conforms to the ancient teachings that one man is entitled to 100 *mu* of land. If we obtain more than that, it would be seen as seizing other people's and no crime is greater than this. There are so many people in the world who do not have anything — neither land nor other property. What are we? Why should we be greedy? If we were also greedy, how could poor people make a living? Someone asked: "There are some people in the world who possess boundless land of several hundred *qing* (over one thousand hectares). What can you do to them?" I answered: "Other people can do things their way but I have my own way. When the society is prosperous, we will wholeheartedly abide by the law. However, if the moral degeneration of the world is getting worse, we will not associate with the evil people. These are also the rules of Banqiao's family." Written by your elder brother.

游三游洞记

刘大櫆

出夷陵州治①，西北陆行二十里，濒②大江之左，所谓下牢之关③也。路狭不可行，舍舆④登舟。舟行里许，闻水声汤汤⑤，出于两崖之间。复舍舟登陆，循仄⑥径曲折以上。穷⑦山之颠，则又自上缒⑧危⑨滑以下。其下地渐平，有大石覆压当道，乃伛⑩俯⑪径⑫石腹以出。出则豁然平旷⑬，而石洞穹起⑭，高六十余尺，广可十二丈。二石柱屹立其口，分为三门，如三楹⑮之室焉。

---

① 夷陵州治：夷陵州的州府所在地（the seat of the local government of Yiling Prefecture）。夷陵州在今湖北宜昌市（Yiling is today's Yichang, Hubei）。
② 濒：临近（close to）。
③ 下牢关：在今宜昌市西北（northwest of Yichang City）。
④ 舆：车或轿（carriage or sedan chair）。
⑤ 汤（shāng）汤：水流的声音（sound of flowing water）。
⑥ 仄：狭窄（narrow）。
⑦ 穷：尽（limit, end）。
⑧ 缒（zhuì）：用绳索攀援而上下（climb up or down with the aid of a rope）。
⑨ 危：高（high）。
⑩ 伛（yǔ）：弯腰（bend one's body）。
⑪ 俯：低头（lower one's head）。
⑫ 径：经过（go through）。
⑬ 平旷：平坦开阔（flat and open）。
⑭ 穹起：高起成拱形（vault）。
⑮ 楹：原指堂屋前明柱，引申为房屋（originally referring to the post before the central room and has by extension come to mean house）。

TRAVEL NOTES ON TOURING THE SANYOU CAVE

Liu Dakui

Coming out from the seat of Yiling Prefecture, I traveled by land northwestward twenty *li* (1 *li* = 0.5 km) until I reached the so called Xialao Pass which was near the left bank of the Yangtze River. From there, the road became so narrow that it was hard to continue the land route. So I abandoned the carriage and took a boat. Hardly had the boat sailed more than one *li* when I heard the sound of a rushing current coming from between the two cliffs. I soon disembarked from the boat and found myself on a narrow and winding path. I walked uphill via this path to reach the top of a hill. Then my companions and I hung a rope and with its aid, we slid from the heights, step by step, to descend the hill. Walking alongside the foot of the hill, I saw the ground gradually become flat. A huge rock, crouching on the ground, blocked our way. Bending my body and lowering my head, I walked through from underneath the rock. Suddenly there appeared in front of me a wide open field where a rock cave, more than sixty *chi* (1 *chi* = 1/3 metre) high and about twelve *zhang* (1 *zhang* = 10 *chi*) wide, bulged out from the level ground. Two stone columns stood erect at the entrance of the cave. They resembled the door frame of a three-

中室如堂①,右室如厨,左室如别馆②。其中一石,乳③而下垂,扣④之,其声如钟。而左室外小石突立正方,扣之如磬。其地石杂以土,撞之则逄逄⑤然鼓音。背有石如床,可坐,予与二三子浩歌⑥其间,其声轰然,如钟磬助之响者。下视深溪,水声泠然⑦出地底。溪之外翠壁千寻⑧,其下有径,薪采⑨者负薪行歌,缕缕不绝焉。

昔白乐天⑩自江州⑪司马徙为忠州⑫刺史,而元微之⑬适自通州⑭将北还⑮,乐天携其弟知退⑯,与微之会于夷陵,饮酒欢甚,留连不忍别去,因共游此洞,洞以此三人得名。其后欧阳永叔⑰暨⑱

---

① 堂:堂屋(central room)。
② 别馆:别墅(villa)。
③ 乳:钟乳石(stalactite)。
④ 扣:敲(knock)。
⑤ 逄(páng)逄:形容扣石的声音(used to describe rock-knocking sound)。
⑥ 浩歌:大声歌唱(sing loudly)。
⑦ 泠(líng)然:水流之声(sound of flowing water)。
⑧ 寻:古代长度单位,八尺为一寻(an ancient measure of length equal to about eight *chi*)。
⑨ 薪采:打柴(collect firewood)。
⑩ 白乐天:白居易,乐天是他的字(Bai Juyi styled himself Letian)。
⑪ 江州:今江西九江(today's Jiujiang in Jiangxi Province)。
⑫ 忠州:今重庆忠县(today's Zhongxian County in Chongqing)。
⑬ 元微之:元稹,微之是他的字(Yuan Zhen styled himself Weizhi)。
⑭ 通州:今四川达县(today's Daxian County in Sichuan Province)。
⑮ 将北还:指由通州司马改任虢(guó)州(今河南灵宝)长史(to have one's official position changed from the minister of war in Tongzhou to the governor of Guozhou, today's Lingbao County, Henan)。
⑯ 知退:白行简的字(Bai Xingjian styled himself Zhitui)。
⑰ 欧阳永叔:欧阳修,永叔是他的字(Ouyang Xiu styled himself Yongshu)。
⑱ 暨:及(and)。

room house.

The middle cave looked like the living room, the right one was the kitchen and the left one the guest room. Inside the cave, a stalactite hung down from the ceiling and when knocked it sounded like a bell. A small square rock protruded outside the left room and it made a beautiful sound like chimes when knocked. When the stony ground, mixed with soil, was stamped, the sound of pang, pang could be heard as if a drum was being beaten. At the rear of the cave lay a rock in the shape of a bed which could serve as a seat. Around here, I, together with a couple of my traveling companions, sang songs at the top of our voices. Our combined voice became deafening and its volume seemed to be amplified by the "bells" and "chimes." Outside the cave I looked down and saw a deep stream. The sound of flowing water came from underground. On the other side of the stream a green cliff towered one thousand *xun* high and a path stretched at its foot. We kept hearing the singing voices of woodcutters who were treading on the path with firewood on their back.

A long long time ago, Bai Letian (a famous poet of the Tang Dynasty) was transferred from the chief military official of Jiangzhou Prefecture to the governor of Zhongzhou Prefecture. It so happened that Yuan Weizhi (Bai Letian's good friend, also a famous poet of the Tang Dynasty) was travelling northward from Tongzhou at that time. So Letian, accompanied by his younger brother Zhitui, went to meet Weizhi at Yiling. Drinking to their hearts' content, they were having such a good time that none of them could tear himself from the others. While lingering on,

黄鲁直①二公皆以摈斥②流离③，相继而履其地，或为诗文以纪之。予自顾而嘻④，谁摈斥予乎？谁使予之流离而至于此乎？偕予而来者，学使陈公⑤之子曰伯思、仲思⑥。予非陈公，虽欲至此无由，而陈公以守其官未能至，然则其至也，其又有幸有不幸邪？

夫乐天、微之辈⑦，世俗之所谓伟人，能赫然⑧取名位于一时，故凡其足迹所经，皆有以传于后世，而地得因人以显。若予者，虽其穷幽陟⑨险，与虫鸟之适⑩去适来何异？虽然，山川之胜，使其生于通都⑪大邑⑫，则好游者踵⑬相接也；顾⑭乃置之于荒遐⑮僻陋之区，美好不外见，而人亦无以亲炙⑯其光。呜呼！此岂一人之不幸也哉！

① 黄鲁直：黄庭坚，鲁直是他的字（Huang Tingjian styled himself Luzhi）。
② 摈斥：被斥逐（be exiled）。
③ 流离：穷困转徙（wander from place to place）。
④ 自顾而嘻：自视而发出叹声（consider oneself and emit a sigh）。
⑤ 学使陈公：指陈浩。学使，即提督学政，也称提学使（Chen Hao, an official in charge of education）。
⑥ 伯思、仲思：指陈浩之长子陈本忠，次子陈本敬（referring to Chen Hao's eldest son Chen Benzhong and next son Chen Benjing）。
⑦ 辈：类（people of a certain kind）。
⑧ 赫然：显盛的样子（impressively）。
⑨ 陟（zhì）：攀登（climb）。
⑩ 适：随处（anywhere）。
⑪ 通都：四通八达的都会（a metropolis radiating in all directions）。
⑫ 大邑：大的城邑（big city）。
⑬ 踵：脚后跟（heel）。
⑭ 顾：但是（but）。
⑮ 遐：远（far）。
⑯ 亲炙：亲自领略（personally have a taste of / get some idea of）。

these three men came to visit this cave which was later named in honour of their visit. Long afterwards, Ouyang Yongshu and Huang Luzhi, both having been dismissed from office and banished to live a vagrant life, came to this place respectively. They wrote poetry and prose to record their visits to the cave. I felt amused while saying to myself: "Who has dismissed me? Who has made me wander from place to place and finally come here?" I was accompanied by the regional education supervisor Mr. Chen Hao's two sons Bosi and Zhongsi. I am not Mr. Chen and I do not have the same reason to come here as did those high officials. Mr. Chen was unable to come here because of his official business. Even if he could come, would that be his good luck or bad luck?

People like Bai Letian and Yuan Weizhi had been considered by conventional views as great men who, enjoying prominent fame and positions, were once high and mighty. Any places which have their footprints left behind have all become heritages to later generations and these places have become famous because of the fame of those people. However, as to people like me, is there any difference between my steps on a secluded and peaceful wonderland or a high and dangerous mountain and the random flying traces of insects and birds which are coming and going there? If a beautiful landscape is endowed with a good location situated in a big city and accessible from all directions, sightseers will come one after another. If it is located in a remote and barren area, its beauty is concealed and most people are unable to go there personally to feast their eyes on the unique sight. Alas! This misfortune is not incurred by one man only.

骡 说

刘大櫆

乘骑者皆贱骡而贵马。夫煦①之以恩，任其然而不然②，迫之以威③使之然，而不得不然者，世之所谓贱者也。煦之以恩，任其然而然，迫之以威使之然而愈不然，行止④出于其心，而坚不可拔⑤者，世之所谓贵者也，然则⑥马贱而骡贵矣。虽然，今夫軼⑦之而不善，榎楚⑧以威之而可以入于善者，非人耶⑨？人岂贱于骡哉？然则骡之刚愎自用，而自以为不屈也久矣。呜呼！此骡之所以贱于马欤？

---

① 煦：温暖，这里用作动词，给人温暖（warmth, here used as a verb, give warmth to sb.）。
② 任其然而不然：不加强迫，让它自动这样做，它却偏不这样做（it would not do anything if you let it act on its own）。然：这样（so, in this way）。
③ 迫之以威：以威力强迫它（force it to do sth. with power）。
④ 行止：一言一行，一举一动（every word and action, every act and every move）。
⑤ 拔：移易（change, alter）。
⑥ 然则：既然这样，那么（in that case, then）。
⑦ 軼（yì）：通"逸"，放任（be equal to 逸, let go unchecked）。
⑧ 榎（jiǎ）楚：用于笞打的一种刑具（an instrument of torture used to beat）。
⑨ 非人耶：不就是人吗（doesn't it resemble the human being）？

ABOUT MULES

Liu Dakui

Most riders are fond of horses but belittle mules. If an animal is well raised and trained but will not do anything without being guided and can only be forced to do something for human need, it is regarded as a lower animal. Whereas another animal is treated in the same way and can easily adapt to human use. However, it will not do anything if it is forced to do so. Possessing a strong will and determination, it always wants to do whatever it likes, hence it is labeled as a noble animal. Being the noble one, mules should be graded higher than horses. Nowadays, if you let a mule do whatever it likes, it would not behave itself properly. The only way to make it perform well is to threaten it with a whip. Does it resemble the human being who surrenders easily under high pressure and behaves worse than others? Unfortunately, mules have long been degraded for being too stubborn, headstrong, uncompromising and self important. Alas, that is why mules are considered lower grade to horses.

为学一首示子侄

彭端淑

天下事有难易乎？为①之，则难者亦易矣；不为，则易者亦难矣。人之为学有难易乎？学之，则难者亦易矣；不学，则易者亦难矣。

吾资②之昏③不逮④人也，吾材⑤之庸⑥不逮人也，旦旦⑦而学之，久而不怠⑧焉，迄⑨乎成⑩，而亦不知其昏与庸也。吾资之聪⑪倍人⑫也，吾材之敏⑬倍人也；屏弃⑭而不用，其与昏与庸无以异⑮也。

---

① 为：求，做（seek, do）。
② 资：天资禀赋（natural endowments, gift）。
③ 昏：愚笨（foolish, stupid）。
④ 逮（dài）：及（can compare with, be up to）。
⑤ 材：才具（ability）。
⑥ 庸：平庸，平凡（commonplace, ordinary）。
⑦ 旦旦：天天（every day）。
⑧ 怠：松懈（relax, slack）。
⑨ 迄：到，至（up to, till）。
⑩ 成：成功（success）。
⑪ 聪：聪明（clever）。
⑫ 倍人：两倍于人（doubly cleverer than ...）。
⑬ 敏：灵敏，敏捷（quick, smart）。
⑭ 屏弃：丢掉（give up）。
⑮ 异：差别（difference）。

A NOTE ABOUT STUDY WRITTEN FOR MY SONS AND NEPHEWS

Peng Duanshu

Among the tasks we do, are there two categories, i.e. "easy to do" and "hard to do"? If you are willing to do it, the difficult thing will become easy but if you are not willing to do it, the easy one will then become difficult. Is there an easy way to obtain knowledge, or is it hard to do so? If you are willing to learn, it will become easy to obtain knowledge but if you are not willing to learn, to study will become difficult.

Imagine I am not as talented and capable as other people but I continue learning and never give up my study. One day when I become successful, I will forget that I do not have very much talent. Whereas if I have more talent and capability than other people but I have never used these abilities, I will be just an ordinary person, similar to many others. Confucius finally had his doctrines pass down to later generations mainly through one of his disciples Zeng Shen, who had actually less talent than Confucius' other disciples. From this example, you can see clearly

圣人①之道,卒②于鲁③也传之。然则昏庸聪敏之用,岂有常④哉?

蜀之鄙⑤有二僧:其一贫,其一富。贫者语⑥于富者曰:"吾欲之⑦南海⑧,何如?"富者曰:"子何恃⑨而往?"曰:"吾一瓶一钵⑩足矣。"富者曰:"吾数年来欲买⑪舟而下,犹未能也。子何恃而往!"越明年⑫,贫者自南海还,以告富者,富者有惭色。

西蜀之去⑬南海,不知几千里也,僧之富者不能至,而贫者至之。人之立志,顾⑭不如蜀鄙之僧哉?是故⑮聪与敏,可恃而不可恃也;自恃其聪与敏而不学者,自败⑯者也。昏与庸,可限⑰而不可限也;不自限其昏与庸而力学不倦者,自力⑱者也。

---

① 圣人:指孔子(referring to Confucius)。
② 卒:终于(finally)。
③ 鲁:钝拙。这里指的是曾参。曾参人并不聪明,却将孔学传了下来(stupid and clumsy. Here referring to Zeng Shen. Although not clever, he handed down Confucianism)。
④ 常:定规(hard and fast rule)。
⑤ 鄙:偏僻的地方(a remote place)。
⑥ 语(yù):告诉(tell)。
⑦ 之:前往(go to)。
⑧ 南海:中国佛教圣地之一,即今浙江省舟山群岛海中的普陀山(one of the sacred places of Buddhism, i.e. today's Mount Putuo in the sea among the Zhoushan Archipelago, off the coast of Zhejiang)。
⑨ 恃:依靠(rely on)。
⑩ 瓶、钵:和尚盛食物的用具,化缘用(utensil for a monk to contain food, used to beg alms)。
⑪ 买:花钱雇用(pay money to hire)。
⑫ 越明年:到了第二年(when the next year comes)。
⑬ 去:距离(the distance between)。
⑭ 顾:难道,岂(how can ...)。
⑮ 是故:因此(therefore, so)。
⑯ 自败:自己打败自己(one defeats oneself)。
⑰ 限:限制(restrict)。
⑱ 自力:自求上进(do one's best to make progress)。

that wisdom and ignorance are not unchangeable.

Two monks lived on the border of Sichuan Province. One was poor and the other rich. One day the poor monk said to the rich one: "I am planning to go to Nanhai. What do you think of my idea?" The rich one asked, "How will you get there?" The poor one answered: "I only need one bottle for drinking and one bowl for eating. That's all." The rich one said: "I have been trying to hire a boat to sail all the way to Nanhai, but I have never succeeded. What are you going to rely on to get there?" In the following year, the poor monk came back from Nanhai. He told the rich one that he had been there and his story made his counterpart feel ashamed.

How far is Nanhai from Sichuan? Several thousand *li* perhaps. The rich monk could not get there but the poor one succeeded in going there. If you have a strong intention toward your study, you will be as good as the poor Sichuan monk. Therefore, you can be proud of your intelligence and ability but you should not be completely reliant on these. If you are only proud of your talent but never study hard, you will ruin yourself. Some people are restricted by their own ignorance and mediocrity but others are not. Those who are not confined by their own lack of talent but study hard can achieve, through their own effort.

梅花岭记（节选）

全祖望

顺治①二年乙酉②四月，江都围急。督相史忠烈公③知势不可为，集诸将而语之曰："吾誓与城为殉④，然仓皇⑤中不可落于敌人之手以死，谁为我临期⑥成此大节⑦者？"副将军⑧史德威⑨慨然任之。忠烈喜曰："吾尚未有子，汝当以同姓为吾后⑩。吾上书太夫人，谱⑪汝诸孙中。"

二十五日，城陷，忠烈拔刀自裁⑫。诸将果争前抱持⑬之。忠

---

① 顺治：清世祖的年号（reign title of the first emperor of the Qing Dynasty）。
② 乙酉：公元 1645 年（AD 1645）。
③ 督相史忠烈公：史可法以宰相身份督师，故称督相；殉节后谥号忠烈（as a prime minister, he supervised army operations, so called; after dying in loyalty to his nation, he was given the posthumous title of "Loyal Martyr"）。
④ 殉：牺牲（die a martyr's death）。
⑤ 仓皇：慌张匆忙（panic and haste）。
⑥ 临期：到城破时（when the city fell）。
⑦ 大节：指以身殉国（give one's life for the country）。
⑧ 副将军：副总兵官（vice commander）。
⑨ 史德威：山西平阳人（a native of Pingyang County, Shanxi）。
⑩ 后：后代（offspring）。
⑪ 谱：家谱，这里用作动词，"列入家谱中"（family tree, here used as a verb, meaning "list one's name on one's family tree"）。
⑫ 自裁：自杀（take one's own life）。
⑬ 抱持：抱住使他不得自杀（hold somebody with both arms to prevent him from committing suicide）。

THE PLUM BLOSSOM RIDGE (EXCERPTS)

Quan Zuwang

In the fourth month of the second year of the Shunzhi Reign (1645), Jiangdu was fatally besieged. The prime minister Shi Kefa (his posthumous title was Loyal Martyr), who was supervising the army operations, knew that the situation was out of control. He summoned all his subordinate generals together and said to them: "I vow to die a martyr's death along with the city but I fear I would be unexpectedly captured and killed by the enemy. If this happens, who will assist me to lay down my life for our nation when the city falls?" The deputy commander Shi Dewei replied that he was willing to fulfil the mission. Filled with happiness, Shi said, "I have no son and you can be my foster son as your family name is the same as mine. I will write to ask my mother to list your name on my family tree as one of her grandsons."

On the 25th of this month, the city fell. Shi drew his sword, intending to kill himself. His subordinates dashed to hold his arms. Shi shouted to Dewei but Dewei, in tears, would not take up his sword. Thus Shi was clutched and surrounded by his subordinates

烈大呼德威,德威流涕,不能执刃,遂为诸将所拥而行。至小东门,大兵①如林而至,马副使鸣禄②、任太守民育③及诸将刘都督肇基④等皆死。忠烈乃瞠目⑤曰:"我史阁部⑥也。"被执至南门,和硕豫亲王⑦以先生呼之,劝之降。忠烈大骂而死。初,忠烈遗言:"我死当葬梅花岭上。"至是,德威求公之骨不可得,乃以衣冠葬之。

或曰,城之破也,有亲见忠烈青衣乌帽,乘白马,出天宁门投江死者,未尝殒于城中也。自有是言,大江南北遂谓忠烈未死。

---

① 大兵:指清兵(referring to the Qing's troops)。
② 马副使鸣禄:按察副使马鸣禄,陕西省襃城县人(Ma Minglu, the assistant surveillance commissioner, was from Baocheng County, Shaanxi)。
③ 任太守民育:太守任民育。太守:官名,这里代指知府。任民育:山东济宁人,当时任扬州知府(Ren Minyu, magistrate of Yangzhou Prefecture, was from Jining County, Shandong)。
④ 刘都督肇基:都督刘肇基,字鼎维,辽东人(Liu Zhaoji, military governor of Yangzhou, was from eastern Liaoning)。
⑤ 瞠(chēng)目:瞪着眼看(open one's eyes wide to look)。
⑥ 史阁部:明朝称大学士为入阁。史可法是大学士兼管兵部,所以称史阁部(in the Ming Dynasty, a grand secretary was a member of the cabinet. Shi Kefa was then a grand secretary, concurrently in charge of the Ministry of War, so called)。
⑦ 和硕豫亲王:清太祖努尔哈赤的第十五子,名多铎。和硕:满洲语,意思是"旗"(部落)。清代亲王、公主名前都冠以"和硕"二字(the 15th son of Nurhachi, the founder of the Qing Dynasty, was named Duoduo. Heshuo, in the Manchu language, means "qi," a tribe. This word was often placed before the name of a prince or a princess in the Qing Dynasty)。

and had to march on with them. When they arrived at the Little Eastern Gate, the enemy troops, relentlessly encroaching like a jungle, were approaching. Ma Minglu, the assistant surveillance commissioner, Ren Minyu, the magistrate of Yangzhou Prefecture, Liu Zhaoji, the military governor of Yangzhou and other officers were killed. Shi, staring angrily at the enemy, yelled, "I am Shi Kefa, Grand Secretary of the Cabinet!" He was taken to the southern gate and Prince Yu (of the Manchu royal family) respectfully called him "Sir" and induced him to surrender. Shi did not stop abusing the enemy until his death. Shi had left behind him such words: "When I die, I would like to be buried on the Plum Blossom Ridge." As Dewei failed to obtain Shi's remains, he buried Shi's clothing and hat instead.

Some people said: On the day when the city was falling, they had seen the Loyal Martyr, wearing a black coat and hat and riding a white horse, leave the city from the Tianning Gate and then jump into the river to drown himself, so they did not believe that Shi had been killed in the city. Due to this story, people living on both north and south of the Yangtze River believed that Shi was still alive. Soon armed uprisings rose in the areas of Yingshan and Huoshan counties all claiming that they were Shi's armed forces. What they did resembled the uprising headed by Chen She who used Xiang Yan's name in an attempt to overthrow the Qin

已而英、霍山师大起①,皆托②忠烈之名,仿佛陈涉之称项燕③。吴中④孙公兆奎⑤以起兵不克,执至白下⑥。经略洪承畴⑦与之有旧⑧,问曰:"先生在兵间,审知⑨故扬州阁部史公果死邪,抑未死邪?"孙公答曰:"经略从北来,审知故松山殉难督师洪公果死邪,抑⑩未死邪?"承畴大恚⑪,急呼麾下⑫驱出斩之。

---

① 英、霍山师大起:英山和霍山(当时安徽省的两个县)一带大起义兵(people in the area of Yingshan and Huoshan, two counties in Anhui Province, rose in armed revolt)。
② 托:假托(usurp the name of)。
③ 陈涉之称项燕:陈涉起义时假借项燕的名义。项燕世代作楚国大将,在楚国有极高的威望(when Chen She rose in revolt, he usurped the name of Xiang Yan, a famous general of the State of Chu, who had high prestige)。
④ 吴中:旧苏州府属的通称,即今江苏省苏州市一带(a former name for Suzhou Prefecture, i.e. today's area of Suzhou City in Jiangsu Province)。
⑤ 孙兆奎:字君昌,吴江举人。吴江被清兵攻下后,率兵起义抗清,后兵败被俘(styled himself Junchang, a successful candidate in the imperial examination at the provincial level in Wujiang County. When Wujiang was captured by the Qing troops, he led an army to rise in revolt but was later captured after having been defeated)。
⑥ 白下:南京的别名(another name for Nanjing)。
⑦ 洪承畴:字亨九,福建南安县人,崇祯十二年总督蓟辽军务,与清军战于松山,兵败被俘降清(Hong Chengchou styled himself Hengjiu and was from Nan'an, Fujian Province. In the 12th year of the Chongzhen Reign [1639], he led the Ming army to fight against the Qing troops but surrendered to the enemy when he was captured after being defeated)。
⑧ 有旧:有老交情(to be an old friend)。
⑨ 审知:确凿地知道(know exactly)。
⑩ 抑:还是(or)。
⑪ 恚(huì):恨,恼(hate, anger)。
⑫ 麾(huī)下:部下(troops under one's command)。麾:军旗(army flag)。

Dynasty (221 BC – 206 BC). Sun Zhaokui of Suzhou was captured and escorted to Nanjing after his rebellion was defeated. Hong Chengchou (the former governor-general of the Ming Dynasty who had surrendered to Manchu troops) used to be Sun's friend and asked him, "You are in the army. Do you know exactly whether Mr. Shi, the former Grand Secretary of the Cabinet, is dead or not?" Sun replied, "You have come from the north, do you know exactly whether Mr. Hong, who has allegedly died a martyr in a battle, is dead or not?" Greatly angered, Hong immediately called his attendants to take him away to be executed.

Alas! Absurd legends about immortals said that Yan Zhenqing (of the Tang Dynasty), teacher of the crown prince, became an immortal because he was killed by a rebel general. Wen Tianxiang (after having been caught by the Mongol troops and put in jail), enlightened by the Taoist secret of becoming an immortal, left his body like a cicada which, having sloughed, was still alive. Few people realise "loyalty and righteousness" are the principal ethics of our saints and their noble spirit is so tremendous that it will exist on earth for ever. Why should it come into existence in the shape of a human being or go to heaven as a celestial being? The story about immortals is as ridiculous as drawing a snake and adding feet to it. What can we say about the fact that the Loyal Martyr's remains have never been found? One hundred years later,

呜呼！神仙诡诞之说，谓颜太师①以兵解②，文少保③亦以悟大光明法④蝉脱⑤，实未尝死。不知忠义者圣贤家法⑥，其气浩然⑦，常留天地之间，何必出世入世⑧之面目？神仙之说，所谓"为蛇画足"。即如忠烈遗骸，不可问也，百年而后，予登岭上，与客述忠烈遗言，无不泪下如雨，想见当日围城光景，此即忠烈之面目，宛然可遇，是不必问其果解脱否也，而况冒其未死之名者哉！

---

① 颜太师：唐颜真卿，官太子太师，招降叛将时被害（referring to Yan Zhenqing of the Tang Dynasty, teacher of the crown prince. He was killed when he tried to summon a general from the rebel army）。
② 以兵解：因被杀而成仙（become an immortal after being killed）。兵：兵器（weapons）。解：解脱躯壳而成仙（free oneself from one's body to become an immortal）。
③ 文少保：指文天祥（Wen Tianxiang）。
④ 大光明法：指佛法（Buddhist doctrine）。
⑤ 蝉脱：像蝉脱壳一样遗下躯壳（leave one's body just as a cicada shedding its skin）。
⑥ 圣贤家法：圣贤人传统的道德准则（traditional code of ethics of the saints）。
⑦ 浩然：正大光明（frank and righteous）。
⑧ 出世入世：都是佛家语（Buddhist saying）。出世：脱离俗世（break away from the world）。入世：生于世上（be born into the world）。

I stood on the hill and told my friends his last words and they all shed a flood of tears. We imagined the scene of the besieged city and seemed to see the Loyal Martyr's face. There is no need to ask whether he really became an immortal, let alone take advantage of his name for whatever purpose.

黄生借书说

袁枚

黄生允修借书。随园主人①授以书而告之曰："书非借不能读也。子不闻藏书者乎？七略②四库③，天子之书，然天子读书者有几？汗牛塞屋④，富贵家之书，然富贵人读书者有几？其他祖父⑤积、子孙弃者无论焉。非独书为然，天下物皆然。非夫人之物而

---

① 随园主人：袁枚的自称（Yuan Mei called himself "Owner of the Sui Garden"）。随园：在江苏南京市北小仓山上，袁枚中年辞官后居住的别墅（name of a villa habituated by Yuan Mei after his resignation from his official position in his middle age, situated on Mount Xiaocang north of Nanjing, Jiangsu）。
② 七略：中国最早的图书目录分类著作，分为辑略、六艺略、诸子略、诗赋略、兵书略、术数略、方技略七部，西汉末年刘歆奉命校录群书而编撰（the earliest book about catalogue classification in ancient China; it is divided into seven parts, such as: the part of edition, the part of Six Learnings, the part of Philosophers, the part of Poetry and *Fu*, the part of the Art of War, the part of Divination and the part of Skills, compiled by Liu Xin at the end of the Han Dynasty who received orders from the emperor to check and copy all kinds of books）。
③ 四库：宫廷收藏图书的地方（the palace library）。
④ 汗牛塞屋：汗牛充栋，形容书籍之多致使运书的牛出汗，书堆至屋梁（so many books as to make the ox carrying them perspire and to fill a house to the rafters）。
⑤ 祖父：祖辈、父辈（generations of grandfather and father）。

ADVICE TO YOUNG SCHOLAR HUANG ON BORROWING BOOKS

Yuan Mei

Huang Yunxiu, a young scholar, came to my place, the Sui Garden, to borrow books. While giving him the books, I said: "Books, unless borrowed, will not be read attentively. Have you heard anything about the book collectors? The sons of Heaven (the kings or emperors) possess all the masterpieces of classical works, such as *The Seven Categories of Books* and *Complete Library in the Four Branches of Literature*. How many of them read books? The wealthy and influential families have so many books as to make the ox carrying them perspire or enough to fill their houses to the rafters. How many wealthy and powerful men read books? There are also stories about sons or grandsons discarding the books which have been collected by their fathers or grandfathers and so on and so forth. It is not books that are such a phenomenon. Everything under heaven is like that too. If you have managed to borrow something beautiful from others, you will keep holding it for fear that its owner will come to take it away. You murmur to yourself, "Today I can hold it but tomorrow it will go and I will not see it any more." However, if the same object

强假①焉,必虑人逼取,而惴惴焉摩玩②之不已,曰:'今日存,明日去,吾不得而见之矣。'若业为吾所有,必高束焉,庋藏③焉,曰'姑俟④异日⑤观'云尔。"

予幼好书,家贫难致。有张氏藏书甚富。往借,不与,归而形诸梦。其切如是。故有所览辄省记。通籍⑥后,俸去书来,落落大满,素蟫⑦灰丝,时蒙卷轴。然后叹借者之用心专,而少时之岁月为可惜也。

今黄生贫类予,其借书亦类予;惟予之公书⑧与张氏之吝书若不相类。然则予固不幸而遇张乎,生固幸而遇予乎?知幸与不幸,则其读书也必专,而其归书也必速。

为一说,使与书俱。

---

① 强假:勉强借来(manage to borrow)。
② 摩玩:摩挲玩赏(gently stroke and enjoy sth.)。
③ 庋(guǐ)藏:收藏(store up)。
④ 俟(sì):等(wait for)。
⑤ 异日:他日(some other day)。
⑥ 通籍:籍,一种竹片,上写姓名、年龄、身份,挂在宫门口,以便进出时查对(a kind of bamboo strip hanging at the palace gate, on which are written one's name, age and identity, so that officials can be verified when they come in and go out)。通籍,是说姓名登记在门上,进出宫门可以无阻,后作为做官的代称(it means that one is not stopped when he comes in and goes out of the palace because his name is registered on the door. Later it became a term for being an official)。
⑦ 素蟫(yín):一种白色蛀书虫(a kind of white borer that eats books)。
⑧ 公书:把书公开出借(lend out one's book publicly)。

belonged to you, you would wrap it up and store it on the top shelf, saying to yourself, "I will bring it down one day to appreciate it."

I already loved reading books when I was a young child but my family was too poor to buy books for me. A man named Zhang had a large collection of books. I went to his place but he refused to lend me any books. I returned home empty-handed and this bad luck appeared in my dream. My desire for books was so eager that whenever I had a book in hand for reading, I would try my best to understand the book and remember it. Later, when I first became an official, much of my salary was spent on books. Now my books are piled everywhere in my house, often covered by white book-worms and grey dust. So I uttered a deep sigh: How attentively we read the books that we borrow and how unforgettable the events that took place during our childhood!

Young Scholar Huang is as poor as I used to be and he is doing the same thing as I did — borrowing books. The only difference lies between my generosity in lending books to others and Zhang's stinginess with his books. It was my bad luck that led me to ask for kindness from a stingy man like Zhang and it is Young Scholar Huang's good luck that leads him to borrow books from me. When you know that there is either good luck or bad luck in borrowing books, you will read attentively the book you have fortunately borrowed and you will return it as soon as possible.

These notes have been written as an attachment to the books Young Scholar Huang wants to borrow.

祭妹文

袁枚

乾隆丁亥①冬，葬三妹素文②于上元③之羊山④，而奠⑤以文曰：

呜呼！汝生于浙而葬于斯，离吾乡七百里矣；当时虽觭梦⑥幻想，宁知此为归骨所耶？

汝以一念之贞，遇人⑦仳离⑧，致孤危⑨托落⑩，虽命之所存，天实为之，然而累汝至此者，未尝非予之过也。予幼从先生授经，汝

---

① 丁亥：乾隆三十二年（1767）（the 32th year of the Qianlong Reign of the Qing Dynasty）。
② 素文：名机，字素文，别号青琳居士（named Ji, styled herself Suwen, alternatively named Lay Buddhist Qinglin）。
③ 上元：清代县名，属江宁府，后并入江宁县，今属南京市（name of a county in the Qing Dynasty, belonging to Jiangning Prefecture, later merged into Jiangning County, today belonging to Nanjing）。
④ 羊山：位于南京市东（situated east of Nanjing）。
⑤ 奠：向死者献上祭品（make offerings to the spirits of the dead）。
⑥ 觭（jī）梦：怪异的梦（strange dream）。
⑦ 遇人：遇人不淑的省略（a woman marrying a bad husband, it is an elliptical form）。
⑧ 仳（pǐ）离：妇女被遗弃而离去（a woman, when abandoned, leaves）。
⑨ 孤危：孤独忧伤（lonely and distressed）。
⑩ 托落：落拓，失意（be frustrated, be unlucky）。

LAMENTING FOR MY YOUNGER SISTER

Yuan Mei

In winter of the 32nd year of the Qianlong Reign (1767), I buried Suwen, my younger sister (the third child in the family), on Mount Sheep in Shangyuan County and then wrote an article lamenting for her.

Alas! You were born in Zhejiang but are buried here, seven hundred *li* from our hometown. When you were alive, how could you know, even in your dream or illusion, the place for your body to be buried would be here?

You had always remained chaste in mind and accepted the family prearranged marriage to a morally degenerate man who later deserted you. This unhappy marriage led you into a lonely and miserable life. Although your misfortune was predestined, as fate would have it, I still blame myself for causing you all these troubles. When I was young, I followed a teacher to learn Confucian classics. You were fond of stories about the faithfulness and staunchness of our forefathers and often sat side by side with me to listen to the lectures. Once you had grown up, you

差肩而坐①,爱听古人节义事;一旦长成,遽②躬蹈③之。呜呼!使汝不识《诗》《书》,或未必艰贞若是。

予捉蟋蟀,汝奋臂出其间;岁寒虫僵,同临其穴④。今予殓⑤汝葬汝,而当日之情形,憬然⑥赴目。予九岁,憩⑦书斋,汝梳双髻,披单缣⑧来,温《缁衣》⑨一章;适先生奓户⑩入,闻两童子音琅琅然⑪,不觉莞尔⑫,连呼"则则"⑬,此七月望日⑭事也。汝在九原⑮,当

---

① 差(cī)肩而坐:依次并肩而坐(sit side by side in the proper order)。
② 遽(jù):骤然(abruptly)。
③ 躬蹈:亲身实践(practice in person)。
④ 同临其穴:同到埋葬蟋蟀处凭吊(go together to pay a visit to the place where the crickets were buried)。
⑤ 殓(liàn):给死人穿衣入棺(dress up the corpse and put it in the coffin)。
⑥ 憬然:清清楚楚地(absolutely clear)。
⑦ 憩(qì):休息(rest)。
⑧ 单缣(jiān):细绢的单衫(thin shirt of fine silk)。
⑨ 《缁衣》:《诗经·郑风》中的篇名(name of a poem from the *Book of Songs*)。
⑩ 奓(zhà)户:开门(open the door)。
⑪ 琅琅然:清脆响亮的读书声(clear and melodious reading voice)。
⑫ 莞(wǎn)尔:微笑(smile)。
⑬ 则则:赞叹的声音(voice of praise)。
⑭ 望日:夏历每月十五日(the fifteenth day of each month according to the lunar calendar)。
⑮ 九原:墓地(graveyard)。

put it into practice. Alas! If you had not known anything about Confucian classics, you might not have remained so faithful to the promise which had been made by the parents and you would not have suffered from all these ordeals.

In our childhood when I was catching crickets, you would stretch out your arms to join me. When the crickets died in cold winter, you would go with me to dig tiny holes for burying the dead crickets. Today, when I was burying you after having your body dressed, the scene of how we buried the dead crickets in the old days appears clearly before my eyes. I was nine at the time when one day I was having a rest in my study and you came in with your hair worn in a pair of buns and a fine silk blouse draped over your shoulders. Together, we reread "The Black Coat" (a poem from the *Book of Songs* — China's first ancient poem collection). My teacher happened to come to my study and he was so pleased to hear two kids' clear and melodious reading voice that he smiled and could not help but praise us. This happened on that year's 15th day of the 7th month. Now you are in the graveyard; you must clearly remember this event. I went to Guangxi at the age of 20. On that day when I was leaving, you pulled me by the sleeve and cried bitterly. Three years later, after having passed the imperial examination, I returned home in silken robes. You came out from the eastern wing-room with your hand supported by the

分明记之。予弱冠①粤行②,汝掎③裳悲恸④。逾三年,予披宫锦⑤还家,汝从东厢扶案出,一家瞠视⑥而笑,不记语从何起,大概说长安⑦登科⑧、函使报信迟早云尔。凡此琐琐,虽为陈迹,然我一日未死,则一日不能忘。旧事填膺⑨,思之凄梗,如影历历,逼取便逝。悔当时不将婗婗⑩情状,罗缕⑪纪存⑫;然而汝已不在人间,则虽年光倒流,儿时可再,而亦无与为证印者矣。

汝之义绝⑬高氏而归也,堂上阿奶,仗汝扶持;家中文墨,眹⑭

---

① 弱冠:古代男子20岁行冠礼,表示已成年(in ancient China, when a man was 20, the crown ceremony would be held for him to indicate his adulthood)。
② 粤行:乾隆元年(1736)春,袁枚20岁时曾去广西看望他的叔父袁鸿(in 1736, the first year of the Qianlong Reign, when 20, the author went to visit his uncle Yuan Hong in Guangxi)。
③ 掎(jǐ):拖住(drag)。
④ 恸(tòng):痛哭(cry bitterly)。
⑤ 披宫锦:唐代进士及第后,披官袍,以示荣耀。后称中进士为"披宫锦"(in the Tang Dynasty, when a person passed the imperial examination, he would put on an official gown, showing glory. Later, "putting on official gown" was referred to passing the imperial examination)。
⑥ 瞠视:瞪着眼看(look with eyes wide opened)。
⑦ 长安:国都的代称,此指北京(synonym for the capital, here referring to Beijing)。
⑧ 登科:考中进士(pass the highest imperial examination)。
⑨ 填膺:充塞胸怀(fill one's heart)。
⑩ 婗婗(yī ní):指年幼(very young)。
⑪ 罗缕:详细排列(list in detail)。
⑫ 纪存:纪录保存(record and preserve)。
⑬ 义绝:指离婚(divorce)。
⑭ 眹(shùn):以目示意(to indicate one's wish or intention by expressions of the eyes)。

long table. All the family members were smiling and staring at each other with wide-open eyes. I do not remember from what we began to talk about at that time. Probably we began with question-and-answer about the imperial examination which I had taken in the capital, or comments on the messengers' work, whether they had delivered the news in time or not, etc. All these were trivial matters and took place long ago but I will always remember them until I die. The happenings of the past load my heart and I become so sad when I am thinking of them that my mind is blocked. They seem to be visible, like shadows but when I try to grasp them, they immediately disappear. I regret that I did not record in writing the happenings of our childhood. However, you are no longer in the human world. Even if time could flow backwards and childhood could come back, there would be no one with me to authenticate them.

Since you cut ties with the Gao family and came back to live with Mother, it became your duty to look after her and to do some family's paperwork. I used to reckon that there were very few females who understood the meaning of Confucian classics or knew well the principles of the old teachings. Your sister-in-law was an easygoing and thoughtful person but she had insufficient knowledge in this area. Therefore when you came back to live with us, I felt sad for you but happy for myself. I was four years older

汝办治。尝谓女流中最少明经义、谙雅故①者。汝嫂非不婉嫕②，而于此微缺然。故自汝归后，虽为汝悲，实为予喜。予又长汝四岁，或人间长者先亡，可将身后托汝；而不谓汝之先予以去也。前年予病，汝终宵刺探，减一分则喜，增一分则忧。后虽小差③，犹尚殗殜④，无所娱遣；汝来床前，为说稗官野史可喜可愕之事，聊资一欢。呜呼！今而后，吾将再病，教从何处呼汝耶？

汝之疾也，予信医言无害，远吊扬州；汝又虑戚吾心⑤，阻人走报；及至绵惙⑥已极，阿奶问："望兄归否？"强应曰："诺。"予已先一日梦汝来诀，心知不祥，飞舟渡江，果予以未时⑦还家，而汝以辰时⑧气绝；四支犹温，一目未瞑，盖犹忍死待予也。呜呼痛哉！早知诀汝，则予岂肯远游？即游，亦尚有几许心中言要汝知闻、共汝筹画也。而今已矣！除吾死外，当无见期。吾又不知何日死，可以见汝；而死后之有知无知，与得见不得见，又卒难明也。然则抱此无涯之憾，天乎人乎！而竟已乎⑨！

---

① 明经义、谙（ān）雅故：了解经书的意义，懂得古训的道理（understand the meaning of Confucian classics and the truth of old teachings）。
② 婉嫕（yì）：柔顺（gentle and agreeable）。
③ 小差（chài）：病稍好些（be slightly better in illness）。
④ 殗殜（yè dié）：病而不甚重，半卧半坐（be ill but not serious; be in a reclining position）。
⑤ 虑戚吾心：怕我忧心（for fear of worrying me）。
⑥ 绵惙（chuò）：指病情沉重，气息微弱（very ill, at one's faint gasp）。
⑦ 未时：下午一点至三点（1 p.m.–3 p.m.）。
⑧ 辰时：上午七点至九点（7 a.m.–9 a.m.）。
⑨ 而竟已乎：终于这样完了吗（has it ended like this）？

than you. Usually the older one dies first. In this case, I would be able to leave my unfulfilled work to you. I did not expect that you would pass away before me. It happened in the year before last that one day I fell ill and you were so worried that you did not go to sleep the whole night. You kept asking how my condition was. You remained anxious when you were told that my condition was not improving and looked happy on hearing that I was a little bit better. Later I was slightly better but could only recline in bed. You came to my bedside and related to me some funny and amazing stories from the anecdotal book, making me relaxed and happy. Alas, from now on, if I fall ill again, from where can I call you to come to see me?

I believed what the doctor said that your illness was nothing serious, so I travelled faraway to Yangzhou. You prevented them from informing me for fear of worrying me. When your gasp was faint, Mother asked, "Do you want your brother to come back?" With an effort you managed to say, "Yes." Just one day before you passed away, I dreamed that you came to say goodbye. Aware of the bad omen in the nightmare, I immediately took a swift boat to cross the river. Ominous as it was, when I arrived home just after midday, you had stopped breathing some time ago soon after daybreak. Your arms and legs were still warm and one of your eyes had not closed. You seemed to be enduring the last pain, waiting

汝之诗，吾已付梓①；汝之女，吾已代嫁；汝之生平，吾已作传②；惟汝之窀穸③，尚未谋耳。先茔在杭，江广河深，势难归葬，故请母命而宁汝于斯，便祭扫也。其傍，葬汝女阿印④；其下两冢：一为阿爷⑤侍者⑥朱氏，一为阿兄⑦侍者陶氏。羊山旷渺⑧，南望原隰⑨，西望栖霞⑩，风雨晨昏，羁魂⑪有伴，当不孤寂。所怜者，吾自戊寅⑫年读汝哭侄诗后，至今无男，两女牙牙，生汝死后，才周晬⑬耳。予虽亲在⑭未敢言老，而齿危发秃，暗里自知；知在人间，尚复几日？

---

① 付梓：付印（sent to the press）。袁枚将素文的诗，附刻于《小仓山房诗文集》中（Yuan Mei attached his sister Suwen's poems to his own *Collected Works of Poetic Prose in the Small Cangshan Study*）。

② 作传：袁枚曾作《女弟素文传》，见《小仓山房文集》卷七（the author wrote "Biography of My Younger Sister Suwen," see Volume 7 of *Collected Works of the Small Cangshan Study*）。

③ 窀穸（zhūn xī）：墓穴（tomb）。

④ 阿印：素文有两女，一名阿印，早死，一由袁枚代嫁（Suwen had two daughters, one was named Ayin, who died early; the other was married off by the author）。

⑤ 阿爷：作者的父亲袁滨，曾为幕僚（the author's father Yuan Bin, once was an assistant to a general）。

⑥ 侍者：侍妾（concubine）。

⑦ 阿兄：作者自称(the term by which the author denotes himself while addressing his sister)。

⑧ 旷渺：空旷辽阔（wide and vast）。

⑨ 原隰（xí）：平原低洼的地方（low-lying land on a plain）。

⑩ 栖霞：山名，在南京市东（name of a mountain, east of Nanjing）。

⑪ 羁魂：寄居他乡的灵魂（soul living away from home）。

⑫ 戊寅：乾隆二十三年（1758），袁枚丧子，素文曾写哭侄诗以哀悼。次年素文死。作者写此文时，尚无子，两年后得男（in the 23th year of the Qianlong Reign, 1758, Yuan Mei lost his son. Suwen wrote a poem to express grief upon her nephew's death. Next year Suwen died. When the author wrote this article, he had no son at that time. His son was born two years later）。

⑬ 周晬（zuì）：周岁（one full year of life）。

⑭ 亲在：此时作者母亲尚健在（the author's mother was still alive）。

for me. Alas, it was painful! If I had known earlier that it was the last moment of your life, I would not have traveled faraway. I was very regretful for being away when I should have been here, telling you what I had in my mind and discussing with you about what we need to do in the future. Now everything is gone! Unless I were also dead, we would never have a chance to see each other again. However I do not know when I will die and be able to see you. Also, it is very hard to be sure whether we are conscious and whether we can meet after we die. Oh, heaven! Oh, man! How miserable it would be if I had to live on with endless remorse! How sad it is if all the good things have suddenly come to an end like this!

I have turned over your poems for printing and I have, on your behalf, married off your daughter. About your life story, I have written a biography. The only thing yet to be done was to find an ideal spot for your final resting place. Our ancestors' graveyard is in Hangzhou and far from here. Wide and deep rivers have to be crossed to get there and it would be difficult to bury you there. Therefore I obtained Mother's permission to bury you here for convenient visiting. Your daughter Ayin's tomb is beside yours and nearby are two other tombs. One is that of our father's concubine, Née Zhu, and the other is that of my concubine, Née Tao. Mount Sheep occupies a vast area. Looking southward, you

阿品①远官河南，亦无子女，九族②无可继者。汝死我葬，我死谁埋？汝倘有灵，可能告我？

呜呼！生前既不可想，身后又不可知；哭汝既不闻汝言，奠汝又不见汝食。纸灰飞扬，朔风野大，阿兄归矣，犹屡屡回头望汝也。呜呼哀哉！呜呼哀哉！

---

① 阿品：袁枚的堂弟，名树，当时任河南正阳县令（the author's younger male cousin, named Shu, was then magistrate of Zhengyang County, Henan）。
② 九族：本身以上的父、祖、曾祖、高祖，本身以下的子、孙、曾孙、玄孙，与本身合称九族（above oneself: father, grandfather, great-grandfather, great-great-grandfather; below oneself: son, grandson, great-grandson, great-great-grandson, and oneself）。

can see a plain of low-lying land and to the west stands Mount Qixia. You will never feel lonely here as your soul has companions day and night, the wind and the rain. It is a pity that I do not have a second son after I lost the only son in the 23th year of the Qianlong Reign (1758) for whose death you wrote a poem of lament. My two daughters were born after you had passed away and they are only one year old. Now that Mother is still alive, I dare not say that I am old. However, my head is already bald and my teeth are shaking badly. I know in my heart that my life will not last long. Our brother Apin is an official, far away in Henan and he also has no son. No one will continue our family line. I buried you when you died. Who will bury me when I die? Can you tell me if your soul can think or talk?

Alas! I cannot bear to think of the happenings that we experienced when you were alive. I do not know what will happen after our death. When I am crying over you, I do not hear you respond; when I am offering you sacrifices, I do not see you come to eat. The north wind is blowing hard in the open field and ashes of burned paper are flying everywhere. Sister, I'm going now but I am looking back again and again to see you. Alas, it is sad indeed! Alas, such is my sorrow!

《鸣机夜课图》记

蒋士铨

吾母姓钟氏，名令嘉，字守箴，出①南昌名族②，行九③。幼与诸兄从先外祖滋生公读书。十八，归④先府君⑤。时府君年四十余，任侠⑥好客，乐施与，散数千金⑦，囊箧萧然⑧，宾从辄⑨满座。吾母脱簪珥⑩，治酒浆⑪，盘罍⑫间未尝有俭色。越二载，生铨，家益落⑬，历困苦穷乏，人所不能堪者，吾母怡然⑭无愁蹙⑮状，戚党

---

① 出：出身（come from a certain family, either rich or poor, official or non-official）。
② 名族：有名的家族（a famous family）。
③ 行（háng）九：排行第九（the ninth child in the family）。
④ 归：女子出嫁（a woman marries a man）。
⑤ 先府君：对死去父亲的敬称（respectful form of address to one's late father）。
⑥ 任侠：喜好侠义（be fond of justice and being ready to help the weak）。
⑦ 金：指一两银子（one liang of silver）。
⑧ 囊箧萧然：把钱物都用空了（spend all one's money）。囊：荷包，口袋（pocket）。箧：箱子（box）。萧然：空无所有（have nothing in it; absolutely empty）。
⑨ 辄（zhé）：常常，总是（always, often）。
⑩ 珥（ěr）：耳环（earrings）。
⑪ 浆：泛指酒（referring to wine in general）。
⑫ 罍（léi）：坛状酒器（drinking vessel like a jar）。
⑬ 落：衰落（decline）。
⑭ 怡然：和悦的样子（kindly; amiable）。
⑮ 蹙（cù）：皱起眉头（to knit or furrow one's brows）。

THE PICTURE OF TEACHING WHILE WEAVING AT NIGHT

Jiang Shiquan

My mother was from a prominent family in Nanchang and she was the ninth child in the family. Zhong was her surname, Lingjia her given name and she styled herself Shouzhen. When she was still under age, my mother, together with her elder brothers, studied at the family school and they were taught by their father (my grandfather), the revered Mr. Zisheng. At the age of 18, my mother married my late father and at that time my father was more than 40. Being chivalrous and hospitable, my father was always glad to give alms to those who required assistance. He was so generous that he gave out plenty of money and had nothing left at home. However, his house was still full of guests all the time. My mother had to pawn her hairpins and earrings in order to be able to wine and dine these guests. The food and drinks provided at the feasts remained as good as before. When I was born two years later, the family fortunes had declined. We began to suffer from poverty and hardships. My mother always kept calm and

人①争贤之②。府君由是计③复游燕、赵间,而归吾母及铨,寄食外祖家。

铨四龄,母日授"四子书"④数句;苦⑤儿幼不能执笔,乃镂⑥竹枝为丝,断之,诘屈⑦作波⑧磔⑨点画⑩,合而成字,抱铨坐膝上教之。既识,即拆去。日训⑪十字,明日,令铨持竹丝合所识字,无误乃已。至六龄,始令执笔学书⑫。先外祖家素不润⑬,历年饥大凶⑭,益窘乏⑮。时铨及小奴衣服冠履,皆出于母。母工纂⑯绣组⑰

---

① 戚党人:亲戚们(kinsmen and neighbors)。
② 争贤之:交口称赞她(shower praise on her)。
③ 计:打算(intend, plan)。
④ 四子书:即四书(the Four Books),《论语》(the *Analects of Confucius*)、《孟子》(*Mencius*)、《大学》(the *Great Learning*)、《中庸》(the *Doctrine of the Mean*)的合称。因内容都是记载孔子、孟子、曾子和子思等人的言行,故又称四子书(the contents of these books are about the words and deeds of Confucius, Mencius, Master Zeng and Master Zisi)。
⑤ 苦:苦于(suffering from)。
⑥ 镂(lòu):刻(carve, slice)。
⑦ 诘屈:曲折(twist)。
⑧ 波:字的笔画"撇"(left-falling stroke of Chinese characters)。
⑨ 磔(zhé):字的笔画"捺"(right-falling stroke of Chinese characters)。
⑩ 画:横画(horizontal stroke of Chinese characters)。
⑪ 训:教(teach)。
⑫ 书:写字(write)。
⑬ 润:富足(rich)。
⑭ 凶:荒年(famine year)。
⑮ 窘乏:穷困(poverty-stricken)。
⑯ 纂:编织(knit, weave)。
⑰ 组:织带(weave a belt)。

never presented a worried look even at the time when we were experiencing difficulties which others could not endure. Because of this she was highly praised by our relatives and neighbors and my father was able to fulfil his plan to revisit the area of Yan and Zhao to seek an official career. He let mother and me live in my maternal grandfather's home.

When I was four years old, each day she taught me several sentences from the Four Books. As I was too young to hold a writing brush, she sliced bamboo branches into thin twigs and then cut them short. She used these short bamboo twigs to form (Chinese) characters by bending or twisting for making all sorts of strokes, such as vertical and horizontal strokes, dots and hooks, etc. She put me on her lap and taught me how to read these characters. A character would be dismantled as soon as I had learnt how to read it. She taught me ten characters a day and the next day she would require me to form, with bamboo twigs, the characters I had learnt. I had to do it again and again until no mistake occurred. I was not taught how to write with a writing brush until I was six. My maternal grandfather's family was never rich and they even became poverty-stricken after having experienced several years of famine. During this period, mother made clothes, shoes and hats for me and the young servants. She was good at knitting, embroidering and weaving and often asked a young servant to take her needlework to the market. They sold

织①，凡所为女红②，令小奴携于市，人辄争购之；以是③铨及小奴无褴褛④状。

先外祖长身白髯⑤，喜饮酒。酒酣⑥，辄大声吟所作诗，令吾母指其疵⑦。母每指一字，先外祖则满引一觥⑧；数⑨指之后，乃陶然⑩捋⑪须大笑，举觞⑫自呼曰："不意阿丈⑬乃有此女！"既而⑭摩铨顶曰："好儿子，尔他日何以报尔母？"铨稚，不能答，投母怀，泪涔涔⑮下，母亦抱儿而悲；檐风几烛⑯，若愀然⑰助人以哀者。

---

① 织：织布（weave cotton cloth）。
② 女红（gōng）：妇女所作纺织、刺绣、缝纫等制品（spinning, weaving, embroidering and sewing products made by women）。
③ 以是：因此（therefore）。
④ 褴褛（lán lǚ）：衣服破烂（shabbily dressed）。
⑤ 髯（rán）：胡须（whiskers, beard）。
⑥ 酒酣：喝足了酒（drinking to one's heart's content）。
⑦ 疵（cī）：缺点（defect, flaw）。
⑧ 满引一觥（gōng）：斟满一杯酒喝了（fill a cup with wine and drink it）。引：吸（draw）。觥：古代用牛角制成的酒器（a drinking vessel made of ox horn）。
⑨ 数：多次（many times）。
⑩ 陶然：快活的样子（happy manner）。
⑪ 捋（lǚ）：用手握着一样东西，顺着抚摩（hold something in the hand and stroke it）。
⑫ 觞（shāng）：酒杯（wine glass）。
⑬ 阿丈：老夫（an old fellow like me）。
⑭ 既而：然后，随又（then）。
⑮ 涔（cén）涔：流的样子（flowing manner）。
⑯ 檐风几烛：屋檐外的风，吹着几上烛火（the wind from the outside eaves blowing the candle on the desk）。
⑰ 愀（qiǎo）然：悲凉的样子（sad and dreary）。

very well in the market. Therefore, neither I nor the servants were shabbily dressed at this difficult time.

My late maternal grandfather was a tall man with white beard and moustache. He liked wine. Whenever he was warmed with wine, he would recite the poems he had written himself and asked my mother to find out if there were any flaws in his writing. Each time when she pointed out a word which needed to be changed, grandpa would have his wine cup filled and drink it all. If one after another flaw had been found out by my mother, grandpa would merrily stroke his beard before bursting into laughter and then raise his cup, saying loudly to himself, "To have such a wonderful daughter is beyond the expectation of an old man like me!" Then he would caress my head, saying, "Good child, how will you repay your mum?" I was too young to give an answer. So what I would do was to throw myself into mother's bosom, shedding a flood of tears. Mother would hold me in her arms and she also was sad. The candle on the desk guttered in the wind which came through the eaves outside the window and this seemed to magnify the dreary melancholic atmosphere.

I remember that when mother was giving me a lecture, she would place all her spinning, weaving and embroidering devices beside her and put a book on her lap, telling me to sit near her knee to read the book. While operating the device, she taught me to read one sentence after another. Our reading voices were in

记①母教铨时,组绣纺绩②之具,毕③陈左右;膝置书,令铨坐膝下读之。母手任操作④,口授句读⑤,咿唔⑥之声,与轧轧⑦相间。儿怠,则少加夏楚⑧,旋⑨复持⑩儿而泣曰:"儿及此不学,我何以见汝⑪父!"至夜分⑫寒甚,母坐于床,拥被覆双足,解衣以胸温儿背,共铨朗诵之;读倦,睡母怀,俄而⑬母摇铨曰:"可以醒矣!"铨张目视母面,泪方纵横落,铨亦泣。少间⑭,复令读;鸡鸣,卧焉。

诸姨尝谓母曰:"妹一儿也,何苦乃尔⑮!"对曰:"子众,可矣;儿一,不肖⑯,妹何托⑰焉!"

庚戌⑱,外祖母病且⑲笃⑳,母侍之,凡汤药饮食,必亲尝之而

---

① 记:回忆(recall)。
② 纺:纺纱(spin cotton threads);绩:纺麻(spin hemp threads)。
③ 毕:都(all)。
④ 手任操作:手里干着活儿(while working with one's hands)。
⑤ 句读(dòu):文句停顿(stop of a sentence)。
⑥ 咿唔(yī wú):读书的声调(reading voice)。
⑦ 轧轧:纺车声(sound of spinning wheels)。
⑧ 夏(jiǎ):木制戒尺(teacher's ruler for beating pupils);楚:荆条(twigs of the chaste tree, also for beating pupils)。
⑨ 旋:不久(soon)。
⑩ 持:抱(carry in breast)。
⑪ 汝:你的(your)。
⑫ 夜分:半夜(midnight)。
⑬ 俄而:一会儿(a little while)。
⑭ 少间:一会儿(after a while)。
⑮ 乃尔:竟至如此(to such an extent)。
⑯ 不肖:不好(unworthy)。
⑰ 托:托付(entrust)。
⑱ 庚戌:清雍正八年(1730)(the 8th year of the Yongzheng Reign)。
⑲ 且:将近(close to)。
⑳ 笃:(病情)严重(the worsening of one's illness)。

harmony with the sound of spinning wheel. I looked tired and she beat me lightly with a ruler before tearfully holding my hands, saying: "You are unwilling to study. What can I tell your father when I see him?" At midnight, when it was cold, mother would sit on the bed, covering her feet with the quilt, and then unbutton her blouse to warm my back with her bosom, reading with me. One time I was so tired that I fell asleep in mother's arms. It was not long before she shook me and told me to wake up. I opened my eyes. On seeing tears streaming down her cheeks, I also sobbed. Soon she told me to read again. We did not go to sleep until the cocks started to crow. My aunts once said to my mother, "You have only one son, why should you bother him so much?" Mother answered: "There would be no anxiety if I had many sons. But I have only one son. If he is no good, whom can I rely on?"

In the eighth year of the Yongzheng Reign (1730), my maternal grandmother was seriously ill and my mother looked after her. Mother tasted all the food and drink as well as medical decoctions prepared for grandma before she gave them to her mother to take. She didn't look tired at all after having waited on grandma for forty days and nights. On her deathbed, grandma said amid tears: "You used to be weak. These days you have been doing more tiring work than your brothers and you must be exhausted by now. When my son-in-law comes back eventually, please tell him on my behalf that I have died without any regret and the only

后进，历四十昼夜，无倦容。外祖母濒危①，泣曰："女②本弱，今劳瘁③过诸兄，惫④矣。他日⑤婿归，为言：'我死无恨，恨不见女子成立。'其善诱⑥之。"语讫⑦而卒。母哀毁骨立⑧，水浆不入口者七日。闾党姻亚⑨，一时咸⑩以"孝女"称，至今弗衰也。

铨九龄，母授以《礼记》⑪《周易》⑫《毛诗》⑬，皆成诵⑭。暇更录唐宋人诗，教之为吟哦声。母与铨皆弱而多病，铨每病，母即抱铨行一室中，未尝寝；少瘥，辄指壁间诗歌，教儿低吟之以为戏。母有病，铨则坐枕侧不去。母视铨，辄无言而悲，铨亦凄楚依恋之。尝问曰："母有忧乎？"曰："然⑮。""然则何以解忧？"曰："儿能背诵所读书，斯⑯解也。"铨诵声琅琅⑰然，争药鼎⑱沸，母微笑曰：

---

① 濒危：临终（approaching one's end）。
② 女：汝（you）。
③ 瘁（cuì）：辛苦（toilsome, laborious）。
④ 惫：疲乏（fatigue）。
⑤ 他日：日后（in the future）。
⑥ 诱：教导（give guidance）。
⑦ 讫（qì）：完毕（finished）。
⑧ 哀毁骨立：因哀伤瘦得皮包骨头（become a mere skeleton after going through mourning for some time）。
⑨ 闾（lú）党：邻里和乡党（people of the neighbourhood）。姻亚：亲眷（one's relatives）。
⑩ 咸：都（all）。
⑪ 礼记：记述中国古代礼仪的书（the *Book of Rites*）。
⑫ 周易：易经（the *Book of Changes*）。
⑬ 毛诗：汉代毛亨所传《诗经》（the *Book of Songs* passed on by Mao Heng in the Han Dynasty）。
⑭ 诵：背诵（recite）。
⑮ 然：是（yes）。
⑯ 斯：这样（thus）。
⑰ 琅琅：读书声（reading voice）。
⑱ 药鼎：煎药锅（pot for decocting medicinal herbs）。

thing that has made me feel bad is that I will not be able to see my grandson get married and start his career. This child needs to be given good guidance." Having finished her words, grandma passed away. Mother was so sorrowful over grandma's death that she did not eat nor drink for seven days. As a result, she became a bag of bones. All our neighbors and relatives called her "filial daughter" and up to now she is still so called.

When I was nine, mother taught me the *Book of Rites*, the *Book of Changes* and the *Book of Songs*. I could repeat all of them from memory. When she was free from housework, mother would copy out poems of the Tang and Song dynasties and teach me how to chant the poetry in cadence. Mother and I were both weak and often fell ill. Whenever I was sick, she would hold me in her arms and kept walking to and fro in the room for the whole night without sleeping. As soon as I was a little better, she would point to the poems copied on the wall and teach me to play a game — chanting poetry in a low voice. When mother was sick, I would sit by her pillow for a long time. Mother stared at me, sad and speechless. I was also feeling upset, unwilling to leave her. Once I asked her, "Do you have anything to worry about?" She said "yes." I asked again, "Then how do you relieve yourself from anxiety?" She answered, "My anxiety will go if you can repeat from memory what you've learnt." Thus my reciting voice was mingled with the sound of a medical concoction boiling in the pot. Mother

"病少①差②矣。"由是,母有病,铨即持书诵于侧,而病辄能愈。

十岁,父归。越一载,复携母及铨,偕游燕、赵、秦、魏、齐、梁、吴、楚③间。先府君苟有过,母必正色婉言规④,或怒不听,则屏息⑤,俟怒少解,复力争之,听而后止。先府君每决⑥大狱⑦,母辄携儿立席⑧前,曰:"幸⑨以此儿为念。"府君数颔之⑩。先府君在客邸⑪,督铨学甚急,稍怠,即怒而弃⑫之,数日不及⑬一言;吾母垂涕扑⑭之,令跪读至熟乃已,未尝倦也。铨故不能荒⑮于嬉⑯,而母教由是益以严。

又十载,归。卜居⑰于鄱阳⑱。铨年且⑲二十。明年,娶妇张氏。

---

① 少:稍微(slightly)。
② 差:瘥,愈(recover)。
③ 燕、赵、秦、魏、齐、梁、吴、楚:春秋战国国名。此处代指今陕西、河南、河北、山东、江苏、安徽、湖北等地(names of the states during the Spring and Autumn Period and the Warring States Period. Here referring to areas of today's Shaanxi, Henan, Hebei, Shandong, Jiangsu, Anhui, Hubei, etc.)。
④ 规:劝告(advise)。
⑤ 屏息:收敛呼吸(hold one's breath)。
⑥ 决:判决(adjudge)。
⑦ 大狱:死刑案(death penalty)。
⑧ 席:座位(seat)。
⑨ 幸:盼望(hope for)。
⑩ 颔之:点头称许(nod assent)。
⑪ 客邸:旅居在外的住宅(residence for living away from home)。
⑫ 弃:不理会(pay no attention to)。
⑬ 及:涉及(relate to)。
⑭ 扑:责打(mete out corporal punishment to)。
⑮ 荒:荒废(neglect)。
⑯ 嬉:游戏(play)。
⑰ 卜居:找新居处(look for a new residence)。
⑱ 鄱阳:江西省鄱阳县(Poyang County, Jiangxi Province)。
⑲ 且:将近(close to)。

smiled and said, "I am feeling a little better now." From then on, whenever mother was ill, I would immediately read books beside her and she always very soon recovered from her illness.

When I was ten, my father returned home. One year later, he took mother and me to his appointed post. We kept moving from one area to another including Hebei, Shanxi, Shaanxi, Henan, Shandong, Jiangsu, Hunan and Hubei. Occasionally father made a mistake. When it happened, mother would give him a serious piece of advice but in a tactful way. If he became angry, she would hold her breath, wait until he was a little calmer and then persuade him again and again until he took her advice. Every time while father was making the court decision on a serious case, mother always took me to stand before his seat, saying, "Please keep in mind that you have this son." Father would nod assent on hearing her words. Once when we were staying in a temporary residence away from our home, father had little patience in supervising my study. One day he saw me lax in my study and immediately left in a huff. He did not talk to anybody for several days after that. With tears running down her cheeks, mother inflicted a punishment by beating me and telling me to kneel on the ground and remain on my knees until I had learnt the text by heart. She never tired of doing so. Therefore, it was impossible for me to indulge in playing games and neglect my study. After this incident, mother became more strict in teaching me.

母,女视之①,训以纺绩织纴②事,一如教儿时。

铨生二十有二年,未尝去③母前,以应童子试④,归铅山,母略无离别可怜之色,旋⑤补弟子员。明年丁卯⑥,食廪饩⑦;秋,荐于乡⑧。归拜母,母色喜。依膝下廿日,遂北行⑨。母念儿辄有诗;未一寄也。明年落第,九月归。十二月,先府君即世⑩,母哭而濒死者十余次,自为文祭之,凡百余言⑪,朴婉沉痛,闻者无⑫亲疏老幼,皆呜咽失声。时行年⑬四十有三也。

己巳⑭,有南昌老画师游鄱阳,八十余,白发垂耳⑮,能图人状貌。铨延⑯之为母写小像,因以位置景物请于母,且问:"母何以行乐?当图之以为娱。"母愀然曰:"呜呼!自为蒋氏妇,尝以不

---

① 女视之:视之如女(regard her as her daughter)。
② 纺绩织纴(rèn):纺织(spinning and weaving)。
③ 去:离开(depart from)。
④ 童子试:低级科举考试(elementary imperial examination)。
⑤ 旋:不久(soon)。
⑥ 丁卯:清乾隆十二年(1747)(the 12th year of the Qianlong Reign, 1737)。
⑦ 食廪饩(xì):吃官府的粮食,即补了廪生(get support from the government)。
⑧ 荐于乡:乡试录取,中了举人(become a successful candidate for the imperial examination at the provincial level in the Qing Dynasty)。
⑨ 北行:往北京(left for Beijing)。
⑩ 即世:去世(pass away)。
⑪ 言:字(word)。
⑫ 无:无论(regardless of)。
⑬ 行年:年岁(age)。
⑭ 己巳:清乾隆十四年(1749)(the 14th year of the Qianlong Reign, 1749)。
⑮ 白发垂耳:指年老(very old)。
⑯ 延:请(invite)。

Another ten years later, we returned to hometown and found a new residence in Poyang County. At that time I was nearly 20. In the following year, I married a girl named Née Zhang. Mother treated her as her own daughter and taught her how to do needlework, such as spinning, weaving and sewing, just like she taught me how to read and write.

In the past twenty two years since I was born, I had never been away from my mother. When I was going back to Qianshan County to take the elementary imperial examination, mother did not look unwilling to part from me at all. Soon I passed the examination and became a *xiucai* (one who passed the imperial examination at the county level). The next year (the 12th year of the Qianlong Reign), I received financial support from the government and in autumn I became a successful candidate for the imperial examination at the provincial level. When I returned home to pay respects to mother, she looked happy. Having stayed with her for twenty days, I left home for the north. Whenever she missed me, she would write a poem but she never sent the poetry to me. In the year after, I failed to pass the imperial exam and came back home in the ninth month of the same year. Three months later father passed away and mother grieved so deeply that she herself almost died a dozen times. Mother personally wrote the funeral oration. Consisting of more than one hundred words, the oration expressed her true feeling and it was so sad

及奉舅姑①盘匜②为恨；而处忧患哀恸③间数十年：凡哭母、哭父、哭儿、哭女夭折④，今且⑤哭夫矣！未亡人⑥欠一死耳，何乐为⑦！"

铨跪曰："虽然，母志有乐得未致⑧者，请寄斯图也，可乎？"母曰："苟吾儿及新妇能习于勤，不亦可乎？鸣机夜课，老妇之愿足矣，乐何有焉！"

铨于是退而语⑨画士。乃图秋夜之景：虚堂⑩四敞⑪，一灯荧荧⑫；高梧萧疏⑬，影落檐际；堂中列一机，画吾母坐而织之，妇执纺车坐母侧；檐底横列一几，剪烛⑭自照，凭画栏而读者则铨也。阶下假山一，砌⑮花盆兰，婀娜⑯相倚，动摇于微风凉月中。其童子蹲树根捕促织⑰为戏，及垂短发、持羽扇，煮茶石上者，则奴子阿同、小婢阿昭也。

---

① 舅姑：丈夫的父母（parents of one's husband）。
② 盘匜（yí）：盥洗盛水器物（utensils for washing faces or containing water）。
③ 恸：大哭（cry bitterly）。
④ 夭折：未成年死去（die young）。
⑤ 且：甚且（even）。
⑥ 未亡人：旧时妇女丧夫后自称（a term used by a woman to call herself after her husband dies）。
⑦ 为：疑问语气词（an interrogative modal particle）。
⑧ 致：达到（achieve, attain）。
⑨ 语（yù）：告诉（tell）。
⑩ 虚堂：空堂屋（empty central room）。
⑪ 四敞：四面敞开（open wide on four sides）。
⑫ 荧荧：火光微弱（faint light）。
⑬ 萧疏：稀稀落落（sparse but graceful）。
⑭ 剪烛：剪掉烧过的蜡烛芯（cut the burnt candlewicks）。
⑮ 砌：台阶（step）。
⑯ 婀娜：优美轻盈（graceful）。
⑰ 促织：蟋蟀（cricket）。

and moving that all the listeners, either friends or acquaintances, young or old, were choked with sobs. Mother was then forty-three years of age.

In the 14th year of the Qianlong Reign (1749), an old painter from Nanchang visited Poyang County. He was in his eighties and had long white hair covering his ears. He was good at portrait painting and I invited him to draw a portrait for my mother. I asked mother about her idea as how to arrange the figures and background in the painting, and also asked what her hobby was so that it could be added to the painting for more fun. Mother said gloomily: "Alas! Since I became a daughter-in-law of the Jiang family, I have often felt sorry for not being able to wait on my parents-in-law. For dozens of years, I have come across one sad event after another which always plunged me into deep sorrow. I cried for my mother's death, then my father's and afterwards my son's. I was overcome with grief over the death of my daughter who died very young and now I still feel sad over my husband's death. They have died but I am still alive. So I owe heaven my death. What fun can I have?" I knelt down and said, "Mother, though you've not attained anything that can make you happy, I wonder if you would allow us to depict your unfulfilled happy things in the painting." Mother answered: "Isn't it a happy thing to see my son and his bride work hard? The experience of teaching my son how to read and write while operating my weaving and

图成，母视之而欢。铨谨按①吾母生平勤劳，为之略②，以进求诸大人先生③之立言④而与⑤人为善者。

---

① 按：根据（according to）。
② 略：事略（biographical sketch）。
③ 大人先生：有声望的人（man with high reputation）。
④ 立言：著书立说（write books and set up a theory）。
⑤ 与：赞助（support, sponsor）。

spinning devices has given me much satisfaction. Is there anything that can make me happy other than this?"

I withdrew from her room and talked to the painter. Thus the picture of an autumn night was painted: A spacious living room with all its doors and windows opened, a lamp twinkling with dim light and the shadow of the sparse branches and leaves of a tall parasol tree falling on the eaves. A loom was laid at the centre of the room and mother, sitting at the machine, was engaged in weaving. My wife, sitting by my mother, was operating the spinning wheel. A desk was put horizontally under the eaves. The man, leaning against the painted windowsill to read at candlelight, was me. Outside the window, a rockery stood near the foot of the staircase. The flowers by the stairs and the orchids in the pots, leaning against each other, were swaying gracefully in the gentle breeze and chilly moonlight. The young boy, squatting at the foot of a tree root to catch crickets, was servant Atong and the short-haired girl, holding a feather fan to boil tea in a pot placed on a rock, was maidservant Azhao.

The painting was completed and mother was happy when she saw it. Mother had been diligent all her life. Based on her life, I have written this biographical sketch. I hope that someone of high reputation will use this material to set forth a theory to encourage people to be well conducted.

弈 喻

钱大昕

予观弈①于友人所②,一客数③败,嗤④其失算,辄⑤欲易⑥置⑦之,以为不逮己⑧也。顷之⑨,客请与予对局⑩,予颇易之⑪。甫⑫下数子,客已得先手⑬。局将半,予思益苦⑭,而客之智尚有余。竟局⑮数之,客胜予十三子,予赧⑯甚,不能出一言。后有招予观弈者,终日默坐而已。

---

① 弈(yì):下棋(play chess)。
② 所:处,地方(place)。
③ 数:屡次(time and again)。
④ 嗤(chī):讥笑(sneer at)。
⑤ 辄:每每(often)。
⑥ 易:改换(replace)。
⑦ 置:指下棋,布子(arrange chess pieces)。
⑧ 不逮己:不及自己(not as good as / inferior to oneself)。
⑨ 顷之:过一会儿(after a little while)。
⑩ 对局:下棋。下一次叫一局(play chess; play a game of chess)。
⑪ 易之:轻视他(look down upon him)。
⑫ 甫:刚刚(just, only)。
⑬ 得先手:占上风(take the wind; prevail over)。
⑭ 思益苦:越来越想不出应付的办法(can't figure out a way to cope with all the more)。
⑮ 竟局:结局,局终(final result)。竟:结束(end)。局:棋局(chess game)。
⑯ 赧(nǎn):因羞愧而脸红(blushing with shame)。

THE METAPHOR OF A CHESS GAME

Qian Daxin

One day I was watching chess games in my friend's house where I witnessed one of his guests losing one game after another. Sneering at his stupid moves in the game and thinking that I was better than he, I was eager to take his place. Not long afterwards, this man invited me to play a game with him and I accepted his invitation, expecting to beat him very easily. We had hardly made some moves when he obtained the upper hand. In the middle of the game, I racked my brains to find a way out while my opponent seemed to be using only half of his wisdom. When the game was over, the result was counted and he beat me by a margin of thirteen pieces. I felt so ashamed that I was rendered speechless. After that, whenever I was invited to watch chess games, I would sit there and keep silent.

Nowadays, while reading ancient books, scholars often find fault with the ancient writers. While getting along with others, they are inclined to criticize their counterpart's errors. Nobody can avoid making mistakes. In all fairness, if I put myself in that

今之学者，读古人书，多訾①古人之失②；与今人居，亦乐称人失。人固不能无失，然试易地③以处④，平心而度⑤之，吾果无一失乎？吾能知人之失而不能见吾之失，吾能指人之小失而不能见吾之大失。吾求吾失且不暇⑥，何暇论人哉！

弈之优劣有定⑦也，一着⑧之失，人皆见之，虽护前⑨者不能讳也。理之所在，各是其所是，各非其所非⑩，世无孔子⑪，谁能定是非之真？然则人之失者未必非得也，吾之无失者未必非大失也，而彼此相嗤，无有已时⑫，曾⑬观弈者之不若⑭已⑮。

---

① 訾（zī）：诋毁（slander）。
② 失：过失，缺点（fault, shortcoming）。
③ 易地：换一下位置（exchange location, here meaning if one were in someone else's position）。
④ 处：居（be in a certain position）。
⑤ 度（duó）：推测，估计（calculate, estimate）。
⑥ 不暇：来不及（there's no time）。暇：空闲，多余的时间（free time）。
⑦ 定：定准，公认的标准（established standard）。
⑧ 一着（zhāo）：一步棋（make a step forward）。
⑨ 护前：回护前此之失（cover / conceal one's last fault）。
⑩ 各是其所是，各非其所非：各人赞成自以为正确的，反对自以为不正确的（each approves of what he thinks right and opposes what he thinks wrong）。
⑪ 孔子：这里是指具有大智慧的人（here referring to a really clever man）。
⑫ 无有已时：没完没了（endless）。
⑬ 曾（zēng）：简直（simply）。
⑭ 不若：不如（not equal to）。
⑮ 已：矣，助词（auxiliary word）。

person's place, could I avoid making the same mistake? I can see other people's mistake but not my own. I can pick up others' tiny fault but cannot see my own big mistake. If I do not have time to find out my mistakes, how can I have time to comment on others' errors?

There is a criterion for judging the skill of a chess player — whether it is good or not. A single bad move in a chess game can be seen by all the viewers. Whatever the loser tries to do in an attempt to cover up the previous defects will end up in vain. To find the reason behind a happening, everybody always takes the one he considers right and rejects the one he thinks wrong. In today's world, there are not sages like Confucius, so how can we judge what is right and what is wrong? Therefore, what in your mind is someone's loss may be a gain while the "non-error" label attached to yourself may turn out to be a big mistake. When people never stop sneering at each other, we can say that they are not as good as the viewers of a chess game.

登泰山记

姚鼐

泰山①之阳②,汶水③西流;其阴④,济水⑤东流。阳谷⑥皆入汶,阴谷皆入济。当其南北分者,古长城⑦也。最高日观峰⑧,在长城南十五里。

---

① 泰山:古称东岳,又称岱山、岱宗,主峰在今泰安城北(Mount Tai was called the Eastern Mountain in the olden days, also called Mount Dai, Daizong; its main peak is to the north of Tai'an City in Shandong Province)。
② 阳:山南为阳(south of a mountain is called Yang)。
③ 汶(wèn)水:即大汶河,发源于山东莱芜东北,向西南流经泰安,至汶上县入运河(i.e. the Big Wen River, originating in the northeast of Laiwu County, Shandong, flows southwestward and passes through Tai'an to Wenshang County, where it enters the Grand Canal)。
④ 阴:山北为阴(north of a mountain is called Yin)。
⑤ 济水:源于河南济源市西之王屋山,流经山东。清代末年,济水河道为黄河所占(coming from the Wangwu Mountain west of Jiyuan City, Henan, passes through Shandong. At the end of the Qing Dynasty its river course was occupied by the Yellow River)。
⑥ 阳谷:指山南谷中水道(referring to the water course in the southern valley of the mountain)。
⑦ 古长城:战国时齐国修筑的长城,西起平阴,经泰山北冈,东至诸城(the old Great Wall built by the State of Qi during the Warring States Period, rising from Pingyin in the west, passing by the Northern Ridge of Mount Tai, to Zhucheng in the east)。
⑧ 日观峰:泰山顶峰,观日出之胜地(the summit of Mount Tai, a scenic spot for viewing the sunrise)。

ASCENDING MOUNT TAI

Yao Nai

To the south of Mount Tai, the Wen River flows westward and to its north the Ji River flows eastward. Water in its southern valley all flows into the Wen River while water in its northern one all flows into the Ji River. The dividing line for the south and north in this area is the ancient Great Wall. The highest peak of Mount Tai, called the Sunrise-Viewing Peak, is fifteen *li* south of the Great Wall.

In the 12th month of the 39th year of the Qianlong Reign, braving wind and snow, I left the capital. I passed Qihe and Changqing and then went through the valley northwest of Mount Tai. Having crossed the Great Wall which lay there like a threshold, I arrived at Tai'an Prefecture. On the 28th of this month, together with Zhu Xiaochun, the magistrate of Tai'an Prefecture, I began to ascend Mount Tai from its southern foot. The whole length of the journey was 45 *li*. It was a road of stone stairs which consisted of more than seven thousand steps.

There were three valleys due south of Mount Tai. The stream

余以乾隆三十九年①十二月,自京师乘②风雪,历齐河、长清③,穿泰山西北谷,越长城之限④,至于泰安⑤。是月丁未⑥,与知府朱孝纯子颖⑦由南麓⑧登。四十五里,道皆砌石为磴⑨,其级七千有余。

泰山正南面有三谷。中谷绕泰安城下,郦道元⑩所谓环水⑪也。余始循⑫以入,道少半,越中岭,复循西谷,遂至其巅⑬。古

---

① 乾隆三十九年:公元 1774 年(in AD 1774)。乾隆,清高宗年号(the reign title of Emperor Gaozong of the Qing Dynasty, 1736–1795)。
② 乘:趁,这里有"冒着"的意思(be equal to 趁, here meaning "to brave")。
③ 齐河、长清:山东两县名,在泰安西北(name of two counties of Shandong, northwest of Tai'an)。
④ 限:门槛,这里指像一道门槛的城墙(threshold, here referring to the city wall like a threshold)。
⑤ 泰安:清代山东府治,辛亥革命后改为县,登泰山者大抵从泰安上去(a prefecture during the Qing Dynasty; after the Revolution of 1911, it was changed into a county. Climbers of Mount Tai usually ascend from Tai'an)。
⑥ 丁未:指乾隆三十九年十二月二十八日(referring to the 28th day of the 12th month in the 39th year of the Qianlong Reign)。
⑦ 朱孝纯:字子颖,号海愚,山东历城人,当时是泰安府的知府,姚鼐挚友(styled himself Ziying, alternatively named Haiyu, from Licheng, Shandong, then magistrate of Tai'an Prefecture, the author's close friend)。
⑧ 麓(lù):山脚(the foot of a mountain)。
⑨ 磴(dèng):山上的石级(stone stairs on the mountain)。
⑩ 郦(lì)道元:字善长,北魏范阳(今河北涿州)人,著有《水经注》(Li Daoyuan styled himself Shanchang, from today's Zhuozhou City, Hebei, and wrote a famous book *Notes on Rivers*)。
⑪ 环水:总名中溪,又名梳洗河(generally named the Central Stream, also the Washing River)。
⑫ 循(xún):沿着(along)。
⑬ 巅(diān):山顶(top of a mountain)。

from the central valley circled the city wall of Tai'an, thus called by Li Daoyuan the Circling Stream. I walked along the central valley to commence the journey. Less than halfway up the mountain we have tramped over the central ridge. Then I walked along the western valley and reached the summit of Mount Tai. In the old days, people usually ascended Mount Tai from the eastern valley. On this mountain path there was a gate with the elegant name of Heavenly Gate and hence the eastern valley was called "Stream under Heavenly Gate" in ancient times. It was a place to which I had never been. Today when we were walking on the mountain path to climb the central ridge and then to scale the summit, we were often blocked by cliffs which stood before us like gates. They were called by everyone "the Gate of Heaven." The whole way was enveloped in mist and the steps were so frozen as to become so slippery that it was almost impossible to walk on them. When we finally reach the summit, I saw the green mountain mostly covered with snow and the southern sky lit up by the reflection from the snow. I sighted the city wall of Tai'an bathed in the glow of sunset and surrounded by the picturesque scenery of the Wen River and Mount Culai. I also saw the beautiful view of fog settling around the mountainside in the shape of a ribbon.

Just before dawn on the last day of this month, I went

时登山，循东谷入，道有天门①。东谷者，古谓之天门溪水，余所不至也。今所经中岭及山巅崖限②当道者，世皆谓之天门云。道中迷雾冰滑，磴几不可登。及既上，苍山负雪，明烛天南；望晚日照城郭，汶水、徂徕③如画，而半山居④雾若带然。

戊申晦⑤，五鼓⑥，与子颖坐日观亭⑦，待日出。大风扬积雪击面。亭东自足下皆云漫。稍见云中白若摴蒱⑧数十立者，山也。极天⑨云一线异色⑩，须臾⑪成五采。日上，正赤⑫如丹⑬，下有红光，动摇承⑭之。或曰，此东海⑮也。回视日观以西峰，或得日⑯或否，

---

① 天门：泰山有南天门、东天门、西天门（on Mount Tai there are the Southern Heaven Gate, the Eastern Heaven Gate and the Western Heaven Gate）。

② 崖限：像门限一样的山崖（cliff like a threshold）。

③ 徂徕（cú lái）：山名，在泰安东南40里（name of a mountain, 40 li southeast of Tai'an）。

④ 居：停留（stay）。

⑤ 晦：农历每月最后一天（the last day of each month according to the traditional Chinese calendar）。戊申晦：戊申这天正值晦日（the day of Wushen, the 29th, happened to be the last day of this month）。

⑥ 五鼓：五更（the fifth watch of the night）。一夜分为五更（one night is divided into five watches or periods）。

⑦ 日观亭：亭名，在日观峰（name of a pavilion, on the Sunrise-Viewing Peak）。

⑧ 摴蒱（chū pú）：赌博工具（gambling devices）。

⑨ 极天：天的尽头，天边（the end of the sky, horizon）。

⑩ 云一线异色：一缕云颜色很特别（a thread of cloud in an unusual color）。

⑪ 须臾（xū yú）：片刻（moment, instant）。

⑫ 正赤：纯红（pure red）。

⑬ 丹：朱砂（cinnabar）。

⑭ 承：托（support from underneath）。

⑮ 东海：泛指东方的大海（generally refer to the sea in the east）。

⑯ 得日：受到太阳照射（shone by the sun）。

to the Sunrise-Viewing Pavilion with Ziying. We sat there to wait for the sun to rise. At this time, a strong wind lifted the accumulated snow which brushed our faces. East of the pavilion, dense clouds pervaded everywhere beneath our feet. Dozens of white objects similar to dice were faintly visible among the clouds. These turned out to be mountains peaks. On the horizon, a thread of cloud, which had been tinted with an unusual color, at this moment became more colourful. Now the sun had risen, pure red like cinnabar, with a swaying scarlet light supporting it from underneath. Some one said that it was the Eastern Sea. I looked back at the peaks west of the Sunrise-Viewing Peak, some were illuminated by the sun, some were not, some were white or red, some were in mixed colors. All these peaks resembled hunchbacked human figures.

There were two temples to the east of the pavilion, one was called the Dai Temple and the other the Temple of Goddess of Bixia. A temporary imperial palace was situated to the east of the second Temple. That day, on viewing the stone tablets on both sides of the road, we could see that many of them had been erected since the Xianqing Reign [656–661] during the Tang Dynasty but the inscriptions of those that dated from earlier years had become illegible owing to the erosional damage. We did not have time to go to see the stone tablets which were not alongside the road.

绛①皓②驳③色，而皆若偻④。

亭西有岱祠⑤，又有碧霞元君⑥祠；皇帝行宫⑦在碧霞元君祠东。是日，观道中石刻，自唐显庆⑧以来，其远古刻尽漫失⑨。僻不当道者，皆不及往。

山多石，少土；石苍黑色，多平方，少圜⑩。少杂树，多松，生石罅⑪，皆平顶。冰雪，无瀑水⑫，无鸟兽音迹。至日观数里内无树，而雪与人膝齐。

桐城姚鼐记。

---

① 绛（jiàng）：红色（red）。
② 皓（hào）：白色（white）。
③ 驳：杂（mixed）。
④ 偻（lǚ）：弯腰曲背（[of one's back] crooked）。
⑤ 岱祠：一名岱庙，祭祀东岳大帝的庙宇（also named Dai Temple, for offering sacrifices to the god of the Eastern Mountain）。
⑥ 碧霞元君：女神，传说为东岳大帝的女儿（a goddess, is said to be daughter of the god of the Eastern Mountain）。
⑦ 行宫：皇帝出巡时的住所（dwelling place for royal progress）。
⑧ 显庆：唐高宗李治的年号（the reign title of Emperor Gaozong of the Tang Dynasty）。
⑨ 漫失：石碑经过风雨剥蚀，字迹模糊不清（eroded by weather the writings on the stone tablets become illegible）。漫：磨灭（wear away）。
⑩ 圜（yuán）：同"圆"（round）。
⑪ 石罅（xià）：石缝（stone crack）。
⑫ 瀑水：瀑布（waterfall）。

On the mountain there're more stones than soil. Greenish black in color, most of the stones were flat and square in shape and round ones were rare. Among very few other species, most of the trees were pine, growing in stone cracks and with flat tops. It was a world of ice and snow, without waterfalls and streams. There was no sound or trace of birds or beasts at all. Within a distance of several *li* from the Sunrise-Viewing Pavilion, we could not find any trees and what we could see was only the knee-deep snow.

Written by Yao Nai from Tongcheng.

问　说

刘　开

　　君子学必好问。问与学，相辅而行者也，非学无以致疑①，非问无以广识②。好学而不勤问，非真能好学者也。理明矣，而或不达③于事，识其大矣，而或不知其细，舍④问，其奚⑤决⑥焉？

　　贤⑦于己者，问焉以破⑧其疑，所谓就⑨有道而正⑩也。不如己者，问焉以求一得⑪，所谓以能问于不能，以多问于寡也。等于己

---

① 致疑：发现问题（discover problems）。
② 广识：增长知识（broaden one's knowledge）。
③ 达：通达（understand）。
④ 舍：除去（abandon）。
⑤ 奚：怎么（how）。
⑥ 决：判断（judge）。
⑦ 贤：胜过（excel, surpass, be better than）。
⑧ 破：破除（do away with; get rid of）。
⑨ 就：接近（be close to）。
⑩ 正：决定是非（to judge right from wrong）。
⑪ 一得：偶然正确的意见（occasionally correct idea）。

THE IMPORTANCE OF ASKING QUESTIONS

Liu Kai

Asking questions is sure to be a gentleman's fondness while he is studying. Asking questions and acquiring knowledge are two aspects of one's study which complement each other. No question will occur if you do not study and no enrichment of knowledge will happen if you do not ask questions. If you are eager to study but do not like asking questions, we cannot say that you study well. If you understand the principle of something but are unable to put it into practice, or if you know the general situation of an event but not its details, how can you make a judgment without asking others for advice?

Seeking advice from someone who is more knowledgeable than yourself will help you solve the problem and this can be described as to judge right or wrong by approaching a learned man. If the person from whom you are asking advice knows less than yourself, you can still gain something from him and we can say that you are asking a less capable person for help or you are seeking advice from a less knowledgeable person. When

者,问焉以资切磋①,所谓交相问难②,审问③而明辨④之也。《书》⑤不云乎,"好问则裕⑥。"孟子论"求放心⑦",而并称曰"学问之道",学即继以问也。子思⑧言"尊德性",而归于"道⑨问学",问且先于学也。

古之人虚中⑩乐善,不择事⑪而问焉,不择人而问焉,取其有益于身⑫而已。是故狂夫⑬之言,圣人择之;刍荛⑭之微,先民⑮询

---

① 切磋(cuō):本谓古代加工玉器的两种方法,后喻朋友间交流学问(originally referring to two methods of the jade carving process, later figuratively meaning to learn from each other by exchanging views)。
② 问难(nàn):提出责难或不同意见(put forward censure or different ideas)。
③ 审问:仔细地讯问(question carefully)。
④ 明辨:明智地辨别是非(distinguish between right and wrong)。
⑤ 《书》:指《尚书》(the *Book of History*, a famous book in ancient China)。
⑥ 裕:丰足(abundant)。
⑦ 求放心:语出《孟子·告子》:"学问之道无他,求其放心而已矣(cited from "Master Gao" of *Mencius*: "Learning is no other than seeking for a lost mind")。放:放任,迷失(abandoned, lost)。
⑧ 子思:孔子的孙子,名伋(jí),孟子曾就学于他的学生。著有《子思》23篇,已佚。相传《礼记》中的《中庸》一篇为他所作。(Confucius' grandson, named Ji. Mencius used to learn from his student. There were 23 articles of *Zisi* but they were already lost. Tradition has it that "the Doctrine of the Mean" in the *Book of Rites* was written by him)。
⑨ 道:遵循(follow, abide by)。
⑩ 虚中:虚心(open-minded)。
⑪ 不择事:不管什么事(regardless of anything)。
⑫ 身:自己(oneself)。
⑬ 狂夫:狂妄的普通人(extremely conceited person)。
⑭ 刍荛(chú ráo):樵夫(woodcutter)。
⑮ 先民:古代贤人(a person of virtue in ancient times)。

the person from whom you are asking advice is about equal to yourself, there will be an opportunity to learn from each other by exchanging views and comparing notes and it will become easier to distinguish right from wrong when different ideas are put forward for debates. The Book says that by asking questions one will become rich in knowledge. While talking about bringing back the drifting mind, Mencius also mentioned the principle of study by saying that learning always followed after asking questions. While emphasizing the importance of self-cultivation and ethical attainments, Zisi (Confucius' grandson) summed up this process by giving first priority to the inclination to ask questions.

Ancient people were always ready to accept good advice with an open mind. They would raise questions under whatever circumstances, never placing too much consideration on whether it was proper to ask the question on this matter or to seek advice from that person. What they cared about was whether it would help their study and self-cultivation. Therefore, a sage would receive some of a conceited man's words. A humble woodcutter would sometimes be consulted by a noble man. As a king, Shun sought advice from ordinary people. He was a man of great wisdom and profound knowledge but was willing to listen to the ideas of ordinary people. He was not temporarily modest but was eager to find good advice from a wide range. After the three

之;舜以天子而询于匹夫①,以大知②而察及迩言③,非苟④为谦,诚取善之弘⑤也。三代⑥而下,有学而无问,朋友之交,至于劝善规过⑦足矣,其以义理⑧相咨访⑨,孜孜⑩焉唯进修是急⑪,未之多见⑫也,况流俗⑬乎?

是己而非人⑭,俗之同病。学有未达⑮,强以为知,理有未安,妄以臆度⑯,如是,则终身几⑰无可问之事。贤于己者,忌之而不愿问焉,不如己者,轻之而不屑问焉,等于己者,狎⑱之而不甘问焉,如是,则天下几无可问之人。人不足服矣,事无可疑矣,此

---

① 匹夫:普通老百姓(common people)。
② 大知:极有智慧的人(an extremely witty person)。
③ 迩言:平常的意见(ordinary idea)。迩:浅近(simple; easy to understand)。
④ 苟:聊且(just, merely)。
⑤ 弘:广阔(vast, wide)。
⑥ 三代:指夏、商、周三个朝代(referring to the three dynasties of Xia, Shang and Zhou)。
⑦ 劝善规过:劝导善行,规诫过失(persuade sb to do good and correct his fault)。
⑧ 义理:指儒家讲求经义、探求名理的学问(referring to the Confucian school's learning about striving for the real meaning of the classics)。
⑨ 相咨(zī)访:互相交换意见(mutually exchange ideas)。
⑩ 孜(zī)孜:勤勉的样子(diligent)。
⑪ 唯进修是急:唯急进修(only considering engaging in advanced studies)。是:语助词,无义(auxiliary word, without meaning)。
⑫ 未之多见:未多见之的倒装句(to say "have not seen it" in an inverted word order)。
⑬ 流俗:世俗之徒(common people)。
⑭ 是己而非人:以自己为是而以别人为非(think oneself right and others wrong)。
⑮ 达:通达(understand)。
⑯ 臆度(duo):猜测(guess)。
⑰ 几:几乎(almost)。
⑱ 狎(xiá):亲近而不尊(be improperly close to)。

dynasties of Xia, Shang and Zhou, people stopped asking questions while learning. The only thing that can be seen between friends is to persuade each other to do good and to correct mistakes. It is rare to see that friends visit each other for exchanging views about Confucian classics or for seeking advice. Very few scholars devote themselves to further study as no one regards it as top priority. Even intellectuals fail to do the right thing, let alone ordinary people.

It is a common failing that people always think themselves right and others wrong. It often occurs in someone's study that when he fails to understand something he will pretend to know the meaning and when his idea is not accepted by others he will make a wishful guess about the reason. Thus, he has hardly any questions to ask all his life. Out of jealousy, he is not willing to seek advice from those who are more knowledgeable than himself. Toward those who know less than himself, he looks down upon them and does not want to ask them for advice. While to those who are much the same as himself, he is too familiar with them and hates to ask them any questions. Therefore, there is hardly anyone in the world to whom he can turn to for advice. Admiring nobody, he will not listen to anybody's advice. Without any questions in mind, he will not make inquiries into anything. Rather conceited, he regards himself as infallible. That attitude of

唯师心自用①耳。夫自用，其小者也；自知其陋而谨护其失，宁使学终不进，不欲虚以下人②，此为害于心术③者大，而蹈④之者常十之八九。

不然，则所问非所学焉：询天下之异文鄙事以快⑤言论；甚且心之所已明者，问之人以试其能，事之至难解者，问之人以穷其短⑥。而非是者，虽有切于身心性命⑦之事，可以收取善之益，求一屈己⑧焉而不可得也。嗟乎！学之所以不能几⑨于古者，非此之由⑩乎？

且夫不好问者，由心不能虚也；心之不虚，由好学之不诚也。亦非不潜心专力之故，其学非古人之学，其好亦非古人之好也，不能问宜⑪也。

智者千虑，必有一失。圣人所不知，未必不为愚人之所知

---

① 师心自用：固执己见，自以为是，以自己的心为老师（adhere to one's opinion, be self-righteous, regard one's heart as a teacher）。
② 下人：承认自己不如人（admit oneself not as good as others）。
③ 心术：指人的品格修养（referring to one's character and morals）。
④ 蹈：陷入（fall into）。
⑤ 快：使痛快（to one's great satisfaction）。
⑥ 穷其短：使对方的短处暴露出来（expose the shortcoming of one's opponent）。
⑦ 身心性命：指自身修养和天性天理等（referring to self-cultivation, the course of nature and one's conscience）。
⑧ 屈己：委屈自己，指求教于人（restrain oneself, referring to asking for advice from others）。
⑨ 几（jī）：接近（be close to）。
⑩ 由：原因（reason）。
⑪ 宜：理所当然（be natural and right）。

considering himself always right is a small mistake. However, if someone is aware of his own shortcoming but tries to conceal it, or would rather make no progress in his study than modestly ask others for advice, he is doing great harm to his moral character. Eight or nine out of ten people make such a big mistake.

Or else, this man may one day raise questions but his questions are not related to what he is learning. For example, he will ask about strange stories and anecdotes to add spice to his talk. He even asks questions to which he already knows the answers, to test others' ability, or asks somebody a perplexing question to make his counterpart feel awkward. If this is not the case, can he compromise a little to ask others for beneficial advice while he is in the depths of a situation concerning life and death? No, he cannot! Alas! This must be the reason why nowadays people are unable to study as effectively as ancient people did.

Nowadays people do not like asking questions because of a lack of modesty in their mind. The lack of modesty in mind is the outcome of the shortage of sincerity in their attitude towards study. We cannot say that these people are not studying hard enough. What we can say is that people of our era are not learning what our ancestors learnt and what we are interested in is not the same thing that our forefathers liked. So it is only natural that nowadays people are not keen to ask questions.

也；愚人之所能，未必非圣人之不能也。理无专在①，而学无止境也，然则问可少耶？《周礼》②，外朝③以询万民，国之政事尚问及庶人④，是故贵可以问贱，贤可以问不肖⑤，而老可以问幼，唯道之所成而已矣。

孔文子⑥不耻下问，夫子⑦贤之。古人以问为美德，而并不见其有可耻也，后之君子反争以问为耻，然则古人所深耻者，后世且行之而不以为耻者多矣，悲夫！

---

① 理无专在：道理不是由某人所专有的（truth does not belong to somebody alone）。
②《周礼》：儒家经书之一（one of the Confucian classics）。
③ 外朝：朝廷外面（outside the royal court）。
④ 庶人：平民百姓（the common people）。
⑤ 不肖：没有才能的人（unworthy）。
⑥ 孔文子：魏国的大夫孔圉（yǔ），谥为"文"。《论语》中孔子解释他为何被谥为"文"说："敏而好学，不耻下问，是以为'文'也"（Kong Yu, a senior official of the State of Wei, whose posthumous title was "Literary." In the *Analects*, Confucius explained why he was given this title by saying, "Bright as he is, he is fond of studying and does not feel ashamed to ask and learn from his subordinates"）。
⑦ 夫子：指孔子（Confucius）。

Even the wise make mistakes sometimes. What a sage does not know is not necessarily what is unknown by ignorant people and what a fool is able to do is not always what a sage can do. Real knowledge and truth do not belong to one person only and there is no end to learning. How can we not ask questions while learning? *The Rites of Zhou* (one of the Confucian classics) says that outside the imperial court common people can be asked for advice; even about state affairs, ordinary people are asked for their advice. Therefore, the noble can ask the humble, the worthy can ask the unworthy and the old can ask the young for advice, as long as their goal of self-cultivation will be reached.

Kong Wenzi (Kong Yu) did not feel ashamed to learn from those in a lower position and his behavior won praise from Confucius. Our ancestors regarded the habit of asking questions as a virtue and they did not see any disgrace in it. On the contrary, gentlemen of our time do not want to be the last to describe it as shameful. However, people of later generations are shamelessly doing many things that were belittled by ancient people as disgraceful. Alas, lamentable!

病梅馆记

龚自珍

江宁①之龙蟠②,苏州之邓尉③,杭州之西溪④,皆产梅。或曰:"梅以曲为美,直则无姿;以欹⑤为美,正则无景;以疏为美,密则无态。"固⑥也。此文人画士,心知其意,未可明⑦诏⑧大号⑨以绳⑩天下之梅也;又不可以使天下之民斫⑪直、删密、锄⑫正,以夭梅病梅⑬为业以

---

① 江宁:清代江宁府,今南京市(Jiangning Prefecture in the Qing Dynasty, today's Nanjing City)。
② 龙蟠:龙蟠里,在南京清凉山下(name of a place, located at the foot of the Cool Hill in Nanjing)。
③ 邓尉:山名,在苏州西南,传说汉代有个叫邓尉的曾隐居于此,故得名(name of a mountain, southwest of Suzhou. It's said there was a man called Deng Wei dwelling here in seclusion in the Han Dynasty)。
④ 西溪:杭州灵隐山西北(northwest of the Lingyin Mountain)。
⑤ 欹(qī):横斜(lean to one side)。
⑥ 固:本来(of course, naturally)。
⑦ 明:公开(publicly)。
⑧ 诏:告诉,一般指上告下(tell, usually the superior tell the inferior)。
⑨ 号:疾呼,喊叫(shout, cry out)。
⑩ 绳:衡量(weigh, measure, judge)。
⑪ 斫(zhuó):砍(cut, chop)。
⑫ 锄:铲除(root out, uproot)。
⑬ 夭(yāo)梅病梅:摧残梅,使之成病态。夭:使弯曲(bend)。这里的"夭"和"病"皆作动词(destroy plums to make them into an abnormal state. Here "夭" and "病" are both used as verbs)。

THE HOME FOR SICK PLUM TREES

Gong Zizhen

The Longpan District of Jiangning, the Deng Wei Hill in Suzhou and the Western Stream in Hangzhou are plum producing areas. Some people say, "A plum is beautiful for its crooked branches but graceless if they are straight; it is pretty when its branches lean to one side but does not look good if they are regular; it is lovely when its branches are sparse but has no posture when dense." The scholars and painters certainly know the reason why this is said but it is not in their interest for them to reveal it to the public and use this criterion to judge plum trees all over the country; they are not supposed to tell the plum growers to cut off the straight branches, delete the dense and cut out the upright in order to make money by harming and ill-treating plum trees. Those who are busy making money do not have the wisdom to cultivate and distort plum trees into the slanting, sparse and crooked style. It was the scholars and painters who secretly told the plum growers about the tricks of how to make plum trees appear unique by chopping off the upright main trunks and

求钱也。梅之欹之疏之曲,又非蠢蠢求钱之民①能以其智力为②也。有以文人画士孤癖③之隐④明告鬻⑤梅者,斫其正,养其旁条⑥,删其密,夭⑦其稚枝⑧,锄其直,遏⑨其生气,以求重价⑩,而江浙之梅皆病。文人画士之祸之烈⑪至此哉!

予购三百盆,皆病者,无一完者。既泣之三日,乃誓疗之:纵之⑫顺之,毁其盆,悉埋于地,解其棕缚⑬;以五年为期,必复之全之⑭。予本非文人画士,甘受诟厉⑮,辟⑯病梅之馆以贮之。

呜呼!安得使予多暇日,又多闲田,以广贮江宁、杭州、苏州之病梅,穷⑰予生之光阴以疗梅也哉!

---

① 蠢蠢求钱之民:这里指梅农(here refers to peasants who grow plums)。蠢蠢:愚昧无知(benighted)。
② 为:办到(get sth. done)。
③ 孤癖:奇特的嗜好(peculiar hobby)。
④ 隐:心理,隐情(psychology, mentality, facts one wishes to hide)。
⑤ 鬻(yù):卖(sell)。
⑥ 旁条:旁逸斜出的枝条(branches stretching on the slant)。
⑦ 夭:伤害、摧残(harm, destroy)。
⑧ 稚枝:幼枝(young twigs)。
⑨ 遏:阻止(stop)。
⑩ 重价:高价(high price)。
⑪ 烈:酷(cruel, brutal)。
⑫ 纵之:解放它,让它生长(set it free, let it grow unrestrained)。
⑬ 棕缚:棕绳的束缚(be bound by coir rope)。
⑭ 复之全之:恢复它自然的形态,保全它的生机(recover its natural form and preserve its vitality)。
⑮ 诟厉(gòu lì):辱骂,斥责(abuse, rebuke)。
⑯ 辟:开设(open, establish)。
⑰ 穷:竭尽(use up, exhaust)。

letting the side ones grow, by damaging the young twigs to allow less branches to remain and eliminating the fast growing sprays to restrain their vitality, so that the plum trees can be sold at a higher price. As a result, all the plum trees in Jiangsu and Zhejiang are ill. So brutal is the disaster caused by the scholars and painters!

I bought 300 pots of plum trees, all of which were ill, not one in good condition. After weeping three days for them, I pledged to treat them: I set them free and let them grow unrestrained, by destroying their pots, undoing the binding ropes and transplanting all of them into the earth. I set a limit of five years within which I am sure to recover their natural form and preserve their vitality. I am neither a scholar nor a painter, therefore I am not afraid of being criticized. I have designated a mansion to house the sick plum trees.

Alas! How may I have more spare time and enough vacant fields to save the sick plum trees from Jiangning, Hangzhou and Suzhou districts so that I can spend the rest of my life treating them!

己亥①六月重过扬州记

龚自珍

居礼曹②，客有过③者曰："卿知今日之扬州乎？读鲍照《芜城赋》④则遇之矣。"余悲其言。

明年，乞假南游，抵扬州，属⑤有告籴⑥谋⑦，舍舟而馆⑧。

既宿，循馆之东墙，步游得小桥，俯溪，溪声讙⑨。过桥，遇

---

① 己亥：清道光十九年（1839）（the 19th year of the Daoguang Reign, 1839）。
② 礼曹：礼部各司。这里指礼部主客司（each department of the Ministry of Rites. Here referring to the Protocol Department）。
③ 过：访（visit）。
④ 鲍照：南朝宋文学家，字明远，东海（今江苏连云港）人。所作《芜城赋》，写广陵故城（即扬州）昔日盛况及后来衰颓景象（Bao Zhao was a writer of the Song Dynasty, one of the four dynasties of the Southern Dynasties, styled himself Mingyuan, from Donghai, today's Lianyungang, Jiangsu Province. The prose writing of "Ode to the Desolate City" he wrote described the spectacular events of Guangling, today's Yangzhou City, in former days and its later waning scenes）。
⑤ 属（zhǔ）：适逢（just when）。
⑥ 告籴（dí）：向人借或买粮，意思是请求资助（borrow / buy grain from others, here referring to asking for aid）。
⑦ 谋：打算（plan）。
⑧ 馆：用为动词，住旅馆（stay in a hotel, used as a verb）。
⑨ 讙（huān）：喧哗（noisy）。

REVISITING YANGZHOU IN EARLY MIDSUMMER OF 1839

Gong Zizhen

When I worked in the Protocol Department, one of my visitors asked me: "Do you know anything about today's Yangzhou? You will know something about it if you read 'The Rhyme Prose on a Desolate City' written by Bao Zhao." I felt sad on hearing his words.

In the following year, I asked for some leave and travelled to the south. When the boat anchored at Yangzhou, the idea of asking for aid in this city came to me. Therefore I left the boat and found a hotel to stay for the night.

Having settled in, I went out of the hotel. Walking along its eastern wall, I found a path leading to a small bridge. I stood on the bridge, looking down at a noisy stream. After crossing the bridge, I saw a parapet of the city wall. Through a gap, I climbed to the top of the parapet. From there, the whole city — either high buildings or low houses, including zigzag streets and water-ways, whether far or near — all came into sight. After a fall of rain in

女墙①啮②可登者，登之，扬州三十里，首尾屈折高下见③。晓雨沐④屋，瓦鳞鳞然，无零甃断甓⑤，心已疑礼曹过客言不实矣。

入市，求熟肉，市声讙。得肉，馆人以酒一瓶、虾一筐馈。醉而歌，歌宋元长短言乐府⑥，俯窗呜呜，惊对岸女夜起，乃止。

客有请吊⑦蜀岗⑧者，舟甚捷，帘幕皆文绣⑨，疑舟窗蠡毈⑩也，审视⑪，玻璃，五色具⑫。舟人时指两岸曰：某园故址也，某家酒肆故址也，约八九处。其实独倚虹园⑬圮⑭无存。曩⑮所信宿⑯之西园，门在，题榜在，尚可识，其可登临者尚八九处，阜⑰有桂，水有芙

---

① 女墙：城墙上之矮墙（parapet on the city wall）。
② 啮（niè）：这里指缺口（here referring to a loophole or gap）。
③ 见：现（show, appear）。
④ 沐：冲洗（wash）。
⑤ 甃（zhòu）甓（pì）：砖瓦（bricks and tiles）。
⑥ 长短言乐府：长短句，即词（a kind of classical poetry consisting chiefly of seven-character lines interspersed with shorter or longer ones, i.e. Ci poem）。
⑦ 吊：吊古（think of ancients or ancient events）。
⑧ 蜀岗：山名，在今江苏扬州市西北，为扬州古城遗址（name of a hill, to the northwest of Yangzhou City, Jiangsu Province. It's the ruins of ancient Yangzhou）。
⑨ 文绣：绣着花纹（embroidered with patterns）。
⑩ 蠡毈（què）：用贝壳镶嵌（inlay with seashell）。
⑪ 审视：仔细看（look carefully）。
⑫ 具：具备（possess）。
⑬ 倚虹园：因靠近横跨瘦西湖的大虹桥而得名（name of a garden, near the Big Rainbow Bridge stretching across the Thin West lake）。
⑭ 圮（pǐ）：坍塌（collapse）。
⑮ 曩（nǎng）：过去（in the past）。
⑯ 信宿：连宿两夜（stay for two nights）。
⑰ 阜：土山（mound）。

the morning, all the houses had been washed and their tiles were glistening like fish scales. No sign of ruined bricks and tiles made me doubt the truth of that visitor's words.

I went to the market to buy cooked meat. When I came back from the noisy market, the hotel owner gave me a bottle of wine and a basket of shrimps. I was soon drunk. Bending over the window, I began to chant rhymed ballads of long and short lines, composed during the Song and Yuan dynasties. I stopped chanting when I noticed with a start that the women on the opposite side of the river had been woken by my voice so late at night.

Someone proposed to pay a visit to the Shu Ridge and we went there by a swift boat. The curtains of the boat were beautifully embroidered. Originally, I thought its windows were inlaid with seashells, but when I went closer to carefully view them, I found they were glazed with multicolored glass. Time and again the boatman pointed to the river bank, alternatively to the right and to the left, telling us: "This is the old site of a garden; that used to be a restaurant"; etc. Eight or nine sites were mentioned by him. In fact, only the Yihong Garden had been leveled to the ground and no longer existed. The Western Garden, in which I used to stay for two nights, still had its gate and the board inscribed with its name which was still recognizable. In the garden there were still eight or nine spots which could still be visited. Cinnamon trees

渠①菱②茨③，是居扬州城外西北隅，最高秀。南览江，北览淮，江淮数十州县治，无如此冶华④也。忆京师言，知有极不然者。

归馆，郡之士皆知余至，则大讙⑤，有以经义请质难者，有发⑥史事见问者，有就询京师近事者，有呈所业若文、若诗、若笔⑦、若长短言、若杂著、若丛书乞为序、为题辞者，有状⑧其先世⑨事行⑩乞为铭⑪者，有求书册子、书扇者，填委⑫塞户牖⑬，居然嘉庆⑭中故态⑮。谁得曰今非承平⑯时耶？惟窗外船过，夜无笙琶声，即有之，声不能彻旦⑰。然而女子有以栀子⑱华发为贽⑲求书者，

---

① 芙渠：荷花（lotus）。
② 菱：菱角（water chestnut）。
③ 茨（qiàn）：俗名"鸡头"（gorgon euryale, popularly named "cock head"）。
④ 冶华：美丽繁华（beautiful and prosperous）。
⑤ 讙：同"欢"（happy）。
⑥ 发：提出，揭示（put forward）。
⑦ 笔：散文。与"文"相对，"文"指韵文（prose, opposite to verse）。
⑧ 状：写成行状（write a brief biographical sketch about a deceased person）。
⑨ 先世：先辈（ancestors）。
⑩ 事行：事迹行为（deeds and behavior）。
⑪ 乞为铭：请求为他们作碑铭（ask to write inscriptions for them）。
⑫ 填委：拥挤（crowded）。
⑬ 户牖（yǒu）：门窗（door and window）。
⑭ 嘉庆：清仁宗年号（reign title of Emperor Renzong of the Qing Dynasty）。
⑮ 态：社会风习（social atmosphere）。
⑯ 承平：太平（peaceful）。
⑰ 彻旦：通宵达旦（all night till dawn）。
⑱ 栀（zhī）子：即栀子花，夏天开，白色（gardenia, white bloom in summer）。
⑲ 贽（zhì）：初次见面所赠之礼（gift presented to a senior on one's first visit as a token of respect）。

were growing on the mounds and water plants such as lotus, water chestnuts and gorgon euryale occupied the ponds. This garden was situated on the northwest corner outside the city. Having a high altitude, it commanded a panoramic and beautiful view. Looking southward we could see the Yangtze River, and to the north the Huaihe River. Scores of prefecture and county seats were scattered throughout the valley between the two rivers, but none of them was as beautiful and prosperous as Yangzhou. I remembered what the visitor from the capital had said about Yangzhou and now I realized that it was untrue.

I returned to the hotel. The scholars in this prefecture were glad to know I was here and came to see me. Some argued with me about the real meaning of certain parts of Confucian classics; some asked me questions about historical events or inquired about current affairs within the capital. There were also visitors who had come to show me what they had written, such as essays, poetry, prose, rhymed ballads of long and short lines, miscellanies and series of books. They asked me to write a preface or some words for their writings. Some people even brought brief biographies of their ancestors and what they wanted from me were inscriptions which were intended to be incised on memorial tablets. I also saw people who came to request my calligraphy to add to their albums or to write on their folding fans. My room was packed

爰①以书画环瑱②互通问③，凡三人，凄馨哀艳之气，缭绕于桥亭舰舫间，虽澹定④，是夕魂摇摇不自持。余既信信⑤，拿流风⑥，捕余韵⑦，乌睹⑧所谓风嗥雨啸、鼯⑨狖⑩悲、鬼神泣者？嘉庆末，尝于此和友人宋翔凤⑪侧艳诗⑫，闻宋君病，存亡弗可知。又问其所谓赋诗者⑬，不可见，引为恨。

卧而思之，余齿⑭垂⑮五十矣，今昔之慨，自然之运，古之美人名士富贵寿考⑯者几人哉？此岂关扬州之盛衰，而独置感慨于江介⑰也哉？抑予赋侧艳则老矣，甄综⑱人物，搜辑⑲文献，仍以自任，

---

① 爰（yuán）：于是（hence）。
② 环瑱（tiàn）：戴在耳垂上的环形玉（jade on one's earlobes）。
③ 互通问：互通音问（exchange news）。
④ 澹定：淡泊稳定（calm）。
⑤ 信信：住了四宿（stay for four nights）。
⑥ 流风：前代流传下来的风俗（the custom handed down from the ancestors）。
⑦ 余韵：余音（lingering charm）。
⑧ 乌睹：哪里看到（from where can be seen）。
⑨ 鼯（wú）：鼯鼠，又叫大飞鼠（flying squirrel）。
⑩ 狖（yòu）：黑色长尾猿（black monkey with a big tail）。
⑪ 宋翔凤（1776—1860）：字虞庭，江苏长洲（今苏州吴中区）人。著名学者（styled himself Yuting, from Changzhou, today's Wuzhong District, Suzhou, a famous scholar）。
⑫ 侧艳诗：艳情诗（poems describing love affairs）。
⑬ 所谓赋诗者：指当年与宋氏及作者和诗之妓（referring to the courtesan who wrote poems in reply to Song and the author in those days）。
⑭ 齿：年龄（age）。
⑮ 垂：将近（close to）。
⑯ 寿考：年高（advanced age）。
⑰ 江介：江边，这里是指扬州（riverside, here referring to Yangzhou）。
⑱ 甄综：甄别（examine and distinguish）。
⑲ 搜辑：搜集编辑（collect and edit）。

with so many people that its door and window could not be shut. Strangely, these people were still doing what the people of the Jiaqing Reign (1796-1820) liked to do. Who can say that it is not now a time of peace and prosperity? The only thing unusual was that at night boats were quietly passing outside my window without any sound of musical instruments. Even when there was the sound of music in the evening, it would not last all night. It was amazing that some girls came to give me gifts of gardenia and beautiful ornaments, asking for my calligraphy. Thus calligraphy, paintings, and jade pendants were exchanged and a hearty chat was held. The three girls left their chilly fragrance and an elegant vein of melancholy lingering in the gaps between the bridge and pavilion as well as over the boat. Though I was usually in possession of myself, on that night I could hardly control myself. I stayed for four nights in Yangzhou and what I saw were beautiful fashions and customs which had been passed down from the past. I did not see or hear anything that would remind me of ruins, such as the howl of wind and rain, or the wail of animals and ghosts. Towards the end of the Jiaqing Reign, I wrote poems here in reply to the erotic poems written by my friend Song Xiangfeng. Later I heard that he had fallen ill. I do not know whether he is still alive. I also asked about the girl who had joined us in the poem exchange at that time. Much to my regret, I failed to find her.

固未老也。天地有四时，莫病①于酷暑，而莫善于初秋；澄汰②其繁缛③淫蒸④，而与之为萧疏澹荡，泠然⑤瑟⑥然，而不遽⑦使人有苍莽⑧寥泬⑨之悲者，初秋也。今扬州，其初秋也欤？予之身世，虽乞籴，自信不遽死，其尚犹丁⑩初秋也欤？作《己亥六月重过扬州记》。

---

① 病：难受（feel unwell）。
② 澄汰：澄清淘汰（clear up and eliminate）。
③ 繁缛：杂乱（mixed and disorderly）。
④ 淫蒸：闷热（oppressively hot）。
⑤ 泠（líng）然：清凉（cool and refreshing）。
⑥ 瑟：萧索（bleak and chilly）。
⑦ 遽：顷刻（in an instant）。
⑧ 苍莽：迷茫空阔（vast and hazy）。
⑨ 寥泬（xuè）：空旷萧条（open and desolate）。
⑩ 丁：遭遇，碰到。（meet with, rush into）

Lying in bed, I was deep in thought. It was the meditation of a man at the age of nearly fifty. I couldn't help sighing with emotion at the past experience and the present event as well as the law of nature. Looking back to the past, were there many beautiful women and talented scholars who could enjoy not only wealth and honors but also a long life? Did this law of nature have any impact on the prosperity and adversity of Yangzhou? Why should I sigh over these happenings when I was on the riverside? I may be too old to write erotic poems now but I am not too old to make an appraisal of a personage and comment on him, or accumulate data and compile books. Among the four seasons of a year, scorching summer is the most unbearable while early autumn is the most pleasant. In early autumn, the nasty heat of summer would be swept away and replaced by cool and refreshing air. Though somewhat bleak and chilly, such a change did not make people feel unprepared and uncomfortable. Does today's Yangzhou resemble early autumn? As for myself, I am confident that even if I had to beg for food, I would not soon die of hunger. Am I in the age of my life similar to early autumn? Thus I have written "Revisiting Yangzhou in Midsummer of 1839."

作家小传

王若虚（1174—1243）：金代文学家，字从之，号慵夫、滹南遗老，藁城（今属河北省石家庄市）人。士承安进士，官翰林学士。金亡不仕。著有《滹南遗老集》。

元好问（1190—1257）：金代文学家，字裕之，号遗山，秀容（今山西省忻州）人。祖系出自北魏托跋氏。兴定进士。曾为金中央政府高级官员。金亡不仕。工诗文，在金元间颇有名望。有《遗山集》等。

戴表元（1244—1310）：元代文学家，字帅初，奉化（今属浙江省）人。宋末咸淳进士，入元任信州教授。有《剡源戴先生文集》。

BRIEF BIOGRAPHIES OF WRITERS

Wang Ruoxu (1174-1243): a writer of the Jin Dynasty (1115-1234); styled himself Congzhi, alternatively named Yongfu and Old Adherent South of the Hutuo River. Born in Gaocheng County (part of today's Shijiazhuang City, Hebei Province), he was a successful candidate for the highest imperial examination of the Cheng'an Reign and became a member of the Imperial Academy. He did not fill an office after the Jin Dynasty was toppled. His works include *Collection of an Old Adherent South of River Hutuo*.

Yuan Haowen (1190-1257): a writer of the Jin Dynasty; styled himself Yuzhi and was alternatively named Yishan, from Xiurong (today's Xinzhou City, Shanxi). His ancestry originated from an ethnic group with Tuoba as their surname during the Northern Wei Dynasty (386-534). He was a successful candidate for the highest imperial examination during the Xingding Reign (1217-1222) and later became a high official in the central government. He did not fill an office after Jin was brought down. He was well versed in poetic prose and famous in the Jin and Yuan dynasties. His works include *Collection of Yishan*, etc.

Dai Biaoyuan (1244-1310): a writer of the Yuan Dynasty (1206-1368); styled himself Shuaichu. Born in Fenghua County of Zhejiang Province, he was a successful candidate for the highest imperial examination in the last year of the Xianchun Reign (1265-1274) of the Song Dynasty (960-1279). He became a professor in Xinzhou Prefecture during the Yuan Dynasty. His works include *Collection of*

刘因（1249—1293）：宋元之际学者，字梦吉，号静修，雄州容城（今河北省保定市徐水区）人。元世祖时曾任赞善大夫，未几即辞归。后拒绝应聘。著作有《静修集》。

钟嗣成（生卒年不详）：字继先，号丑斋，元大梁（今河南开封）人。戏曲家。寄居杭州。累试不第。顺帝时编著《录鬼簿》。

李孝光（1285—1350）：字季和，元代乐清（今属浙江）人。年少博学，隐居雁荡山五峰下。至正七年（1347）应召至北京，为元顺帝赏识，次年升秘书监丞。著有《五峰集》。

宋濂（1310—1381）：明初文学家。字景濂，号潜溪，浦江（今属浙江）人。明初奉命主修元史，官至学士承旨知制诰，深得朱元璋宠信。后因长孙宋慎牵涉胡惟庸案，全家谪茂州，中途死于夔州。有《宋学士文集》。

Mr. Dai from Shanyuan.

Liu Yin (1249-1293): a scholar between the Song and Yuan dynasties; styled himself Mengji and was alternatively named Jingxiu, from Rongcheng (today's Xushui District, Baoding City, Hebei Province) of Xiongzhou. He was appointed to a senior position as Zanshan during the reign of Emperor Shizu of the Yuan Dynasty but soon resigned from his office and refused to be engaged again. His works include *Collection of Jingxiu*.

Zhong Sicheng (birth and death dates unknown) styled himself Jixian and was alternatively named Chouzhai, from Daliang (today's Kaifeng, Henan) during the Yuan Dynasty. He was a dramatist and lived away from home in Hangzhou. He compiled *The Records of Ghosts*.

Li Xiaoguang (1285-1350) styled himself Jihe and was from Yueqing, Zhejiang. He was learned when young and lived in seclusion at the foot of the Five Peaks of Mount Yandang. In the 7th year of the Zhizheng Reign (1347) he was invited to Beijing and appreciated by Emperor Shundi of the Yuan Dynasty. The next year he was promoted to a high official position in charge of the public libraries of the whole nation. His works include *The Five-Peaks Collection*.

Song Lian (1310-1381): a writer at the beginning of the Ming Dynasty (1368-1644). He styled himself Jinglian and was alternatively named Qianxi, from Pujiang, Zhejiang. Following the order of the emperor, he took charge of writing the history of Yuan and held a high official position in charge of drafting imperial mandates and was deeply favoured and trusted by Zhu Yuanzhang (founder of the Ming Dynasty). Later, due to the involvement of his eldest grandson Song Shen in the case of Hu Weiyong, his whole family was banished to Maozhou and he died in Kuizhou on the way to Maozhou. His works

刘基（1311—1375）：字伯温，浙江青田人，元末明初军事谋略家、政治家、文学家和思想家，曾辅佐朱元璋开创明王朝，封诚意伯，被后人比作诸葛亮。洪武四年（1371年）辞官，后为胡惟庸所害，忧愤而死。刘伯温是中国古代的一位传奇人物，至今在中国大陆、港澳台乃至东南亚仍有广泛深厚的民间影响力。

高启（1336—1374）：明初诗人，字季迪，长洲（今江苏省苏州吴中区）人，元末隐居吴淞青丘，自号青丘子，与杨基、张羽、徐贲齐名，称"吴中四杰"。明洪武初，召修《元史》，为翰林院国史编修。授户部右侍郎，不受，回青丘，教书为生。尝赋诗有所讽刺，被太祖借故腰斩。有诗集《高太史大全集》《凫藻集》等。

方孝孺（1357—1402）：字希直，人称正学先生。明浙江宁海人。宋濂弟子。惠帝时任侍讲学士。燕王（成祖）兵入京师（南京）后，他不肯为成祖起草登极诏书，被杀。著有《逊志斋集》。

include *Collected Works of Scholar Song*.

Liu Ji (1311-1375) styled himself Bowen, from Qingtian County in Zhejiang Province; a military strategist, statesman, writer and thinker. He assisted Zhu Yuanzhang in founding the Ming Dynasty and was granted Count of Chengyi; he is compared to Zhuge Liang by later generations. In 1371, he resigned from office and was later framed by Hu Weiyong. He died of grief and indignation. Liu was a legendary figure in ancient China and has up to now a deep influence in China's mainland, Hong Kong, Macao, Taiwan and even Southeast Asia.

Gao Qi (1336-1374): a poet at the beginning of the Ming Dynasty. He styled himself Jidi and was from Changzhou (today's Wuzhong District, Suzhou City, Jiangsu), living in seclusion in Qingqiu of Wusong at the end of the Yuan Dynasty. He was as famous as Yang Ji, Zhang Yu and Xu Ben and they were called the Four Outstanding Scholars in the Area of Wu. At the beginning of the Hongwu Reign (1368-1398), he was invited to compile the *History of Yuan* in the Imperial Academy. He refused the appointment of Deputy Minister of Revenue and returned to Qingqiu, living by teaching. Because of writing satirical poems, he was executed by being cut in half at the waist and his execution was ordered by the first emperor of the Ming Dynasty. His works include a collection of poems *The Complete Works of Gao, the Royal Historian* and *Collection of Fuzao*.

Fang Xiaoru (1357-1402) styled himself Xizhi and was called Teacher Zhengxue, from Ninghai, Zhejiang during the Ming Dynasty, a disciple of Song Lian. In the time of Emperor Huidi, he was appointed to be an official who served as a teaching scholar. When King Yan (later Emperor Chengzu) led troops to capture the capital (Nanjing), due to his refusal to draft an imperial edict for King Yan

薛瑄（1389或1392—1464）：明学者，字德温，号敬轩，河津（今属山西省）人。官至礼部右侍郎。谥文清。性刚直，曾因触怒权贵下狱。著作有《薛文清集》等。

马中锡（？—约1512）：字天禄，号东田，明故城（今属河北省）人。成化进士，官至右都御史。统兵镇压刘六、刘七起义，未成功，被朝廷论罪，下狱死。有《东田集》。

崔铣（1478—1541）：字子钟，又字仲凫，明安阳（今属河南省）人。弘治十八年（1505）进士。官至南京礼部右侍郎。嘉靖三年（1524），上书弹劾新贵，得罪皇帝，因而免官。卒谥文敏。

何景明（1483—1521）：明代文学家。字仲默，号大复山人，河南信阳人。弘治进士，官至陕西提学副史，为"前七子"之一。有《大复集》。

to ascend the throne, he was killed. His works include *Collection from Home Library Xunzhizhai*.

Xue Xuan (1389 or 1392 – 1464): a scholar of the Ming Dynasty, styled himself Dewen and was alternatively named Jingxuan, from Hejin (part of today's Shanxi Province). His utmost official position was Deputy Minister of Rites and his posthumous title was Wenqing. He was upright and outspoken and was once put in prison because of offending an influential official. His works include *Collection of Xue Wenqing*, etc.

Ma Zhongxi (? – circa 1512) styled himself Dongtian and was from Gucheng (in today's Hebei Province) during the Ming Dynasty. He was a successful candidate for the imperial examination and was once appointed to the position of junior president of the censorate. He was later found guilty of not succeeding in suppressing the uprising led by Liu Liu and Liu Qi and was put in prison where he died. His works include *Collection of Dongtian*.

Cui Xian (1478–1541) styled himself Zizhong or Zhongfu and was from Anyang (part of today's Henan Province). He was a successful candidate for the imperial examination in the 18th year of the Hongzhi Reign (1505). His official career reached its pinnacle when he was promoted to be Deputy Minister of Rites in Nanjing. In the 3rd year of the Jiajing Reign (1524), he submitted a statement accusing an upstart official of a crime, thus offending the emperor and consequently he was dismissed from his position. His posthumous title was Wenmin.

He Jingming (1483–1521): a writer of the Ming Dynasty, styled himself Zhongmo and was alternatively named Hermit Dafu, from Xinyang, Henan. A successful candidate for the imperial examination during the Hongzhi Reign, he was promoted to the position of deputy

归有光（1506—1571）：明代散文家。字熙甫，号震川，昆山（今属江苏省）人。35岁中举后，曾八次应进士试皆落第，直到60岁才中进士，曾任湖州长兴知县，南京太仆寺丞。长期居嘉定安亭江上，读书讲学。与唐顺之、王慎中、茅坤等同被称为"唐宋派"。有《震川先生集》。

唐顺之（1507—1560）：明代散文家。字应德，江苏武进人。嘉靖八年（1529）会试第一。曾督领兵船在崇明抵御倭寇，以功升凤阳代巡抚。人称荆川先生。与汪慎中、茅坤、归有光等同被称为"唐宋派"。有《荆川先生文集》。

王世贞（1526—1590）：字元美，号凤洲、弇州山人，明江苏太仓人。嘉靖进士，官至南京刑部尚书。与李攀龙同为"后七子"首领，倡导复古摩拟。有《弇州山人四部稿》等。

director in charge of education in Shaanxi Province. He was one of "The Former Seven Masters" of the Ming Dynasty. His works include *Collection of Dafu*.

Gui Youguang (1506–1571): a writer of the Ming Dynasty. He styled himself Xifu and was alternatively named Zhenchuan, from Kunshan (in Jiangsu Province). After he passed the provincial imperial examination at the age of 35, he failed 8 times before passing the highest imperial examination at the age of 60. He was appointed magistrate of Changxing County in Huzhou Prefecture. For a long time he lived by the Anting River, reading and teaching. He, together with Tang Shunzhi, Wang Shenzhong and Mao Kun etc. established a literary style called "The Tang and Song School." His works include *Collection of Master Zhenchuan*.

Tang shunzhi (1507–1560), a writer of the Ming Dynasty. He styled himself Yingde and was from Wujin, Jiangsu. He won the first place at the metropolitan examination in the 8th year of the Jiajing Reign (1529). Having successfully led the naval fleet to resist Japanese pirates in Chongming, he was promoted to the position of acting imperial inspector in Fengyang District for his military exploits. He was called Mr. Jingchuan and together with Wang Shenzhong, Mao Kun and Gui Youguang etc. established a literary style called "The Tang and Song School." His works include *Collection of Master Jingchuan*.

Wang Shizhen (1526–1590) styled himself Yuanmei and was alternatively named Fengzhou and Hermit Yanzhou. He was from Taicang County, Jiangsu Province. As a successful candidate for the imperial examination during the Jiajing Reign of the Ming Dynasty, the highest position he reached was Minister of Punishments in Nanjing. He, together with Li Panlong, was chieftain of "The Latter

李贽（1527—1602）：明思想家、文学家。号卓吾，又号宏甫，别号温陵居士，福建泉州晋江人。做过云南姚安知府。公开以"异端"自居，大胆揭露封建传统教条和假道学，提出"童心"说。终被统治者以"敢倡乱道，惑世诬民"罪名迫害而死。著有《焚书》《续焚书》等。

袁宗道（1560—1600）：明代文学家。字伯修，湖广公安（今属湖北省）人。万历进士，与弟宏道、中道齐名，并称三袁。前后七子倡导"诗必盛唐"，他们则崇尚本色，反对模拟，世称"公安派"。有《白苏斋》集。

袁宏道（1568—1610）：明代文学家。字中郎，号石公。湖广公安（今属湖北省）人。万历进士，官吏部郎中，与兄宗道、弟中道并称三袁，为公安派创始者，在三袁中宏道成就最大。其思想受李贽影响较深。于诗文不满前后七子模拟、复古主张，强调抒写"性灵"。有《袁中郎全集》。

Seven Masters" and proposed the idea of returning to the ancients and imitating them. His works include *Four Volumes of Hermit Yanzhou*.

Li Zhi (1527-1602): a thinker and writer of the Ming Dynasty. He was alternatively named Zhuowu and also Hongfu, alias Lay Buddhist Wenling, from Jinjiang County of Quanzhou Prefecture in Fujian Province. He was once appointed magistrate of Yaoan Prefecture, Yunnan. He publicly considered himself a heretic and courageously exposed feudalistic traditional dogmas and hypocrite. He put forward the theory of "childlike innocence" and was finally persecuted to death by the ruler with a charge of "Initiating social upheaval, puzzling the world and the people." His works include *Burning Books, Continued Burning of Books* etc.

Yuan Zongdao (1560-1600): a writer of the Ming Dynasty. He styled himself Boxiu and was from Gong'an County, Hubei Province. He was a successful candidate for the highest imperial examination during the Wanli Reign (1573-1620). He was as famous as his two brothers Hongdao and Zhongdao. They were called the "Three Yuan's" by the public. Different from "The Former Seven Masters" and "The Latter Seven Masters" who initiated "poetry must imitate that of the Tang Dynasty," they advocated true qualities and opposed imitation. They were called "The Gong'an School." His works include *Collection from Baisu Study*.

Yuan Hongdao (1568-1610): a writer of the Ming Dynasty. He styled himself Zhonglang and was alternatively named Shigong, from Gong'an County, Hubei Province. As a successful candidate for the highest imperial examination during the Wanli Reign, he later became Deputy Minister of Civil Personnel. He, together with his elder brother Zongdao and younger brother Zhongdao, were called the "Three Yuan's." As the originator of the Gong'an School, his

袁中道（1570—1623）：明代文学家。字小修，湖广公安（今属湖北省）人。万历进士，官南京吏部郎中。与兄宗道、宏道并称"三袁"，同以"公安派"著称。其文学主张，反对模拟，崇尚自然。有《珂雪斋集》。

钟惺（1574—1624）：字伯敬，号退谷，湖广竟陵（今湖北省天门市）人。万历进士，官至福建提学佥事。与谭元春同为"竟陵派"的创始人。有《隐秀轩集》。

张明弼（1584—1652）：明末江苏金坛人。

谭元春（1586—1637）：明代文学家。字友夏，湖北竟陵人。天启年间乡试第一。与钟惺同为竟陵派创始人。论文反对摹古，提倡幽深的风格。有《谭友夏合集》。

literary achievement was greater than his two brothers. His thinking was deeply influenced by Li Zhi. In poetry and prose writing he did not agree with the view of "imitation and back to the ancients." He stressed the expression of natural disposition and intelligence. His works include *Collection of Yuan Zhonglang*.

Yuan Zhongdao (1570–1623): a writer of the Ming Dynasty. He styled himself Xiaoxiu and was from Gong'an County, Hubei Province. As a successful candidate for the highest imperial examination during the Wanli Reign, he was appointed Deputy Minister of Civil Personnel. He and his elder brothers Zongdao and Hongdao were called the "Three Yuan's" and were famous as the Gong'an School. In literature, he opposed imitation and advocated nature. His works include *Collection from Kexue Study* etc.

Zhong Xing (1574–1624) styled himself Bojing and was alternatively named Tuigu, from Jingling (today's Tianmen City, Hubei Province). He was a successful candidate for the highest imperial examination of the Wanli Reign and was appointed a high official in charge of education in Fujian Province. He and Tan Yuanchun were both originators of the Jingling School. His works include *Collection from Home Library Yinxiuxuan*.

Zhang Mingbi (1584–1652) was from Jintan County, Jiangsu Province.

Tan Yuanchun (1586–1637): a writer of the Ming Dynasty. He styled himself Youxia and was from Jingling, Hubei Province. He won the first place in the imperial examination at the provincial level during the Tianqi Reign (1621–1627). He and Zhong Xing were both originators of the Jingling School. In literature he opposed imitating the ancients and advocated a deep and serene style. His works include

徐宏祖（1586—1641）：字振之，号霞客，江苏江阴人。幼年好学，博览图经地志。因见明末政治黑暗，不愿入仕，专心从事旅行，足迹所及，北至燕、晋，南至云、贵、两广。其考察所得，按日记载，死后季会明等整理成富有地理学价值和文学价值的《徐霞客游记》。

魏学洢（1596—1625）：字子敬，浙江嘉善人。其父魏大中因弹劾魏忠贤而入狱，他奔走营救，无效。父死狱中，他亦悲伤而死。著有《茅檐集》。

张岱（1597—1679）：明末清初散文家。字宗子、石公，号陶庵，浙江绍兴人，侨寓杭州。清兵南下，入山著书。有《琅嬛文集》《陶庵梦忆》等。

Collection of Tan Youxia.

Xu Hongzu (1586–1641) styled himself Zhenzhi and was alternatively named Xiake, from Jiangyin, Jiangsu. In childhood, he was fond of learning and had widely read books about topography and cartography. Seeing the dark politics of the last years of the Ming Dynasty, he was unwilling to be an official. Instead he concentrated his attention on travelling. He travelled northward to the area of Yan and Jin and southward to Yunnan, Guizhou, Guangdong and Guangxi. He daily wrote down what he had learned from his investigations. After his death, his writings were compiled by Ji Huiming and others into *Travel Notes of Xu Xiake*, which has a great value in geography and literature.

Wei Xueyi (1596–1625) styled himself Zijing and was from Jiashan, Zhejiang. His father Wei Dazhong was put in prison because of his impeaching against Wei Zhongxian, the powerful eunuch. He rushed here and there to rescue his father but failed. His father died in prison and he died of sorrow. His works include *Collection under the Thatch Eaves*.

Zhang Dai (1597–1679): a prose writer between the Ming and Qing dynasties. He styled himself Zongzi or Shigong and was alternatively named Taoan, from Shaoxing, Zhejiang but lived in Hangzhou. When the Qing troop came southward, he went into the mountains to write books. His works include *Collection of Langhuan* and *Recall and Dream of Taoan*.

张溥(1602—1641):明末文学家。字天如,江苏太仓人。崇祯进士。与同邑张采齐名,于崇祯初年组织复社,进行文学和政治活动。有《七录斋集》。

吴伟业(1609—1672):字骏公,号梅村,别署鹿樵生,江苏太仓人。明崇祯四年(1631)进士,曾任翰林院编修。清顺治十年(1653)被迫应诏北上,被授予秘书院侍讲,后升国子监祭酒。顺治十三年底,以奉嗣母丧为由乞假南归,此后不复出仕。他是明末清初著名诗人,与钱谦益、龚鼎孳并称"江左三大家",又为娄东诗派开创者。后人称之为"梅村体"。

张煌言(1620—1664):南明大臣,字玄著,号苍水,浙江鄞县(今宁波市鄞州区)人。崇祯举人。弘光元年(1645)与钱肃乐等起兵抗清,奉鲁王监国,据守浙东山地和沿海一带。官至兵部尚书。永历十三年(1659)与郑成功合兵,进入长江,围攻南京。他别率一军到芜湖,乘胜攻下四府、三州、二十四县。终因郑成功兵败,孤军无援而退。后鲁王政权覆灭,他又派人与十三家农民军联系

Zhang Pu (1602-1641): a writer in the last years of the Ming Dynasty, styled himself Tianru, from Taicang, Jiangsu. He was a successful candidate for the highest imperial examination during the Chongzhen Reign (1628-1644) and as famous as Zhang Cai from the same county. At the beginning of the Chongzhen Reign he organised a club named the Fu Association and was active in literary and political activities. His works include *Collection from Qilu Study*.

Wu Weiye (1609-1672): styled himself Jungong and was alternately named Meicun, also called himself Luqiaosheng. He was a native of Taicang, Jiangsu. In the 4th year of the Chongzhen Reign (1631) of the Ming Dynasty, he was admitted as one of the successful candidates for the highest imperial examination and later became a compiler in the Imperial Academy. In the 10th year of the Shunzhi Reign (1653) of the Qing Dynasty, appointed by the imperial court, he had to move to the north to hold an official position there. He was first given a senior position in the Imperial Secretariat and then promoted to the presidency of the Imperial College. At the end of the 13th year of the Shunzhi Reign, he asked for a long leave to return to the south under the pretext of carrying out a filial son's mourning rites after his mother's death. He never resumed his official career. He was a famous poet at the changeover of the Ming Dynasty and the Qing Dynasty and enjoyed the good name of one of the three great masters in the areas south of the lower reaches of the Yangtze River (the other two were Qian Qianyi and Gong Dingzi). He was also the originator of the Loudong School and his poetry style is called the Meicun Style by later generations.

Zhang Huangyan (1620-1664) was a minister of the Southern Ming Dynasty. He styled himself Xuanzhu and was alternatively named Cangshui, from Yinxian County (today's Yinzhou District, Ningbo City), Zhejiang. He was a successful candidate for the imperial examinations at the provincial level during the Chongzhen Reign. In the first year of

抗清。至清康熙三年（1664），因见大势已去，遂解散余部，隐居浙江省象山南，不久被俘，遭杀害。有《张苍水集》。

夏完淳（1631—1647）：南明将领、诗人。原名复，字存古，上海松江人。14岁从父夏允彝、师陈子龙起兵抗清。允彝兵败自杀后，又与陈子龙等倡义，受鲁王封中书舍人，参谋太湖吴易军事。易败，他仍为抗清而奔走。被捕后痛骂洪承畴，被杀害。有《夏完淳集》。

黄宗羲（1610—1695）：明清之际思想家、史学家。字太冲，号南雷，学者称梨洲先生，浙江余姚人。其父黄尊素为"东林"名士，被魏忠贤陷害，他受遗命问学于刘宗周。19岁入都讼冤，以铁椎毙伤仇人。领导复社成员坚持反宦官权贵斗争，几遭残杀。清兵南下，他招募义兵，成立"世忠"营，被鲁王任为左副都御史。明亡后隐居著述，屡拒清廷征召。与孙奇逢、李颙并称三大儒。学问极博，对天文、算术、乐律、经史百家以及释道之书，无不研究。著作有《明夷待访录》《南雷文案》等。

Hongguang Reign (1645), together with Qian Sule etc, he led an army to resist the Qing troops and supported King Lu to come to the throne. He occupied the mountainous and coastal regions in the east of Zhejiang. He was promoted as high as the position of Minister of War. In the 13th year of the Yongli Reign (1659), he and Zheng Chenggong merged their troops and they came to the bank of the Yangtze River and besieged Nanjing. He led another troop to Wuhu and followed up the victory by capturing 4 prefectures, 3 districts and 24 counties. In the end, due to the failure of Zheng Chenggong in the battle, he, isolated and cut off from help, had to draw back. After the political power of King Lu had collapsed, he sent his subordinates to get in touch with 13 peasant troops to resist Qing. In the 3rd year of the Kangxi Reign (1664), seeing the situation was hopeless, he dismissed his remaining forces and lived away from society in the south of Xiangshan County of Zhejiang. Before long he was captured and killed. His works include *Collection of Zhang Cangshui*.

Xia Wanchun (1631–1647) was a general and a poet of the Southern Ming Dynasty. He was originally named Fu and styled himself Cungu, from Songjiang, Shanghai. At the age of fourteen he followed his father Xia Yunyi and teacher Chen Zilong to start an armed uprising against the Qing army. After his father Xia Yunyi committed suicide after military failure, he, together with Chen Zilong, continued to resist Qing. He was appointed a high official by King Lu and provided advice for the military struggle led by Wu Yi from the Taihu Lake. After Wu Yi failed, he still worked to resist Qing. When he was captured, he severely scolded Hong Chengchou (an original Ming minister who had surrendered to Qing) and was killed. His works include *Collection of Xia Wanchun*.

Huang Zongxi (1610–1695): a thinker and historian of the period between the Ming and Qing dynasties. He styled himself Taichong and was alternatively named Nanlei, from Yuyao County, Zhejiang

李渔（1611—约1679）：清代戏曲理论家、作家。字笠鸿，谪凡，号笠翁，浙江兰溪人。家设戏班，常往各地达官贵人门下演出。著有《闲情偶记》《笠翁十种曲》等。

顾炎武（1613—1679）：明清之际思想家、学者。初名绛，字宁人，江苏昆山人。学者称亭林先生。少年时参加复社反宦官权贵斗争。清兵南下，又参加昆山、嘉定一带的抗清起义。失败后，十谒明陵，遍游华北，了解风俗，搜集材料，尤致力边防和西北地理的研究，垦荒种地，不忘兴复。晚年卜居曲沃。学问极博，于国家典制、郡邑掌故、天文、河漕、兵农以及经史百家、音韵训诂之学都有研究。著作有《日知录》《亭林诗文集》等。

Province. He was called Scholar Lizhou by the public. After his father Huang Zunsu, a celebrity of "Donglin," was framed and killed by Wei Zhongxian, Huang Zongxi followed his father's instruction to learn from Liu Zongzhou. At the age of 19, he arrived in the capital to appeal for the redressing of a wrong against his father where he wounded a foe with an iron club. He led the members of the Fu Association to continue the struggle against the influential eunuchs and officials, nearly being killed. When the Qing troops marched southward, he enlisted an army of volunteers called "Battalion of Loyalty" to resist Qing and was appointed by King Lu to a high official. After the Ming Dynasty was toppled, he lived in solitude to write books, refusing time and again to be appointed to an official position. He, Sun Qifeng and Li Yong were called "Three Learned Men." He was a man of great learning and an expert in astronomy, arithmetic, music and classics of Confucianism, Buddhism and Taoism. His works include *Waiting for the Dawn: A Plan for the Prince* and *Records about Nanlei*.

Li Yu (1611 – circa 1679): an opera theoretician and writer of the Qing Dynasty (1616–1911). He styled himself Lihong or Zhefan and was alternatively named Liweng, from Lanxi County, Zhejiang Province. He set up a theatrical troupe in his home and often led them to perform in the houses of high officials and noble lords all over the country. His works include *Occasional Writings about a Leisurely Life*, *Ten Operas by Liweng* etc.

Gu Yanwu (1613–1679) was a thinker and scholar who lived between the Ming and Qing dynasties. He was originally named Jiang, styled himself Ningren and was called Scholar Tinglin by others. While young, he joined the Fu Association in the struggle against influential eunuchs. When the Qing troops marched southward, he took part in the anti-Qing uprisings in the areas of Kunshan and Jiading. After defeat, he paid homage to the Ming Tombs ten

侯方域（1618—1683）：字朝宗，河南商丘人。明末与方以智、陈贞慧、冒襄齐名，称"四公子"。入清后曾应河南乡试，并向清总督献策，企图消灭农民军。有《壮悔堂文集》等。

施闰章（1618—1683）：清初诗人。字尚白，号愚山，安徽宣城人。顺治进士。康熙时官至侍读。诗与山东莱阳人宋琬齐名，号"南施北宋"。有《学余堂文集》《学余堂诗集》。

周容（1619—1679）：字茂三，明清之际浙江鄞县（今宁波市鄞州区）人。明亡后，一度削发为僧。后清廷召贤，朝臣力荐，他以死力辞不赴。著有《春酒堂文集》。

times and travelled all over North China, finding out about the local customs, collecting materials and making efforts to research frontier defence and northwestern geography. He opened up virgin soil and did farm work but never forgot his opposition to the Qing Dynasty and the restoration of Ming. In his twilight years, he chose Quwo for his home. He had a very wide range of learning: state systems, anecdotes of prefectures and counties, astronomy, water transportation, classics of Confucianism, Buddhism and Taoism, phonology and exegesis of ancient texts. His works include *Records of Daily Learning* and *Collection of Scholar Tinglin's Poetry and Prose*.

Hou Fangyu (1618-1683) styled himself Chaozong and was from Shangqiu, Henan. In the last years of the Ming Dynasty, he and Fang Yizhi, Chen Zhenhui and Mao Xiang were called "Four Outstanding Youngsters." When entering the Qing Dynasty, he took part in the imperial examination at provincial level and offered advice to a governor of the Qing Dynasty about how to wipe out the peasant uprising. His works include *Collection of the Repentance Hall* etc.

Shi Runzhang (1618-1683): a poet living at the beginning of the Qing Dynasty. He styled himself Shangbai and was alternatively named Yushan, from Xuanchen, Anhui. As a successful candidate for the highest imperial examination during the Shunzhi Reign (1644-1661), he was appointed reading advisor to the emperor during the Kangxi Reign (1662-1722). In poetry, he was as famous as Song Wan from Laiyang, Shandong and they were called "Shi in the South and Song in the North." His works include *Collection of Poetry and Prose from Xueyu Hall*.

Zhou Rong (1619-1679) styled himself Maosan and was born in Yinxian County (today's Yinzhou District, Ningbo City), Zhejiang Province between the Ming and Qing dynasties. After the Ming

魏禧（1624—1681）：清初散文家，字叔子，号裕斋，江西宁都人。入清不仕，隐居翠微峰。有《魏叔子集》。

林嗣环（1607—？）：字铁崖，明清之际福建晋江人。清顺治六年（1649）中进士。曾因事被贬谪，戍守边疆，后遇赦放还，客死武林。著有《铁崖文集》《湖舫存稿》。

汪琬（1624—1691）：清初散文家。字苕文，号钝庵，江苏吴县（今苏州市吴中区）人。顺治进士，曾任刑部郎中等职。曾结庐居太湖尧峰山，时称尧峰先生。有《尧峰文钞》等。

蒲松龄（1640—1715）：清代文学家。字留仙，别号柳泉居士，世称聊斋先生。山东淄川（今属淄博市）人。早岁即有文名，但屡应省试皆落第。71岁始成贡生，除中年一度在宝应做幕客外，都在家乡为塾师。以数十年时间写成短篇小说集《聊斋志异》，又有《聊斋文集》等。

Dynasty was brought down, he shaved his head and became a monk for some time. Later when the Qing government called talented men to service, many courtiers made an effort to recommend him but he refused. His works include *Collection of Spring-Wine Hall*.

Wei Xi (1624-1681): a prose-writer at the beginning of the Qing Dynasty. He styled himself Shuzi and was alternatively named Yuzhai, from Ningdu, Jiangxi. He refused to be an official in the Qing Government and lived away from society in the Cuiwei Mountain. His works include *Collection of Wei Shuzi*.

Lin Sihuan (1607-?) was from Jinjiang, Fujian between the Ming and Qing dynasties. In the 6th year of the Shunzhi Reign (1649), he passed the highest imperial examination. He was banished to the frontiers for garrison duty because of an unexpected event and later was pardoned. He died in Wulin, far from his hometown. His works include *Collection of Tieya* and *Existing Drafts of the Lake Boat*.

Wang Wan (1624-1691): a prose writer at the beginning of the Qing Dynasty, styled himself Tiaowen and was alternatively named Dun'an, from Wuxian County (today's Wuzhong District, Suzhou City), Jiangsu Province. As a successful candidate for the highest imperial examination during the Shunzhi Reign, he was appointed Deputy Minister of Punishments, etc. He built a cottage in the Yaofeng Mountain beside the Taihu Lake and was called Mr. Yaofeng by the public. His works include *Collection of Yaofeng*, etc.

Pu Songling (1640-1715): a writer of the Qing Dynasty. He styled himself Liuxian and was alternatively named Lay Buddhist Liuquan and called by the public "Scholar of the Chatting Room." While young, he was already famous for his writing but failed time and again in the imperial examination at the provincial level. At the age

方苞（1668—1749）：清代散文家。字灵皋，号望溪，安徽桐城人。康熙进士。曾因戴名世《南山集》案牵连入狱，后得赦。官礼部侍郎。桐城派创始人。有《方望溪先生全集》。

郑燮（1693—1765）：清书画家、文学家。字克柔，号板桥，江苏兴化人。早年家贫，应科举为康熙秀才，雍正举人，乾隆进士，曾任山东范县（今属河南省）、潍县知县，后因得罪豪绅罢官。做官前后均居扬州卖画，擅写兰竹。为扬州八怪之一。有《板桥全集》。

刘大櫆（1698—1779）：清代散文家。字才甫，号海峰，安徽桐城人。官黟县教谕。提倡古文，师事方苞，为桐城派重要作家之一。有《海峰文集》《海峰诗集》等。

of 71, he became a student of the imperial college. Except for once in his mid-life when he acted as an assistant to an official in Baoying, he always worked as a teacher in a private school in his hometown. He spent tens of years writing short stories which were later compiled into *Strange Tales from a Make-do Studio* and *Collection of the Make-do Studio*.

Fang Bao (1668–1749): a prose writer of the Qing Dynasty, styled himself Linggao and was alternatively named Wangxi. He was from Tongcheng, Anhui and a successful candidate for the highest imperial examination during the Kangxi Reign. He was put in prison due to his involvement in the case of Dai Mingshi's *Collection of Nanshan*. Later he was pardoned and appointed Deputy Minister of Rites. He was the founder of the Tongcheng School and his works include *Collection of Mr. Fang Wangxi*.

Zheng Xie (1693–1765): a painter, calligrapher and writer of the Qing Dynasty, styled himself Kerou and was alternatively named Banqiao (Wooden Bridge), from Xinghua, Jiangsu. In his early years, his family was poor. He passed the imperial examination at the county level during the Kangxi Reign at the provincial level during the Yongzheng Reign (1723–1735) and at the highest level during the Qianlong Reign (1736–1795). He took up office as magistrate of Fanxian County (part of today's Henan Province) and Weixian County in Shandong Province. Before and after this, he lived in Yangzhou selling paintings. He was good at drawing orchid and bamboo and was one of the Eight Eccentrics of Yangzhou. His works include *Collection of Banqiao*.

Liu Dakui (1698–1779): a prose writer of the Qing Dynasty, styled himself Caifu and was alternatively named Haifeng, from Tongcheng, Anhui. He was an official in charge of education in Yixian County. He

彭端淑（约1699—约1779）：字乐斋，清四川丹棱人。雍正进士，曾任吏部郎中，后辞官回到四川，主持锦江书院。著有《白鹤堂诗文集》。

全祖望（1705—1755）：清代史学家、文学家。字绍农，学者称谢山先生，浙江鄞县（今宁波市鄞州区）人。乾隆进士。初为翰林，旋受权贵排斥，辞官归家，专心著述。研治宋末和南明史事。七校《水经注》。著有《鲒埼亭集》等。

袁枚（1716—1798）：清代诗人。字子才，号简斋、随园老人，浙江钱塘（今杭州）人。乾隆进士，曾任江宁等地知县。辞官后侨居江宁，筑园林于小仓山，号随园。论诗创性灵说。有《小仓山房集》《随园诗话》等。

advocated the ancient style of prose writings and acknowledged Fang Bao as his teacher and he was one of the important writers of the Tongcheng School. His works include *Collection of Haifeng*, etc.

Peng Duanshu (circa 1699 – circa 1779) styled himself Lezhai and was from Danling County, Sichuan. As a successful candidate for the highest imperial examination during the Yongzheng Reign, he was appointed Deputy Minister of Civil Personnel. Later he resigned from office and came back to Sichuan in charge of the Jinjiang Academy of Classical Learning. His works include *Collection of Poetry and Prose in White Crane Hall*.

Quan Zuwang (1705–1755): a historian and writer of the Qing Dynasty. He styled himself Shaonong and was called Scholar Xieshan by the public, from Yinxian County (today's Yinzhou District, Ningbo City), Zhejiang. As a successful candidate for the highest imperial examination during the Qianlong Reign, he was a member of the Imperial Academy. Before long, having been expelled by influential officials, he resigned from office and returned home to be engaged whole-heartedly in writing. He studied historical events of the last years of the Song Dynasty and the Southern Ming Dynasty. He proofread *Notes on Rivers* seven times. His works include *Collection of the Jieqi Pavilion*, etc.

Yuan Mei (1716–1798): a poet of the Qing Dynasty. His styled himself Zicai and was alternatively named Old Man in the Sui Garden, from Qiantang (the present Hangzhou), Zhejiang Province, a successful candidate for the highest imperial examination during the Qianlong Reign. He served as magistrate of Jiangning and some other counties. He lived away from home in Jiangning after resigning from office and built a garden in the Xiaocang Mountain, called the Sui Garden. In poetry, he put forward the Theory of Natural Disposition.

蒋士铨（1725—1785）：清代文学家。字心余、清容、苕生，号藏园，江西铅山人。乾隆二十二年（1757）年进士。曾任翰林院编修。作有传奇、杂剧十六种。其诗与袁枚、赵翼并称"江右三大家"。有《忠雅堂全集》。

钱大昕（1728—1804）：清代学者。字晓征，一字辛楣，号竹汀。江苏嘉定（今属上海市）人。乾隆进士。一度为官。乾隆四十年（1775）以后主讲钟山、娄东、紫阳等书院。治学方面颇广，于音韵训诂尤多创见。著作有《恒言录》等。

姚鼐（1732—1815）：清代散文家。字姬传，一字梦谷，室名惜抱轩，旧时或称惜抱先生，安徽桐城人。乾隆进士，官刑部郎中。历主江宁、扬州等地书院凡四十年。治学以经为主，兼及子史、诗文。曾受业于刘大櫆，为桐城派主要作家。有《惜抱轩全集》。

His works include *Collection of Xiaocang Mountain Cottage* and *Notes on Poetry of Sui Garden*.

Jiang Shiquan (1725–1785): a writer of the Qing Dynasty. He styled himself Xinyu or Qingrong or Tiaosheng and was alternatively named Zangyuan, from Yanshan County, Jiangxi. As a successful candidate for the highest imperial examination in the 22nd year of the Qianlong Reign (1757), he once served as an editor in the Imperial Academy. His poetry, together with that of Yuan Mei and Zhao Yi were labeled works of the "Three Great Masters of Jiangxi." His works include *Collection of Zhongya Hall*.

Qian Daxin (1728–1804): a scholar of the Qing Dynasty. He styled himself Xiaozheng or Xinmei and was alternatively named Zhuting, from Jiading (part of today's Shanghai), Jiangsu, a successful candidate for the highest imperial examination during the Qianlong Reign. He served as an official for some time but after the 40th year of the Qianlong Reign (1775) he gave lectures in the academies of Zhongshan, Loudong and Ziyang, etc. He pursued his studies widely and especially had many creative ideas in phonology and interpretation of ancient texts. His works include *Recording of Hengyan*, etc.

Yao Nai (1732–1815): a prose writer of the Qing Dynasty. He styled himself Jichuan or Menggu. His study was named "Xibao Room" and he was called Master Xibao, from Tongcheng, Anhui. He was a successful candidate for the highest imperial examination during the Qianlong Reign and served in the capacity of Deputy Minister of Punishments. He presided over academies of classical learning in Jiangning, Yangzhou etc. for 40 years. He specialised in Confucian classics and also studied history and poetic prose simultaneously. He learned from Liu Dakui and was the main writer of the Tongcheng

刘开（1784—1824）：清代文学家。字明东，一字孟涂，安徽桐城人。受学于同乡姚鼐。有《孟涂文集》。

龚自珍（1792—1841）：一名巩祚，字璱人，号定盦，浙江仁和（今属杭州）人。清道光进士，官礼部主事。学务博览，为嘉道间提倡"通经致用"的重要人物。当林则徐赴广东查禁鸦片时，他曾预见到英国可能侵犯，建议加强战备。所作诗文，竭力提倡"更法""改图"。散文奥博纵横，诗瑰丽奇肆，有"龚派"之称。著作有《定盦文集》等。今人辑有《龚自珍全集》。

school. His works include *Collection of Xibao Room*.

Liu Kai (1784–1824): a writer of the Qing Dynasty. He styled himself Mingdong or Mengtu, from Tongcheng, Anhui. He received instruction in study from Yao Nai from the same town. His works include *Collection of Mengtu*.

Gong Zizhen (1792–1841): also named Gongzuo, styled himself Seren and alternatively named Ding'an, from Renhe (in the present Hangzhou), Zhejiang. He was a successful candidate for the highest imperial examination during the Daoguang Reign (1821–1850) of the Qing Dynasty. He was broad in learning and the important person who advocated "understanding classics and applying them" between the Jiaqing and Daoguang reigns. When Lin Zexu went to Guangzhou to place a ban on opium, he, foreseeing that England would probably violate, suggested strengthening combat readiness. In his prose and poems, he spared no efforts to promote "changing the law." His prose was profound, broad and free. His poetry was surprisingly beautiful and unrestrained, called "Gong School." His works include *Collected Works of Ding'an* and *Complete Works of Gong Zizhen* (the latter was edited by contemporaries).

本书由扬州大学出版基金资助